SIR WALTER SCOTT was born on 15 August 1771 in Edinburgh, Scotland. He was educated at Edinburgh High School and University, went on to study law and was called to the bar in 1792. In 1797 he married Charlotte Carpenter, with whom he had four children. He was appointed Sheriff-Depute of Selkirk in 1799, and Clerk of Session in Edinburgh in 1806. Four years later he became a partner in James Ballantyne's publishing business, but in the meantime he had published several volumes of his own poetry to such acclaim that in 1813 he was offered the laureateship; he declined it, however, in favour of Southey. Scott subsequently turned to prose, publishing his first historical novel, *Waverley*, in 1814. There followed a tremendous output which included *The Bride of Lammermoor*, *Ivanhoe*, *The Antiquary*, *Heart of Mid-Lothian*, *Quentin Durward*, *Rob Roy* and *Redgauntlet* – known collectively as the Waverley novels since Scott kept his authorship secret until years later.

Scott continued to enjoy considerable literary and social success – he was made a baronet in 1820 – but in 1826 disaster struck when his publishing business went into bankruptcy. Scott felt morally obliged to pay off all the creditors, which he resolved to do through his literary efforts. Over the next six years he published another six novels and two historical works but the strain eventually proved too much. He died on 21 September 1832 at his Abbotsford home and was buried in Dryburgh Abbey.

W. M. PARKER (1891–1973) was Assistant Editor of the Centenary edition of Scott's *Letters* (1932–37), and part editor of Scott's *Journal* (1950). In 1953 Edinburgh University conferred on him an honorary MA degree for his work on Scott.

SIR WALTER SCOTT

The Bride of Lammermoor

Preface by W. M. Parker

J. M. Dent & Sons Ltd
London
Charles E. Tuttle Co., Inc.
Rutland, Vermont

EVERYMAN'S LIBRARY

Made in Great Britain by
The Guernsey Press Co. Ltd, Guernsey, C.I. for
J. M. Dent & Sons Ltd
91 Clapham High Street, London SW4 7TA
and
Charles E. Tuttle Co., Inc.
28, South Main Street, Rutland,
Vermont 05701, U.S.A.

This edition was first published in
Everyman's Library in 1906
Last reprinted 1988
Reissued 1991

ISBN 0 460 87099 8

Everyman's Library
Reg. U.S. Patent Office

PREFACE

THE comparison frequently made between Scott and Shakespeare is perhaps more clearly evident in *The Bride of Lammermoor* than in any other of Scott's works. Hitherto, in the seven preceding Waverley Novels, comedy and pathos had been more or less equally distributed and blended, but when Scott turned to an almost entirely serious theme in the present narrative he made tragedy the predominant element. And it was not only to develop into a tragic chronicle of the south-east Scottish lowlands; it was to be given a universal significance and to be definitely tinctured with the same sublimity and inevitableness which characterize Shakespeare's tragic conceptions.

The circumstances in which the novel was composed were also of tragic import, for, according to Lockhart, Scott dictated the greater portion when he was wracked by violent pain. William Laidlaw, one of his amanuenses, implored him to stop, but Scott replied: 'Nay, Willie. Only see that the doors are fast . . . as to giving over work, that can only be when I am in woollen.' But Scott must have written so much in his own hand. As testimony there is the original MS. which, bequeathed in 1916 by Alexander Sholto Douglas, W.S., to the Library of the Society of Writers to H.M. Signet, Edinburgh, contains definite evidence of Scott's autograph. When the finished novel was first put into Scott's hands, he assured John Ballantyne that he did not remember one incident, character, or conversation in it.

Six months before that acute illness came upon him, Scott was working on the novel, and by September 1818, when brooding over the first chapters, he reported to James Ballantyne: 'The story is a dismal one, and I doubt sometimes whether it will bear working out to much length after all. . . . When the proofs come in, my pen must and shall step out.' [1] The illness intervened in January 1819, and by March there was a violent recurrence of it. But the novel progressed briskly throughout April and May, and in June *The Bride of Lammermoor*, together with *A Legend of Montrose*, appeared in four volumes as the third series of *Tales of my Landlord*. Lockhart tells us that Scott's position at that time was 'what no other man had ever won for himself by the pen alone. His works were the daily food, not only of his countrymen, but of all educated Europe.' It is not surprising, therefore, that *The Bride* was immediately read with avidity and reached a third edition within the year of publication.

It was from his mother that Scott heard the story on which he based his novel. It concerned the tragic event which appeared

---

[1] *Letters of Sir Walter Scott*, vol. v (1933), p. 186.

in a Scottish lampoon, 'Satyre on the Familie of Stairs' in *Three Books of Scotish Pasquils, etc.* (1827–8). Before she came of age, Janet Dalrymple pledged her troth to a poor Scots noble, Lord Rutherfurd, whose suit was not favoured by Janet's parents. Her father was Sir James Dalrymple, a notable Scots lawyer and statesman, who died, Viscount Stair, in 1695. Her mother, Margaret Ross of Balniel, was a proud, strong-willed woman who succeeded in breaking off her daughter's engagement. Thereupon Janet married her parents' choice, David Dunbar, heir of Sir David of Baldoon, and nephew of Lord Rutherfurd. Shortly after the marriage she died, evidently of a broken heart. But there is no allusion to any such tragedy as that which occurs in the novel on the night of the marriage. The bride's remains were moved, it is said, from Kirkinner to Kirkliston Church, Midlothian, where they are now with those of the proud mother who died twenty-three years later.[1]

These scenes and events were transfigured by Scott's great creative imagination into a rich romance. In his fiction he places the scene on the south-east coast of Scotland in the year 1700. The hero, Edgar, Master of Ravenswood, of noble family, is penniless and proud. He has vowed vengeance against the owner of the Ravenswood estates, Sir William Ashton, Lord Keeper, whom he considers guilty of fraud, but he forgoes his plans on falling in love with Ashton's daughter, Lucy. There is a secret betrothal; the ambitious Lady Ashton (the fictitious rendering of Lady Stair) tries to force Lucy to marry another suitor; in the struggle that ensues Lucy goes mad; and Ravenswood, thinking himself rejected, comes to an untimely end. This plot, indeed the whole narrative, reveals a sense of construction unusual with Scott, and the tone and texture are suffused with a glamour that characterizes the tragic Border ballads.

From the time of its publication *The Bride* has been subjected intermittently to many variations of both censure and praise. One of Scott's best critics, his correspondent Lady Louisa Stuart, wrote to him soon after the novel appeared: 'I have had it by heart these five weeks. It possesses the same power of captivating the attention as its predecessors. . . . The Master of Ravenswood is perhaps the best *lover* the author ever yet drew.' Naturally, in a work so fraught with impending fate—a theme repeatedly treated by our great modern tragic novelist, Thomas Hardy—many contemporary critics perceived resemblances to classic drama and to Shakespeare. Although Coleridge referred to the work as a 'wretched abortion,' nevertheless it recalled to him Greek tragic fate, and the *New Monthly* critic thought it 'almost as single and harmonious as a tragedy of Sophocles.' In more recent times Emerson, regarding *The Bride* as Scott's highest achievement, declared that it 'almost goes back to Aeschylus for a counterpart, a painting of Fate.' The simi-

[1] For a detailed account of the story see *The Scott Originals* by W. S. Crockett (third ed., 1932), pp. 249–68.

larities to Shakespeare, too, were seen in Edgar with his Hamlet-like traits; in both him and Lucy as reincarnations of those other 'star-crossed' lovers, Romeo and Juliet; and, of course, in the weird women so like Macbeth's witches.

Indeed, Scott's treatment of the supernatural in this novel (he was well versed in demonology), especially in the scene where Ravenswood meets the hags, won unanimous praise. At times, in most of the earlier parts of the narrative, the reader is conscious of being in a borderland between reality and a dream-world. Then, his poetic vision in the ascendant, Scott conjures up with his wizard's wand an appropriately ghoulish atmosphere, in which the eeriness is increased by the introduction of grimly realistic Scots dialect. (Scott's genius always soared when using the Doric with masterly ease.) 'The old women paid the Master their salutations with a ghastly smile, which reminded him of the meeting betwixt Macbeth and the witches on the blasted heath of Forres.' One beldame, Annie Winnie, mentions the great folk 'that hae breasts like whin-stane. They prick us and they pine us, and they pit us on the pinny-winkles for witches; and, if I say my prayers backwards ten times ower, Satan will never gie me amends o' them' (chapter xxiii). And then there is the saying of the Sibyl when Lucy rides to her deathly bridal: 'I tell ye her winding sheet is up as high as her throat already, believe it wha list. Her sand has but a few grains to rin out, and nae wonder—they've been weel shaken' (chapter xxxiv).

While *Blackwood's Magazine* extolled *The Bride*, observing that perhaps there was more poetry of the finest kind in the last scenes than was ever contained in the same number of pages in any of Scott's prose, both the *Edinburgh* and the *Quarterly* Reviews modified their commendations by deploring the absurdities and buffoonery of Caleb Balderstone, the butler at Ravenswood Castle—a verdict to which not a few later commentators have subscribed. Victorian writers held diverse views about the work. Ruskin stoutly maintained it had been foolishly praised and he objected to its 'prevailing melancholy and fantastic improbability.' But against the charge of improbability Scott could have defended himself by quoting his own sage words on the licence permitted to romance. 'Though an unconnected course of adventures is what most frequently occurs in nature, yet the province of the romance writer, being artificial, there is more required from him than a mere compliance with the simplicity of reality.' [1] Curiously enough, what he considered to be Lucy Ashton's defects as a tragic heroine was a sufficient reason for that staunch Scott devotee, George Saintsbury, to pronounce that the novel was 'not tragic in the true sense of the word.' Jowett and FitzGerald used to read *The Bride* every two years and were deeply affected each time. In the opinions of Tennyson and Gladstone it was the most artistic

---

[1] In the 1830 Introduction to *The Monastery*, and quoted, with variants, as a motto on the title-page of Hardy's *Desperate Remedies*.

of the Waverleys. Again, Thomas Hardy, whose own fiction is so superbly constructed, could not say enough about its beautiful symmetry. '*The Bride of Lammermoor* is an almost perfect specimen of form, which is the more remarkable in that Scott, as a rule, depends more upon episode, dialogue, and description, for exciting interest, than upon the well-knit interdependence of parts.'

The topographical background of *The Bride* has caused much speculation and conjecture. Fast Castle, near St Abb's Head, seems to answer approximately to the description of Wolf's Crag, the last remnant of Ravenswood's property. Although Scott himself, in his 1819 Introduction to the novel, did not entirely repudiate this popular identity, later he intimated that the Kaim of Uric, on the East Coast, had suggested the Crag. Dunglass mansion, near Cockburnspath, occupying the site of a former castle, has also been claimed as the Crag. The original of Ravenswood Castle is uncertain. As it is described to be in a ruined state, the claim of Winton Castle, East Lothian, which is not a ruin, is scarcely acceptable. If, on the other hand, Crichton Castle, Midlothian, be accepted, then Crichton Kirk might be considered as 'the parish church of Ravenswood.' where Lucy Ashton and the Laird of Bucklaw were married. It has been hinted that Coldingham Priory represents the chapel in which Ravenswood's father was buried at the opening of the novel. Again, Eyemouth, on the Berwickshire coast, has features that correspond with those of Wolf's Hope, where the quicksands of 'the Kelpie's Flow' are located, if it were not for the fact that no actual quicksands exist in the Eyemouth vicinity.

Although Scott assured his actor friend, Daniel Terry, that *The Bride* would not lend itself to dramatization, there have been many stage versions from time to time. An episode in the novel inspired Joanna Baillie, the dramatist, to write her prose tragedy, *Witchcraft*. On 28th June 1819, informing Scott that *The Bride* 'left a gloom upon my mind for a long time after I had finished the story,' she added: 'There is one scene between the old Hags, as they are preparing to *straught* [1] the corpse, which struck me as fearfully natural and original. . . . These said Hags have created in me a prodigious hankering after the matter.' But the only stage adaptation which has endured is the popular opera, *Lucia di Lammermoor*, and it has survived rather because of Donizetti's music than on account of Salvatore Cammarano's indifferent libretto, based on Scott's work. All dramatizations, however—successful or unsuccessful—form a group of tributes to the dramatic qualities of *The Bride of Lammermoor*, and it is as essentially the most dramatic of the Scott romances that it has remained a classic in English fiction.

W. M. PARKER.

---

[1] To 'straucht' or 'straughten' is to stretch a corpse.

INTRODUCTION

THE author, on a former occasion,[1] declined giving the real source from which he drew the tragic subject of this history, because, though occurring at a distant period, it might possibly be unpleasing to the feelings of the descendants of the parties. But as he finds an account of the circumstances given in the Notes to Law's *Memorials*,[2] by his ingenious friend Charles Kirkpatrick Sharpe, Esq., and also indicated in his reprint of the Rev. Mr Symson's poems, appended to the *Description of Galloway*, as the original of the Bride of Lammermoor, the author feels himself now at liberty to tell the tale as he had it from connections of his own, who lived very near the period, and were closely related to the family of the Bride.

It is well known that the family of Dalrymple, which has produced, within the space of two centuries, as many men of talent, civil and military, and of literary, political, and professional eminence, as any house in Scotland, first rose into distinction in the person of James Dalrymple, one of the most eminent lawyers that ever lived, though the labours of his powerful mind were unhappily exercised on a subject so limited as Scottish Jurisprudence, on which he has composed an admirable work.

He married Margaret, daughter to Ross of Balniel, with whom he obtained a considerable estate. She was an able, politic, and high-minded woman, so successful in what she undertook, that the vulgar, no way partial to her husband or her family, imputed her success to necromancy. According to the popular belief, this Dame Margaret purchased the temporal prosperity of her family from the Master whom she served, under a singular condition, which is thus

[1] *See* Introduction to the *Chronicles of the Canongate*.
[2] Law's *Memorials*, p. 226.

narrated by the historian of her grandson, the great Earl of Stair. "She lived to a great age, and at her death desired that she might not be put under ground, but that her coffin should be placed upright on one end of it, promising that while she remained in that situation, the Dalrymples should continue in prosperity. What was the old lady's motive for such a request, or whether she really made such a promise, I cannot take upon me to determine; but it is certain her coffin stands upright in the aisle of the church of Kirkliston, the burial place of the family."[1] The talents of this accomplished race were sufficient to have accounted for the dignities which many members of the family attained, without any supernatural assistance. But their extraordinary prosperity was attended by some equally singular family misfortunes, of which that which befell their eldest daughter was at once unaccountable and melancholy.

Miss Janet Dalrymple, daughter of the first Lord Stair, and Dame Margaret Ross, had engaged herself without the knowledge of her parents to the Lord Rutherford, who was not acceptable to them either on account of his political principles, or his want of fortune. The young couple broke a piece of gold together, and pledged their troth in the most solemn manner; and it is said the young lady imprecated dreadful evils on herself should she break her plighted faith. Shortly after, a suitor who was favoured by Lord Stair, and still more so by his lady, paid his addresses to Miss Dalrymple. The young lady refused the proposal, and being pressed on the subject, confessed her secret engagement. Lady Stair, a woman accustomed to universal submission (for even her husband did not dare to contradict her), treated this objection as a trifle, and insisted upon her daughter yielding her consent to marry the new suitor, David Dunbar, son and heir to David Dunbar of Baldoon, in Wigtownshire. The first lover, a man of very high spirit, then interfered by letter, and insisted on the right he had acquired by his troth plighted with the young lady. Lady Stair sent him for answer, that her daughter, sensible of her undutiful behaviour in entering into a contract unsanctioned by her parents, had retracted her unlawful vow, and now refused to fulfil her engagement with him.

[1] *Memoirs of John Earl of Stair*, by an Impartial Hand. London, printed for C. Cobbet, p. 7.

The lover, in return, declined positively to receive such an answer from any one but his mistress in person; and as she had to deal with a man who was both of a most determined character, and of too high condition to be trifled with, Lady Stair was obliged to consent to an interview between Lord Rutherford and her daughter. But she took care to be present in person, and argued the point with the disappointed and incensed lover with pertinacity equal to his own. She particularly insisted on the Levitical law, which declares, that a woman shall be free of a vow which her parents dissent from. This is the passage of Scripture she founded on:—

"If a man vow a vow unto the Lord, or swear an oath to bind his soul with a bond; he shall not break his word, he shall do according to all that proceedeth out of his mouth.

"If a woman also vow a vow unto the Lord, and bind herself by a bond, being in her father's house in her youth;

"And her father hear her vow, and her bond wherewith she hath bound her soul, and her father shall hold his peace at her: then all her vows shall stand, and every bond wherewith she hath bound her soul shall stand.

"But if her father disallow her in the day that he heareth; not any of her vows, or of her bonds wherewith she hath bound her soul, shall stand: and the Lord shall forgive her, because her father disallowed her."—Numbers, xxx. 2, 3, 4, 5.

While the mother insisted on these topics, the lover in vain conjured the daughter to declare her own opinion and feelings. She remained totally overwhelmed, as it seemed, —mute, pale, and motionless as a statue. Only at her mother's command, sternly uttered, she summoned strength enough to restore to her plighted suitor the piece of broken gold, which was the emblem of her troth. On this he burst forth into a tremendous passion, took leave of the mother with maledictions, and as he left the apartment, turned back to say to his weak, if not fickle mistress, "For you, madam, you will be a world's wonder"; a phrase by which some remarkable degree of calamity is usually implied. He went abroad, and returned not again. If the last Lord Rutherford was the unfortunate party, he must have been the third who bore that title, and who died in 1685.

The marriage betwixt Janet Dalrymple and David Dunbar of Baldoon now went forward, the bride showing no repugnance, but being absolutely passive in every thing her mother commanded or advised. On the day of the marriage, which, as was then usual, was celebrated by a great assemblage of friends and relations, she was the same—sad, silent, and resigned, as it seemed, to her destiny. A lady, very nearly connected with the family, told the author that she had conversed on the subject with one of the brothers of the bride, a mere lad at the time, who had ridden before his sister to church. He said her hand, which lay on his as she held her arm round his waist, was as cold and damp as marble. But, full of his new dress, and the part he acted in the procession, the circumstance, which he long afterwards remembered with bitter sorrow and compunction, made no impression on him at the time.

The bridal feast was followed by dancing; the bride and bridegroom retired as usual, when of a sudden the most wild and piercing cries were heard from the nuptial chamber. It was then the custom, to prevent any coarse pleasantry which old times perhaps admitted, that the key of the nuptial chamber should be intrusted to the brideman. He was called upon, but refused at first to give it up, till the shrieks became so hideous that he was compelled to hasten with others to learn the cause. On opening the door, they found the bridegroom lying across the threshold, dreadfully wounded, and streaming with blood. The bride was then sought for: She was found in the corner of the large chimney, having no covering save her shift, and that dabbled in gore. There she sat grinning at them, mopping and mowing, as I heard the expression used; in a word, absolutely insane. The only words she spoke were, "Tak up your bonny bridegroom." She survived this horrible scene little more than a fortnight, having been married on the 24th of August, and dying on the 12th of September 1669.

The unfortunate Baldoon recovered from his wounds, but sternly prohibited all enquiries respecting the manner in which he had received them. If a lady, he said, asked him any question upon the subject, he would neither answer her nor speak to her again while he lived; if a gentleman, he would consider it as a mortal affront, and demand satisfaction as having received such. He did not very long survive the dreadful catastrophe, having met with a fatal injury by a fall from his horse, as he rode between Leith and Holyrood-house, of which he died the next day, 28th March 1682. Thus a few years removed all the principal actors in this frightful tragedy.

Various reports went abroad on this mysterious affair, many of them very inaccurate, though they could hardly be said to be exaggerated. It was difficult at that time to become acquainted with the history of a Scottish family above the lower rank; and strange things sometimes took place there, into which even the law did not scrupulously enquire.

The credulous Mr Law says, generally, that the Lord President Stair had a daughter, who "being married, the night she was *bride in* [that is, bedded bride], was taken from her bridegroom and *harled* [dragged] through the house (by spirits, we are given to understand), and soon afterwards died. Another daughter," he says, "was possessed by an evil spirit."

My friend, Mr Sharpe, gives another edition of the tale. According to his information, it was the bridegroom who wounded the bride. The marriage, according to this account, had been against her mother's inclination, who had given her consent in these ominous words : "You may marry him, but soon shall you repent it."

I find still another account darkly insinuated in some highly scurrilous and abusive verses, of which I have an original copy. They are docketed as being written "Upon the late Viscount Stair and his family, by Sir William Hamilton of Whitelaw. The marginals by William Dunlop, writer in Edinburgh, a son of the Laird of Househill, and nephew to the said Sir William Hamilton." There was a bitter and personal quarrel and rivalry betwixt the author of this libel, a name which it richly deserves, and Lord President Stair; and the lampoon, which is written with much more malice than art, bears the following motto :—

> "Stair's neck, mind, wife, sons, grandson, and the rest,
>   Are   wry,   false, witch, pests, parricide,   possessed."

This malignant satirist, who calls up all the misfortunes of the family, does not forget the fatal bridal of Baldoon.

He seems, though his verses are as obscure as unpoetical, to intimate, that the violence done to the bridegroom was by the intervention of the foul fiend to whom the young lady had resigned herself, in case she should break her contract with her first lover. His hypothesis is inconsistent with the account given in the note upon Law's *Memorials*, but easily reconcilable to the family tradition.

> "In al Stair's offspring we no difference know,
> They doe the females as the males bestow;
> So he of's daughter's marriage gave the ward,
> Like a true vassal, to Glenluce's Laird;
> He knew what she did to her suitor plight,
> If she her faith to Rutherfurd should slight,　}
> Which, like his own, for greed he broke outright.
> Nick did Baldoon's posterior right deride,
> And, as first substitute, did seize the bride;
> Wha'e'er he to his mistress did or said,
> He threw the bridegroom from the nuptial bed,
> Into the chimney did so his rival maul,
> His bruised bones ne'er were cured but by the fall."[1]

One of the marginal notes ascribed to William Dunlop, applies to the above lines. "She had betrothed herself to Lord Rutherfoord under horrid imprecations, and afterwards married Baldoon, his nevoy, and her mother was the cause of her breach of faith."

The same tragedy is alluded to in the following couplet and note:—

> "What train of curses that base brood pursues,
> When the young nephew weds old uncle's spouse.

The note on the word *uncle* explains it as meaning "Rutherfoord, who should have married the Lady Baldoon, was Baldoon's uncle." The poetry of this satire on Lord Stair and his family was, as already noticed, written by Sir William Hamilton of Whitelaw, a rival of Lord Stair for the situation of President of the Court of Session; a person much inferior to that great lawyer in talents, and equally ill-treated by the calumny or just satire of his contemporaries, as an unjust and partial judge. Some of the notes are by that curious and laborious antiquary, Robert Milne.

[1] The fall from his horse, by which he was killed.

who, as a virulent Jacobite, willingly lent a hand to blacken the family of Stair.[1]

Another poet of the period, with a very different purpose, has left an elegy, in which he darkly hints at and bemoans the fate of the ill-starred young person, whose very uncommon calamity Whitelaw, Dunlop, and Milne, thought a fitting subject for buffoonery and ribaldry. This bard of milder mood was Andrew Symson, before the Revolution minister of Kirkinner, in Galloway, and after his expulsion as an Episcopalian, following the humble occupation of a printer in Edinburgh. He furnished the family of Baldoon, with which he appears to have been intimate, with an elegy on the tragic event in their family. In this piece he treats the mournful occasion of the bride's death with mysterious solemnity.

The verses bear this title—"On the unexpected death of the virtuous Lady Mrs Janet Dalrymple, Lady Baldoon, younger," and afford us the precise dates of the catastrophe, which could not otherwise have been easily ascertained. "Nupta August 12. Domum Ducta August 24. Obiit September 12. Sepult. September 30, 1669." The form of the elegy is a dialogue betwixt a passenger and a domestic servant. The first, recollecting that he had passed that way lately, and seen all around enlivened by the appearances of mirth and festivity, is desirous to know what had changed so gay a scene into mourning. We preserve the reply of the servant as a specimen of Mr Symson's verses which are not of the first quality:—

> ————" Sir, 'tis truth, you've told,
> We did enjoy great mirth; but now, ah me!
> Our joyful song's turn'd to an elegie.
> A virtuous lady, not long since a bride,
> Was to a hopeful plant by marriage tied,
> And brought home hither. We did all rejoice,
> Even for her sake. But presently our voice
> Was turn'd to mourning for that little time
> That she'd enjoy: She waned in her prime,

[1] I have compared the satire, which occurs in the first volume of the curious little collection called a *Book of Scottish Pasquils*, 1827, with that which has a more full text, and more extended notes, and which is in my own possession, by gift of Thomas Thomson, Esq., Register-Depute. In the second *Book of Pasquils*, p. 72, is a most abusive epitaph on Sir James Hamilton of Whitelaw.

> For Atropos, with her impartial knife,
> Soon cut her thread, and therewithal her life;
> And for the time we may it will remember,
> It being in unfortunate September;
> Where we must leave her till the resurrection,
> 'Tis then the Saints enjoy their full perfection."[1]

Mr Symson also poured forth his elegiac strains upon the fate of the widowed bridegroom, on which subject, after a long and querulous effusion, the poet arrives at the sound conclusion, that if Baldoon had walked on foot, which it seems was his general custom, he would have escaped perishing by a fall from horseback. As the work in which it occurs is so scarce as almost to be unique, and as it gives us the most full account of one of the actors in this tragic tale which we have rehearsed, we will, at the risk of being tedious, insert some short specimens of Mr Symson's composition. It is entitled,—

"A Funeral Elegie, occasioned by the sad and much lamented death of that worthily respected, and very much accomplished gentleman, David Dunbar, younger of Baldoon, only son and apparent heir to the right worshipful Sir David Dunbar of Baldoon, Knight Baronet. He departed this life on March 28, 1682, having received a bruise by a fall, as he was riding the day preceding betwixt Leith and Holy-Rood-House; and was honourably interred in the Abbey church of Holy-Rood-House, on April 4, 1682."

> "Men might, and very justly too, conclude
> Me guilty of the worst ingratitude,
> Should I be silent, or should I forbear
> At this sad accident to shed a tear;
> A tear! said I? ah! that's a petit thing,
> A very lean, slight, slender offering,
> Too mean, I'me sure, for me, wherewith t'attend
> The unexpected funeral of my friend—
> A glass of briny tears charged up to th' brim,
> Would be too few for me to shed for him."

[1] This elegy is reprinted in the appendix to a topographical work by the same author, entitled *A Large Description of Galloway*, by *Andrew Symson, Minister of Kirkinner*, 8vo, Taits, Edinburgh, 1823. The reverend gentleman's elegies are extremely rare, nor did the author ever see a copy but his own, which is bound up with the "Tripatriarchicon," a religious poem from the *Biblical History*, by the same author.

The poet proceeds to state his intimacy with the deceased, and the constancy of the young man's attendance on public worship, which was regular, and had such effect upon two or three others that were influenced by his example,

> " So that my Muse 'gainst Priscian avers,
>   He, only he, *were* my parishioners;
>   Yea, and my only hearers."

He then describes the deceased in person and manners, from which it appears that more accomplishments were expected in the composition of a fine gentleman in ancient than modern times:

> " His body, though not very large or tall,
>   Was sprightly, active, yea and strong withal.
>   His constitution was, if right I've guess'd,
>   Blood mixt with choler, said to be the best.
>   In's gesture, converse, speech, discourse, attire,
>   He practis'd that which wise men still admire,
>   Commend, and recommend. What's that? you'l say;
>   'Tis this: He ever choos'd the middle way
>   'Twixt both th' extremes. Amost in ev'ry thing
>   He did the like, 'tis worth our noticing:
>   Sparing, yet not a niggard; liberal,
>   And yet not lavish or a prodigal,
>   As knowing when to spend and when to spare;
>   And that's a lesson which not many are
>   Acquainted with. He bashful was, yet daring
>   When he saw cause, and yet therein but sparing:
>   Familiar, yet not common, for he knew
>   To condescend, and keep his distance too.
>   He us'd, and that most commonly, to go
>   On foot; I wish that he had still done so.
>   Th' affairs of court were unto him well known:
>   And yet mean while he slighted not his own.
>   He knew full well how to behave at court,
>   And yet but seldome did thereto resort;
>   But lov'd the country life, choos'd to inure
>   Himself to past'rage and agriculture;
>   Proving, improving, ditching, trenching, draining,
>   Viewing, reviewing, and by those means gaining;
>   Planting, transplanting, levelling, erecting
>   Walls, chambers, houses, terraces; projecting
>   Now this, now that device, this draught, that measure
>   That might advance his profit with his pleasure.
>   Quick in his bargains, honest in commerce,

Just in his dealings, being much averse
From quirks of law, still ready to refer
His cause t' an honest country arbiter.
He was acquainted with cosmography,
Arithmetic, and modern history;
With architecture and such arts as these,
Which I may call specifick sciences
Fit for a gentleman; and surely he
That knows them not, at least in some degree,
May brook the title, but he wants the thing,
Is but a shadow scarce worth noticing.
He learned the French, be't spoken to his praise,
In very little more than fourty days."

Then comes the full burst of woe, in which, instead of saying much himself, the poet informs us what the ancients would have said on such an occasion:

" A heathen poet, at the news, no doubt,
Would have exclaimed, and furiously cry'd out
Against the fates, the destinies and starrs,
What! this the effect of planetarie warrs!
We might have seen him rage and rave, yea worse,
'Tis very like we might have heard him curse
The year, the month, the day, the hour, the place,
The company, the wager, and the race;
Decry all recreations, with the names
Of Isthmian, Pythian, and Olympick games;
Exclaim against them all both old and new,
Both the Nemæan and the Lethæan too;
Adjudge all persons under highest pain,
Always to walk on foot, and then again
Order all horses so be hough'd, that we
Might never more the like adventure see."

Supposing our readers have had enough of Mr Symson's verses, and finding nothing more in his poem worthy of transcription, we return to the tragic story.

It is needless to point out to the intelligent reader, that the witchcraft of the mother consisted only in the ascendency of a powerful mind over a weak and melancholy one, and that the harshness with which she exercised her superiority in a case of delicacy, had driven her daughter first to despair, then to frenzy. Accordingly, the author has endeavoured to explain the tragic tale on this principle. Whatever resemblance Lady Ashton may be supposed to possess to the celebrated Dame Margaret Ross, the reader must not suppose that there was any idea of tracing the portrait of the first Lord Viscount Stair in the tricky and mean-spirited Sir William Ashton. Lord Stair, whatever might be his moral qualities, was certainly one of the first statesmen and lawyers of his age.

The imaginary castle of Wolf's Crag has been identified by some lover of locality with that of Fast Castle. The author is not competent to judge of the resemblance betwixt the real and imaginary scene, having never seen Fast Castle except from the sea. But fortalices of this description are found occupying, like ospreys' nests, projecting rocks, or promontories, in many parts of the eastern coast of Scotland, and the position of Fast Castle seems certainly to resemble that of Wolf's Crag as much as any other, while its vicinity to the mountain ridge of Lammermoor, renders the assimilation a probable one.

We have only to add, that the death of the unfortunate bridegroom by a fall from horseback, has been in the novel transferred to the no less unfortunate lover.

CHAPTER I

By cauk and keel to win your bread,
Wi' whigmaleeries for them wha need,
Whilk is a gentle trade indeed
    To carry the gaberlunzie on.

Old Song.

FEW have been in my secret while I was compiling these narratives, nor is it probable that they will ever become public during the life of their author. Even were that event to happen, I am not ambitious of the honoured distinction, *digito monstrarier.* I confess, that, were it safe to cherish such dreams at all, I should more enjoy the thought of remaining behind the curtain unseen, like the ingenious manager of Punch and his wife Joan, and enjoying the astonishment and conjectures of my audience. Then might I, perchance, hear the productions of the obscure Peter Pattieson praised by the judicious, and admired by the feeling, engrossing the young, and attracting even the old; while the critic traced their fame up to some name of literary celebrity, and the question when, and by whom, these tales were written, filled up the pause of conversation in a hundred circles and coteries. This I may never enjoy during my lifetime; but farther than this, I am certain, my vanity should never induce me to aspire.

I am too stubborn in habits, and too little polished in manners, to envy or aspire to the honours assigned to my literary contemporaries. I could not think a whit more highly of myself, were I even found worthy to "come in place as a lion," for a winter in the great metropolis. I could not rise, turn round, and show all my honours, from the shaggy mane to the tufted tail, roar you an 'twere any nightingale, and so lie down again like a well-behaved beast of show, and all at the cheap and easy rate of a cup of coffee, and a slice of bread and butter as thin as a wafer. And I could ill stomach the fulsome flattery with which the lady of the evening indulges her show-monsters on such occasions, as she crams her parrots with sugar-plums, in order to make them talk before company. I cannot be tempted

13

to "come aloft" for these marks of distinction, and, like imprisoned Samson, I would rather remain—if such must be the alternative—all my life in the mill-house, grinding for my very bread, than be brought forth to make sport for the Philistine lords and ladies. This proceeds from no dislike, real or affected, to the aristocracy of these realms. But they have their place, and I have mine; and, like the iron and earthen vessels, in the old fable, we can scarce come into collision without my being the sufferer in every sense. It may be otherwise with the sheets which I am now writing. These may be opened and laid aside at pleasure; by amusing themselves with the perusal, the great will excite no false hopes; by neglecting or condemning them, they will inflict no pain; and how seldom can they converse with those whose minds have toiled for their delight, without doing either the one or the other.

In the better and wiser tone of feeling, which Ovid only expresses in one line to retract in that which follows, I can address these quires—

Parve, nec invideo, sine me, liber, ibis in urbem.

Nor do I join the regret of the illustrious exile, that he himself could not in person accompany the volume, which he sent forth to the mart of literature, pleasure, and luxury. Were there not a hundred similar instances on record, the fate of my poor friend and school-fellow, Dick Tinto, would be sufficient to warn me against seeking happiness, in the celebrity which attaches itself to a successful cultivator of the fine arts.

Dick Tinto, when he wrote himself artist, was wont to derive his origin from the ancient family of Tinto, of that ilk, in Lanarkshire, and occasionally hinted that he had somewhat derogated from his gentle blood, in using the pencil for his principal means of support. But if Dick's pedigree was correct, some of his ancestors must have suffered a more heavy declension, since the good man his father executed the necessary, and, I trust, the honest, but certainly not very distinguished employment, of tailor in ordinary to the village of Langdirdum in the west. Under his humble roof was Richard born, and to his father's humble trade was Richard, greatly contrary to his inclination, early indentured. Old Mr Tinto had, however, no reason to congratulate himself upon having compelled the youthful genius of his son to forsake its natural bent. He fared like the schoolboy, who attempts to stop with his finger the spout of a water cistern, while the stream, exasperated at this compression, escapes by a thousand uncalculated spirts, and wets him all over for his pains. Even so fared the senior Tinto, when his hopeful apprentice not only exhausted all the chalk in making sketches upon the shopboard, but even executed several caricatures of his father's best customers, who began loudly to murmur, that it was too hard to have their persons deformed by the vestments of the father, and to be at the same time turned into ridicule by the pencil of the son. This led to discredit and loss of practice, until the old tailor, yielding to destiny, and to the entreaties of his son, permitted him to attempt his fortune in a line for which he was better qualified.

There was about this time, in the village of Langdirdum, a peripatetic brother of the brush, who exercised his vocation *sub Jove frigido*, the object of admiration to all the boys of the village, but especially to Dick Tinto. The age had not yet adopted, amongst other unworthy retrenchments, that illiberal measure of economy, which, supplying by written characters the lack of symbolical representation, closes one open and easily accessible avenue of instruction and emolument against the students of the fine arts. It was not yet permitted to write upon the plastered door-way of an ale-house, or the suspended sign of an inn, "The Old Magpie," or "The Saracen's Head," substituting that cold description for the lively effigies of the plumed chatterer, or the turban'd frown of the terrific soldan. That early and more simple age considered alike the necessities of all ranks, and depicted the symbols of good cheer so as to be obvious to all capacities; well judging, that a man, who could not read a syllable, might nevertheless love a pot of good ale as well as his better-educated neighbours, or even as the parson himself. Acting upon this liberal principle, publicans as yet hung forth the painted emblems of their calling, and sign-painters, if they seldom feasted, did not at least absolutely starve.

To a worthy of this decayed profession, as we have already intimated, Dick Tinto became an assistant; and thus, as is not unusual among heaven-born geniuses in this

department of the fine arts, began to paint before he had
any notion of drawing.

His talent for observing nature soon induced him to
rectify the errors, and soar above the instructions, of his
teacher. He particu arly shone in painting horses, that
being a favourite sign in the Scottish villages; and, in
tracing his progress, it is beautiful to observe, how by
degrees he learned to shorten the backs, and prolong the
legs, of these noble animals, until they came to look less
like crocodiles, and more like nags. Detraction, which
always pursues merit with strides proportioned to its ad-
vancement, has indeed alleged, that Dick once upon a time
painted a horse with five legs, instead of four. I might
have rested his defence upon the licence allowed to that
branch of his profession, which, as it permits all sorts of
singular and irregular combinations, may be allowed to
extend itself so far as to bestow a limb supernumerary on a
favourite subject. But the cause of a deceased friend is
sacred; and I disdain to bottom it so superficially. I have
visited the sign in question, which yet swings exalted in the
village of Langdirdum; and I am ready to depone upon
oath, that what has been idly mistaken or misrepresented
as being the fifth leg of the horse, is, in fact, the tail of that
quadruped, and, considered with reference to the posture
in which he is delineated, forms a circumstance, introduced
and managed with great and successful, though daring art.
The nag being represented in a rampant or rearing posture,
the tail, which is prolonged till it touches the ground,
appears to form a *point d'appui*, and gives the firmness of a
tripod to the figure, without which it would be difficult to
conceive, placed as the feet are, how the courser could
maintain his ground without tumbling backwards. This
bold conception has fortunately fallen into the custody of
one by whom it is duly valued; for, when Dick, in his
more advanced state of proficiency, became dubious of the
propriety of so daring a deviation from the established rules
of art, and was desirous to execute a picture of the publican
himself in exchange for this juvenile production, the
courteous offer was declined by his judicious employer,
who had observed, it seems, that when his ale failed to do
its duty in conciliating his guests, one glance at his sign
was sure to put them in good humour.

It would be foreign to my present purpose to trace the steps by which Dick Tinto improved his touch, and corrected, by the rules of art, the luxuriance of a fervid imagination. The scales fell from his eyes on viewing the sketches of a contemporary, the Scottish Teniers, as Wilkie has been deservedly styled. He threw down the brush, took up the crayons, and, amid hunger and toil, and suspense and uncertainty, pursued the path of his profession under better auspices than those of his original master. Still the first rude emanations of his genius (like the nursery rhymes of Pope, could these be recovered) will be dear to the companions of Dick Tinto's youth. There is a tankard and gridiron painted over the door of an obscure change-house in the Back-wynd of Gandercleugh—But I feel I must tear myself from the subject, or dwell on it too long.

Amid his wants and struggles, Dick Tinto had recourse, like his brethren, to levying that tax upon the vanity of mankind which he could not extract from their taste and liberality—in a word, he painted portraits. It was in this more advanced state of proficiency, when Dick had soared above his original line of business, and highly disdained any allusion to it, that, after having been estranged for several years, we again met in the village of Gandercleugh, I holding my present situation, and Dick painting copies of the human face divine at a guinea per head. This was a small premium, yet, in the first burst of business, it more than sufficed for all Dick's moderate wants; so that he occupied an apartment at the Wallace Inn, cracked his jest with impunity even upon mine host himself, and lived in respect and observance with the chamber-maid, hostler, and waiter.

Those halcyon days were too serene to last long. When his honour the Laird of Gandercleugh, with his wife and three daughters, the minister, the gauger, mine esteemed patron Mr Jedediah Cleishbotham, and some round dozen of the feuars and farmers, had been consigned to immortality by Tinto's brush, custom began to slacken, and it was impossible to wring more than crowns and half-crowns from the hard hands of the peasants, whose ambition led them to Dick's painting-room.

Still, though the horizon was overclouded, no storm for

some time ensued. Mine host had Christian faith with a
lodger, who had been a good paymaster as long as he had
the means.   And from a portrait of our landlord himself,
grouped with his wife and daughters, in the style of Rubens,
which suddenly appeared in the best parlour, it was evident
that Dick had found some mode of bartering art for the
necessaries of life.

Nothing, however, is more precarious than resources of
this nature.   It was observed, that Dick became in his turn
the whetstone of mine host's wit, without venturing either
at defence or retaliation; that his easel was transferred to
a garret-room, in which there was scarce space for it to
stand upright; and that he no longer ventured to join the
weekly club, of which he had been once the life and soul.
In short, Dick Tinto's friends feared that he had acted like
the animal called the sloth, which, having eaten up the last
green leaf upon the tree where it has established itself, ends
by tumbling down from the top, and dying of inanition.   I
ventured to hint this to Dick, recommended his transferring
the exercise of his inestimable talent to some other sphere,
and forsaking the common which he might be said to have
eaten bare.

"There is an obstacle to my change of residence," said
my friend, grasping my hand with a look of solemnity.

"A bill due to my landlord, I am afraid?" replied I,
with heartfelt sympathy; "if any part of my slender means
can assist in this emergence"——

"No, by the soul of Sir Joshua!" answered the generous
youth, "I will never involve a friend in the consequences
of my own misfortune.   There is a m de by which I can
regain my liberty; and to creep even through a common
sewer, is better than to remain in prison."

I did not perfectly understand what my friend meant.
The muse of painting appeared to have failed him, and
what other goddess he could invoke in his distress, was a
mystery to me.   We parted, however, without further
explanation, and I did not again see him until three days
after, when he summoned me to partake of the *foy* with
which his landlord proposed to regale him ere his departure
for Edinburgh.

I found Dick in high spirits, whistling while he buckled
the small knapsack, which contained his colours, brushes,

pallets, and clean shirt. That he parted on the best terms
with mine host, was obvious from the cold beef set forth
in the low parlour, flanked by two mugs of admirable brown
stout; and I own my curiosity was excited concerning the
means through which the face of my friend's affairs had
been so suddenly improved. I did not suspect Dick of
dealing with the devil, and by what earthly means he had
extricated himself thus happily, I was at a total loss to
conjecture.

He perceived my curiosity, and took me by the hand.
"My friend," he said, "fain would I conceal, even from
you, the degradation to which it has been necessary to submit, in order to accomplish an honourable retreat from
Gandercleugh. But what avails attempting to conceal that,
which must needs betray itself even by its superior excellence? All the village—all the parish—all the world—will
soon discover to what poverty has reduced Richard Tinto."

A sudden thought here struck me—I had observed that
our landlord wore, on that memorable morning, a pair of
bran new velveteens, instead of his ancient thicksets.

"What," said I, drawing my right hand, with the fore-
finger and thumb pressed together, nimbly from my right
haunch to my left shoulder, "you have condescended to
resume the paternal arts to which you were first bred—long
stitches, ha, Dick?"

He repelled this unlucky conjecture with a frown and a
pshaw, indicative of indignant contempt, and leading me
into another room, showed me, resting against the wall, the
majestic head of Sir William Wallace, grim as when severed
from the trunk by the orders of the felon Edward.

The painting was executed on boards of a substantial
thickness, and the top decorated with irons, for suspending
the honoured effigy upon a sign-post.

"There," he said, "my friend, stands the honour of
Scotland, and my shame—yet not so—rather the shame of
those, who, instead of encouraging art in its proper sphere,
reduce it to these unbecoming and unworthy extremities."

I endeavoured to smooth the ruffled feelings of my misused and indignant friend. I reminded him, that he ought
not, like the stag in the fable, to despise the quality which
had extricated him from difficulties, in which his talents,
as a portrait or landscape painter, had been found unavail-

ing.   Above all, I praised the execution, as well as conception, of his painting, and reminded him, that far from
feeling dishonoured by so superb a specimen of his talents
being exposed to the general view of the public, he ought
rather to congratulate himself upon the augmentation of his
celebrity, to which its public exhibition must necessarily
give rise.

"You are right, my friend—you are right," replied poor
Dick, his eye kindling with enthusiasm; "why should I
shun the name of an—an"—(he hesitated for a phrase)—
"an out-of-doors artist?   Hogarth has introduced himself
in that character in one of his best engravings—Domeni-
chino, or somebody else in ancient times—Moreland in
our own, have exercised their talents in this manner.   And
wherefore limit to the rich and higher classes alone the
delight which the exhibition of works of art is calculated to
inspire into all classes?   Statues are placed in the open
air, why should Painting be more niggardly in displaying
her master-pieces than her sister Sculpture?   And yet, my
friend, we must part suddenly; the carpenter is coming in
an hour to put up the—the emblem; and truly, with all my
philosophy, and your consolatory encouragement to boot,
I would rather wish to leave Gandercleugh before that
operation commences."

We partook of our genial host's parting banquet, and I
escorted Dick on his walk to Edinburgh.   We parted
about a mile from the village, just as we heard the distant
cheer of the boys which accompanied the mounting of the
new symbol of the Wallace-Head.   Dick Tinto mended his
pace to get out of hearing—so little had either early practice
or recent philosophy reconciled him to the character of a
sign-painter.

In Edinburgh, Dick's talents were discovered and appreciated, and he received dinners and hints from several
distinguished judges of the fine arts.   But these gentlemen
dispensed their criticism more willingly than their cash,
and Dick thought he needed cash more than criticism.
He therefore sought London, the universal mart of talent,
and where, as is usual in general marts of most descriptions,
much more of each commodity is exposed to sale than can
ever find purchasers.

Dick, who, in serious earnest, was supposed to have con-

siderable natural talents for his profession, and whose vain
and sanguine disposition never permitted him to doubt for
a moment of ultimate success, threw himself headlong into
the crowd which jostled and struggled for notice and preferment. He elbowed others, and was elbowed himself; and
finally, by dint of intrepidity, fought his way into some
notice, painted for the prize at the Institution, had pictures
at the exhibition at Somerset-house, and damned the hanging committee. But poor Dick was doomed to lose the
field he fought so gallantly. In the fine arts, there is scarce
an alternative betwixt distinguished success and absolute
failure; and as Dick's zeal and industry were unable to
ensure the first, he fell into the distresses which, in his condition, were the natural consequences of the latter alternative. He was for a time patronised by one or two of
those judicious persons who make a virtue of being singular,
and of pitching their own opinions against those of the
world in matters of taste and criticism. But they soon
tired of poor Tinto, and laid him down as a load, upon the
principle on which a spoilt child throws away its plaything.
Misery, I fear, took him up, and accompanied him to a
premature grave, to which he was carried from an obscure
lodging in Swallow-street, where he had been dunned by
his landlady within doors, and watched by bailiffs without,
until death came to his relief. A corner of the *Morning
Post* noticed his death, generously adding, that his manner
displayed considerable genius, though his style was rather
sketchy; and referred to an advertisement, which announced
that Mr Varnish, a well-known print-seller, had still on hand
a very few drawings and paintings by Richard Tinto,
Esquire, which those of the nobility and gentry, who might
wish to complete their collections of modern art, were
invited to visit without delay. So ended Dick Tinto! a
lamentable proof of the great truth, that in the fine arts
mediocrity is not permitted, and that he who cannot ascend
to the very top of the ladder, will do well not to put his
foot upon it at all.

The memory of Tinto is dear to me, from the recollection
of the many conversations which we have had together,
most of them turning upon my present task. He was
delighted with my progress, and talked of an ornamented
and illustrated edition, with heads, vignettes and *culs de*

lampe, all to be designed by his own patriotic and friendly pencil. He prevailed upon an old sergeant of invalids to sit to him in the character of Bothwell, the life-guard's-man of Charles the Second, and the bell-man of Gandercleugh in that of David Deans. But while he thus proposed to unite his own powers with mine for the illustration of these narratives, he mixed many a dose of salutary criticism with the panegyrics which my composition was at times so fortunate as to call forth.

"Your characters," he said, "my dear Pattieson, make too much use of the *gob box*; they *patter* too much—(an elegant phraseology, which Dick had learned while painting the scenes of an itinerant company of players)—there is nothing in whole pages but mere chat and dialogue."

"The ancient philosopher," said I in reply, "was wont to say, 'Speak, that I may know thee;' and how is it possible for an author to introduce his *personæ dramatis* to his readers in a more interesting and effectual manner, than by the dialogue in which each is represented as supporting his own appropriate character?"

"It is a false conclusion," said Tinto; "I hate it, Peter, as I hate an unfilled cann. I will grant you, indeed, that speech is a faculty of some value in the intercourse of human affairs, and I will not even insist on the doctrine of that Pythagorean toper, who was of opinion, that over a bottle speaking spoiled conversation. But I will not allow that a professor of the fine arts has occasion to embody the idea of his scene in language, in order to impress upon the reader its reality and its effect. On the contrary, I will be judged by most of your readers, Peter, should these tales ever become public, whether you have not given us a page of talk for every single idea which two words might have communicated, while the posture, and manner, and incident, accurately drawn, and brought out by appropriate colouring, would have preserved all that was worthy of preservation, and saved these everlasting said he's and said she's, with which it has been your pleasure to encumber your pages."

I replied, "that he confounded the operations of the pencil and the pen; that the serene and silent art, as painting has been called by one of our first living poets, necessarily appealed to the eye, because it had not the organs for addressing the ear; whereas poetry, or that species of composition which approached to it, lay under the necessity of doing absolutely the reverse, and addressed itself to the ear, for the purpose of exciting that interest which it could not attain through the medium of the eye."

Dick was not a whit staggered by my argument, which he contended was founded on misrepresentation. "Description," he said, "was to the author of a romance exactly what drawing and tinting were to a painter; words were his colours, and, if properly employed, they could not fail to place the scene. which he wished to conjure up, as effectually before the mind's eye, as the tablet or canvas presents it to the bodily organ. The same rules," he contended, "applied to both, and an exuberance of dialogue, in the former case, was a verbose and laborious mode of composition which went to confound the proper art of fictitious narrative with that of the drama, a widely different species of composition, of which dialogue was the very essence, because all, excepting the language to be made use of, was presented to the eye by the dresses, and persons, and actions of the performers upon the stage. But as nothing," said Dick, "can be more dull than a long narrative written upon the plan of a drama, so where you have approached most near to that species of composition, by indulging in prolonged scenes of mere conversation, the course of your story has become chill and constrained, and you have lost the power of arresting the attention and exciting the imagination, in which upon other occasions you may be considered as having succeeded tolerably well.

I made my bow in requital of the compliment, which was probably thrown in by way of *placebo*, and expressed myself willing at least to make one trial of a more straightforward style of composition, in which my actors should do more, and say less, than in my former attempts of this kind. Dick gave me a patronising and approving nod, and observed, that, finding me so docile, he would communicate, for the benefit of my muse, a subject which he had studied with a view to his own art.

"The story," he said, "was, by tradition, affirmed to be truth, although, as upwards of a hundred years had passed away since the events took place, some doubts upon the accuracy of all the particulars might be reasonably entertained."

When Dick Tinto had thus spoken, he rummaged his portfolio for the sketch from which he proposed one day to execute a picture of fourteen feet by eight. The sketch, which was cleverly executed, to use the appropriate phrase, represented an ancient hall, fitted up and furnished in what we now call the taste of Queen Elizabeth's age. The light, admitted from the upper part of a high casement, fell upon a female figure of exquisite beauty, who, in an attitude of speechless terror, appeared to watch the issue of a debate betwixt two other persons. The one was a young man, in the Vandyke dress common to the time of Charles I., who, with an air of indignant pride, testified by the manner in which he raised his head and extended his arm, seemed to be urging a claim of right, rather than of favour, to a lady, whose age, and some resemblance in their features, pointed her out as the mother of the younger female, and who appeared to listen with a mixture of displeasure and impatience.

Tinto produced his sketch with an air of mysterious triumph, and gazed on it as a fond parent looks upon a hopeful child, while he anticipates the future figure he is to make in the world, and the height to which he will raise the honour of his family. He held it at arms' length from me,—he held it closer,—he placed it upon the top of a chest of drawers, closed the lower shutters of the casement, to adjust a downward and favourable light,—fell back to the due distance, dragging me after him,—shaded his face with his hand, as if to exclude all but the favourite object,— and ended by spoiling a child's copy book, which he rolled up so as to serve for the darkened tube of an amateur. I fancy my expressions of enthusiasm had not been in proportion to his own, for he presently exclaimed with vehemence, "Mr Pattieson, I used to think you had an eye in your head."

I vindicated my claim to the usual allowance of visual organs.

"Yet, on my honour," said Dick, "I would swear you had been born blind, since you have failed at the first glance to discover the subject and meaning of that sketch.

I do not mean to praise my own performance, I leave these arts to others; I am sensible of my deficiencies, conscious that my drawing and colouring may be improved by the time I intend to dedicate to the art. But the conception— the expression—the positions—these tell the story to every one who looks at the sketch; and if I can finish the picture without diminution of the original conception, the name of Tinto shall no more be smothered by the mists of envy and intrigue."

I replied, "That I admired the sketch exceedingly; but that to understand its full merit, I felt it absolutely necessary to be informed of the subject."

"That is the very thing I complain of," answered Tinto; "you have accustomed yourself so much to these creeping twilight details of yours, that you are become incapable of receiving that instant and vivid flash of conviction, which darts on the mind from seeing the happy and expressive combinations of a single scene, and which gathers from the position, attitude, and countenance of the moment, not only the history of the past lives of the personages represented, and the nature of the business on which they are immediately engaged, but lifts even the veil of futurity, and affords a shrewd guess at their future fortunes."

"In that case," replied I, "Painting excels the Ape of the renowned Gines de Passamont, which only meddled with the past and the present; nay, she excels that very Nature who affords her subjects; for I protest to you, Dick, that were I permitted to peep into that Elizabeth-chamber, and see the persons you have sketched conversing in flesh and blood, I should not be a jot nearer guessing the nature of their business, than I am at this moment while looking at your sketch. Only generally, from the languishing look of the young lady, and the care you have taken to present a very handsome leg on the part of the gentleman, I presume there is some reference to a love affair between them."

"Do you really presume to form such a bold conjecture?" said Tinto. "And the indignant earnestness with which you see the man urge his suit—the unresisting and passive despair of the younger female—the stern air of inflexible determination in the elder woman, whose looks express at once consciousness that she is acting wrong, and a firm determination to persist in the course she has adopted"——

"If her looks express all this, my dear Tinto," replied I, interrupting him, "your pencil rivals the dramatic art of Mr Puff in the *Critic*, who crammed a whole complicated sentence into the expressive shake of Lord Burleigh's head."

"My good friend, Peter," replied Tinto, "I observe you are perfectly incorrigible; however, I have compassion on your dulness, and am unwilling you should be deprived of the pleasure of understanding my picture, and of gaining, at the same time, a subject for your own pen. You must know then, last summer, while I was taking sketches on the coast of East Lothian and Berwickshire, I was seduced into the mountains of Lammermoor by the account I received of some remains of antiquity in that district. Those with which I was most struck, were the ruins of an ancient castle in which that Elizabeth-chamber, as you call it, once existed. I resided for two or three days at a farm-house in the neighbourhood, where the aged goodwife was well acquainted with the history of the castle, and the events which had taken place in it. One of these was of a nature so interesting and singular, that my attention was divided between my wish to draw the old ruins in landscape, and to represent, in a history-piece, the singular events which have taken place in it. Here are my notes of the tale," said poor Dick, handing a parcel of loose scraps, partly scratched over with his pencil, partly with his pen, where outlines of caricatures, sketches of turrets, mills, old gables, and dovecots, disputed the ground with his written memoranda.

I proceeded, however, to decipher the substance of the manuscript as well as I could, and wove it into the following Tale, in which, following in part, though not entirely, my friend Tinto's advice, I endeavoured to render my narrative rather descriptive than dramatic. My favourite propensity, however, has at times overcome me, and my persons, like many others in this talking world, speak now and then a great deal more than they act.

CHAPTER II

Well, lords, we have not got that which we have;
'Tis not enough our foes are this time fled,
Being opposites of such repairing nature.
                    Second Part of Henry VI.

IN the gorge of a pass or mountain glen, ascending from the
fertile plains of East Lothian, there stood in former times
an extensive castle, of which only the ruins are now visible.
Its ancient proprietors were a race of powerful and warlike
barons, who bore the same name with the castle itself, which
was Ravenswood. Their line extended to a remote period
of antiquity, and they had intermarried with the Douglasses,
Humes, Swintons, Hays, and other families of power and
distinction in the same country. Their history was frequently involved in that of Scotland itself, in whose annals
their feats are recorded. The Castle of Ravenswood,
occupying, and in some measure commanding, a pass
betwixt Berwickshire or the Merse, as the south-eastern
province of Scotland is termed, and the Lothians, was of
importance both in times of foreign war and domestic discord. It was frequently besieged with ardour, and defended
with obstinacy, and, of course, its owners played a con-
spicuous part in story. But their house had its revolutions,
like all sublunary things; it became greatly declined from
its splendour about the middle of the 17th century; and
towards the period of the Revolution, the last proprietor of
Ravenswood Castle saw himself compelled to part with the
ancient family seat, and to remove himself to a lonely and
sea-beaten tower, which, situated on the bleak shores
between Saint Abb's Head and the village of Eyemouth,
looked out on the lonely and boisterous German Ocean.
A black domain of wild pasture-land surrounded their new
residence, and formed the remains of their property.

Lord Ravenswood, the heir of this ruined family, was far
from bending his mind to his new condition of life. In
the civil war of 1689, he had espoused the sinking side, and
although he had escaped without the forfeiture of life or
land, his blood had been attainted, and his title abolished.
He was now called Lord Ravenswood only in courtesy.

This forfeited nobleman inherited the pride and turbulence, though not the fortune of his house, and, as he imputed the final declension of his family to a particular individual, he honoured that person with his full portion of hatred. This was the very man who had now become, by purchase, proprietor of Ravenswood, and the domains of which the heir of the house now stood dispossessed. He was descended of a family much less ancient than that of Lord Ravenswood, and which had only risen to wealth and political importance during the great civil wars. He himself had been bred to the bar, and had held high offices in the state, maintaining through life the character of a skilful fisher in the troubled waters of a state divided by factions, and governed by delegated authority ; and of one who contrived to amass considerable sums of money in a country where there was but little to be gathered, and who equally knew the value of wealth, and the various means of augmenting it, and using it as an engine of increasing his power and influence.

Thus qualified and gifted, he was a dangerous antagonist to the fierce and imprudent Ravenswood. Whether he had given him good cause for the enmity with which the Baron regarded him, was a point on which men spoke differently. Some said the quarrel arose merely from the vindictive spirit and envy of Lord Ravenswood, who could not patiently behold another, though by just and fair purchase, become the proprietor of the estate and castle of his forefathers. But the greater part of the public, prone to slander the wealthy in their absence, as to flatter them in their presence. held a less charitable opinion. They said, that the Lord Keeper (for to this height Sir William Ashton had ascended) had, previous to the final purchase of the estate of Ravenswood, been concerned in extensive pecuniary transactions with the former proprietor ; and, rather intimating what was probable, than affirming any thing positively, they a ked which party was likely to have the advantage in staring and enforcing the claims arising out of these complicated affairs, and more than hinted the advantages which the cool lawyer and able politician must necessarily possess over the hot, fiery, and imprudent character, whom he had involved in legal toils and pecuniary snares.

The character of the times aggravated these suspicions. "In those days there was no king in Israel." Since the departure of James VI. to assume the richer and more powerful crown of England, there had existed in Scotland contending parties, formed among the aristocracy, by whom, as their intrigues at the court of St James's chanced to prevail, the delegated powers of sovereignty were alternately swayed. The evils attending upon this system of government, resemble those which afflict the tenants of an Irish estate, the property of an absentee. There was no supreme power, claiming and possessing a general interest with the community at large, to whom the oppressed might appeal from subordinate tyranny, either for justice or for mercy. Let a monarch be as indolent, as selfish, as much disposed to arbitrary power as he will, still, in a free country, his own interests are so clearly connected with those of the public at large, and the evil consequences to his own authority are so obvious and imminent when a different course is pursued, that common policy, as well as common feeling, point to the equal distribution of justice, and to the establishment of the throne in righteousness. Thus, even sovereigns, remarkable for usurpation and tyranny, have been found rigorous in the administration of justice among their subjects, in cases where their own power and passions were not compromised.

It is very different when the powers of sovereignty are delegated to the head of an aristocratic faction, rivalled and pressed closely in the race of ambition by an adverse leader. His brief and precarious enjoyment of power must be employed in rewarding his partisans, in extending his influence, in oppressing and crushing his adversaries. Even Abou Hassan, the most disinterested of all viceroys, forgot not, during his caliphate of one day, to send a *douceur* of one thousand pieces of gold to his own household; and the Scottish vicegerents raised to power by the strength of their faction, failed not to embrace the same means of rewarding them.

The administration of justice, in particular, was infected by the most gross partiality. A case of importance scarcely occurred, in which there was not some ground for bias or partiality on the part of the judges, who were so little able to withstand the temptation, that the adage, "Show me the man, and I will show you the law," became as prevalent as it was scandalous. One corruption led the way to others still more gross and profligate. The judge who lent his sacred authority in one case to support a friend, and in another to crush an enemy, and whose decisions were founded on family connexions, or political relations, could not be supposed inaccessible to direct personal motives; and the purse of the wealthy was too often believed to be thrown into the scale to weigh down the cause of the poor litigant. The subordinate officers of the law affected little scruple concerning bribery. Pieces of plate, and bags of money, were sent in presents to the king's counsel, to influence their conduct, and poured forth, says a contemporary writer, like billets of wood upon their floors, without even the decency of concealment.

In such times, it was not over uncharitable to suppose, that the statesman, practised in courts of law, and a powerful member of a triumphant cabal, might find and use means of advantage over his less skilful and less favoured adversary; and if it had been supposed that Sir William Ashton's conscience had been too delicate to profit by these advantages, it was believed that his ambition and desire of extending his wealth and consequence, found as strong a stimulus in the exhortations of his lady, as the daring aim of Macbeth in the days of yore.

Lady Ashton was of a family more distinguished than that of her lord, an advantage which she did not fail to use to the uttermost, in maintaining and extending her husband's influence over others, and, unless she was greatly belied, her own over him. She had been beautiful, and was stately and majestic in her appearance. Endowed by nature with strong powers and violent passions, experience had taught her to employ the one, and to conceal, if not to moderate, the other. She was a severe and strict observer of the external forms, at least, of devotion; her hospitality was splendid, even to ostentation; her address and manners, agreeable to the pattern most valued in Scotland at the period, were grave, dignified, and severely regulated by the rules of etiquette. Her character had always been beyond the breath of slander. And yet, with all these qualities to excite respect, Lady Ashton was seldom mentioned in the terms of love or affection. Interest,—the interest of her family, if not her own,—seemed too obviously the motive of her actions; and where this is the case, the sharp-judging

and malignant public are not easily imposed upon by outward show. It was seen and ascertained, that, in her most
graceful courtesies and compliments, Lady Ashton no more
lost sight of her object than the falcon in his airy wheel
turns his quick eyes from his destined quarry; and hence,
something of doubt and suspicion qualified the feelings
with which her equals received her attentions. With her
inferiors these feelings were mingled with fear; an impression useful to her purposes, so far as it enforced ready
compliance with her requests, and implicit obedience to
her commands, but detrimental, because it cannot exist
with affection or regard.

Even her husband, it is said, upon whose fortunes her
talents and address had produced such emphatic influence,
regarded her with respectful awe rather than confiding
attachment; and report said, there were times when he
considered his grandeur as dearly purchased at the expense
of domestic thraldom. Of this, however, much might be
suspected, but little could be accurately known; Lady
Ashton regarded the honour of her husband as her own,
and was well aware how much that would suffer in the
public eye should he appear a vassal to his wife. In all
her arguments, his opinion was quoted as infallible; his
taste was appealed to, and his sentiments received, with
the air of deference which a dutiful wife might seem to
owe to a husband of Sir William Ashton's rank and character. But there was something under all this which rung
false and hollow; and to those who watched this couple
with close, and perhaps malicious scrutiny, it seemed
evident, that, in the haughtiness of a firmer character,
higher birth, and more decided views of aggrandisement,
the lady looked with some contempt on her husband, and
that he regarded her with jealous fear, rather than with love
or admiration.

Still, however, the leading and favourite interests of Sir
William Ashton and his lady were the same, and they failed
not to work in concert, although without cordiality, and to
testify, in all exterior circumstances, that respect for each
other, which they were aware was necessary to secure that
of the public.

Their union was crowned with several children, of whom
three survived. One, the eldest son, was absent on his

travels; the second, a girl of seventeen, and the third, a boy about three years younger, resided with their parents in Edinburgh, during the sessions of the Scottish Parliament and Privy-council, at other times in the old Gothic castle of Ravenswood, to which the Lord Keeper had made large additions in the style of the seventeenth century.

Allan Lord Ravenswood, the late proprietor of that ancient mansion and the large estate annexed to it, continued for some time to wage ineffectual war with his successor concerning various points to which their former transactions had given rise, and which were successively determined in favour of the wealthy and powerful competitor, until death closed the litigation, by summoning Ravenswood to a higher bar. The thread of life, which had been long wasting, gave way during a fit of violent and impotent fury, with which he was assailed on receiving the news of the loss of a cause, founded, perhaps, rather in equity than in law, the last which he had maintained against his powerful antagonist. His son witnessed his dying agonies, and heard the curses which he breathed against his adversary, as if they had conveyed to him a legacy of vengeance. Other circumstances happened to exasperate a passion, which was, and had long been, a prevalent vice in the Scottish disposition.

It was a November morning, and the cliffs which overlooked the ocean were hung with thick and heavy mist, when the portals of the ancient and half-ruinous tower, in which Lord Ravenswood had spent the last and troubled years of his life, opened, that his mortal remains might pass forward to an abode yet more dreary and lonely. The pomp of attendance, to which the deceased had, in his latter years, been a stranger, was revived as he was about to be consigned to the realms of forgetfulness.

Banner after banner, with the various devices and coats of this ancient family and its connexions, followed each other in mournful procession from under the low-browed archway of the court-yard. The principal gentry of the country attended in the deepest mourning, and tempered the pace of their long train of horses to the solemn march befitting the occasion. Trumpets, with banners of crape attached to them, sent forth their long and melancholy notes to regulate the movements of the procession. An immense train of inferior mourners and menials closed the rear, which had not yet issued from the castle-gate, when the van had reached the chapel where the body was to be deposited.

Contrary to the custom, and even to the law of the time, the body was met by a priest of the Scottish Episcopal communion, arrayed in his surplice, and prepared to read over the coffin of the deceased the funeral service of the church. Such had been the desire of Lord Ravenswood in his last illness, and it was readily complied with by the tory gentlemen, or cavaliers, as they affected to style themselves, in which faction most of his kinsmen were enrolled. The presbyterian church-judicatory of the bounds, considering the ceremony as a bravading insult upon their authority, had applied to the Lord Keeper, as the nearest privy-councillor, for a warrant to prevent its being carried into effect ; so that, when the clergyman had opened his prayer-book, an officer of the law, supported by some armed men, commanded him to be silent. An insult, which fired the whole assembly with indignation, was particularly and instantly resented by the only son of the deceased, Edgar, popularly called the Master of Ravenswood, a youth of about twenty years of age. He clapped his hand on his sword, and, bidding the official person to desist at his peril from farther interruption, commanded the clergyman to proceed. The man attempted to enforce his commission, but as an hundred swords at once glittered in the air, he contented himself with protesting against the violence which had been offered to him in the execution of his duty, and stood aloof, a sullen and moody spectator of the ceremonial, muttering as one who should say, " You'll rue the day that clogs me with this answer."

The scene was worthy of an artist's pencil. Under the very arch of the house of death, the clergyman, affrighted at the scene, and trembling for his own safety, hastily and unwillingly rehearsed the solemn service of the church, and spoke dust to dust, and ashes to ashes, over ruined pride and decayed prosperity. Around stood the relations of the deceased, their countenances more in anger than in sorrow, and the drawn swords which they brandished forming a violent contrast with their deep mourning habits. In the countenance of the young man alone, resentment seemed for the moment overpowered by the deep agony with which he beheld his nearest, and almost his only friend, consigned to the tomb of his ancestry. A relative observed him turn deadly pale, when, all rites being now duly observed, it became the duty of the chief mourner to lower down into the charnel vault, where mouldering coffins showed their tattered velvet and decayed plating, the head of the corpse which was to be their partner in corruption. He stept to the youth and offered his assistance, which, by a mute motion, Edgar Ravenswood rejected. Firmly, and without a tear, he performed that last duty. The stone was laid on the sepulchre, the door of the aisle was locked, and the youth took possession of its massive key.

As the crowd left the chapel, he paused on the steps which led to its Gothic chancel. "Gentlemen and friends," he said, "you have this day done no common duty to the body of your deceased kinsman. The rites of due observance, which, in other countries, are allowed as the due of the meanest Christian, would this day have been denied to the body of your relative—not certainly sprung of the meanest house in Scotland—had it not been assured to him by your courage. Others bury their dead in sorrow and tears, in silence and in reverence; our funeral rites are marred by the intrusion of bailiffs and ruffians, and our grief —the grief due to our departed friend—is chased from our cheeks by the glow of just indignation. But it is well that I know from what quiver this arrow has come forth. It was only he that dug the grave who could have the mean cruelty to disturb the obsequies; and Heaven do as much to me and more, if I requite not to this man and his house the ruin and disgrace he has brought on me and mine!"

A numerous part of the assembly applauded this speech, as the spirited expression of just resentment; but the more cool and judicious regretted that it had been uttered. The fortunes of the heir of Ravenswood were too low to brave the farther hostility which they imagined these open expressions of resentment must necessarily provoke. Their apprehensions, however, proved groundless, at least in the immediate consequences of this affair.

The mourners returned to the tower, there, acccording to a custom but recently abolished in Scotland, to carouse deep healths to the memory of the deceased, to make the house of sorrow ring with sounds of joviality and debauch, and to diminish, by the expense of a large and profuse entertainment, the limited revenues of the heir of him whose funeral they thus strangely honoured. It was the custom, however, and on the present occasion it was fully observed. The tables swam in wine, the populace feasted in the court-yard, the yeomen in the kitchen and buttery; and two years' rent of Ravenswood's remaining property hardly defrayed the charge of the funeral revel. The wine did its office on all but the Master of Ravenswood, a title which he still retained, though forfeiture had attached to that of his father. He, while passing around the cup which he himself did not taste, soon listened to a thousand exclamations against the Lord Keeper, and passionate protestations of attachment to himself, and to the honour of his house. He listened with dark and sullen brow to ebullitions which he considered justly as equally evanescent with the crimson. bubbles on the brink of the goblet, or at least with the vapours which its contents excited in the brains of the revellers around him.

When the last flask was emptied, they took their leave, with deep protestations—to be forgotten on the morrow, if, indeed, those who made them should not think it necessary for their safety to make a more solemn retractation.

Accepting their adieus with an air of contempt which he could scarce conceal, Ravenswood at length beheld his ruinous habitation cleared of this confluence of riotous guests, and returned to the deserted hall, which now appeared doubly lonely from the cessation of that clamour to which it had so lately echoed. But its space was peopled by phantoms, which the imagination of the young heir conjured up before him—the tarnished honour and degraded fortunes of his house, the destruction of his own hopes, and the triumph of that family by whom they had been ruined. To a mind naturally of a gloomy cast, here was ample room for meditation, and the musings of young Ravenswood were deep and unwitnessed.

The peasant who shows the ruins of the tower, which still crown the beetling cliff and behold the war of the waves, though no more tenanted save by the sea-mew and cormorant, even yet affirms, that on this fatal night the Master of Ravenswood, by the bitter exclamations of his despair, evoked some evil fiend, under whose malignant influence the future tissue of incidents was woven. Alas! what fiend can suggest more desperate counsels, than those adopted under the guidance of our own violent and unresisted passions?

CHAPTER III

Over Gods forebode, then said the King,
That thou shouldst shoot at me.
William Bell.   Clim o' the Cleugh, &c.

ON the morning after the funeral, the legal officer, whose authority had been found insufficient to effect an interruption of the funeral solemnities of the late Lord Ravenswood, hastened to state before the Keeper the resistance which he had met with in the execution of his office.

The statesman was seated in a spacious library, once a banqueting-room in the old Castle of Ravenswood, as was evident from the armorial insignia still displayed on the carved roof, which was vaulted with Spanish chestnut, and on the stained glass of the casement, though which gleamed a dim yet rich light, on the long rows of shelves, bending under the weight of legal commentators and monkish historians, whose ponderous volumes formed the chief and most valued contents of a Scottish historian of the period. On the massive oaken table and reading-desk, lay a confused mass of letters, petitions, and parchments; to toil amongst which was the pleasure at once and the plague of Sir William Ashton's life. His appearance was grave and even noble, well becoming one who held an high office in the state; and it was not, save after long and intimate conversation with him upon topics of pressing and personal interest, that a stranger could have discovered something vacillating and uncertain in his resolutions; an infirmity of purpose, arising from a cautious and timid disposition, which, as he was conscious of its internal influence on his mind, he was, from pride as well as policy, most anxious to conceal from others.

He listened with great apparent composure to an exaggerated account of the tumult which had taken place at the funeral, of the contempt thrown on his own authority, and that of the church and state; nor did he seem moved even by the faithful report of the insulting and threatening language which had been uttered by young Ravenswood and others, and obviously directed against himself. He heard, also, what the man had been able to collect, in a very distorted and aggravated shape, of the toasts which had been drunk, and the menaces uttered, at the subsequent entertainment. In fine, he made careful notes of all these particulars, and of the names of the persons by whom, in case of need, an accusation, founded upon these violent proceedings, could be witnessed and made good, and dismissed his informer, secure that he was now master of the remaining fortune, and even of the personal liberty, of young Ravenswood.

When the door had closed upon the officer of the law, the Lord Keeper remained for a moment in deep meditation; then, starting from his seat, paced the apartment as one about to take a sudden and energetic resolution. "Young Ravenswood," he muttered, "is now mine—he is my own—he has placed himself in my hand, and he shall bend or break. I have not forgotten the determined and dogged obstinacy with which his father fought every point to the last, resisted every effort at compromise, embroiled me in lawsuits, and attempted to assail my character when he could not otherwise impugn my rights. This boy he has left behind him—this Edgar—this hot-headed, hare-brained fool, has wrecked his vessel before she has cleared the harbour. I must see that he gains no advantage of some turning tide which may again float him off. These memoranda, properly stated to the Privy Council, cannot but be construed into an aggravated riot, in which the dignity both of the civil and ecclesiastical authorities stand committed. A heavy fine might be imposed; an order for committing him to Edinburgh or Blackness Castle seems not improper; even a charge of treason might be laid on many of these words and expressions, though God forbid I should prosecute the matter to that extent. No, I will not;—I will not touch his life, even if it should be in my power;—and yet, if he lives till a change of times, what follows?—Restitution—perhaps revenge. I know Athole promised his interest to old Ravenswood, and here is his son already bandying and making a faction by his own contemptible influence. What a ready tool he would be for tne use of those who are watching the downfall of our administration ! "

While these thoughts were agitating the mind of the wily statesman, and while he was persuading himself that his own interest and safety, as well as those of his friends and party, depended on using the present advantage to the uttermost against young Ravenswood, the Lord Keeper sate down to his desk, and proceeded to draw up, for the information of the Privy Council, an account of the disorderly proceedings which, in contempt of his warrant, had taken place at the funeral of Lord Ravenswood. The names of most of the parties concerned, as well as the fact itself, would, he was well aware, sound odiously in the ears of his colleagues in administration, and most likely instigate them to make an example of young Ravenswood, at least, *in terrorem.*

It was a point of delicacy, however, to select such expressions as might infer the young man's culpability, without seeming directly to urge it, which, on the part of Sir William Ashton, his father's ancient antagonist, could not but appear odious and invidious. While he was in the act of composition, labouring to find words which might indicate Edgar Ravenswood to be the cause of the uproar, without specifically making such a charge, Sir William, in a pause of his task, chanced, in looking upward, to see the crest of the family (for whose heir he was whetting the arrows, and disposing the toils of the law), carved upon one of the corbeilles from which the vaulted roof of the apartment sprung. It was a black bull's head, with the legend, " I bide my time "; and the occasion upon which it was adopted mingled itself singularly and impressively with the subject of his present reflections.

It was said by a constant tradition, that a Malisius de Ravenswood had, in the thirteenth century, been deprived of his castle and lands by a powerful usurper, who had for a while enjoyed his spoils in quiet. At length, on the eve of a costly banquet, Ravenswood, who had watched his opportunity, introduced himself into the castle with a small band of faithful retainers. The serving of the expected feast was impatiently looked for by the guests, and clamorously demanded by the temporary master of the castle. Ravenswood, who had assumed the disguise of a sewer upon the occasion, answered, in a stern voice, " I bide my time " ; and at the same moment a bull's head, the ancient symbol of death, was placed upon the table. The explosion of the conspiracy took place upon the signal, and the usurper and his followers were put to death. Perhaps there was something in this still known and often repeated story, which came immediately home to the breast and conscience of the Lord Keeper ; for, putting from him the paper on which he had begun his report, and carefully locking the memoranda which he had prepared, into a cabinet which stood beside him, he proceeded to walk abroad, as if for the purpose of collecting his ideas, and reflecting farther on the consequences of the step which he was about to take, ere yet they became inevitable.

In passing through a large Gothic anteroom, Sir William Ashton heard the sound of his daughter's lute. Music, when the performers are concealed, affects us with a pleasure mingled with surprise, and reminds us of the natural concert of birds among the leafy bowers. The statesman, though little accustomed to give way to emotions of this natural and simple class, was still a man and a father. He stopped, therefore, and listened, while the silver tones of Lucy Ashton's voice mingled with the accompaniment in an ancient air, to which some one had adapted the following words :—

> " Look not thou on beauty's charming,—
> Sit thou still when king's are arming,—
> Taste not when the wine-cup glistens,—
> Speak not when the people listens,—
> Stop thine ear against the singer,—
> From the red gold keep thy finger,—
> Vacant heart, and hand, and eye,—
> Easy live and quiet die."

The sounds ceased, and the Keeper entered his daughter's apartment.

The words she had chosen seemed particularly adapted to her character ; for Lucy Ashton's exquisitely beautiful, yet somewhat girlish features, were formed to express peace of mind, serenity, and indifference to the tinsel of worldly pleasure. Her locks, which were of shadowy gold, divided on a brow of exquisite whiteness, like a gleam of broken and pallid sunshine upon a hill of snow. The expression of the countenance was in the last degree gentle, soft, timid, and feminine, and seemed rather to shrink from the most casual look of a stranger, than to court his admiration. Something there was of a Madonna cast, perhaps the result of delicate health, and of residence in a family, where the dispositions of the inmates were fiercer, more active, and energetic, than her own.

Yet her passiveness of disposition was by no means owing to an indifferent or unfeeling mind. Left to the impulse of her own taste and feelings, Lucy Ashton was peculiarly accessible to those of a romantic cast. Her secret delight was in the old legendary tales of ardent devotion and unalterable affection, chequered as they so often are with strange adventures and supernatural horrors. This was her favoured fairy realm, and here she erected her aerial palaces. But it was only in secret that she laboured at this delusive, though delightful architecture. In her retired chamber, or in the woodland bower which she had chosen for her own, and called after her name, she was in fancy distributing the prizes at the tournament, or raining down influence from her eyes on the valiant combatants; or she was wandering in the wilderness with Una, under escort of the generous lion; or she was identifying herself with the simple, yet noble-minded Miranda, in the isle of wonder and enchantment.

But in her exterior relations to things of this world, Lucy willingly received the ruling impulse from those around her. The alternative was, in general, too indifferent to her to render resistance desirable, and she willingly found a motive for decision in the opinion of her friends, which perhaps she might have sought for in vain in her own choice. Every reader must have observed in some family of his acquaintance, some individual of a temper soft and yielding, who, mixed with stronger and more ardent minds, is borne along by the will of others, with as little power of opposition as the flower which is flung into a running stream. It usually happens that such a compliant and easy disposition, which resigns itself without murmur to the guidance of others, becomes the darling of those to whose inclinations its own seem to be offered, in ungrudging and ready sacrifice.

This was eminently the case with Lucy Ashton. Her politic, wary, and worldly father, felt for her an affection, the strength of which sometimes surprised him into an unusual emotion. Her elder brother, who trod the path of ambition with a haughtier step than his father, had also more of human affection. A soldier, and in a dissolute age, he preferred his sister Lucy even to pleasure, and to military preferment and distinction. Her younger brother, at an age when trifles chiefly occupied his mind, made her the confidant of all his pleasures and anxieties, his success in field-sports, and his quarrels with his tutors and instructors. To these details, however trivial, Lucy lent patient and not indifferent attention. They moved and interested Henry, and that was enough to secure her ear.

Her mother alone did not feel that distinguished and predominating affection, with which the rest of the family cherished Lucy. She regarded what she termed her daughter's want of spirit, as a decided mark, that the more plebeian blood of her father predominated in Lucy's veins, and used to call her in derision her Lammermoor Shepherdess. To dislike so gentle and inoffensive a being was impossible; but Lady Ashton preferred her eldest son, on whom had descended a large portion of her own ambitious and undaunted disposition, to a daughter whose softness of temper seemed allied to feebleness of mind. Her eldest son was the more partially beloved by his mother, because, contrary to the usual custom of Scottish families of distinction, he had been named after the head of the house.

"My Sholto," she said, "will support the untarnished honour of his maternal house, and elevate and support that of his father. Poor Lucy is unfit for courts, or crowded halls. Some country laird must be her husband, rich enough to supply her with every comfort, without an effort on her own part, so that she may have nothing to shed a tear for but the tender apprehension lest he may break his neck in a fox-chase. It was not so, however, that our house was raised, nor is it so that it can be fortified and augmented. The Lord Keeper's dignity is yet new; it must be borne as if we were used to its weight, worthy of it, and prompt to assert and maintain it. Before ancient authorities, men bend, from customary and hereditary deference; in our presence, they will stand erect, unless they are compelled to prostrate themselves. A daughter fit for the sheep-fold or the cloister, is ill qualified to exact respect where it is yielded with reluctance; and since Heaven refused us a third boy, Lucy should have held a character fit to supply his place. The hour will be a happy one which disposes her hand in marriage to some one whose energy is greater than her own, or whose ambition is of as low an order."

So meditated a mother, to whom the qualities of her children's hearts, as well as the prospect of their domestic happiness, seemed light in comparison to their rank and temporal greatness. But, like many a parent of hot and impatient character, she was mistaken in estimating the feelings of her daughter, who, under a semblance of extreme indifference, nourished the germ of those passions which sometimes spring up in one night, like the gourd of the prophet, and astonish the observer by their unexpected ardour and intensity. In fact, Lucy's sentiments seemed chill, because nothing had occurred to interest or awaken them. Her life had hitherto flowed on in a uniform and gentle tenor, and happy for her had not its present smoothness of current resembled that of the stream as it glides downwards to the waterfall!

"So, Lucy," said her father, entering as her song was ended, "does your musical philosopher teach you to contemn the world before you know it?—that is surely something premature. Or did you but speak according to the fashion of fair maidens, who are always to hold the pleasures of life in contempt till they are pressed upon them by the address of some gentle knight?"

Lucy blushed, disclaimed any inference respecting her own choice being drawn from her selection of a song, and readily laid aside her instrument at her father's request that she would attend him in his walk.

A large and well-wooded park, or rather chase, stretched along the hill behind the castle, which occupying, as we have noticed, a pass ascending from the plain, seemed built in its very gorge to defend the forest ground which arose behind it in shaggy majesty. Into this romantic region the

father and daughter proceeded, arm in arm, by a noble
avenue overarched by embowering elms, beneath which
groups of the fallow-deer were seen to stray in distant per-
spective. As they paced slowly on, admiring the different
points of view, for which Sir William Ashton, notwithstanding
the nature of his usual avocations, had considerable taste
and feeling, they were overtaken by the forester, or park-
keeper, who, intent on silvan sport, was proceeding with his
cross-bow over his arm, and a hound led in leash by his
boy, into the interior of the wood.

"Going to shoot us a piece of venison, Norman?" said
his master, as he returned the woodman's salutation.

"Saul, your honour, and that I am. Will it please you
to see the sport?"

"O no," said his lordship, after looking at his daughter,
whose colour fled at the idea of seeing the deer shot,
although had her father expressed his wish that they should
accompany Norman, it was probable she would not even
have hinted her reluctance.

The forester shrugged his shoulders. "It was a dis-
heartening thing," he said, "when none of the gentles came
down to see the sport. He hoped Captain Sholto would
be soon hame, or he might shut up his shop entirely; for
Mr Harry was kept sae close wi' his Latin nonsense,
that, though his will was very gude to be in the wood from
morning till night, there would be a hopeful lad lost, and
and no making a man of him. It was not so, he had heard,
in Lord Ravenswood's time—when a buck was to be killed,
man and mother's son ran to see; and when the deer fell,
the knife was always presented to the knight, and
he never gave less than a dollar for the compliment. And
there was Edgar Ravenswood—Master of Ravenswood
that is now—when he goes up to the wood—there
hasna been a better hunter since Tristrem's time—
when Sir Edgar hauds out,[1] down goes the deer, faith.
But we hae lost a' sense of wood-craft on this side of the
hill."

There was much in this harangue highly displeasing to
the Lord Keeper's feelings; he could not help observing
that his menial despised him almost avowedly for not
possessing that taste for sport, which in those times was

[1] *Hauds out.* Holds out, *i.e.* presents his piece.

deemed the natural and indispensable attribute of a real gentleman. But the master of the game is, in all country houses, a man of great importance, and entitled to use considerable freedom of speech. Sir William, therefore, only smiled and replied, he had something else to think upon to-day than killing deer; meantime, taking out his purse, he gave the ranger a dollar for his encouragement. The fellow received it as the waiter of a fashionable hotel receives double his proper fee from the hands of a country gentleman,—that is, with a smile, in which pleasure at the gift is mingled with contempt for the ignorance of the donor. "Your honour is the bad paymaster," he said, "who pays before it is done. What would you do were I to miss the buck after you have paid me my wood-fee?"

"I suppose," said the Keeper, smiling, "you would hardly guess what I mean were I to tell you of a *condictio indebiti?*"

"Not I, on my saul—I guess it is some law phrase—but sue a beggar, and—your honour knows what follows.—Well, but I will be just with you, and if bow and brach fail not, you shall have a piece of game two fingers fat on the brisket."

As he was about to go off, his master again called him, and asked, as if by accident, whether the Master of Ravenswood was actually so brave a man and so good a shooter as the world spoke him?

"Brave!—brave enough, I warrant you," answered Norman; "I was in the wood at Tyninghame, when there was a sort of gallants hunting with my lord; on my saul, there was a buck turned to bay made us all stand back; a stout old Trojan of the first head, ten-tyned branches, and a brow as broad as e'er a bullock's. Egad, he dashed at the old lord, and there would have been inlake among the peerage, if the Master had not whipt roundly in, and hamstrung him with his cutlass. He was but sixteen then, bless his heart!"

"And is he as ready with the gun as with the couteau?" said Sir William.

"He'll strike this silver dollar out from between my finger and thumb at fourscore yards, and I'll hold it out for a gold merk; what more would ye have of eye, hand, lead, and gunpowder?"

"O no more to be wished, certainly," said the Lord Keeper; "but we keep you from your sport, Norman. Good-morrow, good Norman."

And humming his rustic roundelay, the yeoman went on his road, the sound of his rough voice gradually dying away as the distance betwixt them increased :—

> The monk must arise when the matins ring,
>   The abbot may sleep to their chime ;
> But the yeoman must start when the bugles sing,
>   'Tis time, my hearts, 'tis time.
>
> There's bucks and raes on Bilhope braes,
>   There's a herd on Shortwood Shaw ;
> But a lily-white doe in the garden goes,
>   She's fairly worth them a'.

"Has this fellow," said the Lord Keeper, when the yeoman's song had died on the wind, "ever served the Ravenswood people, that he seems so much interested in them? I suppose you know, Lucy, for you make it a point of conscience to record the special history of every boor about the castle."

"I am not quite so faithful a chronicler, my dear father; but I believe that Norman once served here while a boy, and before he went to Ledington, whence you hired him. But if you want to know any thing of the former family, old Alice is the best authority."

"And what should I have to do with them, pray, Lucy," said her father, "or with their history or accomplishments?"

"Nay, I do not know, sir; only that you were asking questions of Norman about young Ravenswood."

"Pshaw, child!"—replied her father, yet immediately added, "And who is old Alice? I think you know all the old women in the country."

"To be sure I do, or how could I help the old creatures when they are in hard times? And as to old Alice, she is the very empress of old women, and queen of gossips, so far as legendary lore is concerned. She is blind, poor old soul, but when she speaks to you, you would think she has some way of looking into your very heart. I am sure I often cover my face, or turn it away, for it seems as if she saw one change colour, though she has been blind these twenty years. She is worth visiting, were it but to say you have seen a blind and paralytic old woman have so much acuteness of perception, and dignity of manners. I assure you, she might be a countess from her language and behaviour.—Come, you must go to see Alice; we are not a quarter of a mile from her cottage."

"All this, my dear," said the Lord Keeper, "is no answer to my question, who this woman is, and what is her connexion with the former proprietor's family?"

"O, it was something of a nourice-ship, I believe; and she remained here, because her two grandsons were engaged in your service. But it was against her will, I fancy; for the poor old creature is always regretting the change of times and of property."

"I am much obliged to her," answered the Lord Keeper. "She and her folk eat my bread and drink my cup, and are lamenting all the while that they are not still under a family which never could do good, either to themselves or any one else!"

"Indeed," replied Lucy, "I am certain you do old Alice injustice. She has nothing mercenary about her, and would not accept a penny in charity, if it were to save her from being starved. She is only talkative, like all old folk, when you put them upon stories of their youth; and she speaks about the Ravenswood people, because she lived under them so many years. But I am sure she is grateful to you, sir, for your protection, and that she would rather speak to you, than to any other person in the whole world beside. Do, sir, come and see old Alice."

And with the freedom of an indulged daughter, she dragged the Lord Keeper in the direction she desired.

CHAPTER IV

Through tops of the high trees she did descry
A little smoke, whose vapour, thin, and light,
Reeking aloft, uprolled to the sky,
Which cheerful sign did send unto her sight,
That in the same did wonne some living wight.

Spenser.

LUCY acted as her father's guide, for he was too much engrossed with his political labours, or with society, to be perfectly acquainted with his own extensive domains, and, moreover, was generally an inhabitant of the city of Edinburgh; and she, on the other hand, had, with her mother, resided the whole summer in Ravenswood, and, partly from taste, partly from want of any other amusement, had, by her frequent rambles, learned to know each lane, alley, dingle, or bushy dell,

"And every bosky bourne from side to side."

We have said that the Lord Keeper was not indifferent to the beauties of nature; and we add, in justice to him, that he felt them doubly, when pointed out by the beautiful, simple, and interesting girl, who, hanging on his arm with filial kindness, now called him to admire the size of some ancient oak, and now the unexpected turn, where the path, developing its maze from glen or dingle, suddenly reached an eminence commanding an extensive view of the plains beneath them, and then gradually glided away from the prospect to lose itself among rocks and thickets, and guide to scenes of deeper seclusion.

It was when pausing on one of those points of extensive and commanding view, that Lucy told her father they were close by the cottage of her blind protegée; and on turning from the little hill, a path which led around it, worn by the daily steps of the infirm inmate, brought them in sight of the hut, which, embosomed in a deep and obscure dell, seemed to have been so situated purposely to bear a correspondence with the darkened state of its inhabitant.

The cottage was situated immediately under a tall rock, which in some measure beetled over it, as if threatening to drop some detached fragment from its brow on the frail tenement beneath. The hut itself was constructed of turf and stones, and rudely roofed over with thatch, much of which was in a dilapidated condition. The thin blue smoke rose from it in a light column, and curled upward along the white face of the incumbent rock, giving the scene a tint of exquisite softness. In a small and rude garden, surrounded by straggling elder-bushes, which formed a sort of imperfect hedge, sat near to the bee-hives, by the produce of which she lived, that "woman old," whom Lucy had brought her father hither to visit.

Whatever there had been which was disastrous in her fortune—whatever there was miserable in her dwelling, it was easy to judge, by the first glance, that neither years, poverty, misfortune, nor infirmity, had broken the spirit of this remarkable woman.

She occupied a turf-seat, placed under a weeping birch of unusual magnitude and age, as Judah is represented sitting under her palm-tree, with an air at once of majesty and of dejection. Her figure was tall, commanding, and but little bent by the infirmities of old age. Her dress, though that of a peasant, was uncommonly clean, forming in that particular a strong contrast to most of her rank, and was disposed with an attention to neatness, and even to taste, equally unusual. But it was her expression of countenance which chiefly struck the spectator, and induced most persons to address her with a degree of deference and civility very inconsistent with the miserable state of her dwelling, and which, nevertheless, she received with that easy composure which showed she felt it to be her due. She had once been beautiful, but her beauty had been of a bold and masculine cast, such as does not survive the bloom of youth; yet her features continued to express strong sense, deep reflection, and a character of sober pride, which, as we have already said of her dress, appeared to argue a conscious superiority to those of her own rank. It scarce seemed possible that a face, deprived of the advantage of sight, could have expressed character so strongly; but her eyes, which were almost totally closed, did not, by the display of their sightless orbs, mar the countenance to which they could add nothing. She seemed in a ruminating posture, soothed, perhaps, by the murmurs of the busy tribe around her, to abstraction, though not to slumber.

Lucy undid the latch of the little garden gate, and solicited the old woman's attention. "My father, Alice, is come to see you."

"He is welcome, Miss Ashton, and so are you." said the old woman, turning and inclining her head towards her visitors.

"This is a fine morning for your bee-hives, mother," said the Lord Keeper, who, struck with the outward appearance of Alice, was somewhat curious to know if her conversation would correspond with it.

"I believe so, my lord," she replied; "I feel the air breathe milder than of late."

"You do not," resumed the statesman, "take charge of these bees yourself, mother?—How do you manage them?"

"By delegates, as kings do their subjects," resumed Alice; "and I am fortunate in a prime minister—Here, Babie."

She whistled on a small silver call which hung around her neck, and which at that time was sometimes used to summon domestics, and Babie, a girl of fifteen, made her appearance from the hut, not altogether so cleanly arrayed as she would probably have been had Alice had the use of her eyes, but with a greater air of neatness than was upon the whole to have been expected.

"Babie," said her mistress, "offer some bread and honey to the Lord Keeper and Miss Ashton—they will excuse your awkwardness, if you use cleanliness and dispatch."

Babie performed her mistress's command with the grace which was naturally to have been expected, moving to and fro with a lobster-like gesture, her feet and legs tending one way, while her head, turned in a different direction, was fixed in wonder upon the laird, who was more frequently heard of than seen by his tenants and dependants. The bread and honey, however, deposited on a plantain leaf, was offered and accepted in all due courtesy. The Lord Keeper, still retaining the place which he had occupied on the decayed trunk of a fallen tree, looked as if he wished to prolong the interview, but was at a loss how to introduce a suitable subject.

"You have been long a resident on this property?" he said, after a pause.

"It is now nearly sixty years since I first knew Ravenswood," answered the old dame, whose conversation, though perfectly civil and respectful, seemed cautiously limited to the unavoidable and necessary task of replying to Sir William.

"You are not, I should judge by your accent, of this country originally?" said the Lord Keeper, in continuation.

"No; I am by birth an Englishwoman."

"Yet you seem attached to this country as if it were your own"

"It is here," replied the blind woman, "that I have drank the cup of joy and of sorrow which Heaven destined for me. I was here the wife of an upright and affectionate husband for more than twenty years—I was here the mother of six promising children—it was here that God deprived me of all these blessings—it was here they died, and yonder, by yon ruined chapel, they lie all buried—I had no country but theirs while they lived—I have none but theirs now they are no more."

"But your house," said the Lord Keeper, looking at it, "is miserably ruinous?"

"Do, my dear father," said Lucy, eagerly, yet bashfully, catching at the hint, "give orders to make it better,—that is, if you think it proper."

"It will last my time, my dear Miss Lucy," said the blind woman; "I would not have my lord give himself the least trouble about it."

"But," said Lucy, "you once had a much better house, and were rich, and now in your old age to live in this hovel!"

"It is as good as I deserve, Miss Lucy; if my heart has not broke with what I have suffered, and seen others suffer, it must have been strong enough, and the rest of this old frame has no right to call itself weaker."

"You have probably witnessed many changes," said the Lord Keeper; "but your experience must have taught you to expect them."

"It has taught me to endure them, my lord," was the reply.

"Yet you knew that they must needs arrive in the course of years?" said the statesman.

"Ay; as I know that the stump, on or beside which you sit, once a tall and lofty tree, must needs one day fall by decay, or by the axe; yet I hoped my eyes might not witness the downfall of the tree which overshadowed my dwelling"

"Do not suppose," said the Lord Keeper, "that you will lose any interest with me, for looking back with regret to the days when another family possessed my estates. You had reason, doubtless, to love them, and I respect your gratitude. I will order some repairs in your cottage, and I hope we shall live to be friends when we know each other better."

"Those of my age," returned the dame, "make no new friends. I thank you for your bounty—it is well intended undoubtedly; but I have all I want, and I cannot accept more at your lordship's hands."

"Well, then," continued the Lord Keeper, "at least allow me to say, that I look upon you as a woman of sense and education beyond your appearance, and that I hope you will continue to reside on this property of mine rent-free for your life."

"I hope I shall," said the old dame, composedly; "I believe that was made an article in the sale of Ravenswood to your lordship, though such a trifling circumstance may have escaped your recollection."

"I remember—I recollect," said his lordship, somewhat confused. "I perceive you are too much attached to your old friends to accept any benefit from their successor."

"Far from it, my lord; I am grateful for the benefits which I decline, and I wish I could pay you for offering them, better than what I am now about to say." The Lord Keeper looked at her in some surprise, but said not a word. "My lord," she continued, in an impressive and solemn tone, "take care what you do; you are on the brink of a precipice."

"Indeed?" said the Lord Keeper, his mind reverting to the political circumstances of the country. "Has any thing come to your knowledge—any plot or conspiracy?"

"No, my lord; those who traffic in such commodities do not call into their councils the old, blind, and infirm. My warning is of another kind. You have driven matters hard with the house of Ravenswood. Believe a true tale—they are a fierce house, and there is danger in dealing with men when they become desperate."

"Tush," answered the Keeper; "what has been between us has been the work of the law, not my doing; and to the law they must look, if they would impugn my proceedings."

"Ay, but they may think otherwise, and take the law into their own hand, when they fail of other means of redress."

"What mean you?" said the Lord Keeper. "Young Ravenswood would not have recourse to personal violence?"

"God forbid I should say so! I know nothing of the youth but what is honourable and open—honourable and open, said I?—I should have added free, generous, noble.

But he is still a Ravenswood, and may bide his time. Remember the fate of Sir George Lockhart."[1]

The Lord Keeper started as she called to his recollection a tragedy so deep and so recent. The old woman proceeded : "Chiesley, who did the deed, was a relative of Lord Ravenswood. In the hall of Ravenswood, in my presence, and in that of others, he avowed publicly his determination to do the cruelty which he afterwards committed. I could not keep silence, though to speak it ill became my station. 'You are devising a dreadful crime,' I said, 'for which you must reckon before the judgment-seat.' Never shall I forget his look, as he replied, 'I must reckon then for many things, and will reckon for this also.' Therefore I may well say, beware of pressing a desperate man with the hand of authority. There is blood of Chiesley in the veins of Ravenswood, and one drop of it were enough to fire him in the circumstances in which he is placed—I say, beware of him."

The old dame had, either intentionally or by accident, harped aright the fear of the Lord Keeper. The desperate and dark resource of private assassination, so familar to a Scottish baron in former times, had even in the present age been too frequently resorted to under the pressure of

[1] President of the Court of Session. He was pistolled in the High Street of Edinburgh, by John Chiesley of Dalry, in the year 1689. The revenge of this desperate man was stimulated by an opinion that he had sustained injustice in a decreet-arbitral pronounced by the President, assigning an alimentary provision of about L. 93 in favour of his wife and children. He is said at first to have designed to shoot the judge while attending upon divine worship, but was diverted by some feeling concerning the sanctity of the place. After the congregation was dismissed, he dogged his victim as far as the head of the close on the south side of the Lawnmarket, in which the President's house was situated, and shot him dead as he was about to enter it. This act was done in the presence of numerous spectators. The assassin made no attempt to fly, but boasted of the deed, saying, "I have taught the President how to do justice." He had at least given him fair warning, as Jack Cade says on a similar occasion. The murderer, after undergoing the torture, by a special act of the Estates of Parliament, was tried before the Lord Provost of Edinburgh, as high sheriff, and condemned to be dragged on a hurdle to the place of execution, to have his right hand struck off while he yet lived, and, finally, to be hung on the gallows with the pistol wherewith he shot the President tied round his neck. This execution took place on the 3d of April 1689; and the incident was long remembered as a dreadful instance of what the law books call the *perfervidum ingenium Scotorum*.

unusual temptation, or where the mind of the actor was prepared for such a crime. Sir William Ashton was aware of this; as also that young Ravenswood had received injuries sufficient to prompt him to that sort of revenge, which becomes a frequent though fearful consequence of the partial administration of justice. He endeavoured to disguise from Alice the nature of the apprehensions which he entertained; but so ineffectually, that a person even of less penetration than nature had endowed her with must necessarily have been aware that the subject lay near his bosom. His voice was changed in its accent as he replied to her, that the Master of Ravenswood was a man of honour; and, were it otherwise, that the fate of Chiesley of Dalry was a sufficient warning to any one who should dare to assume the office of avenger of his own imaginary wrongs. And having hastily uttered these expressions, he rose and left the place without waiting for a reply.

CHAPTER V

———Is she a Capulet?
O dear account! my life is my foe's debt.
Shakspeare.

THE Lord Keeper walked for nearly a quarter of a mile in profound silence. His daughter, naturally timid, and bred up in those ideas of filial awe and implicit obedience which were inculcated upon the youth of that period, did not venture to interrupt his meditations.

"Why do you look so pale, Lucy?" said her father, turning suddenly round and breaking silence.

According to the ideas of the time, which did not permit a young woman to offer her sentiments on any subject of importance unless especially required to do so, Lucy was bound to appear ignorant of the meaning of all that had passed betwixt Alice and her father, and imputed the emotion he had observed to the fear of the wild cattle which grazed in that part of the extensive chase through which they were now walking.

Of these animals, the descendants of the savage herds which anciently roamed free in the Caledonian forests, it was formerly a point of state to preserve a few in the parks of the Scottish nobility. Specimens continued within the memory of man to be kept at least at three houses of distinction, Hamilton namely, Drumlanrick, and Cumbernauld. They had degenerated from the ancient race in size and strength, if we are to judge from the accounts of old chronicles, and from the formidable remains frequently discovered in bogs and morasses when drained and laid open. The bull had lost the shaggy honours of his mane, and the race was small and light made, in colour a dingy white, or rather a pale yellow, with black horns and hoofs. They retained, however, in some measure, the ferocity of their ancestry, could not be domesticated on account of their antipathy to the human race, and were often dangerous if approached unguardedly, or wantonly disturbed. It was this last reason which has occasioned their being extirpated at the places we have mentioned, where probably they would otherwise have been retained as appropriate inhabitants of a Scottish woodland, and fit tenants for a baronial forest. A few, if I mistake not, are still preserved at Chillingham Castle, in Northumberland, the seat of the Earl of Tankerville.

It was to her finding herself in the vicinity of a group of three or four of these animals, that Lucy thought proper to impute those signs of fear, which had arisen in her countenance for a different reason. For she had been familiarised with the appearance of the wild cattle, during her walks in the chase; and it was not then, as it may be now, a necessary part of a young lady's demeanour, to indulge in causeless tremors of the nerves. On the present occasion, however, she speedily found cause for real terror.

Lucy had scarcely replied to her father in the words we have mentioned, and he was just about to rebuke her supposed timidity, when a bull, stimulated either by the scarlet colour of Miss Ashton's mantle, or by one of those fits of capricious ferocity to which their dispositions are liable, detached himself suddenly from the group which was feeding at the upper extremity of a grassy glade, that seemed to lose itself among the crossing and entangled boughs. The animal approached the intruders on his pasture ground, at first slowly, pawing the ground with his hoof, bellowing from time to time, and tearing up the sand with his horns, as if to lash himself up to rage and violence.

The Lord Keeper, who observed the animal's demeanour, was aware that he was about to become mischievous, and, drawing his daughter's arm under his own, began to walk fast along the avenue, in hopes to get out of his sight and his reach. This was the most injudicious course he could have adopted, for, encouraged by the appearance of flight, the bull began to pursue them at full speed. Assailed by a danger so imminent, firmer courage than that of the Lord Keeper might have given way. But paternal tenderness, "love strong as death," sustained him. He continued to support and drag onward his daughter, until, her fears altogether depriving her of the power of flight, she sunk down by his side; and when he could no longer assist her to escape, he turned round and placed himself betwixt her and the raging animal, which advancing in full career, its brutal fury enhanced by the rapidity of the pursuit, was now within a few yards of them. The Lord Keeper had no weapons; his age and gravity dispensed even with the usual appendage of a walking sword,—could such appendage have availed him any thing.

It seemed inevitable that the father or daughter, or both, should have fallen victims to the impending danger, when a shot from the neighbouring thicket arrested the progress of the animal. He was so truly struck between the junction of the spine with the skull, that the wound, which in any other part of his body might scarce have impeded his career, proved instantly fatal. Stumbling forward with a hideous bellow, the progressive force of his previous motion, rather than any operation of his limbs, carried him up to within three yards of the astonished Lord Keeper, where he rolled on the ground, his limbs darkened with the black death-sweat, and quivering with the last convulsions of muscular motion.

Lucy lay senseless on the ground, insensible of the wonderful deliverance which she had experienced. Her father was almost equally stupefied, so rapid and unexpected had been the transition from the horrid death which seemed inevitable, to perfect security. He gazed on the animal, terrible even in death, with a species of mute and confused astonishment, which did not permit him distinctly to understand what had taken place; and so inaccurate was his consciousness of what had passed, that he might have supposed the bull had been arrested in its career by a thunderbolt, had he not observed among the branches of the thicket the figure of a man, with a short gun or musquetoon in his hand.

This instantly recalled him to a sense of their situation —a glance at his daughter reminded him of the necessity of procuring her assistance. He called to the man, whom he concluded to be one of his foresters, to give immediate attention to Miss Ashton, while he himself hastened to call assistance. The huntsman approached them accordingly, and the Lord Keeper saw he was a stranger, but was too much agitated to make any farther remarks. In a few hurried words, he directed the shooter, as stronger and more active than himself, to carry the young lady to a neighbouring fountain, while he went back to Alice's hut to procure more aid.

The man to whose timely interference they had been so much indebted, did not seem inclined to leave his good work half finished. He raised Lucy from the ground in his arms, and conveying her through the glades of the forest by paths with which he seemed well acquainted, stopped not until he laid her in safety by the side of a plentiful and pellucid fountain, which had been once covered in, screened and decorated with architectural ornaments of a Gothic character. But now the vault which had covered it being broken down and riven, and the Gothic font ruined and demolished, the stream burst forth from the recess of the earth in open day, and winded its way among the broken sculpture and moss-grown stones which lay in confusion around its source.

Tradition, always busy, at least in Scotland, to grace with a legendary tale a spot in itself interesting, had ascribed a cause of peculiar veneration to this fountain. A beautiful young lady met one of the Lords of Ravenswood while hunting near this spot, and, like a second Egeria, had captivated the affections of the feudal Numa. They met frequently afterwards, and always at sunset, the charms of the nymph's mind completing the conquest which her beauty had begun, and the mystery of the intrigue adding zest to both. She always appeared and disappeared close by the fountain, with which, therefore, her lover judged she had some inexplicable connexion. She

placed certain restrictions on their intercourse, which also
savoured of mystery. They met only once a-week—Friday
was the appointed day—and she explained to the Lord of
Ravenswood, that they were under the necessity of separat-
ing so soon as the bell of a chapel, belonging to a hermitage
in the adjoining wood, now long ruinous, should toll the
hour of vespers. In the course of his confession, the Baron
of Ravenswood intrusted the hermit with the secret of this
singular amour, and Father Zachary drew the necessary
and obvious consequence, that his patron was enveloped in
the toils of Satan, and in danger of destruction, both to
body and soul. He urged these perils to the Baron with
all the force of monkish rhetoric, and described, in the
most frightful colours, the real character and person of the
apparently lovely Naiad, whom he hesitated not to denounce
as a limb of the kingdom of darkness. The lover listened
with obstinate incredulity; and it was not until worn out
by the obstinacy of the anchoret, that he consented to put
the state and condition of his mistress to a certain trial,
and for that purpose acquiesced in Zachary's proposal, that
on their next interview the vespers bell should be rung half
an hour later than usual. The hermit maintained and
bucklered his opinion, by quotations from *Malleus, Mali-
ficarum, Sprengerus, Remigius,* and other learned demono-
logists, that the Evil One, thus seduced to remain behind
the appointed hour, would assume her true shape, and,
having appeared to her terrified lover as a fiend of hell,
would vanish from him in a flash of sulphurous lightning.
Raymond of Ravenswood acquiesced in the experiment,
not incurious concerning the issue, though confident it
would disappoint the expectations of the hermit.

At the appointed hour the lovers met, and their interview
was protracted beyond that at which they usually parted,
by the delay of the priest to ring his usual curfew. No
change took place upon the nymph's outward form; but
as soon as the lengthening shadows made her aware that
the usual hour of the vespers chime was passed, she tore
herself from her lover's arms with a shriek of despair, bid
him adieu for ever, and, plunging into the fountain, disappeared from his eyes. The bubbles occasioned by her
descent were crimsoned with blood as they arose, leading
the distracted Baron to infer, that his ill-judged curiosity

had occasioned the death of this interesting and mysterious being. The remorse which he felt, as well as the recollection of her charms, proved the penance of his future life, which he lost in the Battle of Flodden not many months after. But, in memory of his Naiad, he had previously ornamented the fountain in which she appeared to reside, and secured its waters from profanation or pollution, by the small vaulted building of which the fragments still remained scattered around it. From this period the house of Ravenswood was supposed to have dated its decay.

Such was the generally received legend, which some, who would seem wiser than the vulgar, explained, as obscurely intimating the fate of a beautiful maid of plebeian rank, the mistress of this Raymond, whom he slew in a fit of jealousy, and whose blood was mingled with the waters of the locked fountain, as it was commonly called. Others imagined that the tale had a more remote origin in the ancient heathen mythology. All however agreed, that the spot was fatal to the Ravenswood family; and that to drink of the waters of the well, or even approach its brink, was as ominous to a descendant of that house, as for a Grahame to wear green, a Bruce to kill a spider, or a St Clair to cross the Ord on a Monday.

It was on this ominous spot that Lucy Ashton first drew breath after her long and almost deadly swoon. Beautiful and pale as the fabulous Naiad in the last agony of separation from her lover, she was seated so as to rest with her back against a part of the ruined wall, while her mantle, dripping with the water which her protector had used profusely to recall her senses, clung to her slender and beautifully proportioned form.

The first moment of recollection brought to her mind the danger which had overpowered her senses—the next called to remembrance that of her father. She looked around—he was nowhere to be seen—" My father—my father!" was all that she could ejaculate.

" Sir William is safe," answered the voice of a stranger—" perfectly safe, and will be with you instantly."

" Are you sure of that?" exclaimed Lucy—"the bull was close by us—do not stop me—I must go to seek my father!"

And she arose with that purpose; but her strength was

so much exhausted, that, far from possessing the power to execute her purpose, she must have fallen against the stone on which she had leant, probably not without sustaining serious injury.

The stranger was so near to her, that, without actually suffering her to fall, he could not avoid catching her in his arms, which, however, he did with a momentary reluctance, very unusual when youth interposes to prevent beauty from danger. It seemed as if her weight, slight as it was, proved too heavy for her young and athletic assistant, for, without feeling the temptation of detaining her in his arms even for a single instant, he again placed her on the stone from which she had risen, and retreating a few steps, repeated hastily, " Sir William Ashton is perfectly safe, and will be here instantly. Do not make yourself anxious on his account—Fate has singularly preserved him. You, madam, are exhausted, and must not think of rising until you have some assistance more suitable than mine."

Lucy, whose senses were by this time more effectually collected, was naturally led to look at the stranger with attention. There was nothing in his appearance which should have rendered him unwilling to offer his arm to a young lady who required support, or which could have induced her to refuse his assistance; and she could not help thinking, even in that moment, that he seemed cold and reluctant to offer it. A shooting-dress of dark cloth intimated the rank of the wearer, though concealed in part by a large and loose cloak of a dark brown colour. A Montero cap and a black feather drooped over the wearer's brow, and partly concealed his features, which, so far as seen, were dark, regular, and full of majestic, though somewhat sullen, expression. Some secret sorrow, or the brooding spirit of some moody passion had quenched the light and ingenuous vivacity of youth in a countenance singularly fitted to display both, and it was not easy to gaze on the stranger without a secret impression either of pity or awe, or at least of doubt and curiosity allied to both.

The impression which we have necessarily been long in describing, Lucy felt in the glance of a moment, and had no sooner encountered the keen black eyes of the stranger, than her own were bent on the ground with a mixture of bashful embarrassment and fear. Yet there was a necessity to speak, or at least she thought so, and in a fluttered accent she began to mention her wonderful escape, in which she was sure that the stranger must, under Heaven, have been her father's protector, and her own.

He seemed to shrink from her expressions of gratitude, while he replied abruptly, "I leave you, madam,"—the deep melody of his voice rendered powerful, but not harsh, by something like a severity of tone—"I leave you to the protection of those to whom it is possible you may have this day been a guardian angel."

Lucy was surprised at the ambiguity of his language, and, with a feeling of artless and unaffected gratitude, began to deprecate the idea of having intended to give her deliverer any offence, as if such a thing had been possible. "I have been unfortunate," she said, "in endeavouring to express my thanks—I am sure it must be so, though I cannot re-collect what I said—but would you but stay till my father —till the Lord Keeper comes—would you only permit him to pay you his thanks, and to enquire your name?"

"My name is unnecessary," answered the stranger; "your father—I would rather say Sir William Ashton—will learn it soon enough, for all the pleasure it is likely to afford him."

"You mistake him," said Lucy earnestly; "he will be grateful for my sake and for his own. You do not know my father, or you are deceiving me with a story of his safety, when he has already fallen a victim to the fury of that animal."

When she had caught this idea, she started from the ground, and endeavoured to press towards the avenue in which the accident had taken place, while the stranger, though he seemed to hesitate between the desire to assist and the wish to leave her, was obliged, in common humanity, to oppose her both by entreaty and action.

"On the word of a gentleman, madam, I tell you the truth; your father is in perfect safety; you will expose yourself to injury if you venture back where the herd of wild cattle grazed.—If you will go"—for, having once adopted the idea that her father was still in danger, she pressed forward in spite of him—"If you *will* go, accept my arm, though I am not perhaps the person who can with most propriety offer you support."

But, without heeding this intimation, Lucy took him at his word. "O if you be a man," she said,—"if you be a gentleman, assist me to find my father! You shall not leave me—you must go with me—he is dying perhaps while we are talking here!"

Then, without listening to excuse or apology, and holding fast by the stranger's arm, though unconscious of any thing save the support which it gave, and without which she could not have moved, mixed with a vague feeling of preventing his escape from her, she was urging, and almost dragging him forward, when Sir William Ashton came up, followed by the female attendant of blind Alice, and by two woodcutters, whom he had summoned from their occupation to his assistance. His joy at seeing his daughter safe, overcame the surprise with which he would at another time have beheld her hanging as familiarly on the arm of a stranger, as she might have done upon his own.

"Lucy, my dear Lucy, are you safe?—are you well?" were the only words that broke from him as he embraced her in ecstasy.

"I am well, sir, thank God! and still more that I see you so;—but this gentleman," she said, quitting his arm, and shrinking from him, "what must he think of me?" and her eloquent blood, flushing over neck and brow, spoke how much she was ashamed of the freedom with which she had craved, and even compelled his assistance.

"This gentleman," said Sir William Ashton, "will, I trust, not regret the trouble we have given him, when I assure him of the gratitude of the Lord Keeper for the greatest service which one man ever rendered to another—for the life of my child—for my own life, which he has saved by his bravery and presence of mind. He will, I am sure, permit us to request"——

"Request nothing of ME, my lord," said the stranger, in a stern and peremptory tone; "I am the Master of Ravenswood."

There was a dead pause of surprise, not unmixed with less pleasant feelings. The Master wrapt himself in his cloak, made a haughty inclination towards Lucy, muttering a few words of courtesy, as indistinctly heard as they seemed to be reluctantly uttered, and, turning from them, was immediately lost in the thicket.

"The Master of Ravenswood!" said the Lord Keeper, when he had recovered his momentary astonishment— "Hasten after him—stop him—beg him to speak to me for a single moment."

The two foresters accordingly set off in pursuit of the stranger. They speedily reappeared, and, in an embarrassed and awkward manner, said the gentleman would not return. The Lord Keeper took one of the fellows aside, and questioned him more closely what the Master of Ravenswood had said.

"He just said he wadna come back," said the man, with the caution of a prudent Scotchman, who cared not to be the bearer of an unpleasant errand.

"He said something more, sir," said the Lord Keeper, "and I insist on knowing what it was."

"Why, then, my lord," said the man, looking down, "he said—But it wad be nae pleasure to your lordship to hear it, for I daresay the Master meant nae ill."

"That's none of your concern, sir; I desire to hear the very words."

"Weel, then," replied the man, "he said, Tell Sir William Ashton, that the next time he and I forgather, he will not be half sae blithe of our meeting as of our parting."

"Very well, sir," said the Lord Keeper, "I believe he alludes to a wager we have on our hawks—it is a matter of no consequence."

He turned to his daughter, who was by this time so much recovered as to be able to walk home. But the effect which the various recollections, connected with a scene so terrific, made upon a mind which was susceptible in an extreme degree, was more permanent than the injury which her nerves had sustained. Visions of terror, both in sleep and in waking reveries, recalled to her the form of the furious animal, and the dreadful bellow with which he accompanied his career; and it was always the image of the Master of Ravenswood, with his native nobleness of countenance and form, that seemed to interpose betwixt her and assured death. It is, perhaps, at all times dangerous for a young person to suffer recollection to dwell repeatedly, and with too much complacency, on the same individual; but in Lucy's situation it was almost unavoidable. She had never happened to see a young man of mien and features so

romantic and so striking as young Ravenswood; but had
she seen an hundred his equals or his superiors in those
particulars, no one else could have been linked to her
heart by the strong associations of remembered danger and
escape, of gratitude, wonder, and curiosity. I say curiosity,
for it is likely that the singularly restrained and unaccom-
modating manners of the Master of Ravenswood, so much
at variance with the natural expression of his features and
grace of his deportment, as they excited wonder by the
contrast, had their effect in riveting her attention to the
recollection. She knew little of Ravenswood, or the disputes
which had existed betwixt her father and his, and perhaps
could in her gentleness of mind hardly have comprehended
the angry and bitter passions which they had engendered.
But she knew that he was come of noble stem; was poor,
though descended from the noble and the wealthy; and
she felt that she could sympathise with the feelings of a
proud mind, which urged him to recoil from the proffered
gratitude of the new proprietors of his father's house and
domains. Would he have equally shunned their acknowledgments, and avoided their intimacy, had her father's
request been urged more mildly, less abruptly, and softened
with the grace which women so well know how to throw
into their manner, when they mean to mediate betwixt the
headlong passions of the ruder sex? This was a perilous
question to ask her own mind—perilous both in the idea
and in its consequences.

Lucy Ashton, in short, was involved in those mazes of
the imagination which are most dangerous to the young
and the sensitive. Time, it is true, absence, change of
scene and new faces, might probably have destroyed the
illusion in her instance as it has done in many others; but
her residence remained solitary, and her mind without
those means of dissipating her pleasing visions. This
solitude was chiefly owing to the absence of Lady Ashton,
who was at this time in Edinburgh, watching the progress
of some state-intrigue; the Lord Keeper only received
society out of policy or ostentation, and was by nature
rather reserved and unsociable; and thus no cavalier appeared to rival or to obscure the ideal picture of chivalrous
excellence which Lucy had pictured to herself in the Master
of Ravenswood.

While Lucy indulged in these dreams, she made frequent visits to old blind Alice, hoping it would be easy to lead her to talk on the subject, which at present she had so imprudently admitted to occupy so large a portion of her thoughts. But Alice did not in this particular gratify her wishes and expectations. She spoke readily, and with pathetic feeling, concerning the family in general, but seemed to observe an especial and cautious silence on the subject of the present representative. The little she said of him was not altogether so favourable as Lucy had anticipated. She hinted that he was of a stern and unforgiving character, more ready to resent than to pardon injuries; and Lucy combined with great alarm the hints which she now dropped of these dangerous qualities, with Alice's advice to her father, so emphatically given, "to beware of Ravenswood."

But that very Ravenswood, of whom such unjust suspicions had been entertained, had, almost immediately after they had been uttered, confuted them, by saving at once her father's life and her own. Had he nourished such black revenge as Alice's dark hints seemed to indicate, no deed of active guilt was necessary to the full gratification of that evil passion. He needed but to have withheld for an instant his indispensable and effective assistance, and the object of his resentment must have perished, without any direct aggression on his part, by a death equally fearful and certain. She conceived, therefore, that some secret prejudice, or the suspicions incident to age and misfortune, had led Alice to form conclusions injurious to the character, and irreconcilable both with the generous conduct and noble features of the Master of Ravenswood. And in this belief Lucy reposed her hope, and went on weaving her enchanted web of fairy tissue, as beautiful and transient as the film of the gossamer, when it is pearled with the morning dew, and glimmering to the sun.

Her father, in the meanwhile, as well as the Master of Ravenswood, were making reflections, as frequent though more solid than those of Lucy, upon the singular event which had taken place. The Lord Keeper's first task, when he returned home, was to ascertain by medical advice that his daughter had sustained no injury from the dangerous and alarming situation in which she had been placed. Satisfied on this topic, he proceeded to revise the memoranda which he had taken down from the mouth of the person employed to interrupt the funeral service of the late Lord Ravenswood. Bred to casuistry, and well accustomed to practise the ambidexter ingenuity of the bar, it cost him little trouble to soften the features of the tumult which he had been at first so anxious to exaggerate. He preached to his colleagues of the Privy Council the necessity of using conciliatory measures with young men, whose blood and temper were hot, and their experience of life limited. He did not hesitate to attribute some censure to the conduct of the officer, as having been unnecessarily irritating.

These were the contents of his public dispatches. The letters which he wrote to those private friends into whose management the matter was likely to fall, were of a yet more favourable tenor. He represented that lenity in this case would be equally politic and popular, whereas, considering the high respect with which the rites of interment are regarded in Scotland, any severity exercised against the Master of Ravenswood for protecting those of his father from interruption, would be on all sides most unfavourably construed. And, finally, assuming the language of a generous and high-spirited man, he made it his particular request that this affair should be passed over without severe notice. He alluded with delicacy to the predicament in which he himself stood with young Ravenswood, as having succeeded in the long train of litigation by which the fortunes of that noble house had been so much reduced, and confessed it would be most peculiarly acceptable to his own feelings, could he find means in some sort to counterbalance the disadvantages which he had occasioned the family, though only in the prosecution of his just and lawful rights. He therefore made it his particular and personal request that the matter should have no farther consequences, and insinuated a desire that he himself should have the merit of having put a stop to it by his favourable report and intercession. It was particularly remarkable, that, contrary to his uniform practice, he made no special communication to Lady Ashton upon the subject of the tumult; and although he mentioned the alarm which Lucy had received from one of the wild cattle, yet he gave no detailed account of an incident so interesting and terrible.

There was much surprise among Sir William Ashton's

political friends and colleagues on receiving letters of a tenor so unexpected. On comparing notes together, one smiled, one put up his eyebrows, a third nodded acquiescence in the general wonder, and a fourth asked, if they were sure these were *all* the letters the Lord Keeper had written on the subject. "It runs strangely in my mind, my lords, that none of these advices contain the root of the matter."

But no secret letters of a contrary nature had been received, although the question seemed to imply the possibility of their existence.

"Well," said an old grey-headed statesman, who had contrived, by shifting and trimming, to maintain his post at the steerage through all the changes of course which the vessel had held for thirty years, "I thought Sir William would hae verified the auld Scottish saying, 'as soon comes the lamb's skin to market as the auld tup's.'"

"We must please him after his own fashion," said another, "though it be an unlooked-for one."

"A wilful man maun hae his way," answered the old counsellor.

"The Keeper will rue this before year and day are out," said a third; "the Master of Ravenswood is the lad to wind him a pirn."[1]

"Why, what would you do, my lords, with the poor young fellow?" said a noble Marquis present; "the Lord Keeper has got all his estates—he has not a cross to bless himself with."

On which the ancient Lord Turntippet replied,

> "'If he hasna gear to fine,
> He has shins to pine'—

And that was our way before the Revolution—*Luitur cum persona, qui luere non potest cum crumena*[2]—Hegh, my lords, that's gude law Latin."

"I can see no motive," replied the Marquis, "that any noble lord can have for urging this matter farther; let the Lord Keeper have the power to deal in it as he pleases."

"Agree, agree—remit to the Lord Keeper, with any

---

[1] *Wind him a pirn*, proverbial for preparing a troublesome business for some person.

[2] *i.e.* Let him pay with his person, who cannot pay with his purse.

other person for fashion's sake—Lord Hirple-hooly, who is bed-ridden—one to be a quorum—Make your entry in the minutes, Mr Clerk—And now, my lords, there is that young scattergood, the Laird of Bucklaw's fine to be disponed upon—I suppose it goes to my Lord Treasurer?"

"Shame be in my meal-poke, then," exclaimed Lord Turntippet, "and your hand aye in the nook of it! I had set that down for a by bit between meals for mysell."

"To use one of your favourite saws, my lord," replied the Marquis, "you are like the miller's dog, that licks his lips before the bag is untied—the man is not fined yet."

"But that costs but twa skarts of a pen," said Lord Turntippet; "and surely there is nae noble lord that will presume to say, that I, wha hae complied wi' a' compliances, tane all manner of tests, abjured all that was to be abjured, and sworn a' that was to be sworn, for these thirty years bypast, sticking fast by my duty to the state through good report and bad report, shouldna hae something now and then to synd my mouth wi' after sic drouthy wark? Eh?"

"It would be very unreasonable indeed, my lord," replied the Marquis, "had we either thought that your lordship's drought was quenchable, or observed any thing stick in your throat that required washing down."

And so we close the scene on the Privy Council of that period.

CHAPTER VI

> For this are all these warriors come,
>   To hear an idle tale;
> And o'er our death-accustom'd arms
>   Shall silly tears prevail?
>
> *Henry Mackenzie.*

ON the evening of the day when the Lord Keeper and his daughter were saved from such imminent peril, two strangers were seated in the most private apartment of a small obscure inn, or rather alehouse, called the Tod's Den, about three or four miles from the Castle of Ravenswood, and as far from the ruinous tower of Wolf's Crag, betwixt which two places it was situated.

One of these strangers was about forty years of age, tall,

and thin in the flanks, with an aquiline nose, dark, penetrating eyes, and a shrewd but sinister cast of countenance. The other was about fifteen years younger, short, stout, ruddy-faced, and red-haired, with an open, resolute, and cheerful eye, to which careless and fearless freedom, and inward daring, gave fire and expression, notwithstanding its light grey colour. A stoup of wine (for in those days it was served out from the cask in pewter flagons), was placed on the table, and each had his quaigh or bicker [1] before him. But there was little appearance of conviviality. With folded arms, and looks of anxious expectation, they eyed each other in silence, each wrapt in his own thoughts, and holding no communication with his neighbour.

At length the younger broke silence by exclaiming, "What the foul fiend can detain the Master so long? he must have miscarried in his enterprise.—Why did you dissuade me from going with him?"

"One man is enough to right his own wrong," said the taller and older personage; "we venture our lives for him in coming thus far on such an errand."

"You are but a craven after all, Craigengelt," answered the younger, "and that's what many folk have thought you before now."

"But what none has dared to tell me," said Craigengelt, laying his hand on the hilt of his sword; "and, but that I hold a hasty man no better than a fool, I would"—he paused for his companion's answer.

"*Would* you?" said the other coolly; "and why do you not then?"

Craigengelt drew his cutlass an inch or two, and then returned it with violence into the scabbard—"Because there is a deeper stake to be played for, than the lives of twenty harebrained gowks like you."

"You are right there," said his companion, "for if it were not that these forfeitures, and that last fine that the old driveller Turntippet is gaping for, and which, I daresay, is laid on by this time, have fairly driven me out of house and home, I were a coxcomb and a cuckoo to boot, to trust

---

[1] Drinking cups of different sizes, made out of staves hooped together. The *quaigh* was used chiefly for drinking wine or brandy; it might hold about a gill, and was often composed of rare wood, and curiously ornamented with silver.

your fair promises of getting me a commission in the Irish
brigade,—what have I to do with the Irish brigade? I am
a plain Scotchman, as my father was before me; and my
grand-aunt, Lady Girnington, cannot live for ever."

"Ay, Bucklaw," observed Craigengelt, "but she may live
for many a long day; and for your father, he had land and
living, kept himself close from wadsetters and money-
lenders, paid each man his due, and lived on his own."

"And whose fault is it that I have not done so too?"
said Bucklaw—"whose but the devil's and yours, and such
like as you, that have led me to the far end of a fair estate?
and now I shall be obliged, I suppose, to shelter and shift
about like yourself—live one week upon a line of secret
intelligence from Saint Germains—another upon a report
of a rising in the Highlands—get my breakfast and morning-
draught of sack from old Jacobite ladies, and give them
locks of my old wig for the Chevalier's hair—second my
friend in his quarrel till he comes to the field, and then
flinch from him lest so important a political agent should
perish from the way. All this I must do for bread, besides
calling myself a captain!"

"You think you are making a fine speech now," said
Craigengelt, "and showing much wit at my expense. Is
starving or hanging better than the life I am obliged to
lead, because the present fortunes of the king cannot
sufficiently support his envoys?"

"Starving is honester, Craigengelt, and hanging is like
to be the end on't—But what you mean to make of this
poor fellow Ravenswood, I know not—he has no money
left, any more than I—his lands are all pawned and pledged,
and the interest eats up the rents, and is not satisfied, and
what do you hope to make by meddling in his affairs?"

"Content yourself, Bucklaw; I know my business,"
replied Craigengelt. "Besides that his name, and his
father's services in 1689, will make such an acquisition
sound well both at Versailles and Saint Germains—you
will also please be informed, that the Master of Ravenswood
is a very different kind of a young fellow from you. He
has parts and address, as well as courage and talents, and
will present himself abroad like a young man of head as
well as heart, who knows something more than the speed
of a horse or the flight of a hawk. I have lost credit of

late, by bringing over no one that had sense to know more than how to unharbour a stag, or take and reclaim an eyess. The Master has education, sense, and penetration."

"And yet is not wise enough to escape the tricks of a kidnapper, Craigengelt?" replied the younger man. "But don't be angry; you know you will not fight, and so it is as well to leave your hilt in peace and quiet, and tell me in sober guise how you drew the Master into your confidence?"

"By flattering his love of vengeance, Bucklaw," answered Craigengelt. "He has always distrusted me, but I watched my time, and struck while his temper was red-hot with the sense of insult and of wrong. He goes now to expostulate, as he says, and perhaps thinks, with Sir William Ashton. I say, that if they meet, and the lawyer puts him to his defence, the Master will kill him; for he had that sparkle in his eye which never deceives you when you would read a man's purpose. At any rate, he will give him such a bullying as will be construed into an assault on a privy-councilior; so there will be a total breach betwixt him and government; Scotland will be too hot for him, France will gain him, and we will all set sail together in the French brig *L'Espoir*, which is hovering for us off Eyemouth."

"Content am I," said Bucklaw; "Scotland has little left that I care about; and if carrying the Master with us will get us a better reception in France, why, so be it, a God's name. I doubt our own merits will procure us slender preferment; and I trust he will send a ball through the Keeper's head before he joins us. One or two of these scoundrel statesmen should be shot once a-year, just to keep the others on their good behaviour."

"That is very true," replied Craigengelt; "and it reminds me that I must go and see that our horses have been fed, and are in readiness; for should such deed be done, it will be no time for grass to grow beneath their heels." He proceeded as far as the door, then turned back with a look of earnestness, and said to Bucklaw, "Whatever should come of this business, I am sure you will do me the justice to remember, that I said nothing to the Master which could imply my accession to any act of violence which he may take it into his head to commit."

"No, no, not a single word like accession," replied Buck-law; "you know too well the risk belonging to these two terrible words, art and part." Then, as if to himself, he recited the following lines:

> "The dial spoke not, but it made shrewd signs
> And pointed full upon the stroke of murder."

"What is that you are talking to yourself?" said Craigengelt, turning back with some anxiety.

"Nothing—only two lines I have heard upon the stage," replied his companion.

"Bucklaw," said Craigengelt, "I sometimes think you should have been a stage-player yourself; all is fancy and frolic with you."

"I have often thought so myself," said Bucklaw, "I believe it would be safer than acting with you in the Fatal Conspiracy.—But away, play your own part, and look after the horses like a groom as you are.—A play-actor—a stage-player!" he repeated to himself; "that would have deserved a stab, but that Craigengelt's a coward—And yet I should like the profession well enough—Stay—let me see—ay—I would come out in Alexander—

> "'Thus from the grave I rise to save my love,
> Draw all your swords, and quick as lightning move;
> When I rush on, sure none will dare to stay,
> 'Tis love commands, and glory leads the way.'"

As with a voice of thunder, and his hand upon his sword, Bucklaw repeated the ranting couplets of poor Lee, Craigengelt re-entered with a face of alarm.

"We are undone, Bucklaw! the Master's led horse has cast himself over his halter in the stable, and is dead lame—his hackney will be set up with the day's work, and now he has no fresh horse; he will never get off."

"Egad, there will be no moving with the speed of lightning this bout," said Bucklaw, drily. "But stay, you can give him yours."

"What! and be taken myself? I thank you for the proposal," said Craigengelt.

"Why," replied Bucklaw, "if the Lord Keeper should have met with a mischance, which for my part I cannot suppose, for the Master is not the lad to shoot an old and unarmed man—but *if* there should have been a fray at the Castle, you are neither art nor part in it, you know, so have nothing to fear."

"True, true," answered the other, with embarrassment; "but consider my commission from Saint Germains."

"Which many men think is a commission of your own making, noble captain.—Well, if you will not give him your horse, why, d—n it, he must have mine."

"Yours?" said Craigengelt.

"Ay, mine," repeated Bucklaw; "it shall never be said that I agreed to back a gentleman in a little affair of honour, and neither helped him on with it nor off from it."

"You will give him your horse? and have you considered the loss?"

"Loss! why, Grey Gilbert cost me twenty Jacobuses, that's true; but then his hackney is worth something, and his Black Moor is worth twice as much were he sound, and I know how to handle him. Take a fat sucking mastiff whelp, flay and bowel him, stuff the body full of black and grey snails, roast a reasonable time, and baste with oil of spikenard, saffron, cinnamon and honey, anoint with the dripping, working it in"——

"Yes, Bucklaw; but in the meanwhile, before the sprain is cured, nay, before the whelp is roasted, you will be caught and hung. Depend on it, the chase will be hard after Ravenswood. I wish we had made our place of rendezvous nearer to the coast."

"On my faith, then," said Bucklaw, "I had best go off just now, and leave my horse for him—Stay, stay, he comes, I hear a horse's feet."

"Are you sure there is only one?" said Craigengelt; "I fear there is a chase; I think I hear three or four galloping together—I am sure I hear more horses than one."

"Pooh, pooh, it is the wench of the house clattering to the well in her pattens. By my faith, Captain, you should give up both your captainship and your secret service, for you are as easily scared as a wild-goose. But here comes the Master alone, and looking as gloomy as a night in November."

The Master of Ravenswood entered the room accordingly, his cloak muffled around him, his arms folded, his looks stern, and at the same time dejected. He flung his cloak from him as he entered, threw himself upon a chair, and appeared sunk in a profound reverie.

"What has happened? What have you done?" was

hastily demanded by Craigengelt and Bucklaw in the same moment.

"Nothing," was the short and sullen answer.

"Nothing? and left us, determined to call the old villain to account for all the injuries that you, we, and the country, have received at his hand? Have you seen him?"

"I have," replied the Master of Ravenswood.

"Seen him? and come away without settling scores which have been so long due?" said Bucklaw; "I would not have expected that at the hand of the Master of Ravenswood."

"No matter what you expected," replied Ravenswood; "it is not to you, sir, that I shall be disposed to render any reason for my conduct."

"Patience, Bucklaw," said Craigengelt, interrupting his companion, who seemed about to make an angry reply. "The Master has been interrupted in his purpose by some accident; but he must excuse the anxious curiosity of friends, who are devoted to his cause like you and me."

"Friends, Captain Craigengelt!" retorted Ravenswood, haughtily; "I am ignorant what familiarity has passed betwixt us to entitle you to use that expression. I think our friendship amounts to this, that we agreed to leave Scotland together, so soon as I should have visited the alienated mansion of my fathers, and had an interview with its present possessor, I will not call him proprietor."

"Very true, Master," answered Bucklaw; "and as we thought you had a mind to do something to put your neck in jeopardy, Craigie and I very courteously agreed to tarry for you, although ours might run some risk in consequence. As to Craigie, indeed, it does not very much signify, he had gallows written on his brow in the hour of his birth; but I should not like to discredit my parentage by coming to such an end in another man's cause."

"Gentlemen," said the Master of Ravenswood, "I am sorry if I have occasioned you any inconvenience, but I must claim the right of judging what is best for my own affairs, without rendering explanations to any one. I have altered my mind, and do not design to leave the country this season."

"Not to leave the country, Master!" exclaimed Craigengelt. "Not to go over, after all the trouble and expense I have incurred—after all the risk of discovery, and the expense of freight and demurrage!"

"Sir," replied the Master of Ravenswood, "when I designed to leave this country in this haste, I made use of your obliging offer to procure me means of conveyance; but I do not recollect that I pledged myself to go off, if I found occasion to alter my mind. For your trouble on my account, I am sorry, and I thank you; your expense," he added, putting his hand into his pocket, "admits a more solid compensation—freight and demurrage are matters with which I am unacquainted, Captain Craigengelt, but take my purse and pay yourself according to your own conscience." And accordingly he tendered a purse with some gold in it to the soi-disant captain.

But here Bucklaw interposed in his turn. "Your fingers, Craigie, seem to itch for that same piece of green net-work," said he; "but I make my vow to God, that if they offer to close upon it, I will chop them off with my whinger. Since the Master has changed his mind, I suppose we need stay here no longer; but in the first place I beg leave to tell him"——

"Tell him any thing you will," said Craigengelt, "if you will first allow me to state the inconveniences to which he will expose himself by quitting our society, to remind him of the obstacles to his remaining here, and of the difficulties attending his proper introduction at Versailles and Saint Germains, without the countenance of those who have established useful connexions."

"Besides forfeiting the friendship," said Bucklaw, "of at least one man of spirit and honour."

"Gentlemen," said Ravenswood, "permit me once more to assure you, that you have been pleased to attach to our temporary connexion more importance than I ever meant that it should have. When I repair to foreign courts, I shall not need the introduction of an intriguing adventurer, nor is it necessary for me to set value on the friendship of a hot-headed bully." With these words, and without waiting for an answer, he left the apartment, remounted his horse, and was heard to ride off.

"Mortbleu!" said Captain Craigengelt, "my recruit is lost!"

"Ay, Captain," said Bucklaw, "the salmon is off with

hook and all. But I will after him, for I have had more of his insolence than I can well digest."

Craigengelt offered to accompany him; but Bucklaw replied, "No, no, Captain, keep you the cheek of the chimney-nook till I come back; it's good sleeping in a haill skin.

"'Little kens the auld wife that sits by the fire,
  How cauld the wind blaws in hurle-burle swire.'"

And singing as he went, he left the apartment.

CHAPTER VII

Now, Billy Bewick, keep good heart,
  And of thy talking let me be;
But if thou art a man, as I am sure thou art,
  Come over the dike and fight with me.
                    Old Ballad.

THE Master of Ravenswood had mounted the ambling hackney which he before rode, on finding the accident which had happened to his led horse, and, for the animal's ease, was proceeding at a slow pace from the Tod's Den towards his old tower of Wolf's Crag, when he heard the galloping of a horse behind him, and, looking back, perceived that he was pursued by young Bucklaw, who had been delayed a few minutes in the pursuit by the irresistible temptation of giving the hostler at the Tod's Den some recipe for treating the lame horse. This brief delay he had made up by hard galloping, and now overtook the Master where the road traversed a waste moor. "Halt, sir," cried Bucklaw; "I am no political agent—no Captain Craigengelt, whose life is too important to be hazarded in defence of his honour. I am Frank Hayston of Bucklaw, and no man injures me by word, deed, sign, or look, but he must render me an account of it."

"This is all very well, Mr Hayston of Bucklaw," replied the Master of Ravenswood, in a tone the most calm and indifferent; "but I have no quarrel with you, and desire to have none. Our roads homeward, as well as our roads through life, lie in different directions; there is no occasion for us crossing each other."

"Is there not?" said Bucklaw, impetuously. "By Heaven! but I say that there is, though—you called us intriguing adventurers."

"Be correct in your recollection, Mr Hayston; it was to your companion only I applied that epithet, and you know him to be no better."

"And what then? He was my companion for the time, and no man shall insult my companion, right or wrong, while he is in my company."

"Then, Mr Hayston," replied Ravenswood, with the same composure, "you should choose your society better, or you are like to have much work in your capacity of their champion. Go home, sir, sleep, and have more reason in your wrath to-morrow."

"Not so, Master, you have mistaken your man; high airs and wise saws shall not carry it off thus. Besides, you termed me bully, and you shall retract the word before we part."

"Faith, scarcely," said Ravenswood, "unless you show me better reason for thinking myself mistaken than you are now producing."

"Then, Master," said Bucklaw, "though I should be sorry to offer it to a man of your quality, if you will not justify your incivility, or retract it, or name a place of meeting, you must here undergo the hard word and the hard blow."

"Neither will be necessary," said Ravenswood; "I am satisfied with what I have done to avoid an affair with you. If you are serious, this place will serve as well as another."

"Dismount then, and draw," said Bucklaw, setting him an example. "I always thought and said you were a pretty man; I should be sorry to report you otherwise."

"You shall have no reason, sir," said Ravenswood, alighting, and putting himself into a posture of defence.

Their swords crossed, and the combat commenced with great spirit on the part of Bucklaw, who was well accustomed to affairs of the kind, and distinguished by address and dexterity at his weapon. In the present case, however, he did not use his skill to advantage; for, having lost his temper at the cool and contemptuous manner in which the Master of Ravenswood had long refused, and at length granted him satisfaction, and urged by his impatience, he

adopted the part of an assailant with inconsiderate eagerness. The Master, with equal skill, and much greater composure, remained chiefly on the defensive, and even declined
to avail himself of one or two advantages afforded him by
the eagerness of his adversary. At length, in a desperate
lunge, which he followed with an attempt to close, Bucklaw's foot slipped, and he fell on the short grassy turf on
which they were fighting. "Take your life sir," said the
Master of Ravenswood, "and mend it, if you can."

"It would be but a cobbled piece of work, I fear," said
Bucklaw, rising slowly and gathering up his sword, much
less disconcerted with the issue of the combat than could
have been expected from the impetuosity of his temper. "I
thank you for my life, Master," he pursued. "There is my
hand, I bear no ill-will to you, either for my bad luck or
your better swordsmanship."

The Master looked steadily at him for an instant, then
extended his hand to him.—"Bucklaw," he said, "you are
a generous fellow, and I have done you wrong. I heartily
ask your pardon for the expression which offended you; it
was hastily and incautiously uttered, and I am convinced it
is totally misapplied."

"Are you indeed, Master?" said Bucklaw, his face resuming at once its natural expression of light-hearted care-
lessness and audacity; "that is more than I expected of
you; for, Master, men say you are not ready to retract your
opinions and your language."

"Not when I have well considered them," said the
Master.

"Then you are a little wiser than I am, for I always give
my friend satisfaction first, and explanation afterwards. If
one of us falls, all accounts are settled; if not, men are
never so ready for peace as after war.—But what does that
bawling brat of a boy want?" said Bucklaw. "I wish to
Heaven he had come a few minutes sooner! and yet it
must have been ended some time, and perhaps this way is
as well as any other."

As he spoke, the boy he mentioned came up, cudgelling
an ass, on which he was mounted, to the top of its speed,
and sending, like one of Ossian's heroes, his voice before
him,—"Gentlemen,—gentlemen, save yourselves! for the
gudewife bade us tell ye there were folk in her house had

taen Captain Craigengelt, and were seeking for Bucklaw, and that ye behoved to ride for it."

"By my faith, and that's very true, my man," said Bucklaw; "and there's a silver sixpence for your news, and I would give any man twice as much would tell me which way I should ride."

"That will I, Bucklaw," said Ravenswood; "ride home to Wolf's Crag with me. There are places in the old tower where you might lie hid, were a thousand men to seek you."

"But that will bring you into trouble yourself, Master; and unless you be in the Jacobite scrape already, it is quite needless for me to drag you in."

"Not a whit; I have nothing to fear."

"Then I will ride with you blithely, for, to say the truth, I do not know the rendezvous that Craigie was to guide us to this night; and I am sure that, if he is taken, he will tell all the truth of me, and twenty lies of you, in order to save himself from the withie."

They mounted, and rode off in company accordingly, striking off the ordinary road, and holding their way by wild moorish unfrequented paths, with which the gentlemen were well acquainted from the exercise of the chase, but through which others would have had much difficulty in tracing their course. They rode for some time in silence, making such haste as the condition of Ravenswood's horse permitted, until night having gradually closed around them, they discontinued their speed, both from the difficulty of discovering their path, and from the hope that they were beyond the reach of pursuit or observation.

"And now that we have drawn bridle abit," said Bucklaw, "I would fain ask you a question, Master."

"Ask, and welcome," said Ravenswood, "but forgive my not answering it, unless I think proper."

"Well, it is simply this," answered his late antagonist,— "What, in the name of old Sathan, could make you, who stand so highly on your reputation, think for a moment of drawing up with such a rogue as Craigengelt, and such a scape-grace as folk call Bucklaw?"

"Simply, because I was desperate, and sought desperate associates."

"And what made you break off from us at the nearest?" again demanded Bucklaw.

"Because I had changed my mind," said the Master, "and renounced my enterprise, at least for the present. And now that I have answered your questions fairly and frankly, tell me what makes you associate with Craigengelt, so much beneath you both in birth and in spirit?"

"In plain terms," answered Bucklaw, "because I am a fool, who have gambled away my land in these times. My grand-aunt, Lady Girnington, has taen a new tack of life, I think, and I could only hope to get something by a change of government. Craigie was a sort of gambling acquaintance; he saw my condition; and, as the devil is always at one's elbow, told me fifty lies about his credentials from Versailles, and his interest at Saint Germains, promised me a captain's commission at Paris, and I have been ass enough to put my thumb under his belt. I daresay, by this time, he has told a dozen pretty stories of me to the government. And this is what I have got by wine, women, and dice, cocks, dogs, and horses."

"Yes, Bucklaw," said the Master, "you have indeed nourished in your bosom the snakes that are now stinging you."

"That's home as well as true, Master," replied his companion; "but, by your leave, you have nursed in your bosom one great goodly snake that has swallowed all the rest, and is as sure to devour you as my half dozen are to make a meal on all that's left of Bucklaw, which is but what lies between bonnet and boot-heel."

"I must not," answered the Master of Ravenswood, "challenge the freedom of speech in which I have set example. What, to speak without a metaphor, do you call this monstrous passion, which you charge me with fostering?"

"Revenge, my good sir, revenge; which, if it be as gentleman-like a sin as wine and wassail, with their *et cæteras*, is equally unchristian, and not so bloodless. It is better breaking a park-pale to watch a doe or damsel, than to shoot an old man."

"I deny the purpose," said the Master of Ravenswood. "On my soul, I had no such intention; I meant but to confront the oppressor ere I left my native land, and upbraid him with his tyranny and its consequences. I would have stated my wrongs so that they would have shaken his soul within him."

"Yes," answered Bucklaw, "and he would have collared you, and cried help, and then you would have shaken the soul *out* of him, I suppose. Your very look and manner would have frightened the old man to death."

"Consider the provocation," answered Ravenswood— "consider the ruin and death procured and caused by his hard-hearted cruelty—an ancient house destroyed, an affectionate father murdered! Why, in our old Scottish days, he that sat quiet under such wrongs, would have been held neither fit to back a friend nor face a foe."

"Well, Master, I am glad to see that the devil deals as cunningly with other folk as he deals with me; for whenever I am about to commit any folly, he persuades me it is the most necessary, gallant, gentlemanlike thing on earth, and I am up to saddlegirths in the bog before I see that the ground is soft. And you, Master, might have turned out a murd——a homicide, just out of pure respect for your father's memory."

"There is more sense in your language, Bucklaw," replied the Master, "than might have been expected from your conduct. It is too true, our vices steal upon us in forms outwardly as fair as those of the demons whom the superstitious represent as intriguing with the human race, and are not discovered in their native hideousness until we have clasped them in our arms."

"But we may throw them from us, though," said Bucklaw, "and that is what I shall think of doing one of these days,—that is, when old Lady Girnington dies."

"Did you ever hear the expression of the English divine?" said Ravenswood—"'Hell is paved with good intentions'—as much as to say, "they are more often formed than executed."

"Well," replied Bucklaw, "but I will begin this blessed night, and have determined not to drink above one quart of wine, unless your claret be of extraordinary quality."

"You will find little to tempt you at Wolf's Crag," said the Master. "I know not that I can promise you more than the shelter of my roof; all, and more than all, our stock of wine and provisions was exhausted at the late occasion."

"Long may it be ere provision is needed for the like purpose," answered Bucklaw; "but you should not drink up the last flask at a dirge; there is ill luck in that."

"There is ill luck, I think, in whatever belongs to me," said Ravenswood. "But yonder is Wolf's Crag, and whatever it still contains is at your service."

The roar of the sea had long announced their approach to the cliffs, on the summit of which, like the nest of some sea-eagle, the founder of the fortalice had perched his eyry. The pale moon, which had hitherto been contending with flitting clouds, now shone out, and gave them a view of the solitary and naked tower, situated on a projecting cliff that beetled on the German Ocean. On three sides the rock was precipitous; on the fourth, which was that towards the land, it had been originally fenced by an artificial ditch and drawbridge, but the latter was broken down and ruinous, and the former had been in part filled up, so as to allow passage for a horseman into the narrow court-yard, encircled on two sides with low offices and stables, partly ruinous, and closed on the landward front by a low embattled wall, while the remaining side of the quadrangle was occupied by the tower itself, which, tall and narrow, and built of a greyish stone, stood glimmering in the moonlight, like the sheeted spectre of some huge giant. A wilder, or more disconsolate dwelling, it was perhaps difficult to conceive. The sombrous and heavy sound of the billows, successively dashing against the rocky beach at a profound distance beneath, was to the ear what the landscape was to the eye—a symbol of unvaried and monotonous melancholy, not unmingled with horror.

Although the night was not far advanced, there was no sign of living inhabitant about this forlorn abode, excepting that one, and only one, of the narrow and stanchelled windows which appeared at irregular heights and distances in the walls of the building, showed a small glimmer of light.

"There," said Ravenswood, "sits the only male domestic that remains to the house of Ravenswood; and it is well that he does remain there, since otherwise, we had little hope to find either light or fire: But follow me cautiously, the road is narrow, and admits only one horse in front."

In effect, the path led along a kind of isthmus, at the peninsular extremity of which the tower was situated, with that exclusive attention to strength and security, in preference to every circumstance of convenience, which dictated to the Scottish barons the choice of their situations, as well as their style of building.

By adopting the cautious mode of approach recommended by the proprietor of this wild hold, they entered the court-yard in safety. But it was long ere the efforts of Ravenswood, though loudly exerted by knocking at the low-browed entrance, and repeated shouts to Caleb to open the gate and admit them, received any answer.

"The old man must be departed," he began to say, "or fallen into some fit; for the noise I have made would have waked the seven sleepers."

At length a timid and hesitating voice replied,—"Master—Master of Ravenswood, is it you?"

"Yes, it is I, Caleb; open the door quickly."

"But is it you in very blood and body? For I would sooner face fifty deevils as my master's ghaist, or even his wraith,—wherefore, aroint ye, if ye were ten times my master, unless ye come in bodily shape, lith and limb."

"It is I, you old fool," answered Ravenswood, "in bodily shape, and alive, save that I am half dead with cold."

The light at the upper window disappeared, and glancing from loop-hole to loop-hole in slow succession, gave intimation that the bearer was in the act of descending, with great deliberation, a winding staircase occupying one of the turrets which graced the angles of the old tower. The tardiness of his descent extracted some exclamations of impatience from Ravenswood, and several oaths from his less patient and more mercurial companion. Caleb again paused ere he unbolted the door, and once more asked, if they were men of mould that demanded entrance at this time of night?

"Were I near you, you old fool," said Bucklaw, "I would give you sufficient proofs of *my* bodily condition."

"Open the gate, Caleb," said his master, in a more soothing tone, partly from his regard to the ancient and faithful seneschal, partly perhaps because he thought that angry words would be thrown away, so long as Caleb had a stout iron-clenched oaken door betwixt his person and the speakers.

At length Caleb, with a trembling hand, undid the bars, opened the heavy door, and stood before them, exhibiting his thin grey hairs, bald forehead, and sharp high features, illuminated by a quivering lamp which he held in one hand, while he shaded and protected its flame with the other. The timorous courteous glance which he threw around him —the effect of the partial light upon his white hair and illumined features, might have made a good painting; but our travellers were too impatient for security against the rising storm, to permit them to indulge themselves in studying the picturesque. "Is it you, my dear master? is it you yourself, indeed?" exclaimed the old domestic. "I am wae ye suld hae stude waiting at your ain gate; but wha wad hae thought o' seeing ye sae sune, and a strange gentleman with a—(Here he exclaimed apart, as it were, and to some inmate of the tower, in a voice not meant to be heard by those in the court)—Mysie—Mysie woman! stir for dear life, and get the fire mended; take the auld three-legged stool, or ony thing that's readiest that will make a lowe.—I doubt we are but puirly provided, no expecting ye this some months, when doubtless ye wad hae been received conform till your rank, as gude right is; but natheless"——

"Natheless, Caleb," said the master, "we must have our horses put up, and ourselves too, the best way we can. I hope you are not sorry to see me sooner than you expected?"

"So , my lord!—I am sure ye sall aye be my lord wi' honest folk, as your noble ancestors hae been these three hundred years, and never asked a whig's leave. Sorry to see the Lord of Ravenswood at ane o' his ain castles!—(Then again apart to his unseen associate behind the screen)—Mysie, kill the brood-hen without thinking twice on it; let them care that come ahint.—No to say it's our best dwelling," he added. turning to Bucklaw; "but just a strength for the Lord of Ravenswood to flee until,—that is no to *flee*, but to retreat until in troublous times, like the present, when it was ill convenient for him to live farther in the country in ony of his better and mair principal manors; but, for its antiquity, maist folk think that the outside of Wolf's Crag is worthy of a large perusal."

"And you are determined we shall have time to make it," said Ravenswood, somewhat amused with the shift- the old man used to detain them without doors, until his confederate Mysie had made her preparations within.

"O, never mind the outside of the house, my good friend," said Bucklaw; "let's see the inside, and let our horses see the stable, that's all."

"O yes, sir—ay, sir,—unquestionably, sir—my lord and ony of his honourable companions"——

"But our horses, my old friend—our horses; they will be dead-foundered by standing here in the cold after riding hard, and mine is too good to be spoiled; therefore, once more, our horses," exclaimed Bucklaw.

"True—ay—your horses—yes—I will call the grooms;" and sturdily did Caleb roar till the old tower rang again,—"John—William—Saunders!—The lads are gane out, or sleeping," he observed, after pausing for an answer, which he knew that he had no human chance of receiving. . "A' gaes wrang when the Master's out by; but I'll take care o' your cattle mysell."

"I think you had better," said Ravenswood, "otherwise I see little chance of their being attended to at all."

"Whisht, my lord,—whisht, for God's sake," said Caleb, in an imploring tone, and apart to his master; "if ye dinna regard your ain credit, think on mine; we'll hae hard eneugh wark to mak a decent night o't, wi' a' the lees I can tell."

"Well, well, never mind," said his master; "go to the stable. There is hay and corn, I trust?"

"Ou ay, plenty of hay and corn:" this was uttered boldly and aloud, and, in a lower tone, "there was some half fous o' aits, and some taits o' meadow-hay, left after the burial."

"Very well," said Ravenswood, taking the lamp from his domestic's unwilling hand, "I will show the stranger up stairs myself."

"I canna think o' that, my lord;—if ye wad but have five minutes, or ten minutes, or, at maist, a quarter of an hour's patience, and look at the fine moonlight prospect of the Bass and North-Berwick Law till I sort the horses, I would marshal ye up, as reason as ye suld be marshalled, your lordship and your honourable visitor. And I hae lockit up the siller candlesticks, and the lamp is not fit"——

"It will do very well in the meantime," said Ravenswood, "and you will have no difficulty for want of light in the stable, for, if I recollect, half the roof is off."

"Very true, my lord," replied the trusty adherent, and

with ready wit instantly added, "and the lazy sclater loons have never come to put it on a' this while, your lordship."

"If I were disposed to jest at the calamities of my house," said Ravenswood, as he led the way up stairs, "poor old Caleb would furnish me with ample means. His passion consists in representing things about our miserable *menage*, not as they are, but as, in his opinion, they ought to be; and, to say the truth, I have been often diverted with the poor wretch's expedients to supply what he thought was essential for the credit of the family, and his still more generous apologies for the want of those articles for which his ingenuity could discover no substitute. But though the tower is none of the largest, I shall have some trouble without him to find the apartment in which there is a fire."

As he spoke thus, he opened the door of the hall. "Here, at least," he said, "there is neither hearth nor harbour."

It was indeed a scene of desolation. A large vaulted room, the beams of which, combined like those of West-minster-Hall, were rudely carved at the extremities, remained nearly in the situation in which it had been left after the entertainment at Allan Lord Ravenswood's funeral. Overturned pitchers, and black jacks, and pewter stoups, and flagons, still cumbered the large oaken table; glasses, those more perishable implements of conviviality, many of which had been voluntarily sacrificed by the guests in their enthusiastic pledges to favourite toasts, strewed the stone floor with their fragments. As for the articles of plate, lent for the purpose by friends and kinsfolk, those had been carefully withdrawn so soon as the ostentatious display of festivity, equally unnecessary and strangely timed, had been made and ended. Nothing, in short, remained that indicated wealth; all the signs were those of recent wastefulness, and present desolation. The black cloth hangings, which, on the late mournful occasion, replaced the tattered moth-eaten tapestries, had been partly pulled down, and, dangling from the wall in irregular festoons, disclosed the rough stone-work of the building, unsmoothed either by plaster or the chisel. The seats thrown down, or left in disorder, intimated the careless confusion which had concluded the mournful revel. "This room," said Ravenswood, holding up the lamp—"this room, Mr Hayston, was riotous when it should have been sad; it is a just retribution that it should now be sad when it ought to be cheerful."

They left this disconsolate apartment, and went up stairs, where, after opening one or two doors in vain, Ravenswood led the way into a little matted anteroom, in which, to their great joy, they found a tolerably good fire, which Mysie, by some such expedient as Caleb had suggested, had supplied with a reasonable quantity of fuel. Glad at the heart to see more of comfort than the castle had yet seemed to offer, Bucklaw rubbed his hands heartily over the fire, and now listened with more complacency to the apologies which the Master of Ravenswood offered. "Comfort," he said, "I cannot provide for you, for I have it not for myself; it is long since these walls have known it, if, indeed, they were ever acquainted with it. Shelter and safety, I think, I can promise you."

"Excellent matters, Master," replied Bucklaw, "and, with a mouthful of food and wine, positively all I can require to-night."

"I fear," said the Master, "your supper will be a poor one; I hear the matter in discussion betwixt Caleb and Mysie. Poor Balderston is something deaf, amongst his other accomplishments, so that much of what he means should be spoken aside is overheard by the whole audience, and especially by those from whom he is most anxious to conceal his private manœuvres— Hark!"

They listened, and heard the old domestic's voice in conversation with Mysie to the following effect. "Just mak the best o't, mak the best o't, woman; it's easy to put a fair face on ony thing."

"But the auld brood-hen?—she'll be as teugh as bow-strings and bend-leather!"

"Say ye made a mistake—say ye made a mistake, Mysie," replied the faithful seneschal, in a soothing and undertoned voice; "tak it a' on yoursell; never let the credit o' the house suffer."

"But the brood-hen," remonstrated Mysie,—"ou, she's sitting some gate aneath the dais in the hall, and I am feared to gae in in the dark for the bogle; and if I didna see the bogle, I could as ill see the hen, for it's pit-mirk, and there's no another light in the house, save that very blessed lamp whilk the Master has in his ain hand. And if I had the hen, she's to pu', and to draw, and to dress; how can I do that, and them sitting by the only fire we have?"

"Weel, weel, Mysie," said the butler, "bide ye there a wee, and I'll try to get the lamp wiled away frae them."

Accordingly, Caleb Balderston entered the apartment, little aware that so much of his by-play had been audible there. "Well, Caleb, my old friend, is there any chance of supper?" said the Master of Ravenswood.

"*Chance* of supper, your lordship?" said Caleb, with an emphasis of strong scorn at the implied doubt,—"How should there be ony question of that, and us in your lordship's house?—Chance of supper, indeed!—But ye'll no be for butcher-meat? There's walth o' fat poultry, ready either for spit or brander—The fat capon, Mysie!" he added, calling out as boldly as if such a thing had been in existence.

"Quite unnecessary," said Bucklaw, who deemed himself bound in courtesy to relieve some part of the anxious butler's perplexity, "if you have any thing cold, or a morsel of bread."

"The best of bannocks!" exclaimed Caleb, much relieved; "and, for cauld meat, a' that we hae is cauld eneugh,—howbeit maist of the cauld meat and pastry was gien to the poor folk after the ceremony of interment, as gude reason was; nevertheless"——

"Come, Caleb," said the Master of Ravenswood, "I must cut this matter short. This is the young laird of Bucklaw; he is under hiding, and therefore, you know"——

"He'll be nae nicer than your lordship's honour, I'se warrant." answered Caleb, cheerfully, with a nod of intelligence; "I am sorry that the gentleman is under distress, but I am blithe that he canna say muckle agane our housekeeping, for I believe his ain pinches may match ours;—no that we are pinched, thank God," he added, retracting the admission which he had made in his first burst of joy, "but nae doubt we are waur aff than we hae been, or suld be. And for eating,—what signifies telling a lee? there's just the hinder end of the mutton-ham that has been but three times on the table, and the nearer the bane the sweeter, as your honours weel ken; and—there's the heel of the ewe-milk kebbuck, wi' a bit of nice butter, and—and —that's a' that's to trust to." And with great alacrity he produced his slender stock of provisions, and placed them with much formality upon a small round table betwixt the two gentlemen, who were not deterred either by the homely quality or limited quantity of the repast from doing it full justice. Caleb in the meanwhile waited on them with grave officiousness, as if anxious to make up, by his own respectful assiduity, for the want of all other attendance.

But alas! how little on such occasions can form, however anxiously and scrupulously observed, supply the lack of substantial fare! Bucklaw, who had eagerly eaten a considerable portion of the thrice-sacked mutton-ham, now began to demand ale.

"I wadna just presume to recommend our ale," said Caleb; "the maut was ill made, and there was awfu' thunner last week; but siccan water as the Tower well has ye'll seldom see, Bucklaw, and that I'se engage for."

"But if your ale is bad, you can let us have some wine," said Bucklaw, making a grimace at the mention of the pure element which Caleb so earnestly recommended.

"Wine?" answered Caleb, undauntedly, "eneugh of wine; it was but twa days syne—wae's me for the cause— there was as much wine drunk in this house as would have floated a pinnace. There never was lack of wine at Wolf's Crag."

"Do fetch us some then," said his master, "instead of talking about it." And Caleb boldly departed.

Every expended butt in the old cellar did he set a-tilt, and shake with the desperate expectation of collecting enough of the grounds of claret to fill the large pewter measure which he carried in his hand. Alas! each had been too devoutly drained; and, with all the squeezing and manœuvring which his craft as a butler suggested, he could only collect about half a quart that seemed presentable. Still, however, Caleb was too good a general to renounce the field without a stratagem to cover his retreat. He undauntedly threw down an empty flagon, as if he had stumbled at the entrance of the apartment; called upon Mysie to wipe up the wine that had never been spilt, and placing the other vessel on the table, hoped there was still enough left for their honours. There was indeed; for even Bucklaw, a sworn friend to the grape, found no encouragement to renew his first attack upon the vintage of Wolf's Crag, but contented himself, however reluctantly, with a draught of fair water. Arrangements were now made for his repose; and as the secret chamber was assigned for this purpose, it furnished Caleb with a first-rate and most plausible apology for all deficiencies of furniture, bedding, &c.

"For wha," said he, "would have thought of the secret chaumer being needed? it has not been used since the time of the Gowrie Conspiracy, and I durst never let a woman ken of the entrance to it, or your honour will allow that it wad not hae been a secret chaumer lang."

CHAPTER VIII

> The hearth in hall was black and dead,
>   No board was dight in bower within,
> Nor merry bowl, nor welcome bed;
>   "Here's sorry cheer," quoth the Heir of Linne.
>   *Old Ballad.*

THE feelings of the prodigal Heir of Linne, as expressed in that excellent old song, when, after dissipating his whole fortune, he found himself the deserted inhabitant of "the lonely lodge," might perhaps have some resemblance to those of the Master of Ravenswood in his deserted mansion of Wolf's Crag. The Master, however, had this advantage over the spendthrift in the legend, that if he was in similar distress, he could not impute it to his own imprudence. His misery had been bequeathed to him by his father, and, joined to his high blood, and to a title which the courteous might give, or the churlish withhold, at their pleasure, it was the whole inheritance he had derived from his ancestry.

Perhaps this melancholy, yet consolatory reflection, crossed the mind of the unfortunate young nobleman with a breathing of comfort. Favourable to calm reflection, as well as to the Muses, the morning, while it dispelled the shades of night, had a composing and sedative effect upon the stormy passions by which the Master of Ravenswood had been agitated on the preceding day. He now felt

himself able to analyse the different feelings by which he
was agitated, and much resolved to combat and to subdue
them. The morning, which had arisen calm and bright,
gave a pleasant effect even to the waste moorland view
which was seen from the castle on looking to the landward;
and the glorious ocean, crisped with a thousand rippling
waves of silver, extended on the other side, in awful yet
complacent majesty, to the verge of the horizon. With
such scenes of calm sublimity the human heart sympathises
even in its most disturbed moods, and deeds of honour
and virtue are inspired by their majestic influence.

To seek out Bucklaw in the retreat which he had
afforded him was the first occupation of the Master, after
he had performed, with a scrutiny unusually severe, the
important task of self-examination. "How now, Bucklaw?" was his morning's salutation—"how like you the
couch in which the exiled Earl of Angus once slept in
security, when he was pursued by the full energy of a
king's resentment?"

"Umph!" returned the sleeper awakened; "I have
little to complain of where so great a man was quartered
before me, only the mattress was of the hardest, the vault
somewhat damp, the rats rather more mutinous than I
would have expected from the state of Caleb's larder; and
if there had been shutters to that grated window, or a
curtain to the bed, I should think it, upon the whole, an
improvement in your accommodations."

"It is, to be sure, forlorn enough," said the Master,
looking around the small vault; "but if you will rise and
leave it, Caleb will endeavour to find you a better breakfast than your supper of last night."

"Pray, let it be no better," said Bucklaw, getting up, and
endeavouring to dress himself as well as the obscurity of
the place would permit,—"let it, I say, be no better, if you
mean me to persevere in my proposed reformation. The
very recollection of Caleb's beverage has done more to
suppress my longing to open the day with a morning-
draught than twenty sermons would have done. And you,
Master, have you been able to give battle valiantly to your
bosom-snake? You see I am in the way of smothering
my vipers one by one."

"I have commenced the battle, at least, Bucklaw, and I

have had a fair vision of an angel who descended to my assistance," replied the Master.

"Woe's me!" said his guest, "no vision can I expect, unless my aunt, Lady Girnington, should betake herself to the tomb; and then it would be the substance of her heritage rather than the appearance of her phantom that I should consider as the support of my good resolutions.—But this same breakfast, Master,—does the deer that is to make tne pasty run yet on foot, as the ballad has it?"

"I will enquire into that matter," said his entertainer; and, leaving the apartment, he went in search of Caleb, whom, after some difficulty, he found in an obscure sort of dungeon, which had been in former times the buttery of the castle. Here the old man was employed busily in the doubtful task of burnishing a pewter flagon until it should take the hue and semblance of silver-plate. "I think it may do—I think it might pass, if they winna bring it ower muckle in the light o' the window!" were the ejaculations which he muttered from time to time, as if to encourage himself in his undertaking, when he was interrupted by the voice of his master. "Take this," said the Master of Ravenswood, "and get what is necessary for the family." And with these words he gave to the old butler the purse which had on the preceding evening so narrowly escaped the fangs of Craigengelt. The old man shook his silvery and thin locks, and looked with an expression of the most heartfelt anguish at his master as he weighed in his hand the slender treasure, and said in a sorrowful voice, "And is this a' that's left?"

"All that is left at present," said the Master, affecting more cheerfulness than perhaps he really felt, "is just the green purse and the wee pickle gowd, as the old song says; but we shall do better one day, Caleb."

"Before that day comes," said Caleb, "I doubt there will be an end of an auld sang. and an auld serving man to boot. But it disna become me to speak that gate to your honour, and you looking so pale. Tak back the purse, and keep it to be making a show before company; for if your honour would just take a bidding, and be whiles taking it out afore folk and putting it up again, there's naebody would refuse us trust, for a' that's come and gane yet."

"But, Caleb," said the Master, "I still intend to leave

this country very soon, and desire to do so with the reputation of an honest man, leaving no debt behind me, at least or my own contracting."

"And gude right ye suld gang away as a true man, and so ye shall; for auld Caleb can tak the wyte of whatever is taen on for the house, and then it will be a' just ae man's burden; and I will live just as weel in the tolbooth as out of it, and the credit of the family will be a' safe and sound."

The master endeavoured, in vain, to make Caleb comprehend, that the butler's incurring the responsibility of debts in his own person, would rather add to than remove the objections which he had to their being contracted. He spoke to a premier, too busy in devising ways and means to puzzle himself with refuting the arguments offered against their justice or expediency.

"There's Eppie Sma'trash will trust us for ale," said Caleb to himself; "she has lived a' her life under the family—and maybe wi' a soup brandy—I canna say for wine—she is but a lone woman, and gets her claret by a runlet at a time—but I'll work a wee drap out o' her by fair means or foul. For doos, there's the doocot—there will be poultry amang the tenants, though Lucky Chirnside says she has paid the kain twice ower. We'll mak shift, an it like your honour—we'll mak shift—keep your heart abune, for the house sall haud its credit as lang as auld Caleb is to the fore."

The entertainment which the old man's exertions of various kinds enabled him to present to the young gentlemen for three or four days, was certainly of no splendid description, but it may readily be believed it was set before no critical guests; and even the distresses, excuses, evasions, and shifts of Caleb, afforded amusement to the young men, and added a sort of interest to the scrambling and irregular style of their table. They had indeed occasion to seize on every circumstance that might serve to diversify or enliven time, which otherwise passed away so heavily.

Bucklaw, shut out from his usual field-sports and joyous carouses by the necessity of remaining concealed within the walls of the castle, became a joyless and uninteresting companion. When the Master of Ravenswood would no longer fence or play at shovel-board—when he himself had polished to the extremity the coat of his palfrey with brush, curry-comb, and hair-cloth—when he had seen him eat his provender, and gently lie down in his stall, he could hardly help envying the animal's apparent acquiescence in a life so monotonous. "The stupid brute," he said, "thinks neither of the race-ground or the hunting-field, or his green paddock at Bucklaw, but enjoys himself as comfortably when haltered to the rack in this ruinous vault, as if he had been foaled in it; and I, who have the freedom of a prisoner at large, to range through the dungeons of this wretched old tower, can hardly, betwixt whistling and sleeping, contrive to pass away the hour till dinner-time."

And with this disconsolate reflection, he wended his way to the bartizan or battlements of the tower, to watch what objects might appear on the distant moor, or to pelt, with pebbles and pieces of lime, the sea-mews and cormorants which established themselves incautiously within the reach of an idle young man.

Ravenswood, with a mind incalculably deeper and more powerful than that of his companion, had his own anxious subjects of reflection, which wrought for him the same unhappiness that sheer ennui and want of occupation inflicted on his companion. The first sight of Lucy Ashton had been less impressive than her image proved to be upon reflection. As the depth and violence of that revengeful passion, by which he had been actuated in seeking an interview with the father, began to abate by degrees, he looked back on his conduct towards the daughter as harsh and unworthy towards a female of rank and beauty. Her looks of grateful acknowledgment, her words of affectionate courtesy, had been repelled with something which approached to disdain; and if the Master of Ravenswood had sustained wrongs at the hand of Sir William Ashton, his conscience told him they had been unhandsomely resented towards his daughter. When his thoughts took this turn of self-reproach, the recollection of Lucy Ashton's beautiful features, rendered yet more interesting by the circumstances in which their meeting had taken place, made an impression upon his mind at once soothing and painful. The sweetness of her voice, the delicacy of her expressions, the vivid glow of her filial affection, embittered his regret at having repulsed her gratitude with rudeness, while, at the same time, they placed before his imagination a picture of the most seducing sweetness.

Even young Ravenswood's strength of moral feeling and rectitude of purpose at once increased the danger of cherishing these recollections, and the propensity to entertain them. Firmly resolved as he was to subdue, if possible, the predominating vice in his character, he admitted with willingness—nay, he summoned up in his imagination, the ideas by which it could be most powerfully counteracted; and, while he did so, a sense of his own harsh conduct towards the daughter of his enemy naturally induced him, as if by way of recompense, to invest her with more of grace and beauty than perhaps she could actually claim.

Had any one at this period told the Master of Ravenswood that he had so lately vowed vengeance against the whole lineage of him whom he considered, not unjustly, as author of his father's ruin and death, he might at first have repelled the charge as a foul calumny; yet, upon serious self-examination, he would have been compelled to admit, that it had, at one period, some foundation in truth, though, according to the present tone of his sentiments, it was difficult to believe that this had really been the case.

There already existed in his bosom two contradictory passions,—a desire to revenge the death of his father, strangely qualified by admiration of his enemy's daughter. Against the former feeling he had struggled, until it seemed to him upon the wane; against the latter he used no means of resistance, for he did not suspect its existence. That this was actually the case, was chiefly evinced by his resuming his resolution to leave Scotland. Yet, though such was his purpose, he remained day after day at Wolf's Crag, without taking measures for carrying it into execution. It is true, that he had written to one or two kinsmen, who resided in a distant quarter of Scotland, and particularly to the Marquis of A——, intimating his purpose; and when pressed upon the subject by Bucklaw, he was wont to allege the necessity of waiting for their reply, especially that of the Marquis, before taking so decisive a measure.

The Marquis was rich and powerful; and although he was suspected to entertain sentiments unfavourable to the government established at the Revolution, he had nevertheless address enough to head a party in the Scottish

Privy Council, connected with the high church faction in England, and powerful enough to menace those to whom the Lord Keeper adhered, with a probable subversion of their power. The consulting with a personage of such importance was a plausible excuse, which Ravenswood used to Bucklaw, and probably to himself, for continuing his residence at Wolf's Crag; and it was rendered yet more so by a general report which began to be current, of a probable change of ministers and measures in the Scottish administration. These rumours, strongly asserted by some, and as resolutely denied by others, as their wishes or interest dictated, found their way even to the ruinous Tower of Wolf's Crag, chiefly through the medium of Caleb the butler, who, among his other excellences, was an ardent politician, and seldom made an excursion from the old fortress to the neighbouring village of Wolf's-hope, without bringing back what tidings were current in the vicinity.

But if Bucklaw could not offer any satisfactory objections to the delay of the Master in leaving Scotland, he did not the less suffer with impatience the state of inaction to which it confined him; and it was only the ascendency which his new companion had acquired over him, that induced him to submit to a course of life so alien to his habits and inclinations.

"You were wont to be thought a stirring active young fellow, Master," was his frequent remonstrance; "yet here you seem determined to live on and on like a rat in a hole, with this trifling difference, that the wiser vermin chooses a hermitage where he can find food at least; but as for us, Caleb's excuses become longer as his diet turns more spare, and I fear we shall realise the stories they tell of the sloth, —we have almost eat up the last green leaf on the plant, and have nothing left for it but to drop from the tree and break our necks."

"Do not fear it," said Ravenswood; "there is a fate watches for us, and we too have a stake in the revolution that is now impending, and which already has alarmed many a bosom."

"What fate—what revolution?" enquired his companion. "We have had one revolution too much already, I think."

Ravenswood interrupted him by putting into his hands a letter.

"O," answered Bucklaw, "my dream's out—I thought I heard Caleb this morning pressing some unfortunate fellow to a drink of cold water, and assuring him it was better for his stomach in the morning than ale or brandy."

"It was my Lord of A——'s courier," said Ravenswood, "who was doomed to experience his ostentatious hospitality, which I believe ended in sour beer and herrings—Read, and you will see the news he has brought us."

"I will as fast as I can," said Bucklaw; "but I am no great clerk, nor does his lordship seem to be the first of scribes."

The reader will peruse, in a few seconds, by the aid of our friend Ballantyne's types, what took Bucklaw a good half hour in perusal, though assisted by the Master of Ravenswood. The tenor was as follows:—

" *Right Honourable our Cousin,*

"Our hearty commendations premised, these come to assure you oi the interest which we take in your welfare, and in your purposes towards its augmentation. If we have been less active in showing forth our effective good will towards you than, as a loving kinsman and blood-relative, we would willingly have desired, we request that you will impute it to lack of opportunity to show our good-liking, not to any coldness of our will. Touching your resolution to travel in foreign parts, as at this time we hold the same little advisable, in respect that your ill-willers may, according to the custom of such persons, impute motives for your journey, whereof, although we know and believe you to be as clear as ourselves, yet natheless their words may find credence in places where the belief in them may much prejudice you, and which we should see with more unwillingness and displeasure than with means of remedy.

"Having thus, as becometh our kindred, given you our poor mind on the subject of your journeying forth of Scotland, we would willingly add reasons of weight, which might materially advantage you and your father's house, thereby to determine you to abide at Wolf's Crag, until this harvest season shall be passed over. But what sayeth the proverb, *verbum sapienti,*—a word is more to him that hath wisdom than a sermon to a fool. And albeit we have written this poor scroll with our own hand, and are well assured of the fidelity of our messenger, as him that is many ways bounden to us, yet so it is, that sliddery ways crave wary walking, and that we may not peril upon paper matters which we would gladly impart to you by word of mouth. Wherefore, it was our purpose to have prayed you heartily to come to this our barren Highland country to kill a stag, and to treat of the matters which we are now more painfully inditing to you anent. But commodity does not serve at present for such our meeting, which, therefore, shall be deferred intil sic time as we may in all mirth rehearse those things whereof we now keep silence. Meantime, we pray you to think that we are, and will still be, your good kinsman and well-wisher, waiting but for times of whilk we do, as it were, entertain a twilight prospect, and appear and hope to be also your effectual well-doer. And in which hope we heartily write ourselves,

"Right Honourable,

"Your loving cousin,

"A————

"Given from our poor
house of B————, &c."

Superscribed — "For the right honourable, and our honoured kinsman, the Master of Ravenswood—These with haste, haste, post haste—ride and run until these be delivered."

"What think you of this epistle, Bucklaw?" said the Master, when his companion had hammered out all the sense, and almost all the words of which it consisted.

"Truly, that the Marquis's meaning is as great a riddle as his manuscript. He is really in much need of *Wit's Interpreter*, or the *Complete Letter-Writer*, and were I you, I would send him a copy by the bearer. He writes you very kindly to remain wasting your time and your money in this vile, stupid, oppressed country, without so much as offering you the countenance and shelter of his house. In my opinion, he has some scheme in view in which he supposes you can be useful, and he wishes to keep you at hand, to make use of you when it ripens, reserving the power of turning you adrift, should his plot fail in the concoction."

"His plot?—then you suppose it is a treasonable business," answered Ravenswood.

"What else can it be?" replied Bucklaw; "the Marquis has been long suspected to have an eye to Saint Germains."

"He should not engage me rashly in such an adventure," said Ravenswood; "when I recollect the times of the first and second Charles, and of the last James, truly I see little reason, that, as a man or a patriot, I should draw my sword for their descendants."

"Humph!" replied Bucklaw; "so you have set yourself down to mourn over the crop-eared dogs, whom honest Claver'se treated as they deserved?"

"They first gave the dogs an ill name, and then hanged them," replied Ravenswood. "I hope to see the day when justice shall be open to Whig and Tory, and when these nick-names shall only be used among coffee - house politicians, as slut and jade are among apple-women, as cant terms of idle spite and rancour."

"That will not be in our days, Master—the iron has entered too deeply into our sides and our souls."

"It will be, however, one day," replied the Master; "men will not always start at these nick-names as at a trumpet-sound. As social life is better protected, its comforts will become too dear to be hazarded without some better reason than speculative politics."

"It is fine talking," answered Bucklaw; "but my heart is with the old song,—

> "To see good corn upon the rigs,
> And a gallows built to hang the Whigs,
> And the right restored where the right should be
> O, that is the thing that would wanton me."

"You may sing as loudly as you will, *cantabit vacuus*,"— answered the Master; "but I believe the Marquis is too wise, at least too wary, to join you in such a burden. suspect he alludes to a revolution in the Scottish Privy Council, rather than in the British kingdoms."

"O, confusion to your state-tricks!" exclaimed Bucklaw, "your cold calculating manœuvres, which old gentlemen in wrought nightcaps and furred gowns execute like so many games at chess, and displace a treasurer or lord commissioner as they would take a rook or a pawn. Tennis for my sport, and battle for my earnest! My racket and my sword for my plaything and bread-winner! And you, Master, so deep and considerate as you would seem, you have that within you makes the blood boil faster than suits your present humour of moralising on political truths. You are one of those wise men who see every thing with great composure till their blood is up, and then—woe to any one who should put them in mind of their own prudential maxims!"

"Perhaps," said Ravenswood, "you read me more rightly than I can myself. But to think justly will certainly go some length in helping me to act so. But hark! I hear Caleb tolling the dinner-bell."

"Which he always does with the more sonorous grace, in proportion to the meagreness of the cheer which he has provided," said Bucklaw; "as if that infernal clang and jangle, which will one day bring the belfry down the cliff, could convert a starved hen into a fat capon, and a blade-bone of mutton into a haunch of venison."

"I wish we may be so well off as your worst conjectures surmise, Bucklaw, from the extreme solemnity and ceremony with which Caleb seems to place on the table that solitary covered dish."

"Uncover, Caleb! uncover, for Heaven's sake!" said Bucklaw; "let us have what you can give us without preface—Why, it stands well enough, man," he continued, addressing impatiently the ancient butler, who, without reply, kept shifting the dish, until he had at length placed it with mathematical precision in the very midst of the table.

"What have we got here, Caleb?" enquired the Master in his turn.

"Ahem! sir, ye suld have known before; but his honour the Laird of Bucklaw is so impatient," answered Caleb, still holding the dish with one hand, and the cover with the other, with evident reluctance to disclose its contents.

"But what is it, a God's name—not a pair of clean spurs, I hope, in the Border fashion of old times?"

"Ahem! ahem!" reiterated Caleb, "your honour is pleased to be facetious—natheless, I might presume to say it was a convenient fashion, and used, as I have heard, in an honourable and thriving family. But touching your present dinner, I judged that this being Saint Magdalen's Eve, who was a worthy queen of Scotland in her day, your honours might judge it decorous, if not altogether to fast, yet only to sustain nature with some slight refection, as ane saulted herring or the like." And, uncovering the dish, he displayed four of the savoury fishes which he mentioned, adding, in a subdued tone, "that they were no just common herring neither, being every ane melters, and sauted with uncommon care by the housekeeper (poor Mysie) for his honour's especial use."

"Out upon all apologies!" said the Master, "let us eat the herrings, since there is nothing better to be had—but I begin to think with you, Bucklaw, that we are consuming the last green leaf, and that, in spite of the Marquis's political machinations, we must positively shift camp for want of forage, without waiting the issue of them."

CHAPTER IX

Ay, and when huntsmen wind the merry horn,
And from its covert starts the fearful prey,
Who, warm'd with youth's blood in his swelling veins,
Would, like a lifeless clod, outstretched lie,
Shut out from all the fair creation offers?
Ethwald, Act I. Scene I.

LIGHT meals procure light slumbers; and therefore it is not surprising, that, considering the fare which Caleb's conscience, or his necessity, assuming, as will sometimes happen, that disguise, had assigned to the guests of Wolf's Crag, their slumbers should have been short.

In the morning Bucklaw rushed into his host's apartment with a loud haloo, which might have awaked the dead.

"Up! up! in the name of heaven—the hunters are out, the only piece of sport I have seen this month; and you lie here, Master, on a bed that has little to recommend it, except that it may be something softer than the stone floor of your ancestor's vault."

"I wish," said Ravenswood, raising his head peevishly,

"you had forborne so early a jest, Mr Hayston—it is really no pleasure to lose the very short repose which I had just begun to enjoy, after a night spent in thoughts upon fortune far harder than my couch, Bucklaw."

"Pshaw, pshaw!" replied his guest; "get up—get up—the hounds are abroad—I have saddled the horses myself, for old Caleb was calling for grooms and lackeys, and would never have proceeded without two hours' apology, for the absence of men that were a hundred miles off.—Get up, Master—I say the hounds are out—get up, I say—the hunt is up." And off ran Bucklaw.

"And I say," said the Master, rising slowly, "that nothing can concern me less. Whose hounds come so near to us?"

"The Honourable Lord Bittlebrains'," answered Caleb, who had followed the impatient Laird of Bucklaw into his master's bedroom, "and truly I ken nae title they have to be yowling and howling within the freedoms and immunities of your lordship's right of free forestry."

"Nor I, Caleb," replied Ravenswood, "excepting that they have bought both the lands and the right of forestry, and may think themselves entitled to exercise the rights they have paid their money for."

"It may be sae, my lord," replied Caleb; "but it's no gentleman's deed of them to come here and exercise such like right, and your lordship living at your ain castle of Wolf's Crag. Lord Bittlebrains would do weel to remember what his folk have been."

"And we what we now are," said the Master, with suppressed bitterness of feeling. "But reach me my cloak, Caleb, and I will indulge Bucklaw with a sight of this chase. It is selfish to sacrifice my guest's pleasure to my own."

"Sacrifice!" echoed Caleb, in a tone which seemed to imply the total absurdity of his master making the least concession in deference to any one—"Sacrifice, indeed!—but I crave your honour's pardon—and whilk doublet is it your pleasure to wear?"

"Any one you will, Caleb—my wardrobe, I suppose, is not very extensive."

"Not extensive!" echoed his assistant; "when there is the grey and silver that your lordship bestowed on Hew Hildebrand, your outrider—and the French velvet that went

with my lord your father—(be gracious to him!)—my lord
your father's auld wardrobe to the puir friends of the family,
and the drap-de-berry"—

"Which I gave to you, Caleb, and which, I suppose, is
the only dress we have any chance to come at, except that
I wore yesterday—pray, hand me that, and say no more
about it."

"If your honour has a fancy," replied Caleb, "and
doubtless it's a sad-coloured suit, and you are in mourning
—nevertheless, I have never tried on the drap-de-berry—ill
wad it become me—and your honour having no change of
claiths at this present—and it's weel brushed, and as there
are leddies down yonder"—

"Ladies!" said Ravenswood; "and what ladies, pray?"

"What do I ken, your lordship?—looking down at them
from the Warden's Tower, I could but see them glent by
wi' their bridles ringing, and their feathers fluttering, like
the court of Elfland."

"Well, well, Caleb," replied the Master, "help me on
with my cloak, and hand me my sword-belt.—What clatter
is that in the courtyard?"

"Just Bucklaw bringing out the horses," said Caleb, after
a glance through the window, "as if there werena men
eneugh in the castle, or is if I couldna serve the turn of ony
o' them that are out o' the gate."

"Alas! Caleb, we should want little, if your ability were
equal to your will," replied his master.

"And I hope your lordship disna want that muckle," said
Caleb; "for, considering a' things, I trust we support the
credit of the family as weel as things will permit of,—only
Bucklaw is aye sae frank and sae forward.—And there he
has brought out your lordship's palfrey, without the saddle
being decored wi' the broidered sumpter-cloth! and I could
have brushed it in a minute."

"It is all very well," said his master, escaping from him,
and descending the narrow and steep winding staircase,
which led to the court-yard.

"It *may* be a' very weel," said Caleb, somewhat peevishly;
"but if your lordship wad tarry a bit, I will tell you what
will *not* be very weel."

"And what is that?" said Ravenswood, impatiently, but
stopping at the same time.

"Why, just that ye suld speer ony gentleman hame to dinner; for I canna mak anither fast on a feast day, as when I cam ower Bucklaw wi' Queen Margaret—and, to speak truth, if your lordship wad but please to cast yoursell in the way of dining wi' Lord Bittlebrains, I'se warrand I wad cast about brawly for the morn; or if, stead o' that, ye wad but dine wi' them at the change-house, ye might mak your shift for the lawing; ye might say ye had forgot your purse—or that the carline awed ye rent, and that ye wad allow it in the settlement."

"Or any other lie that came uppermost, I suppose?" said his master. "Good-bye, Caleb; I commend your care for the honour of the family." And, throwing himself on his horse, he followed Bucklaw, who, at the manifest risk of his neck, had begun to gallop down the steep path which led from the Tower, as soon as he saw Ravenswood have his foot in the stirrup.

Caleb Balderstone looked anxiously after them, and shook his thin grey locks—"And I trust they will come to no evil —but they have reached the plain, and folk cannot say but that the horse are hearty and in spirits."

Animated by the natural impetuosity and fire of his temper, young Bucklaw rushed on with the careless speed of a whirlwind. Ravenswood was scarce more moderate in his pace, for his was a mind unwillingly roused from contemplative inactivity, but which, when once put into motion, acquired a spirit of forcible and violent progression. Neither was his eagerness proportioned in all cases to the motive of impulse, but might be compared to the speed of a stone, which rushes with like fury down the hill, whether it was first put in motion by the arm of a giant or the hand of a boy. He felt, therefore, in no ordinary degree, the headlong impulse of the chase, a pastime so natural to youth of all ranks, that seems rather to be an inherent passion in our animal nature, which levels all differences of rank and education, than an acquired habit of rapid exercise.

The repeated bursts of the French horn, which was then always used for the encouragement and direction of the hounds—the deep, though distant baying of the pack—the half-heard cries of the huntsmen—the half-seen forms which were discovered, now emerging from glens which crossed the moor, now sweeping over its surface, now picking their way where it was impeded by morasses; and, above all, the feeling of his own rapid motion, animated the Master of Ravenswood, at least for the moment, above the recollections of a more painful nature by which he was surrounded. The first thing which recalled him to those unpleasing circumstances, was feeling that his horse, notwithstanding all the advantages which he received from his rider's knowledge of the country, was unable to keep up with the chase. And he drew his bridle up with the bitter feeling, that his poverty excluded him from the favourite recreation of his forefathers, and indeed their sole employment when not engaged in military pursuits, he was accosted by a well-mounted stranger, who, unobserved, had kept near him during the earlier part of his career.

"Your horse is blown," said the man, with a complaisance seldom used in a hunting-field. "Might I crave your honour to make use of mine?"

"Sir," said Ravenswood, more surprised than pleased at such a proposal, "I really do not know how I have merited such a favour at a stranger's hands."

"Never ask a question about it, Master," said Bucklaw, who, with great unwillingness, had hitherto reined in his own gallant steed, not to outride his host and entertainer. "Take the goods the gods provide you, as the great John Dryden says—or stay—here, my friend, lend me that horse; I see you have been puzzled to rein him up this last half hour. I'll take the devil out of him for you. Now, Master, do you ride mine, which will carry you like an eagle."

And throwing the reins of his own horse to the Master of Ravenswood, he sprung upon that which the stranger resigned to him, and continued his career at full speed.

"Was ever so thoughtless a being!" said the Master; "and you, my friend, how could you trust him with your horse?"

"The horse," said the man, "belongs to a person who will make your honour, or any of your honourable friends, most welcome to him, flesh and fell."

"And the owner's name is——?" asked Ravenswood.

"Your honour must excuse me, you will learn that from himself.—If you please to take your friend's horse, and leave me your galloway, I will meet you after the fall of the stag, for I hear they are blowing him at bay."

"I believe, my friend, it will be the best way to recover your good horse for you," answered Ravenswood; and mounting the nag of his friend Bucklaw, he made all the haste in his power to the spot where the blast of the horn announced that the stag's career was nearly terminated.

These jovial sounds were intermixed with the huntsmen's shouts of "Hyke a Talbot! Hyke a Teviot! now, boys, now!" and similar cheering halloos of the olden hunting-field, to which the impatient yelling of the hounds, now close on the object of their pursuit, gave a lively and unremitting chorus. The straggling riders began now to rally towards the scene of action, collecting from different points as to a common centre.

Bucklaw kept the start which he had gotten, and arrived first at the spot, where the stag, incapable of sustaining a more prolonged flight, had turned upon the hounds, and, in the hunter's phrase, was at bay. With his stately head bent down, his sides white with foam, his eyes strained betwixt rage and terror, the hunted animal had now in his turn become an object of intimidation to his pursuers. The hunters came up one by one, and watched an opportunity to assail him with some advantage, which, in such circumstances, can only be done with caution. The dogs stood aloof and bayed loudly, intimating at once eagerness and fear, and each of the sportsmen seemed to expect that his comrade would take upon him the perilous task of assaulting and disabling the animal. The ground, which was a hollow in the common or moor, afforded little advantage for approaching the stag unobserved; and general was the shout of triumph when Bucklaw, with the dexterity proper to an accomplished cavalier of the day sprang from his horse, and dashing suddenly and swiftly at the stag, brought him to the ground by a cut on the hind leg with his short hunting sword. The pack, rushing in upon their disabled enemy, soon ended his painful struggles, and solemnised his fall with their clamour—the hunters, with their horns and voices, whooping and blowing a *mort*, or death-note, which resounded far over the billows of the adjacent ocean.

The huntsman then withdrew the hounds from the throttled stag, and on his knee presented his knife to a fair female form, on a white palfrey, whose terror, or perhaps her compassion, had till then kept her at some distance. She wore a black silk riding mask, which was then a common fashion, as well for preserving the complexion from sun and rain, as from an idea of decorum, which did not permit a lady to appear barefaced while engaged in a boisterous sport, and attended by a promiscuous company.

The richness of her dress, however, as well as the mettle and form of her palfrey, together with the silvan compliment paid to her by the huntsmen, pointed her out to Bucklaw as the principal person in the field. It was not without a feeling of pity, approaching even to contempt, that this enthusiastic hunter observed her refuse the huntsman's knife presented to her for the purpose of making the first incision in the stag's breast, and thereby discovering the quality of the venison. He felt more than half inclined to pay his compliments to her; but it had been Bucklaw's misfortune, that his habits of life had not rendered him familiarly acquainted with the higher and better classes of female society, so that, with all his natural audacity, he felt sheepish and bashful when it became necessary to address a lady of distinction.

Taking unto himself heart of grace (to use his own phrase), he did at length summon up resolution enough to give the fair huntress good time of the day, and trust that her sport had answered her expectation. Her answer was very courteously and modestly expressed, and testified some gratitude to the gallant cavalier, whose exploit had terminated the chase so adroitly, when the hounds and huntsmen seemed somewhat at a stand.

"Uds daggers and scabbard, madam," said Bucklaw, whom this observation brought at once upon his own ground, "there is no difficulty or merit in that matter at all, so that a fellow is not too much afraid of having a pair of antlers in his guts. I have hunted at force five hundred times, madam; and I never yet saw the stag at bay, by land or water, but I durst have gone roundly in on him. It is all use and wont, madam; and I'll tell you, madam, for all that, it must be done with good heed and caution; and you will do well, madam, to have your hunting-sword both right sharp and double-edged, that you may strike either fore-handed or back-handed, as you see reason, for a hurt with a buck's horn is a perilous and somewhat venomous matter."

"I am afraid, sir," said the young lady, and her smile was scarce concealed by her vizard, "I shall have little use for such careful preparation."

"But the gentleman says very right for all that, my lady," said an old huntsman, who had listened to Bucklaw's harangue with no small edification; "and I have heard my father say, who was a forester at the Cabrach, that a wild boar's gaunch is more easily healed than a hurt from the deer's horn, for so says the old woodman's rhyme,—

"'If thou be hurt with horn of hart, it brings thee to thy bier;
But tusk of boar shall leeches heal—thereof have lesser fear.'"

"An I might advise," continued Bucklaw, who was now in his element, and desirous of assuming the whole management, "as the hounds are surbated and weary, the head of the stag should be cabaged in order to reward them; and if I may presume to speak, the huntsman, who is to break up the stag, ought to drink to your good ladyship's health a good lusty bicker of ale, or a tass of brandy; for if he breaks him up without drinking, the venison will not keep well."

This very agreeable prescription received, as will be readily believed, all acceptation from the huntsman, who, in requital, offered to Bucklaw the compliment of his knife, which the young lady had declined. This polite proffer was seconded by his mistress.

"I believe, sir," she said, withdrawing herself from the circle, "that my father, for whose amusement Lord Bittle-brains' hounds have been out to-day, will readily surrender all care of these matters to a gentleman of your experience."

Then, bending gracefully from her horse, she wished him good morning, and, attended by one or two domestics, who seemed immediately attached to her service, retired from the scene of action, to which Bucklaw, too much delighted with an opportunity of displaying his wood-craft to care about man or woman either, paid little attention; but was soon stript to his doublet, with tucked-up sleeves, and naked arms up to the elbows in blood and grease, slashing, cutting, hacking, and hewing, with the precision of Sir

Tristrem himself, and wrangling and disputing with all around him concerning nombles, briskets, flankards, and raven-bones, then usual terms of the art of hunting, or of butchery, whichever the reader chooses to call it, which are now probably antiquated.

When Ravenswood, who followed a short space behind his friend, saw that the stag had fallen, his temporary ardour for the chase gave way to that feeling of reluctance which he endured, at encountering in his fallen fortunes the gaze whether of equals or inferiors. He reined up his horse on the top of a gentle eminence, from which he observed the busy and gay scene beneath him, and heard the whoops of the huntsmen gaily mingled with the cry of the dogs, and the neighing and trampling of the horses. But these jovial sounds fell sadly on the ear of the ruined nobleman. The chase, with all its train of excitations, has ever since feudal times been accounted the almost exclusive privilege of the aristocracy, and was anciently their chief employment in times of peace. The sense that he was excluded by his situation from enjoying the silvan sport, which his rank assigned to him as a special prerogative, and the feeling that new men were now exercising it over the downs, which had been jealously reserved by his ancestors for their own amusement, while he, the heir of the domain, was fain to hold himself at a distance from their party, awakened reflections calculated to depress deeply a mind like Ravenswood's, which was naturally contemplative and melancholy. His pride, however, soon shook off this feeling of dejection, and it gave way to impatience upon finding that his volatile friend Bucklaw seemed in no hurry to return with his borrowed steed, which Ravenswood, before leaving the field, wished to see restored to the obliging owner. As he was about to move towards the group of assembled huntsmen, he was joined by a horseman, who like himself had kept aloof during the fall of the deer.

This personage seemed stricken in years. He wore a scarlet cloak, buttoning high upon his face, and his hat was unlooped and slouched, probably by way of defence against the weather. His horse, a strong and steady palfrey, was calculated for a rider who proposed to witness the sport of the day, rather than to share it. An attendant waited at some distance, and the whole equipment was that of an elderly gentleman of rank and fashion. He accosted Ravenswood very politely, but not without some embarrassment.

"You seem a gallant young gentleman, sir," he said, "and yet appear as indifferent to this brave sport as if you had my load of years on your shoulders."

"I have followed the sport with more spirit on other occasions," replied the Master; "at present, late events in my family must be my apology—and besides," he added, "I was but indifferently mounted at the beginning of the sport."

"I think," said the stranger, "one of my attendants had the sense to accommodate your friend with a horse."

"I am much indebted to his politeness and yours," replied Ravenswood. "My friend is Mr Hayston of Bucklaw, whom I daresay you will be sure to find in the thick of the keenest sportsmen. He will return your servant's horse and take my pony in exchange—and will add," he concluded, turning his horse's head from the stranger, "his best acknowledgments to mine for the accommodation."

The Master of Ravenswood, having thus expressed himself, began to move homeward, with the manner of one who has taken leave of his company. But the stranger was not so to be shaken off. He turned his horse at the same time, and rode in the same direction so near to the Master, that, without outriding him, which the formal civility of the time, and the respect due to the stranger's age and recent civility, would have rendered improper, he could not easily escape from his company.

The stranger did not long remain silent. "This, then," he said, "is the ancient Castle of Wolf's Crag, often mentioned in the Scottish records," looking to the old tower, then darkening under the influence of a stormy cloud, that formed its background; for at the distance of a short mile, the chase, having been circuitous, had brought the hunters nearly back to the point which they had attained, when Ravenswood and Bucklaw had set forward to join them.

Ravenswood answered this observation with a cold and distant assent.

"It was, as I have heard," continued the stranger, unabashed by his coldness, "one of the most early possessions of the honourable family of Ravenswood."

"Their earliest possession," answered the Master, "and probably their latest."

"I—I—I should hope not, sir," answered the stranger, clearing his voice with more than one cough, and making an effort to overcome a certain degree of hesitation,—"Scotland knows what she owes to this ancient family, and remembers their frequent and honourable achievements. I have little doubt, that, were it properly represented to her majesty that so ancient and noble a family were subjected to dilapidation—I mean to decay—means might be found, *ad re-ædificandum antiquam domum*"——

"I will save you the trouble, sir, of discussing this point farther," interrupted the Master, haughtily. "I am the heir of that unfortunate House—I am the Master of Ravenswood. And you, sir, who seem to be a gentleman of fashion and education, must be sensible, that the next mortification after being unhappy, is the being loaded with undesired commiseration."

"I beg your pardon, sir," said the elder horseman—"I did not know—I am sensible I ought not to have mentioned—nothing could be farther from my thoughts than to suppose"——

"There are no apologies necessary sir," answered Ravenswood, "for here, I suppose, our roads separate, and I assure you that we part in perfect equanimity on my side."

As speaking these words, he directed his horse's head towards a narrow causeway, the ancient approach to Wolf's Crag, of which it might be truly said, in the words of the Bard of Hope, that

> "Frequented by few was the grass-cover'd road,
> Where the hunter of deer and the warrior trode,
> To his hills that encircle the sea."

But, ere he could disengage himself from his companion, the young lady we have already mentioned came up to join the stranger, followed by her servants.

"Daughter," said the stranger to the masked damsel, "this is the Master of Ravenswood."

It would have been natural that the gentleman should have replied to this introduction; but there was something in the graceful form and retiring modesty of the female to whom he was thus presented, which not only prevented him from enquiring to whom, and by whom, the annunciation had been made, but which even for the time struck him absolutely mute. At this moment the cloud which had long lowered above the height on which Wolf's Crag is situated, and which now, as it advanced, spread itself in darker and denser folds both over land and sea, hiding the distant objects and obscuring those which were nearer, turning the sea to a leaden complexion, and the heath to a darker brown, began now, by one or two distant peals, to announce the thunders with which it was fraught; while two flashes of lightning, following each other very closely, showed in the distance the grey turrets of Wolf's Crag, and, more nearly, the rolling billows of the ocean, crested suddenly with red and dazzling light.

The horse of the fair huntress showed symptoms of impatience and restiveness, and it became impossible for Ravenswood, as a man or a gentleman, to leave her abruptly to the care of an aged father or her menial attendants. He was, or believed himself, obliged in courtesy to take hold of her bridle, and assist her in managing the unruly animal. While he was thus engaged, the old gentleman observed that the storm seemed to increase—that they were far from Lord Bittlebrains', whose guests they were for the present—and that he would be obliged to the Master of Ravenswood to point him the way to the nearest place of refuge from the storm. At the same he cast a wistful and embarrassed look towards the Tower of Wolf's Crag, which seemed to render it almost impossible for the owner to avoid offering an old man and a lady, in such an emergency, the temporary use of his house. Indeed, the condition of the young huntress made this courtesy indispensable; for, in the course of the services which he rendered, he could not but perceive that she trembled much, and was extremely agitated, from her apprehensions, doubtless, of the coming storm.

I know not if the Master of Ravenswood shared her terrors, but he was not entirely free from something like a similar disorder of nerves, as he observed, "The Tower of Wolf's Crag has nothing to offer beyond the shelter of its roof, but if that can be acceptable at such a moment"—

he paused, as if the rest of the invitation stuck in his throat. But the old gentleman, his self-constituted companion, did not allow him to recede from the invitation, which he had rather suffered to be implied than directly expressed.

"The storm," said the stranger, "must be an apology for waiving ceremony—his daughter's health was weak—she had suffered much from a recent alarm—he trusted their intrusion on the Master of Ravenswood's hospitality would not be altogether unpardonable in the circumstances of the case—his child's safety must be dearer to him than ceremony."

There was no room to retreat. The Master of Ravenswood led the way, continuing to keep hold of the lady's bridle to prevent her horse from starting at some unexpected explosion of thunder. He was not so bewildered in his own hurried reflections, but that he remarked, that the deadly paleness which had occupied her neck and temples, and such of her features as the riding-mask left exposed, gave place to a deep and rosy suffusion; and he felt with embarrassment that a flush was by tacit sympathy excited in his own cheeks. The stranger, with watchfulness which he disguised under apprehensions for the safety of his daughter, continued to observe the expression of the Master's countenance as they ascended the hill to Wolf's Crag. When they stood in front of that ancient fortress, Ravenswood's emotions were of a very complicated description; and as he led the way into the rude court-yard, and halloo'd to Caleb to give attendance, there was a tone of sternness, almost of fierceness, which seemed somewhat alien from the courtesies of one who is receiving honoured guests.

Caleb came; and not the paleness of the fair stranger at the first approach of the thunder, nor the paleness of any other person, in any other circumstances whatever, equalled that which overcame the thin cheeks of the disconsolate seneschal, when he beheld this accession of guests to the castle, and reflected that the dinner hour was fast approaching. "Is he daft?" he muttered to himself,—"is he clean daft a'thegither, to bring lords and leddies, and a host of folk behint them, and twal-o'-clock chappit?" Then approaching the Master, he craved pardon for having permitted the rest of his people to go out to see the hunt, observing, that "they wad never think of his lordship coming back till mirk night, and that· he dreaded they might play the truant."

"Silence, Balderstone!" said Ravenswood, sternly; "your folly is unseasonable.—Sir and madam," he said, turning to his guests, " this old man, and a yet older and more imbecile female domestic, form my. whole retinue. Our means of refreshing you are more scanty than even so miserable a retinue, and a dwelling so dilapidated, might seem to promise you ; but, such as they may chance to be, you may command them."

The elder stranger, struck with the ruined and even savage appearance of the Tower, rendered still more disconsolate by the lowering and gloomy sky, and perhaps not altogether unmoved by the grave and determined voice in which their host addressed them, looked round him anxiously, as if he half repented the readiness with which he had accepted the offered hospitality. But there was now no opportunity of receding from the situation in which he had placed himself.

As for Caleb, he was so utterly stunned by his master's public and unqualified acknowledgment of the nakedness of the land, that for two minutes he could only mutter within his hebdomadal beard, which had not felt the razor for six days, " He's daft—clean daft—red wud, and awa wi't! But deil hae Caleb Balderstone," said he, collecting his powers of invention and resource, "if the family shall lose credit, if he were as mad as the seven wise masters !" He then boldly advanced, and in spite of his master's frowns and impatience, gravely asked, "if he should not serve up some slight refection for the young leddy, and a glass of tokay, or old sack—or "——

"Truce to this ill-timed foolery," said the Master, sternly, —"put the horses into the stable, and interrupt us no more with your absurdities."

"Your honour's pleasure is to be obeyed aboon a things," said Caleb ; "nevertheless, as for the sack and tokay which it is not your noble guests' pleasure to accept "——

But here the voice of Bucklaw, heard even above the clattering of hoofs and braying of horns with which it mingled, announced that he was scaling the pathway to the Tower at the head of the greater part of the gallant hunting train.

"The deil be in me," said Caleb, taking heart in spite of this new invasion of Philistines, "if they shall beat me yet! The hellicat ne'er-do-weel!—to bring such a crew here, that will expect to find brandy as plenty as ditch-water, and he kenning sae absolutely the case in whilk we stand for the present! But I trow, could I get rid of thae gaping gowks of flunkies that hae won into the court-yard at the back of their betters, as mony a man gets preferment, I could make a' right yet."

The measures which he took to execute this dauntless resolution, the reader shall learn in the next chapter.

CHAPTER X

With throat unslaked, with black lips baked,
   Agape they heard him call ;
Gramercy they for joy did grin,
And all at once their breath drew in,
   As they had been drinking all !
      Coleridge's " Rime of the Ancient Mariner."

HAYSTON of Bucklaw was one of the thoughtless class who never hesitate between their friend and their jest. When it was announced that the principal persons of the chase had taken their route towards Wolf's Crag, the huntsmen, as a point of civility, offered to transfer the venison to that mansion ; a proffer which was readily accepted by Bucklaw, who thought much of the astonishment which their arrival in full body would occasion poor old Caleb Balderstone, and very little of the dilemma to which he was about to expose his friend the Master, so ill circumstanced to receive such a party. But in old Caleb he had to do with a crafty and alert antagonist, prompt at supplying, upon all emergencies, evasions and excuses suitable, as he thought, to the dignity of the family.

"Praise be blest!." said Caleb to himself, "ae leaf of the muckle gate has been swung to wi' yestreen's wind, and I think I can manage to shut the ither."

But he was desirous, like a prudent governor, at the

same time to get rid, if possible, of the internal enemy, in which light he considered almost every one who eat and drank, ere he took measures to exclude those whom their jocund noise now pronounced to be near at hand. He waited, therefore, with impatience until his master had shown his two principal guests into the Tower, and then commenced his operations.

"I think," he said to the stranger menials, "that as they are bringing the stag's head to the castle in all honour, we, who are in-dwellers, should receive them at the gate."

The unwary grooms had no sooner hurried out, in compliance with this insidious hint, than, one folding-door of the ancient gate being already closed by the wind, as has been already intimated, honest Caleb lost no time in shutting the other with a clang, which resounded from donjon-vault to battlement. Having thus secured the pass, he forthwith indulged the excluded huntsmen in brief parley, from a small projecting window, or shot-hole, through which, in former days, the warders were wont to reconnoitre those who presented themselves before the gates. He gave them to understand, in a short and pithy speech, that the gate of the castle was never on any account opened during meal-times—that his honour, the Master of Ravenswood, and some guests of quality, had just sat down to dinner—that there was excellent brandy at the hostler-wife's at Wolf's-hope down below—and he held out some obscure hint that the reckoning would be discharged by the Master; but this was uttered in a very dubious and oracular strain, for, like Louis XIV., Caleb Balder-stone hesitated to carry finesse so far as direct falsehood, and was content to deceive, if possible, without directly lying.

This annunciation was received with surprise by some, with laughter by others, and with dismay by the expelled lackeys, who endeavoured to demonstrate that their right of re-admission, for the purpose of waiting upon their master and mistress, was at least indisputable. But Caleb was not in a humour to understand or admit any distinctions. He stuck to his original proposition with that dogged, but convenient pertinacity, which is armed against all conviction, and deaf to all reasoning. Bucklaw now came from the rear of the party, and demanded admittance in a very angry tone. But the resolution of Caleb was immovable.

" If the king on the throne were at the gate," he declared, " his ten fingers should never open it contrair to the established use and wont of the family of Ravenswood, and his duty as their head-servant."

Bucklaw was now extremely incensed, and with more oaths and curses than we care to repeat, declared himself most unworthily treated, and demanded peremptorily to speak with the Master of Ravenswood himself. But to this, also, Caleb turned a deaf ear.

" He's as soon a-bleeze as a tap of tow the lad Bucklaw," he said; " but the deil of ony master's face he shall see till he has sleepit and waken'd on't. He'll ken himsell better the morn's morning. It sets the like o' him, to be bringing a crew of drunken hunters here, when he kens there is but little preparation ·to sloken his ain drought." And he disappeared from the window, leaving them all to digest their exclusion as they best might.

But another person, of whose presence Caleb, in the animation of the debate, was not aware, had listened in silence to its progress. This was the principal domestic of the stranger—a man of trust and consequence—the same, who, in the hunting-field, had accommodated Bucklaw with the use of his horse. He was in the stable when Caleb had contrived the expulsion of his fellow-servants, and thus avoided sharing the same fate from which his personal importance would certainly not have otherwise saved him.

This personage perceived the manœuvre of Caleb, easily appreciated the motive of his conduct, and knowing his master's intentions towards the family of Ravenswood, had no difficulty as to the line of conduct he ought to adopt. He took the place of Caleb (unperceived by the latter) at the post of audience which he had just left, and announced to the assembled domestics, "that it was his master's pleasure that Lord Bittlebrains' retinue and his own should go down to the adjacent change-house, and call for what refreshments they might have occasion for, and he should take care to discharge the lawing."

The jolly troop of huntsmen retired from the inhospitable gate of Wolf's Crag, execrating, as they descended the steep pathway, the niggard and unworthy disposition of the proprietor, and damning, with more than silvan license, both the castle and its inhabitants. Bucklaw, with many qualities which would have made him a man of worth and judgment in more favourable circumstances, had been so utterly neglected in point of education, that he was apt to think and feel according to the ideas of the companions of his pleasures. The praises which had recently been heaped upon himself he contrasted with the general abuse now levelled against Ravenswood—he recalled to his mind the dull and monotonous days he had spent in the Tower of Wolf's Crag, compared with the joviality of his usual life— he felt, with great indignation, his exclusion from the castle, which he considered as a gross affront, and every mingled feeling led him to break off the union which he had formed with the Master of Ravenswood.

On arriving at the change-house of the village at Wolf's-hope, he unexpectedly met with an old acquaintance just alighting from his horse. This was no other than the very respectable Captain Craigengelt, who immediately came up to him, and, without appearing to retain any recollection of the indifferent terms on which they had parted, shook him by the hand in the warmest manner possible. A warm grasp of the hand was what Bucklaw could never help returning with cordiality, and no sooner had Craigengelt felt the pressure of his fingers than he knew the terms on which he stood with him.

"Long life to you, Bucklaw!" he exclaimed; "there's life for honest folk in this bad world yet!"

The Jacobites at this period, with what propriety I know not, used, it must be noticed, the term of *honest men* as peculiarly descriptive of their own party.

"Ay, and for others besides, it seems," answered Bucklaw; "otherways, how came you to venture hither, noble Captain?"

"Who—I?—I am as free as the wind at Martinmas, that pays neither land-rent nor annual; all is explained—all settled with the honest old drivellers yonder of Auld Reekie—Pooh! pooh! they dared not keep me a week of days in durance. A certain person has better friends among them than you wot of, and can serve a friend when it is least likely."

"Pshaw!" answered Hayston, who perfectly knew and thoroughly despised the character of this man, "none of your cogging gibberish—tell me truly, are you at liberty and in safety?"

"Free and safe as a whig bailie on the causeway of his own borough, or a canting presbyterian minister in his own pulpit—and I came to tell you that you need not remain in hiding any longer."

"Then I suppose you call yourself my friend, Captain Craigengelt?" said Bucklaw.

"Friend!" replied Craigengelt, "my cock of the pit? why, I am thy very Achates, man, as I have heard scholars say—hand and glove—bark and tree—thine to life and death!"

"I'll try that in a moment," answered Bucklaw. "Thou art never without money, however thou comest by it. Lend me two pieces to wash the dust out of these honest fellows' throats in the first place, and then"——

"Two pieces? twenty are at thy service, my lad—and twenty to back them."

"Ay, say you so?" said Bucklaw, pausing, for his natural penetration led him to suspect some extraordinary motive lay couched under such an excess of generosity. "Craigengelt, you are either an honest fellow in right good earnest, and I scarce know how to believe that—or you are cleverer than I took you for, and I scarce know how to believe that either."

"*L'un n'empeche pas l'autre*," said Craigengelt, "touch. and try—the gold is good as ever was weighed."

He put a quantity of gold pieces into Bucklaw's hand, which he thrust into his pocket without either counting or looking at them, only observing, "that he was so circumstanced that he must enlist, though the devil offered the press-money;" and then turning to the huntsmen, he called out, "Come along, my lads—all is at my cost."

"Long life to Bucklaw!" shouted the men of the chase.

"And confusion to him that takes his share of the sport, and leaves the hunters as dry as a drum-head," added another, by way of corollary.

"The house of Ravenswood was ance a gude and an honourable house in this land," said an old man, "but it's lost its credit this day, and the Master has shown himself no better than a greedy cullion."

And with this conclusion, which was unanimously agreed to by all who heard it, they rushed tumultuously into the house of entertainment, where they revelled till a late hour. The jovial temper of Bucklaw seldom permitted him to be nice in the choice of his associates; and on the present occasion, when his joyous debauch received additional zest from the intervention of an unusual space of sobriety, and almost abstinence, he was as happy in leading the revels, as if his comrades had been sons of princes. Craigengelt had his own purposes, in fooling him up to the top of his bent; and having some low humour, much impudence, and the power of singing a good song, understanding besides thoroughly the disposition of his regained associate, he readily succeeded in involving him bumper-deep in the festivity of the meeting.

A very different scene was in the meantime passing in the Tower of Wolf's Crag. When the Master of Ravenswood left the court-yard, too much busied with his own perplexed reflections to pay attention to the manœuvre of Caleb, he ushered his guests into the great hall of the castle.

The indefatigable Balderstone, who, from choice or habit, worked on from morning to night, had, by degrees, cleared this desolate apartment of the confused relics of the funeral banquet, and restored it to some order. But not all his skill and labour, in disposing to advantage the little furniture which remained, could remove the dark and disconsolate appearance of those ancient and disfurnished walls. The narrow windows, flanked by deep indentures into the wall, seemed formed rather to exclude than to admit the cheerful light; and the heavy and gloomy appearance of the thunder-sky added still farther to the obscurity.

As Ravenswood, with the grace of a gallant of that period, but not without a certain stiffness and embarrassment of manner, handed the young lady to the upper end of the apartment, her father remained standing more near to the door, as if about to disengage himself from his hat and cloak. At this moment the clang of the portal was heard, a sound at which the stranger started, stepped hastily to the window, and looked with an air of alarm at

Ravenswood, when he saw that the gate of the court was shut, and his domestics excluded.

"You have nothing to fear, sir," said Ravenswood, gravely; "this roof retains the means of giving protection, though not welcome. Methinks," he added, "it is time that I should know who they are that have thus highly honoured my ruined dwelling?"

The young lady remained silent and motionless, and the father, to whom the question was more directly addressed, seemed in the situation of a performer who has ventured to take upon himself a part which he finds himself unable to present, and who comes to a pause when it is most to be expected that he should speak. While he endeavoured to cover his embarrassment with the exterior ceremonials of a well-bred demeanour, it was obvious, that in making his bow, one foot shuffled forward, as if to advance—the other backward, as if with the purpose of escape—and as he undid the cape of his coat, and raised his beaver from his face, his fingers fumbled as if the one had been linked with rusted iron, or the other had weighed equal with a stone of lead. The darkness of the sky seemed to increase, as if to supply the want of those mufflings which he laid aside with such evident reluctance. The impatience of Ravenswood increased also in proportion to the delay of the stranger, and he appeared to struggle under agitation, though probably from a very different cause. He laboured to restrain his desire to speak, while the stranger, to all appearance, was at a loss for words to express what he felt it necessary to say. At length Ravenswood's impatience broke the bounds he had imposed upon it.

"I perceive," he said, "that Sir William Ashton is unwilling to announce himself in the Castle of Wolf's Crag."

"I had hoped it was unnecessary," said the Lord Keeper, relieved from his silence, as a spectre by the voice of the exorcist; "and I am obliged to you, Master of Ravenswood, for breaking the ice at once, where circumstances— unhappy circumstances, let me call them—rendered self-introduction peculiarly awkward."

"And I am not then," said the Master of Ravenswood, gravely, "to consider the honour of this visit as purely accidental?"

"Let us distinguish a little," said the Keeper, assuming

an appearance of ease which perhaps his heart was a stranger to; "this is an honour which I have eagerly desired for some time, but which I might never have obtained, save for the accident of the storm. My daughter and I are alike grateful for this opportunity of thanking the brave man, to whom she owes her life and I mine."

The hatred which divided the great families in the feudal times had lost little of its bitterness, though it no longer expressed itself in deeds of open violence. Not the feelings which Ravenswood had begun to entertain towards Lucy Ashton, not the hospitality due to his guests, were able entirely to subdue, though they warmly combated, the deep passions which arose within him, at beholding his father's foe standing in the hall of the family of which he had in a great measure accelerated the ruin. His looks glanced from the father to the daughter with an irresolution of which Sir William Ashton did not think it proper to await the conclusion. He had now disembarrassed himself of his riding-dress, and walking up to his daughter, he undid the fastening of her mask.

"Lucy, my love," he said, raising her and leading her towards Ravenswood, "lay aside your mask, and let us express our gratitude to the Master openly and barefaced."

"If he will condescend to accept it," was all that Lucy uttered; but in a tone so sweetly modulated, and which seemed to imply at once a feeling and a forgiving of the cold reception to which they were exposed, that, coming from a creature so innocent and so beautiful, her word cut Ravenswood to the very heart for his harshness. He muttered something of surprise, something of confusion, and, ending with a warm and eager expression of his happiness at being able to afford her shelter under his roof, he saluted her, as the ceremonial of the time enjoined upon such occasions. Their cheeks had touched and were withdrawn from each other—Ravenswood had not quitted the hand which he had taken in kindly courtesy—a blush, which attached more consequence by far than was usual to such ceremony, still mantled on Lucy Ashton's beautiful cheek, when the apartment was suddenly illuminated by a flash of lightning, which seemed absolutely to swallow the darkness of the hall. Every object might have been for an instant seen distinctly. The slight and half-sinking form of Lucy

Ashton, the well-proportioned and stately figure of Ravenswood, his dark features, and the fiery, yet irresolute expression of his eyes,—the old arms and scutcheons which hung on the walls of the apartment, were for an instant distinctly visible to the Keeper by a strong red brilliant glare of light. Its disappearance was almost instantly followed by a burst of thunder, for the storm-cloud was very near the castle; and the peal was so sudden and dreadful, that the old tower rocked to its foundation, and every inmate concluded it was falling upon them. The soot, which had not been disturbed for centuries, showered down the huge tunnelled chimneys—lime and dust flew in clouds from the wall; and, whether the lightning had actually struck the castle, or whether through the violent concussion of the air, several heavy stones were hurled from the mouldering battlements into the roaring sea beneath. It might seem as if the ancient founder of the castle were bestriding the thunder-storm, and proclaiming his displeasure at the reconciliation of his descendant with the enemy of his house.

The consternation was general, and it required the efforts of both the Lord Keeper and Ravenswood to keep Lucy from fainting. Thus was the Master a second time engaged in the most delicate and dangerous of all tasks, that of affording support and assistance to a beautiful and helpless being, who, as seen before in a similar situation, had already become a favourite of his imagination, both when awake and when slumbering. If the Genius of the House really condemned a union betwixt the Master and his fair guest, the means by which he expressed his sentiments were as unhappily chosen as if he had been a mere mortal. The train of little attentions, absolutely necessary to soothe the young lady's mind, and aid her in composing her spirits, necessarily threw the Master of Ravenswood into such an intercourse with her father, as was calculated, for the moment at least, to break down the barrier of feudal enmity which divided them. To express himself churlishly, or even coldly, towards an old man, whose daughter (and *such* a daughter) lay before them, overpowered with natural terror—and all this under his own roof—the thing was impossible; and by the time that Lucy, extending a hand to each, was able to thank them for their kindness, the Master felt that his sentiments of hostility towards the Lord

Keeper were by no means those most predominant in his bosom.

The weather, her state of health, the absence of her attendants, all prevented the possibility of Lucy Ashton renewing her journey to Bittlebrains-House, which was full five miles distant; and the Master of Ravenswood could not but, in common courtesy, offer the shelter of his roof for the rest of the day and for the night. But a flush of less soft expression, a look much more habitual to his features, resumed predominance when he mentioned how meanly he was provided for the entertainment of his guests.

"Do not mention deficiencies," said the Lord Keeper, eager to interrupt him and prevent his resuming an alarming topic; "you are preparing to set out for the Continent and your house is probably for the present unfurnished. All this we understand; but if you mention inconvenience, you will oblige us to seek accommodations in the hamlet."

As the Master of Ravenswood was about to reply, the door of the hall opened, and Caleb Balderstone rushed in.

CHAPTER XI

> Let them have meat enough, woman—half a hen;
> There be old rotten pilchards—put them off too;
> 'Tis but a little new anointing of them,
> And a strong onion, that confounds the savour.
> *Love's Pilgrimage.*

THE thunderbolt, which had stunned all who were within hearing of it, had only served to awaken the bold and inventive genius of the flower of Majors-Domo. Almost before the clatter had ceased, and while there was yet scarce an assurance whether the castle was standing or falling, Caleb exclaimed, "Heavens be praised!—this comes to hand like the boul of a pint stoup." He then barred the kitchen door in the face of the Lord Keeper's servant, whom he perceived returning from the party at the gate, and muttering, "How the deil cam he in?—but deil may care—Mysie, what are ye sitting shaking and greeting in the chimney-neuk for? Come here—or stay where ye are, and skirl as loud as ye can—it's a' ye're gude for—I say, ye auld deevil, skirl — skirl — louder — louder, woman — gar the gentles hear ye in the ha'—I have heard ye as far off as the Bass for a less matter. And stay—down wi' that crockery"—

And with a sweeping blow, he threw down from a shelf some articles of pewter and earthenware. He exalted his voice amid the clatter, shouting and roaring in a manner which changed Mysie's hysterical terrors of the thunder into fears that her old fellow-servant was gone distracted. "He has dung down a' the bits o' pigs, too—the only thing we had left to haud a soup milk—and he has spilt the hatted kitt that was for the Master's dinner. Mercy save us, the auld man's gaen clean and clear wud wi' the thunner!"

"Haud your tongue, ye b——!" said Caleb, in the impetuous and overbearing triumph of successful invention, "a's provided now—dinner and a' thing—the thunner's done a' in a clap of a hand!"

"Puir man, he's muckle astray," said Mysie, looking at him with a mixture of pity and alarm; "I wish he may ever come hame to himsell again."

"Here, ye auld doited deevil," said Caleb, still exulting in his extrication from a dilemma which had seemed insurmountable; "keep the strange man out of the kitchen—swear the thunner came down the chimney, and spoiled the best dinner ye ever dressed—beef—bacon—kid—lark—leveret—wild fowl—venison, and what not. Lay it on thick, and never mind expenses. I'll awa up to the ha'—make a' the confusion ye can—but be sure ye keep out the strange servant."

With these charges to his ally, Caleb posted up to the hall, but stopping to reconnoitre through an aperture, which time, for the convenience of many a domestic in succession, had made in the door, and perceiving the situation of Miss Ashton, he had prudence enough to make a pause, both to avoid adding to her alarm, and in order to secure attention to his account of the disastrous effects of the thunder.

But when he perceived that the lady was recovered, and heard the conversation turn upon the accommodation and refreshment which the castle afforded, he thought it time to burst into the room in the manner announced in the last chapter.

"Wull a wins!—wull a wins!—such a misfortune to befa'
the House of Ravenswood, and I to live to see it!"

"What is the matter, Caleb?" said his master, somewhat
alarmed in his turn; "has any part of the castle fallen?"

"Castle fa'an?—na, but the sute's fa'an, and the thunner's
come right down the kitchen-lumm, and the things are a'
lying here awa, there awa, like the Laird o' Hotchpotch's
lands—and wi' brave guests of honour and quality to entertain"—a low bow here to Sir William Ashton and his
daughter—"and naething left in the house fit to present for
dinner—or for supper either, for aught that I can see!"

"I verily believe you, Caleb," said Ravenswood, drily.

Balderstone here turned to his master a half-upbraiding,
half-imploring countenance, and edged towards him as he
repeated, "It was nae great matter of preparation; but just
something added to your honour's ordinary course of fare
—petty cover, as they say at the Louvre—three courses and
the fruit."

"Keep your intolerable nonsense to yourself, you old
fool!" said Ravenswood, mortified at his officiousness, yet
not knowing how to contradict him, without the risk of
giving rise to scenes yet more ridiculous.

Caleb saw his advantage, and resolved to improve it.
But first, observing that the Lord Keeper's servant entered
the apartment, and spoke apart with his master, he took the
same opportunity to whisper a few words into Ravenswood's
ear—"Haud your tongue, for heaven's sake, sir—if it's my
pleasure to hazard my soul in telling lees for the honour of
the family, it's nae business o' yours—and if ye let me gang
on quietly, I'se be moderate in my banquet; but if ye contradict me, deil but I dress ye a dinner fit for a duke!"

Ravenswood, in fact, thought it would be best to let his
officious butler run on, who proceeded to enumerate upon
his fingers,—"No muckle provision—might hae served four
persons of honour,—first course, capons in white broth—
roast kid—bacon with reverence,—second course, roasted
leveret—butter crabs—a veal florentine,—third course,
black-cock—it's black eneugh now wi' the sute—plumdamas
—a tart—a flam—and some nonsense sweet things, and
comfits—and that's a'," he said, seeing the impatience of
his master; "that's just a' was o't—forby the apples and
pears."

Miss Ashton had by degrees gathered her spirits, so far as to pay some attention to what was going on; and observing the restrained impatience of Ravenswood, contrasted with the peculiar determination of manner with which Caleb detailed his imaginary banquet, the whole struck her as so ridiculous, that, despite every effort to the contrary, she burst into a fit of incontrollable laughter, in which she was joined by her father, though with more moderation, and finally by the Master of Ravenswood himself, though conscious that the jest was at his own expense. Their mirth—for a scene which we read with little emotion often appears extremely ludicrous to the spectators—made the old vault ring again. They ceased —they renewed—they ceased—they renewed again their shouts of laughter! Caleb, in the meantime, stood his ground with a grave, angry, and scornful dignity, which greatly enhanced the ridicule of the scene, and the mirth of the spectators.

At length, when the voices, and nearly the strength of the laughers, were exhausted, he exclaimed, with very little ceremony, "The deil's in the gentles! they breakfast sae lordly, that the loss of the best dinner ever cook pat fingers to, makes them as merry as if it were the best jeest in a' George Buchanan. If there was as little in your honours' wames, as there is in Caleb Balderstone's, less caickling wad serve ye on sic a gravaminous subject."

Caleb's blunt expression of resentment again awakened the mirth of the company, which, by the way, he regarded not only as an aggression upon the dignity of the family, but a special contempt of the eloquence with which he himself had summed up the extent of their supposed losses;—"a description of a dinner," as he said afterwards to Mysie, "that wad hae made a fu' man hungry, and them to sit there laughing at it!"

"But," said Miss Ashton, composing her countenance as well as she could, "are all these delicacies so totally destroyed, that no scrap can be collected?"

"Collected my leddy! what wad ye collect out of the sute and the ass? Ye may gang down yoursell, and look into our kitchen—the cookmaid in the trembling exies— the gude vivers lying a' about—beef—capons, and white broth—florentine and flams—bacon, wi' reverence, and a' the sweet confections and whim-whams; ye'll see them a', my leddy—that is," said he, correcting himself, "ye'll no see ony of them now, for the cook has soopit them up, as was weel her part; but ye'll see the white broth where it was spilt. I pat my fingers in it, and it tastes as like sour-milk as ony thing else; if that isna the effect of thunner, I kenna what is.—This gentleman here couldna but hear the clash of our haill dishes, china and silver thegither?"

The Lord Keeper's domestic, though a statesman's attendant, and of course trained to command his countenance upon all occasions, was somewhat discomposed by this appeal, to which he only answered by a bow.

"I think, Mr Butler," said the Lord Keeper, who began to be afraid lest the prolongation of this scene should at length displease Ravenswood,—"I think, that were you to retire with my servant Lockhard—he has travelled, and is quite accustomed to accidents and contingencies of every kind, and I hope betwixt you, you may find out some mode of supply at this emergency."

"His honour kens,"—said Caleb, who, however hopeless of himself of accomplishing what was desirable, would, like the high-spirited elephant, rather have died in the effort, than brooked the aid of a brother in commission,—"his honour kens weel I need nae counsellor, when the honour of the house is concerned."

"I should be unjust if I denied it, Caleb," said his master; "but your art lies chiefly in making apologies, upon which we can no more dine, than upon the bill of fare of our thunder-blasted dinner. Now, possibly, Mr Lockhard's talent may consist in finding some substitute for that, which certainly is not, and has in all probability never been."

"Your honour is pleased to be facetious," said Caleb, "but I am sure, that for the warst, for a walk as far as Wolf's hope, I could dine forty men,—no that the folk there deserve your honour's custom. They hae been ill advised in the matter of the duty-eggs and butter, I winna deny that."

"Do go consult together," said the Master, "go down to the village, and do the best you can. We must not let our guests remain without refreshment, to save the honour of a ruined family. And here, Caleb—take my purse; I believe that will prove your best ally."

"Purse? purse, indeed?" quoth Caleb, indignantly flinging out of the room,—"what suld I do wi' your honour's purse, on your ain grund? I trust we are no to pay for our ain?"

The servants left the hall; and the door was no sooner shut, than the Lord Keeper began to apologise for the rudeness of his mirth; and Lucy to hope she had given no pain or offence to the kind-hearted faithful old man.

"Caleb and I must both learn, madam, to undergo with good humour, or at least with patience, the ridicule which everywhere attaches itself to poverty."

"You do yourself injustice, Master of Ravenswood, on my word of honour," answered his elder guest. "I believe I know more of your affairs than you do yourself, and I hope to show you, that I am interested in them; and that —in short, that your prospects are better than you apprehend. In the meantime, I can conceive nothing so respectable, as the spirit which rises above misfortune, and prefers honourable privations to debt or dependence."

Whether from fear of offending the delicacy, or awakening the pride of the Master, the Lord Keeper made these allusions with an appearance of fearful and hesitating reserve, and seemed to be afraid that he was intruding too far, in venturing to touch, however lightly, upon such a topic, even when the Master had led to it. In short, he appeared at once pushed on by his desire of appearing friendly, and held back by the fear of intrusion. It was no wonder that the Master of Ravenswood, little acquainted as he then was with life, should have given this consummate courtier credit for more sincerity than was probably to be found in a score of his cast. He answered, however, with reserve, that he was indebted to all who might think well of him; and, apologising to his guests, he left the hall, in order to make such arrangements for their entertainment as circumstances admitted.

Upon consulting with old Mysie, the accommodations for the night were easily completed, as indeed they admitted of little choice. The Master surrendered his apartment for the use of Miss Ashton, and Mysie (once a person of consequence), dressed in a black satin gown which had belonged of yore to the Master's grandmother, and had figured in the court-balls of Henrietta Maria, went to attend her as lady's maid. He next enquired after Bucklaw, and understanding he was at the change-house with the huntsmen and some companions, he desired Caleb to call there, and acquaint him how he was circumstanced at Wolf's Crag—to intimate to him that it would be most convenient if he could find a bed in the hamlet, as the elder guest must necessarily be quartered in the secret chamber, the only spare bedroom which could be made fit to receive him. The Master saw no hardship in passing the night by the hall-fire, wrapt in his campaign-cloak; and to Scottish domestics of the day, even of the highest rank, nay, to young men of family or fashion, on any pinch, clean straw, or a dry hay-loft, was always held good night-quarters.

For the rest, Lockhard had his master's orders to bring some venison from the inn, and Caleb was to trust to his wits for the honour of his family. The Master, indeed, a second time held out his purse; but, as it was in sight of the strange servant, the butler thought himself obliged to decline what his fingers itched to clutch. "Couldna he hae slippit it gently into my hand?" said Caleb—"but his honour will never learn how to bear himsell in siccan cases."

Mysie, in the meantime, according to a uniform custom in remote places in Scotland, offered the strangers the produce of her little dairy, "while better meat was getting ready." And according to another custom, not yet wholly in desuetude, as the storm was now drifting off to leeward, the Master carried the Keeper to the top of his highest tower to admire a wide and waste extent of view, and to "weary for his dinner."

CHAPTER XII

"Now dame," quoth he, " Je vous dis sans doute,
Had I nought of a capon but the liver,
And of your white bread nought but a shiver,
And after that a roasted pigge's head,
(But I ne wold for me no beast were dead,)
Then had I with you homely sufferaunce."
Chaucer, Sumner's Tale.

IT was not without some secret misgivings that Caleb set out upon his exploratory expedition. In fact, it was attended with a treble difficulty. He dared not tell his master the offence which he had that morning given to Bucklaw (just for the honour of the family)—he dared not acknowledge he had been too hasty in refusing the purse—and, thirdly, he was somewhat apprehensive of unpleasant consequences upon his meeting Hayston under the impression of an affront, and probably by this time under the influence also of no small quantity of brandy.

Caleb, to do him justice, was as bold as any lion where the honour of the family of Ravenswood was concerned; but his was that considerate valour which does not delight in unnecessary risks. This, however, was a secondary consideration; the main point was to veil the indigence of the house-keeping at the castle, and to make good his vaunt of the cheer which his resources could procure, without Lockhard's assistance, and without supplies from his master. This was as prime a point of honour with him, as with the generous elephant with whom we have already compared him, who, being over-tasked, broke his skull through the desperate exertions which he made to discharge his duty, when he perceived they were bringing up another to his assistance.

The village which they now approached had frequently afforded the distressed butler resources upon similar emergencies; but his relations with it had been of late much altered.

It was a little hamlet which straggled along the side of a creek formed by the discharge of a small brook into the sea, and was hidden from the castle, to which it had been in former times an appendage, by the intervention of the shoulder of a hill forming a projecting headland. It was called Wolf's-hope (*i.e.* Wolf's Haven), and the few inhabitants gained a precarious subsistence by manning two or three fishing-boats in the herring season, and smuggling gin and brandy during the winter months. They paid a kind of hereditary respect to the Lords of Ravenswood; but, in the difficulties of the family, most of the inhabitants of Wolf's-hope had contrived to get feu-rights [1] to their little possessions, their huts, kail-yards, and rights of commonty,

[1] That is, absolute rights of property for the payment of a sum annually, which is usually a trifle in such cases as are alluded to in the text.

so that they were emancipated from the chains of feudal dependence, and free from the various exactions with which, under every possible pretext, or without any pretext at all, the Scottish landlords of the period, themselves in great poverty, were wont to harass their still poorer tenants at will. They might be, on the whole, termed independent, a circumstance peculiarly galling to Caleb, who had been wont to exercise over them the same sweeping authority in levying contributions which was exercised in former times in England, when "the royal purveyors, sallying forth from under the Gothic portcullis to purchase provisions with power and prerogative, instead of money, brought home the plunder of an hundred markets, and all that could be seized from a flying and hiding country, and deposited their spoil in an hundred caverns." [1]

Caleb loved the memory and resented the downfall o. that authority, which mimicked, on a petty scale, the grand contributions exacted by the feudal sovereigns. And as he fondly flattered himself that the awful rule and right supremacy which assigned to the Barons of Ravenswood the first and most effective interest in all productions of nature within five miles of their castle, only slumbered, and was not departed for ever, he used every now and then to give the recollection of the inhabitants a little jog by some petty exaction. These were at first submitted to, with more or less readiness, by the inhabitants of the hamlet; for they had been so long used to consider the wants of the Baron and his family as having a title to be preferred to their own, that their actual independence did not convey to them an immediate sense of freedom. They resembled a man that has been long fettered, who, even at liberty, feels, in imagination, the grasp of the handcuffs still binding his wrists. But the exercise of freedom is quickly followed with the natural consciousness of its immunities, as the enlarged prisoner, by the free use of his limbs, soon dispels the cramped feeling they had acquired when bound.

The inhabitants of Wolf's-hope began to grumble, to resist, and at length positively to refuse compliance with the exactions of Caleb Balderstone. It was in vain he reminded them, that when the eleventh Lord Ravenswood, called the Skipper, from his delight in naval matters, had

[1] Burke's "Speech on Economical Reform."—Works, vol. iii. p. 250.

encouraged the trade of their port by building the pier (a bulwark of stones rudely piled together), which protected the fishing-boats from the weather, it had been matter of understanding, that he was to have the first stone of butter after the calving of every cow within the barony, and the first egg, thence called the Monday's egg, laid by every hen on every Monday in the year.

The feuars heard and scratched their heads, coughed, sneezed, and being pressed for answer, rejoined with one voice, "They could not say;"—the universal refuge of a Scottish peasant, when pressed to admit a claim which his conscience owns, or perhaps his feelings, and his interest inclines him to deny.

Caleb, however, furnished the notables of Wolf's-hope with a note of the requisition of butter and eggs, which he claimed as arrears of the aforesaid subsidy, or kindly aid, payable as above mentioned; and having intimated that he would not be averse to compound the same for goods or money, if it was inconvenient to them to pay in kind, left them, as he hoped, to debate the mode of assessing themselves for that purpose. On the contrary, they met with a determined purpose of resisting the exaction, and were only undecided as to the mode of grounding their opposition, when the cooper, a very important person on a fishing station, and one of the Conscript Fathers of the village, observed, "That their hens had caickled mony a day for the Lords of Ravenswood, and it was time they suld caickle for those that gave them roosts and barley." An unanimous grin intimated the assent of the assembly. "And," continued the orator, "if it's your wull, I'll just tak a step as far as Dunse for Davie Dingwall the writer, that's come frae the North to settle amang us, and he'll pit this job to rights, I'se warrant him."

A day was accordingly fixed for holding a grand *palaver* at Wolf's-hope on the subject of Caleb's requisitions, and he was invited to attend at the hamlet for that purpose.

He went with open hands and empty stomach, trusting to fill the one on his master's account, and the other on his own score, at the expense of the feuars of Wolf's-hope. But, death to his hopes! as he entered the eastern end of the straggling village, the awful form of Davie Dingwall, a sly, dry, hard-fisted, shrewd country attorney, who had already acted against the family of Ravenswood, and was a principal agent of Sir William Ashton, trotted in at the western extremity, bestriding a leathern portmanteau stuffed with the feu-charters of the hamlet, and hoping he had not kept Mr Balderstone waiting, "as he was instructed and fully empowered to pay or receive, compound or compensate, and, in fine, to *agé*[1] as accords, respecting all mutual and unsettled claims whatsoever, belonging or competent to the Honourable Edgar Ravenswood, commonly called the Master of Ravenswood"——

"The *Right* Honourable Edgar *Lord Ravenswood*," said Caleb, with great emphasis; for, though conscious he had little chance of advantage in the conflict to ensue, he was resolved not to sacrifice one jot of honour.

"Lord Ravenswood, then," said the man of business; "we shall not quarrel with you about titles of courtesy— commonly called Lord Ravenswood or Master of Ravenswood, heritable proprietor of the lands and barony of Wolf's Crag, on the one part, and to John Whitefish and others, feuars in the town of Wolf's-hope, within the barony aforesaid, on the other part."

Caleb was conscious, from sad experience, that he would wage a very different strife with this mercenary champion, than with the individual feuars themselves, upon whose old recollections, predilections, and habits of thinking, he might have wrought by an hundred indirect arguments, to which their deputy-representative was totally insensible. The issue of the debate proved the reality of his apprehensions. It was in vain he strained his eloquence and ingenuity, and collected into one mass all arguments arising from antique custom and hereditary respect, from the good deeds done by the Lord of Ravenswood to the community of Wolf's-hope in former days, and from what might be expected from them in future. The writer stuck to the contents of his feu-charters—he could not see it—'twas not in the bond. And when Caleb, determined to try what a little spirit would do, deprecated the consequences of Lord Ravenswood's withdrawing his protection from the burgh, and even hinted at his using active measures of resentment, the man of law sneered in his face.

"His clients," he said, "had determined to do the best

[1] *i.e.* To act as may be necessary and legal, a Scottish law phrase.

they could for their own town, and he thought Lord
Ravenswood, since he was a lord, might have enough to
do to look after his own castle. As to any threats of
stouthrief oppression, by rule of thumb, or *via facti*, as the
law termed it, he would have Mr Balderstone recollect,
that new times were not as old times—that they lived on
the south of the Forth, and far from the Highlands—that
his clients thought they were able to protect themselves;
but should they find themselves mistaken, they would
apply to the government for the protection of a corporal
and four red-coats, who," said Mr Dingwall, with a grin,
"would be perfectly able to secure them against Lord
Ravenswood, and all that he or his followers could do by
the strong hand."

If Caleb could have concentrated all the lightnings of
aristocracy in his eye, to have struck dead this contemner
of allegiance and privilege, he would have lodged them at
his head, without respect to the consequences. As it was,
he was compelled to turn his course backward to the castle;
and there he remained for full half a day invisible and inaccessible even to Mysie, sequestered in his own peculiar
dungeon, where he sat burnishing a single pewter-plate, and
whistling " Maggie Lauder " six hours without intermission.

The issue of this unfortunate requisition had shut against
Caleb all resources which could be derived from Wolf's-
hope and its purlieus, the El Dorado, or Peru, from which,
in all former cases of exigence, he had been able to extract
some assistance. He had, indeed, in a manner vowed that
the deil should have him, if ever he put the print of his
foot within its causeway again. He had hitherto kept his
word; and, strange to tell, this secession had, as he
intended, in some degree, the effect of a punishment upon
the refractory feuars. Mr Balderstone had been a person
in their eyes connected with a superior order of beings,
whose presence used to grace their little festivities, whose
advice they found useful on many occasions, and whose
communications gave a sort of credit to their village. The
place, they acknowledged, "didna look as it used to do,
and should do, since Mr Caleb keepit the castle sae closely
—but doubtless, touching the eggs and butter, it was a
most unreasonable demand, as Mr Dingwall had justly made
manifest."

Thus stood matters betwixt the parties, when the old butler, though it was gall and wormwood to him, found himself obliged either to acknowledge before a strange man of quality, and, what was much worse, before that stranger's servant, the total inability of Wolf's Crag to produce a dinner, or he must trust to the compassion of the feuars of Wolf's-hope. It was a dreadful degradation, but necessity was equally imperious and lawless. With these feelings he entered the street of the village.

Willing to shake himself from his companion as soon as possible, he directed Mr Lockhard to Luckie Sma'trash's change-house, where a din, proceeding from the revels of Bucklaw, Craigengelt, and their party, sounded half-way down the street, while the red glare from the window overpowered the grey twilight which was now settling down, and glimmered against a parcel of old tubs, kegs, and barrels, piled up in the cooper's yard, on the other side of the way.

"If you, Mr Lockhard," said the old butler to his companion, "will be pleased to step to the change-house where that light comes from, and where, as I judge, they are now singing 'Cauld Kail in Aberdeen,' ye may do your master's errand about the venison, and I will do mine about Bucklaw's bed, as I return frae getting the rest of the vivers. —It's no that the venison is actually needfu'," he added, detaining his colleague by the button, "to make up the dinner; but, as a compliment to the hunters, ye ken—and, Mr Lockhard—if they offer ye a drink o' yill, or a cup o' wine, or a glass o' brandy, ye'll be a wise man to take it, in case the thunner should hae soured ours at the castle,— whilk is ower muckle to be dreaded."

He then permitted Lockhard to depart; and with foot heavy as lead, and yet far lighter than his heart, stepped on through the unequal street of the straggling village, meditating on whom he ought to make his first attack. It was necessary he should find some one, with whom old acknowledged greatness should weigh more than recent independence, and to whom his application might appear an act of high dignity, relenting at once and soothing. But he could not recollect an inhabitant of a mind so constructed. "Our kail is like to be cauld enough too," he reflected, as the chorus of "Cauld Kail in Aberdeen" again reached his ears. The minister—he had got his presentation from the late lord, but they had quarrelled about teinds;—the brewster's wife—she had trusted long—and the bill was aye scored up—and unless the dignity of the family should actually require it, it would be a sin to distress a widow woman. None was so able—but, on the other hand, none was likely to be less willing, to stand his friend upon the present occasion, than Gibbie Girder, the man of tubs and barrels already mentioned, who had headed the insurrection in the matter of the egg and butter subsidy.—"But a' comes o' taking folk on the right side, I trow," quoth Caleb to himself; "and I had ance the ill hap to say he was but a Johnnie Newcome in our town, and the carle bore the family an ill-will ever since. But he married a bonny young quean, Jean Lightbody, auld Lightbody's daughter, him that was in the steading of Loup-the-Dyke,—and auld Lightbody was married himsell to Marion, that was about my lady in the family forty years syne—I hae had mony a day's daffing wi' Jean's mither, and they say she bides on wi' them—the carle has Jacobuses and Georgiuses baith, an ane could get at them—and sure I am, it's doing him an honour him or his never deserved at our hand, the ungracious sumph; and if he loses by us a'thegither, he is e'en cheap o't, he can spare it brawly."

Shaking off irresolution, therefore, and turning at once upon his heel, Caleb walked hastily back to the cooper's house, lifted the latch without ceremony, and, in a moment, found himself behind the *hallan*, or partition, from which position he could, himself unseen, reconnoitre the interior of the *but*, or kitchen apartment, of the mansion.

Reverse of the sad menage at the Castle of Wolf's Crag, a bickering fire roared up the cooper's chimney. His wife on the one side, in her pearlings and pudding sleeves, put the last finishing touch to her holiday's apparel, while she contemplated a very handsome and good-humoured face in a broken mirror, raised upon the *bink* (the shelves on which the plates are disposed) for her special accommodation. Her mother, old Luckie Loup-the-Dyke, "a canty carline" as was within twenty miles of her, according to the unanimous report of the *cummers*, or gossips, sat by the fire in the full glory of a grogram gown, lammer beads, and a clean cockernony, whiffing a snug pipe of tobacco, and superin-

tending the affairs of the kitchen. For—sight more interesting to the anxious heart and craving entrails of the de-
sponding Seneschal, than either buxom dame or canty
cummer—there bubbled on the aforesaid bickering fire, a
huge pot, or rather cauldron, steaming with beef and
brewis; while before it revolved two spits, turned each by
one of the cooper's apprentices, seated in the opposite
corners of the chimney; the one loaded with a quarter of
mutton, while the other was graced with a fat goose and a
brace of wild ducks. The sight and scent of such a land
of plenty almost wholly overcame the drooping spirits of
Caleb. He turned, for a moment's space, to reconnoitre
the *ben*, or parlour end of the house, and there saw a sight
scarce less affecting to his feelings;—a large round table,
covered for ten or twelve persons, *decored* (according to his
own favourite term) with *napery* as white as snow; grand
flagons of pewter, intermixed with one or two silver cups,
containing, as was probable, something worthy the brilliancy
of their outward appearance; clean trenchers, cutty spoons,
knives and forks, sharp, burnished, and prompt for action,
which lay all displayed as for an especial festival.

"The devil's in the pedling tub-coopering carle!" muttered Caleb, in all the envy of astonishment; "it's a shame
to see the like o' them gusting their gabs at sic a rate. But
if some o' that gude cheer does not find its way to Wolf's
Crag this night, my name is not Caleb Balderstone."

So resolving, he entered the apartment, and, in all
courteous greeting, saluted both the mother and the
daughter. Wolf's Crag was the court of the barony, Caleb
prime minister at Wolf's Crag; and it has ever been remarked, that though the masculine subject who pays the
taxes, sometimes growls at the courtiers by whom they are
imposed, the said courtiers continue, nevertheless, welcome
to the fair sex, to whom they furnish the newest small-talk
and the earliest fashions. Both the dames were, there-ore,
at once about old Caleb's neck, setting up their throats
together by way of welcome.

"Ay, sirs, Mr Balderstone, and is this you?—A sight of
you is guide for sair een—sit down—sit down—the guide-
man will be blithe to see you—ye nar saw him sae cadgy in
your life; but we are to christen our bit wean the night, as
ye will hae heard, and doubtless ye will stay and see the

ordinance.—We hae killed a wether, and ane o' our lads has been out wi' his gun at the moss—ye used to like wildfowl."

"Na—na—guidewife," said Caleb, "I just keekit in to wish ye joy, and I wad be glad to hae spoken wi' the gudeman, but "—— moving as if to go away.

"The ne'er a fit ye's gang," said the elder dame, laughing and holding him fast, with a freedom which belonged to their old acquaintance; "wha kens what ill it may bring to the bairn, if ye owerlook it in that gate?"

"But I'm in a preceese hurry, gudewife," said the butler, suffering himself to be dragged to a seat without much resistance; "and as to eating"—for he observed the mistress of the dwelling bustling about to place a trencher for him—"as for eating—lack-a-day, we are just killed up yonder wi' eating frae morning to night—it's shamefu' epicurism; but that's what we hae gotten frae the English pock-puddings."

"Hout—never mind the English pock-puddings," said Luckie Lightbody; "try our puddings, Mr Balderstone—there is black pudding and whitehass—try whilk ye like best."

"Baith gude—baith excellent—canna be better; but the very smell is eneugh for me that hae dined sae lately (the faithful wretch had fasted since daybreak). But I wadna affront your housewifeskep, gudewife; and, with your permission, I'se e'en pit them in my napkin, and eat them to my supper at e'en, for I am wearied of Mysie's pastry and nonsense—ye ken landward dainties aye pleased me best, Marion—and landward lasses too—(looking at the cooper's wife)—Ne'er a bit but she looks far better than when she married Gilbert, and then she was the bonniest lass in our parochine and the neest till't—But gawsie cow, goodly calf."

The women smiled at the compliment each to herself, and they smiled again to each other as Caleb wrapt up the puddings in a towel which he had brought with him, as a dragoon carries his foraging bag to receive what may fall in his way.

"And what news at the castle?" quo' the gudewife.

"News?—the bravest news ye ever heard—the Lord Keeper's up yonder wi' his fair daughter, just ready to fling her at my lord's head, if he winna tak her out o' his arms;

and I'se warrant he'll stitch our auld lands of Ravenswood to her petticoat tail."

"Eh! sirs—ay!—and will he hae her?—and is she weel-favoured?—and what's the colour o' her hair?—and does she wear a habit or a railly?" were the questions which the females showered upon the butler.

"Hout tout!—it wad tak a man a day to answer a' your questions, and I hae hardly a minute. Where's the gudeman?"

"Awa to fetch the minister," said Mrs Girder, "precious Mr Peter Bide-the-Bent, frae the Mosshead—the honest man has the rheumatism wi' lying in the hills in the persecution."

"Ay!—a whig and a mountain-man—nae less?" said Caleb, with a peevishness he could not suppress; "I hae seen the day, Luckie, when worthy Mr Cuffcushion and the service-book would hae served your turn (to the elder dame), or ony honest woman in like circumstances."

"And that's true too," said Mrs Lightbody, "but what can a body do?—Jean maun baith sing her psalms and busk her cockernony the gate the gudeman likes, and nae ither gate; for he's maister and mair at hame, I can tell ye, Mr Balderstone."

"Ay, ay, and does he guide the gear too?" said Caleb, to whose projects masculine rule boded little good.

"Ilka penny on't—but he'll dress her as dink as a daisy, as ye see—sae she has little reason to complain—where there's ane better aff there's ten waur."

"Aweel, gudewife," said Caleb, crest-fallen, but not beaten off, "that wasna the way ye guided your gudeman; but ilka land has its ain lauch. I maun be ganging—I just wanted to round in the gudeman's lug, that I heard them say up by yonder, that Peter Puncheon, that was cooper to the Queen's stores at the Timmer Burse at Leith, is dead—sae I thought that maybe a word frae my lord to the Lord Keeper might hae served Gilbert; but since he's frae hame"——

"O but ye maun stay his hame-coming," said the dame, "I aye tell d the gudeman ye meant weel to him; but he taks the tout at every bit lippening word." *trusting*

"Aweel, I'll stay the last minute I can."

"And so," said the handsome young spouse of Mr Girder,

SWK

"ye think this Miss Ashton is weel-favoured?—troth, and sae should she, to set up for our young lord, with a face, and a hand, and a seat on his horse, that might become a king's son—d'ye ken that he aye glowers up at my window, Mr Balderstone, when he chaunces to ride thro' the town, sae I hae a right to ken what like he is, as weel as ony body."

"I ken that brawly," said Caleb, "for I hae heard his lordship say the cooper's wife had the blackest ee in the barony; and I said, Weel may that be, my lord, for it was her mither's afore her, as I ken to my cost—Eh, Marion? Ha, ha, ha!—Ah! these were merry days!"

"Hout awa, auld carle," said the old dame, "to speak sic daffing to young folk.—But, Jean—fie, woman, dinna ye hear the bairn greet? I'se warrant it's that dreary weid [1] has come ower't again."

Up got mother and grandmother, and scoured away, jostling each other as they ran, into some remote corner of the tenement, where the young hero of the evening was deposited. When Caleb saw the coast fairly clear, he took an invigorating pinch of snuff, to sharpen and confirm his resolution.

Cauld be my cast, thought he, if either Bide-the-Bent or Girder taste that broche of wild-fowl this evening; and then addressing the eldest turnspit, a boy of about eleven years old, and putting a penny into his hand, he said, "Here is twal pennies,[2] my man; carry that ower to Mrs Sma'trash, and bid her fill my mill wi' snishing, and I'll turn the broche for ye in the meantime—and she will gie ye a gingerbread snap for your pains."

No sooner was the elder boy departed on this mission, than Caleb, looking the remaining turnspit gravely and steadily in the face, removed from the fire the spit bearing the wild-fowl of which he had undertaken the charge, clapped his hat on his head, and fairly marched off with it. He stopped at the door of the change-house only to say, in a few brief words, that Mr Hayston of Bucklaw was not to expect a bed that evening in the castle.

If this message was too briefly delivered by Caleb, it became absolute rudeness when conveyed through the

---

[1] *Weid*, a feverish cold; a disorder incident to infants and to females, is so called.

[2] Monetæ Scoticæ, scilicet.

medium of a suburb landlady; and Bucklaw was, as a more calm and temperate man might have been, highly incensed. Captain Craigengelt proposed, with the unanimous applause of all present, that they should course the old fox (meaning Caleb) ere he got to cover, and toss him in a blanket. But Lockhard intimated to his master's servants, and those of Lord Bittlebrains, in a tone of authority, that the slightest impertinence to the Master of Ravenswood's domestic, would give Sir William Ashton the highest offence. And having so said, in a manner sufficient to prevent any aggression on their part, he left the public-house, taking along with him two servants loaded with such provisions as he had been able to procure, and overtook Caleb just when he had cleared the village.

CHAPTER XIII

Should I take aught of you?—'tis true I begged now;
And what is worse than that, I stole a kindness;
And, what is worst of all, I lost my way in't.
Wit without Money.

THE face of the little boy, sole witness of Caleb's infringement upon the laws at once of property and hospitality, would have made a good picture. He sat motionless, as if he had witnessed some of the spectral appearances which he had heard told of in a winter's evening; and as he forgot his own duty, and allowed his spit to stand still, he added to the misfortunes of the evening, by suffering the mutton to burn as black as a coal. He was first recalled from his trance of astonishment by a hearty cuff, administered by Dame Lightbody, who (in whatever other respects she might conform to her name) was a woman strong of person, and expert in the use of her hands, as some say her deceased husband had known to his cost.

"What gar'd ye let the roast burn, ye ill-cleckit, gude-for-nought?"

"I dinna ken," said the boy.

"And where's that ill-deedy gett, Giles?"

"I dinna ken," blubbered the astonished declarant.

"And where's Mr Balderstone?—and abune a', and in

the name of council and kirk-session, that I suld say sae, where's the broche wi' the wild-fowl?"

As Mrs Girder here entered, and joined her mother's exclamations, screaming into one ear while the old lady deafened the other, they succeeded in so utterly confounding the unhappy urchin, that he could not for some time tell his story at all, and it was only when the elder boy returned, that the truth began to dawn on their minds.

"Weel, sirs!" said Mrs Lightbody, "wha wad hae thought o' Caleb Balderstone playing an auld acquaintance sic a pliskie!"

"O, weary on him!" said the spouse of Mr Girder; "and what am I to say to the gudeman?—he'll brain me, if there wasna another woman in a' Wolf's-hope."

"Hout tout, silly quean," said the mother; "na, na—it's come to muckle, but it's no come to that neither; for an he brain you he maun brain me, and I have gar'd his betters stand back—hands aff is fair play—we maunna heed a bit flyting." _scolding_

The tramp of horses now announced the arrival of the cooper, with the minister. They had no sooner dismounted than they made for the kitchen fire, for the evening was cool after the thunder storm, and the woods wet and dirty. The young gudewife, strong in the charms of her Sunday gown and biggonets, threw herself in the way of receiving the first attack, while her mother, like the veteran division of the Roman legion, remained in the rear, ready to support her in case of necessity. Both hoped to protract the discovery of what had happened—the mother, by interposing her bustling person betwixt Mr Girder and the fire, and the daughter, by the extreme cordiality with which she received the minister and her husband, and the anxious fears which she expressed lest they should have "gotten cauld."

"Cauld?" quoth the husband surlily—for he was not of that class of lords and masters whose wives are viceroys over them—"we'll be cauld eneugh, I think, if ye dinna let us in to the fire."

And so saying, he burst his way through both lines of defence; and, as he had a careful eye over his property of every kind, he perceived at one glance the absence of the spit with its savoury burden. "What the deil, woman"——

"Fie for shame!" exclaimed both the women; "and before Mr Bide-the-Bent!"

"I stand reproved," said the cooper; "but "——

"The taking in our mouths the name of the great enemy of our souls," said Mr Bide-the-Bent——

"I stand reproved," said the cooper.

"Is an exposing ourselves to his temptations," continued the reverend monitor, "and an inviting, or, in some sort, a compelling, of him to lay aside his other trafficking with unhappy persons, and wait upon those in whose speech his name is frequent."

"Weel, weel, Mr Bide-the-Bent, can a man do mair than stand reproved?" said the cooper; "but just let me ask the women what for they hae dished the wild-fowl before we came."

"They arena dished, Gilbert," said his wife; "but—but an accident"——

"What accident?" said Girder, with flashing eyes—"Nae ill come ower them, I trust? Uh?"

His wife, who stood much in awe of him, durst not reply, but her mother bustled up to her support, with arms disposed as if they were about to be a-kimbo at the next reply.—"I gied them to an acquaintance of mine, Gibbie Girder; and what about it now?"

Her excess of assurance struck Girder mute for an instant.—"And *ye* gied the wild-fowl, the best end of our christening dinner, to a friend of yours, ye auld rudas! And what might *his* name be, I pray ye?"

"Just worthy Mr Caleb Balderstone, frae Wolf's Crag," answered Marion, prompt and prepared for battle.

Girder's wrath foamed over all restraint. If there was a circumstance which could have added to the resentment he felt, it was, that this extravagant donation had been made in favour of our friend Caleb, towards whom, for reasons to which the reader is no stranger, he nourished a decided resentment. He raised his riding-wand against the elder matron, but she stood firm, collected in herself, and undauntedly brandished the iron ladle with which she had just been *flambing* (*Anglicè*, basting) the roast of mutton. Her weapon was certainly the better, and her arm not the weakest of the two; so that Gilbert thought it safest to turn short off upon his wife, who had by this time hatched a sort of hysterical whine, which greatly moved the minister, who was in fact as simple and kind-hearted a creature as ever breathed.—"And you, ye thow-less jadd, to sit still and see my substance disponed upon to an idle, drunken, reprobate, worm-eaten serving-man, just because he kittles the lugs o' a silly auld wife wi' use-less clavers, and every twa words a lee?—I'll gar you as gude"——

Here the minister interposed, both by voice and action, while Dame Lightbody threw herself in front of her daughter, and flourished her ladle.

"Am I no to chastise my ain wife?" exclaimed the cooper, very indignantly.

"Ye may chastise your ain wife if ye like," answered Dame Lightbody; "but ye shall never lay finger on my daughter, and that ye may found upon."

"For shame, Mr Girder!" said the clergyman; "this is what I little expected to have seen of you, that you suld give rein to your sinful passions against your nearest and your dearest; and this night too, when ye are called to the most solemn duty of a Christian parent—and a' for what? for a redundancy of creature-comforts, as worthless as they are unneedful."

"Worthless!" exclaimed the cooper; "a better guse never walkit on stubble; twa finer dentier wild-ducks never wat a feather"

"Be it sae, neighbour," rejoined the minister; "but see what superfluities are yet revolving before your fire. I have seen the day when ten of the bannocks which stand upon that board would have been an acceptable dainty to as many men, that were starving on hills and bogs, and in caves of the earth, for the Gospel's sake."

"And that's what vexes me maist of a'," said the cooper, anxious to get some one to sympathise with his not alto-gether causeless anger; "an the quean had gien it to ony suffering sant, or to ony body ava but that reaving, lying, oppressing tory villain, that rade in the wicked troop of militia when it was commanded out against the sants at Bothwell Brigg by the auld tyrant Allan Ravenswood, that is gane to his place, I wad the less hae minded it. But to gie the principal part o' the feast to the like o' him!"——

"Aweel, Gilbert," said the minister, "and dinna ye see a high judgment in this?—The seed of the righteous are not seen begging their bread—think of the son of a powerful oppressor being brought to the pass of supporting his household from your fulness."

"And, besides," said the wife, "it wasna for Lord Ravenswood neither, an he wad hear but a body speak— it was to help to entertain the Lord Keeper, as they ca' him, that's up yonder at Wolf's Crag."

"Sir William Ashton at Wolf's Crag!" ejaculated the astonished man of hoops and staves.

"And hand and glove wi' Lord Ravenswood," added Dame Lightbody.

"Doited idiot!—that auld clavering sneck-drawer wad gar ye trow the moon is made of green cheese. The Lord Keeper and Ravenswood! they are cat and dog, hare and hound."

"I tell ye they are man and wife, and gree better than some others that are sae," retorted the mother-in-law; "forby, Peter Puncheon, that's cooper to the Queen's stores, is dead, and the place is to fill, and "——

"Od guide us, wull ye haud your skirling tongues!" said Girder,—for we are to remark, that this explanation was given like a catch for two voices, the younger dame, much encouraged by the turn of the debate, taking up, and repeating in a higher tone, the words as fast as they were uttered by her mother.

"The gudewife says naething but what's true, maister," said Girder's foreman, who had come in during the fray. "I saw the Lord Keeper's servants drinking and driving ower at Luckie Sma'trash's, ower by yonder."

"And is their maister up at Wolf's Crag?" said Girder.

"Ay, troth is he," replied his man of confidence.

"And friends wi' Ravenswood?"

"It's like sae," answered the foreman, "since he is putting up [1] wi' him."

"And Peter Puncheon's dead?"

"Ay, ay—Puncheon has leaked out at last, the auld carle," said the foreman; "mony a dribble o' brandy has gaen through him in his day.—But as for the broche and the wild-fowl, the saddle's no aff your mare yet, maister,

[1] Taking up his abode.

and I could follow and bring it back, for Mr Balderstone's no far aff the town yet."

"D sae, Will—and come here—I'll tell ye what to do when ye owertake him."

He relieved the females of his presence, and gave Will his private instructions.

"A bonny-like thing," said the mother-in-law, as the cooper re-entered the apartment, "to send the innocent lad after an armed man, when ye ken Mr Balderstone aye wears a rapier, and whiles a dirk into the bargain."

"I trust," said the minister, "ye have reflected weel on what ye have done, lest you should minister cause of strife, of which it is my duty to say, he who affordeth matter, albeit he himself striketh not, is in no manner guiltless."

"Never fash your beard, Mr Bide-the-Bent," replied Girder; "ane canna get their breath out here between wives and ministers—I ken best how to turn my ain cake. —Jean, serve up the dinner, and nae mair about it."

Nor did he again allude to the deficiency in the course of the evening.

Meantime, the foreman, mounted on his master's steed, and charged with his special orders, pricked swiftly forth in pursuit of the marauder Caleb. That personage, it may be imagined, did not linger by the way. He intermitted even his dearly-beloved chatter, for the purpose of making more haste—only assuring Mr Lockhard that he had made the purveyor's wife give the wild-fowl a few turns before the fire, in case that Mysie, who had been so much alarmed by the thunder, should not have her kitchen-grate in full splendour. Meanwhile, alleging the necessity of being at Wolf's Crag as soon as possible, he pushed on so fast that his companions could scarcely keep up with him. He began already to think he was safe from pursuit, having gained the summit of the swelling eminence which divides Wolf's Crag from the village, when he heard the distant tread of a horse, and a voice which shouted at intervals, "Mr Caleb—Mr Balderstone—Mr Caleb Balderstone—hollo—bide a wee!"

Caleb, it may be well believed, was in no hurry to acknowledge the summons. First, he would not hear it, and faced his companions down, that it was the echo of the wind; then he said it was not worth stopping for; and, at length,

halting reluctantly, as the figure of the horseman appeared
through the shades of the evening, be bent up his whole
soul to the task of defending his prey, threw himself into
an attitude of dignity, advanced the spit, which in his grasp
might with its burden seem both spear and shield, and
firmly resolved to die rather than surrender it.

What was his astonishment, when the cooper's foreman,
riding up and addressing him with respect, told him, "his
master was very sorry he was absent when he came to his
dwelling, and grieved that he could not tarry the christening dinner; and that he had taen the freedom to send a
sma' rundlet of sack, and ane anker of brandy, as he understood there were guests at the castle, and that they were
short of preparation."

I have heard somewhere a story of an elderly gentleman,
who was pursued by a bear that had gotten loose from its
muzzle, until completely exhausted. In a fit of desperation,
he faced round upon Bruin and lifted his cane; at the
sight of which the instinct of discipline prevailed, and the
animal, instead of tearing him to pieces, rose up upon his
hind-legs, and instantly began to shuffle a saraband. Not
less than the joyful surprise of the senior, who had supposed
himself in the extremity of peril from which he was thus
unexpectedly relieved, was that of our excellent friend
Caleb, when he found the pursuer intended to add to his
prize, instead of bereaving him of it. He recovered his
latitude, however, instantly, so soon as the foreman, stooping from his nag, where he sate perched betwixt the two
barrels, whispered in his ear,—"If ony thing about Peter
Puncheon's place could be airted their way, John Girder
wad mak it better to the Master of Ravenswood than a pair
of new gloves; and that he would be blithe to speak wi'
Maister Balderstone on that head, and he wad find him as
pliant as a hoop-willow in a' that he could wish of him."

Caleb heard all this without rendering any answer,
except that all great men from Louis XIV. downwards,
namely, "we will see about it;" and then added aloud, for
the edification of Mr Lockhard.—"Your master has acted
with becoming civility and attention in forwarding the
liquors, and I will not fail to represent it properly to my
Lord Ravenswood. And, my lad," he said, "you may ride
on to the castle, and if none of the servants are returned,

airt - direct

whilk is to be dreaded, as they make day and night of it
when they are out of sight, ye may put them into the
porter's lodge, whilk is on the right hand of the great entry
—the porter has got leave to go to see his friends, sae ye
will meet no ane to steer ye."

The foreman, having received his orders, rode on ; and
having deposited the casks in the deserted and ruinous
porter's lodge, he returned unquestioned by any one.
Having thus executed his master's commission, and doffed
his bonnet to Caleb and his company as he repassed them
in his way to the village, he returned to have his share of
the christening festivity.[1]

CHAPTER XIV

> As, to the Autumn breeze's bugle sound,
> Various and vague the dry leaves dance their round ;
> Or, from the garner-door, on ether borne,
> The chaff flies devious from the winnow'd corn ;
> So vague, so devious, at the breath of heaven,
> From their fix'd aim are mortal counsels driv'n.
>
> *Anonymous.*

WE left Caleb Balderstone in the extremity of triumph at
the success of his various achievements for the honour of
the house of Ravenswood. When he had mustered and
marshalled his dishes of divers kinds, a more royal provision had not been seen in Wolf's Crag, since the funeral
feast of its deceased lord. Great was the glory of the
serving-man, as he *decored* the old oaken table with a clean
cloth, and arranged upon it carbonaded venison and roasted
wild-fowl, with a glance, every now and then, as if to upbraid the incredulity of his master and his guests ; and with
many a story, more or less true, was Lockhard that evening
regaled concerning the ancient grandeur of Wolf's Crag,
and the sway of its Barons over the country in their
neighbourhood.

"A vassal scarce held a calf or a lamb his ain, till he had
first asked if the Lord of Ravenswood was pleased to
accept it ; and they were obliged to ask the lord's consent
before they married in these days, and mony a merry tale

[1] Note I.—Raid of Caleb Balderstone.

they tell about that right as weel as others. And although," said Caleb, "these times are not like the gude auld times, when authority had its right, yet true it is, Mr Lockhard, and you yoursell may partly have remarked, that we of the House of Ravenswood do our endeavour in ke ping up, by all just and lawful exertion of our baronial authority, that due and fitting connexion betwixt superior and vassal, whilk is in some danger of falling into desuetude, owing to the general license and misrule of these present unhappy times."

"Umph!" said Mr Lockhard; "and if I may enquire, Mr Balderstone, pray do you find your people at the village yonder amenable? for I must needs say, that at Ravenswood Castle, now pertaining to my master, the Lord Keeper, ye have not left behind ye the most compliant set of tenantry."

"Ah! but Mr Lockhard," replied Caleb, "ye must consider there has been a change of hands, and the auld lord might expect twa turns frae them, when the new comer canna get ane. A dour and fractious set they were, thae tenants of Ravenswood, and ill to live wi' when they dinna ken their master—and if your master put them mad ance, the whole country will not put them down."

"Troth," said Mr Lockhard, "an such be the case, I think the wisest thing for us a' wad be to hammer up a match between your young lord and our winsome young leddy up by there; and Sir William might just stitch your auld barony to her gown-sleeve, and he wad soon cuitle [1] another out o' somebody else, sic a lang head as he has."

Caleb shook his head.—"I wish," he said, "I wish that may answer, Mr Lockhard. There are auld prophecies about this house I wad like ill to see fulfilled wi' my auld een, that has seen evil eneugh already."

"Pshaw! never mind freits," said his brother butler; "if the young folk liked ane anither, they wad make a winsome couple. But, to say truth, there is a leddy sits in our hall-neuk, maun have her hand in that as weel as in every other job. But there's no harm in drinking to their healths, and I will fill Mrs Mysie a cup of Mr Girder's canary."

While they thus enjoyed themselves in the kitchen, the

[1] *Cuitle* may answer to the elegant modern phrase *diddle*.

company in the hall were not less pleasantly engaged. So soon as Ravenswood had determined upon giving the Lord Keeper such hospitality as he had to offer, he deemed it incumbent on him to assume the open and courteous brow of a well-pleased host. It has been often remarked, that when a man commences by acting a character, he frequently ends by adopting it in good earnest. In the course of an hour or two, Ravenswood, to his own surprise, found himself in the situation of one who frankly does his best to entertain welcome and honoured guests. How much of this change in his disposition was to be ascribed to the beauty and simplicity of Miss Ashton, to the readiness with which she accommodated herself to the inconveniences of her situation—how much to the smooth and plausible conversation of the Lord Keeper, remarkably gifted with those words which win the ear, must be left to the reader's ingenuity to conjecture. But Ravenswood was insensible to neither.

The Lord Keeper was a veteran statesman, well acquainted with courts and cabinets, and intimate with all the various turns of public affairs during the last eventful years of the seventeenth century. He could talk, from his own knowledge, of men and events, in a way which failed not to win attention, and had the peculiar art, while he never said a word which committed himself, at the same time to persuade the hearer that he was speaking without the least shadow of scrupulous caution or reserve. Ravenswood, in spite of his prejudices and real grounds of resentment, felt himself at once amused and instructed in listening to him, while the statesman, whose inward feelings had at first so much impeded his efforts to make himself known, had now regained all the ease and fluency of a silver-tongued lawyer of the very highest order.

His daughter did not speak much, but she smiled; and what she did say argued a submissive gentleness, and a desire to give pleasure, which, to a proud man like Ravenswood, was more fascinating than the most brilliant wit. Above all, he could not but observe, that, whether from gratitude, or from some other motive, he himself, in his deserted and unprovided hall, was as much the object of respectful attention to his guests, as he would have been when surrounded by all the appliances and means of

hospitality proper to his high birth. All deficiencies passed
unobserved, or, if they did not escape notice, it was to
praise the substitutes which Caleb had contrived to supply
the want of the usual accommodations. Where a smile
was unavoidable, it was a very good-humoured one, and
often coupled with some well-turned compliment, to show
how much the guests esteemed the merits of their noble
host, how little they thought of the inconveniences with
which they were surrounded. I am not sure whether the
pride of being found to outbalance, in virtue of his own
personal merit, all the disadvantages of fortune, did not
make as favourable an impression upon the haughty heart
of the Master of Ravenswood, as the conversation of the
father and the beauty of Lucy Ashton.

The hour of repose arrived. The Keeper and his daughter
retired to their apartments, which were "decored" more
properly than could have been anticipated. In making the
necessary arrangements, Mysie had indeed enjoyed the
assistance of a gossip who had arrived from the village
upon an exploratory expedition, but had been arrested by
Caleb, and impressed into the domestic drudgery of the
evening. So that, instead of returning home to describe
the dress and person of the grand young lady, she found
herself compelled to be active in the domestic economy of
Wolf's Crag.

According to the custom of the time, the Master of
Ravenswood attended the Lord Keeper to his apartment,
followed by Caleb, who placed on the table, with all the
ceremonials due to torches of wax, two rudely-framed
tallow-candles, such as in those days were only used by the
peasantry, hooped in paltry clasps of wire, which served
for candlesticks. He then disappeared, and presently
entered with two earthen flagons (the china, he said, had
been little used since my lady's time), one filled with canary
wine, the other with brandy.[1] The canary sack, unheeding
all probabilities of detection, he declared had been twenty
years in the cellars of Wolf's Crag, "though it was not for
him to speak before their honours; the brandy—it was
weel-kend liquor, as mild as mead, and as strong as Samson
—it had been in the house ever since the memorable revel,
in which auld Micklestob had been slain at the head of the

[1] Note II.—Ancient Hospitality.

stair by Jamie of Jenklebrae, on account of the honour of
the worshipful Lady Muirend, wha was in some sort an
ally of the family; natheless"——

"But to cut that matter short, Mr Caleb," said the
Keeper, "perhaps you will favour me with a ewer of
water."

"God forbid your lordship should drink water in this
family," replied Caleb, "to the disgrace of so honourable
an house!"

"Nevertheless, if his lordship have a fancy," said the
Master, smiling, "I think you might indulge him; for, if I
mistake not, there has been water drank here at no distant
date, and with good relish too."

"To be sure, if 's lordship has a fancy," said Caleb;
and re-entering with a jug of pure element—"He will scarce
find such water onywhere as is drawn frae the well at Wolf's
Crag—nevertheless"——

"Nevertheless, we must leave the Lord Keeper to his
repose in this poor chamber of ours," said the Master of
Ravenswood, interrupting his talkative domestic, who
immediately turning to the doorway, with a profound
reverence, prepared to usher his master from the secret
chamber.

But the Lord Keeper prevented his host's departure.—
"I have but one word to say to the Master of Ravenswood,
Mr Caleb, and I fancy he will excuse your waiting."

With a second reverence, lower than the former, Caleb
withdrew—and his master stood motionless, expecting,
with considerable embarrassment, what was to close the
events of a day fraught with unexpected incidents.

"Master of Ravenswood," said Sir William Ashton, with
some embarrassment, "I hope you understand the Christian
law too well to suffer the sun to set upon your anger."

The Master blushed and replied, "He had no occasion
that evening to exercise the duty enjoined upon him by his
Christian faith."

"I should have thought otherwise," said his guest,
"considering the various subjects of dispute and litigation
which have unhappily occurred more frequently than was
desirable or necessary betwixt the late honourable lord,
your father, and myself."

"I could wish, my lord," said Ravenswood, agitated by

suppressed emotion, "that reference to these circumstances should be made anywhere rather than under my father's roof."

"I should have felt the delicacy of this appeal at another time," said Sir William Ashton, "but now I must proceed with what I mean to say.—I have suffered too much in my own mind, from the false delicacy which prevented my soliciting with earnestness, what indeed I frequently requested, a personal communing with your father—much distress of mind to him and to me might have been prevented."

"It is true," said Ravenswood, after a moment's reflection; "I have heard my father say your lordship had proposed a personal interview."

"Proposed, my dear Master? I did indeed propose it, but I ought to have begged, entreated, beseeched it. I ought to have torn away the veil which interested persons had stretched betwixt us, and shown myself as I was, willing to sacrifice a considerable part even of my legal rights, in order to conciliate feelings so natural as his must be allowed to have been. Let me say for myself, my young friend, for so I will call you, that had your father and I spent the same time together which my good fortune has allowed me to-day to pass in your company, it is possible the land might yet have enjoyed one of the most respectable of its ancient nobility, and I should have been spared the pain of parting in enmity from a person whose general character I so much admired and honoured."

He put his handkerchief to his eyes. Ravenswood also was moved, but awaited in silence the progress of this extraordinary communication.

"It is necessary," continued the Lord Keeper, "and proper that you should understand, that there have been many points betwixt us, in which, although I judged it proper that there should be an exact ascertainment of my legal rights by the decree of a court of justice, yet it was never my intention to press them beyond the verge of equity."

"My lord," said the Master of Ravenswood, "it is unnecessary to pursue this topic farther. What the law will give you, or has given you, you enjoy—or you shal' enjoy; neither my father, nor I myself, would have received any thing on the footing of favour."

"Favour?—no—you misunderstand me," resumed the Keeper; "or rather you are no lawyer. A right may be good in law, and ascertained to be so, which yet a man of honour may not in every case care to avail himself of."

"I am sorry for it, my lord," said the Master.

"Nay, nay," retorted his guest, "you speak like a young counsellor; your spirit goes before your wit. There are many things still open for decision betwixt us. Can you blame me, an old man desirous of peace, and in the castle of a young nobleman who has saved my daughter's life and my own, that I am desirous, anxiously desirous, that these should be settled on the most liberal principles?"

The old man kept fast hold of the Master's passive hand as he spoke, and made it impossible for him, be his predetermination what it would, to return any other than an acquiescent reply; and wishing his guest good-night, he postponed farther conference until the next morning.

Ravenswood hurried into the hall, where he was to spend the night, and for a time traversed its pavement with a disordered and rapid pace. His mortal foe was under his roof, yet his sentiments towards him were neither those of a feudal enemy nor of a true Christian. He felt as if he could neither forgive him in the one character, nor follow forth his vengeance in the other, but that he was making a base and dishonourable composition betwixt his resentment against the father and his affection for his daughter. He cursed himself, as he hurried to and fro in the pale moonlight, and more ruddy gleams of the expiring wood-fire. He threw open and shut the latticed windows with violence, as if alike impatient of the admission and exclusion of free air. At length, however, the torrent of passion foamed off its madness, and he flung himself into the chair, which he proposed as his place of repose for the night.

If, in reality,—such were the calmer thoughts that followed the first tempest of his passion,—If, in reality, this man desires no more than the law allows him—if he is willing to adjust even his acknowledged rights upon an equitable footing, what could be my father's cause of complaint?—what is mine?—Those from whom we won

our ancient possessions fell under the sword of my ancestors, and left lands and livings to the conquerers; we
sink under the force of the law, now too powerful for the
Scottish chivalry.   Let us parley with the victors of the
day, as if we had been besieged in our fortress, and without hope of relief.   This man may be other than I have
thought him; and his daughter—but I have resolved not
to think of her.

He wrapt his cloak around him, fell asleep, and dreamed
of Lucy Ashton till daylight gleamed through the lattices.

CHAPTER XV

> We worldly men, when we see friends and kinsmen
> Past hope sunk in their fortunes, lend no hand
> To lift them up, but rather set our feet
> Upon their heads to press them to the bottom,
> As I must yield with you I practised it;
> But now I see you in a way to rise,
> I can and will assist you.
>
> *New Way to Pay Old Debts.*

THE Lord Keeper carried with him to a couch harder than
he was accustomed to stretch himself upon, the same
ambitious thoughts and political perplexities, which drive
sleep from the softest down that ever spread a bed of state.
He had sailed long enough amid the contending tides and
currents of the time to be sensible of their peril, and of the
necessity of trimming his vessel to the prevailing wind, if
he would have her escape shipwreck in the storm.   The
nature of his talents, and the timorousness of disposition
connected with them, had made him assume the pliability
of the versatile old Earl of Northampton, who explained the
art by which he kept his ground during all the changes of
state, from the reign of Henry VIII. to that of Elizabeth,
by the frank avowal, that he was born of the willow, not of
the oak.   It had accordingly been Sir William Ashton's
policy, on all occasions, to watch the changes in the political
horizon, and, ere yet the conflict was decided, to negotiate
some interest for himself with the party most likely to prove
victorious.   His time-serving disposition was well known,
and excited the contempt of the more daring leaders of

both factions in the state.   But his talents were of a useful
and practical kind, and his legal knowledge held in high
estimation; and they so far counter-balanced other deficiencies, that those in power were glad to use and to
reward, though without absolutely trusting or greatly
respecting him.

Tne Marquis of A—— had used his utmost influence to
effect a change in the Scottish cabinet, and his schemes
had been of late so well laid and so ably supported, that
there appeared a very great chance of his proving ultimately
successful.   He did not, however, feel so strong or so confident as to neglect any means of drawing recruits to his
standard.   The acquisition of the Lord Keeper was deemed
of some importance, and a friend, perfectly acquainted with
his circumstances and character, became responsible for
his political conversion.

When this gentleman arrived at Ravenswood Castle upon
a visit, the real purpose of which was disguised under
general courtesy, he found the prevailing fear which at
present beset the Lord Keeper, was that of danger to his
own person from the Master of Ravenswood.   The language
which the blind sibyl, old Alice, had used; the sudden
appearance of the Master, armed, and within his precincts,
immediately after he had been warned against danger from
him; the cold and haughty return received in exchange for
the acknowledgments with which he loaded him for his
timely protection, had all made a strong impression on his
imagination.

So soon as the Marquis's political agent found how the
wind sate, he began to insinuate fears and doubts of another
kind, scarce less calculated to affect the Lord Keeper.   He
enquired with seeming interest, whether the proceedings in
Sir William's complicated litigation with the Ravenswood
family was out of court, and settled without the possibility
of appeal?   The Lord Keeper answered in the affirmative;
but his interrogator was too well informed to be imposed
upon.   He pointed out to him, by unanswerable arguments,
that some of the most important points which had been
decided in his favour against the house of Ravenswood,
were liable, under the Treaty of Union, to be reviewed by
the British House of Peers, a court of equity of which the
Lord Keeper felt an instinctive dread.   This course came

instead of an appeal to the old Scottish Parliament, or, as it was technically termed, "a protestation for remeid in law."

The Lord Keeper, after he had for some time disputed the legality of such a proceeding, was compelled, at length, to comfort himself with the improbability of the young Master of Ravenswood's finding friends in parliament capable of stirring in so weighty an affair.

"Do not comfort yourself with that false hope," said his wily friend; "it is possible that, in the next session of Parliament, young Ravenswood may find more friends and favour even than your lordship."

"That would be a sight worth seeing," said the Keeper, scornfully.

"And yet," said his friend, "such things have been seen ere now, and in our own time. There are many at the head of affairs even now, that a few years ago were under hiding for their lives; and many a man now dines on plate of silver, that was fain to eat his crowdy without a bicker; and many a high head has been brought full low among us in as short a space. Scott of Scotstarvet's 'Staggering State of Scots Statesmen,' of which curious memoir you showed me a manuscript, has been outstaggered in our time."

The Lord Keeper answered with a deep sigh, "that these mutations were no new sights in Scotland, and had been witnessed long before the time of the satirical author he had quoted. It was many a long year," he said, "since Fordun had quoted as an ancient proverb, '*Neque dives, neque fortis, sed nec sapiens Scotus, praedominante invidia, diu durabit in terra.*'"

"And be assured, my esteemed friend," was the answer, "that even your long services to the state, or deep legal knowledge, will not save you, or render your estate stable, if the Marquis of A—— comes in with a party in the British Parliament. You know that the deceased Lord Ravenswood was his near ally, his lady being fifth in descent from the Knight of Tillibardine; and I am well assured that he will take young Ravenswood by the hand, and be his very good lord and kinsman. Why should he not?—The Master is an active and stirring young fellow, able to help himself with tongue and hands; and it is such as he that finds friends among their kindred, and not those unarmed and unable Mephibosheths, that are sure to be a burden to every one that takes them up. And so, if these Ravenswood cases be called over the coals in the House of Peers, you will find that the Marquis will have a crow to pluck with you."

"That would be an evil requittal," said the Lord Keeper, "for my long services to the state, and the ancient respect in which I have held his lordship's honourable family and person."

"Ay, but," rejoined the agent of the Marquis, "it is in vain to look back on past service and auld respect, my lord—it will be present service and immediate proofs of regard, which, in these sliddery times, will be expected by a man like the Marquis."

The Lord Keeper now saw the full drift of his friend's argument, but he was too cautious to return any positive answer.

"He knew not," he said, "the service which the Lord Marquis could expect from one of his limited abilities, that had not always stood at his command, still saving and reserving his duty to his king and country."

Having thus said nothing, while he seemed to say every thing, for the exception was calculated to cover whatever he might afterwards think proper to bring under it, Sir William Ashton changed the conversation, nor did he again permit the same topic to be introduced. His guest departed, without having brought the wily old statesman the length of committing himself, or of pledging himself to any future line of conduct, but with the certainty that he had alarmed his fears in a most sensible point, had laid a foundation for future and farther treaty.

When he rendered an account of his negotiation to the Marquis, they both agreed that the Keeper ought not to be permitted to relapse into security, and that he should be plied with new subjects of alarm, especially during the absence of his lady. They were well aware that her proud, vindictive, and predominating spirit, would be likely to supply him with the courage in which he was deficient— that she was immovably attached to the party now in power, with whom she maintained a close correspondence and alliance, and that she hated, without fearing, the Ravenswood family (whose more ancient dignity threw discredit on the newly acquired grandeur of her husband), to

such a degree, that she would have periled the interest o
her own house, to have the prospect of altogether crushing
that of her enemy.

But Lady Ashton was now absent. The business which
had long detained her in Edinburgh, had afterwards induced her to travel to London, not without the hope that
she might contribute her share to disconcert the intrigues
of the Marquis at court; for she stood high in favour with
the celebrated Sarah, Duchess of Marlborough, to whom,
in point of character, she bore considerable resemblance.
It was necessary to press her husband hard before her
return; and, as a preparatory step, the Marquis wrote to
the Master of Ravenswood the letter which we rehearsed
in a former chapter. It was cautiously worded, so as to
leave it in the power of the writer hereafter to take as deep,
or as slight an interest in the fortunes of his kinsman, as
the progress of his own schemes might require. But however unwilling, as a statesman, the Marquis might be to
commit himself, or assume the character of a patron, while
he had nothing to give away, it must be said to his honour
that he felt a strong inclination effectually to befriend the
Master of Ravenswood, as well as to use his name as a
means of alarming the terrors of the Lord Keeper.

As the messenger who carried this letter was to pass near
the house of the Lord Keeper, he had it in direction, that
in the village adjoining to the park-gate of the castle, his
horse should lose a shoe, and that, while it was replaced by
the smith of the place, he should express the utmost regret
for the necessary loss of time, and in the vehemence of his
impatience, give it to be understood, that he was bearing a
message from the Marquis of A—— to the Master of
Ravenswood, upon a matter of life and death.

This news, with exaggerations, was speedily carried from
various quarters to the ears of the Lord Keeper, and each
reporter dwelt upon the extreme impatience of the courier,
and the surprising short time in which he had executed his
journey. The anxious statesman heard in silence; but in
private Lockhard received orders to watch the courier on
his return, to waylay him in the village, to ply him with
liquor if possible, and to use all means, fair or foul, to learn
the contents of the letter of which he was the bearer. But
as this plot had been foreseen, the messenger returned by

a different and distant road, and thus escaped the snare that was laid for him.

After he had been in vain expected for some time, Mr Dingwall had orders to make especial enquiry among his clients at Wolf's-hope, whether such a domestic belonging to the Marquis of A—— had actually arrived at the neighbouring castle. This was easily ascertained; for Caleb had been in the village one morning by five o'clock, to borrow "twa chappins of ale and a kipper" for the messenger's refreshment, and the poor fellow had been ill for twenty-four hours at Luckie Sma'trash's, in consequence of dining upon "saut saumon and sour drink." So that the existence of a correspondence betwixt the Marquis and his distressed kinsman, which Sir William Ashton had sometimes treated as a bugbear, was proved beyond the possibility of further doubt.

The alarm of the Lord Keeper became very serious. Since the Claim of Right, the power of appealing from the decisions of the civil court to the Estates of Parliament, which had formerly been held incompetent, had in many instances been claimed, and in some allowed, and he had no small reason to apprehend the issue, if the English House of Lords should be disposed to act upon an appeal from the Master of Ravenswood "for remeid in law." It would resolve into an equitable claim, and be decided, perhaps, upon the broad principles of justice, which were not quite so favourable to the Lord Keeper as those of strict law. Besides, judging, though most inaccurately, from courts which he had himself known in the unhappy times preceding the Scottish Union, the Keeper might have too much right to think, that in the House to which his lawsuits were to be transferred, the old maxim might prevail in Scotland which was too well recognised in former times,—"Show me the man, and I'll show you the law." The high and unbiassed character of English judicial proceedings was then little known in Scotland; and the extension of them to that country was one of the most valuable advantages which it gained by the Union. But this was a blessing which the Lord Keeper, who had lived under another system, could not have the means of foreseeing. In the loss of his political consequence, he anticipated the loss of his lawsuit. Meanwhile, every report which reached him served to render the success of the Marquis's intrigues the more probable, and the Lord Keeper began to think it indispensable, that he should look round for some kind of protection against the coming storm. The timidity of his temper induced him to adopt measures of compromise and conciliation. The affair of the wild bull, properly managed, might, he thought, be made to facilitate a personal communication and reconciliation betwixt the Master and himself. He would then learn, if possible, what his own ideas were of the extent of his rights, and the means of enforcing them; and perhaps matters might be brought to a compromise, where one party was wealthy and the other so very poor. A reconciliation with Ravenswood was likely to give him an opportunity to play his own game with the Marquis of A——. "And besides," said he to himself, "it will be an act of generosity to raise up the heir of this distressed family; and if he is to be warmly and effectually befriended by the new government, who knows but my virtue may prove its own reward?"

Thus thought Sir William Ashton, covering with no unusual self-delusion his interested views with a hue of virtue; and having attained this point, his fancy strayed still farther. He began to bethink himself, "that if Ravenswood was to have a distinguished place of power and trust—and if such a union would sopite the heavier part of his unadjusted claims—there might be worse matches for his daughter Lucy—the Master might be reponed against the attainder—Lord Ravenswood was an ancient title, and the alliance would, in some measure, legitimate his own possession of the greater part of the Master's spoils, and make the surrender of the rest a subject of less bitter regret."

With these mingled and multifarious plans occupying his head, the Lord Keeper availed himself of my Lord Bittlebrains's repeated invitation to his residence, and thus came within a very few miles of Wolf's Crag. Here he found the lord of the mansion absent, but was courteously received by the lady, who expected her husband's immediate return. She expressed her particular delight at seeing Miss Ashton, and appointed the hounds to be taken out for the Lord Keeper's special amusement. He readily entered into the proposal, as giving him an opportunity to reconnoitre Wolf's Crag, and perhaps to make some acquaintance with the owner, if he should be tempted from his desolate mansion by the chase. Lockhard had his orders to endeavour on his part to make some acquaintance with the inmates of the castle, and we have seen how he played his part.

The accidental storm did more to further the Lord Keeper's plan of forming a personal acquaintance with young Ravenswood, than his most sanguine expectations could have anticipated. His fear of the young nobleman's personal resentment had greatly decreased, since he considered him as formidable from his legal claims, and the means he might have of enforcing them. But although he thought, not unreasonably, that only desperate circumstances drove men on desperate measures, it was not without a secret terror, which shook his heart within him, that he first felt himself enclosed within the desolate Tower of Wolf's Crag; a place so well fitted, from solitude and strength, to be a scene of violence and vengeance. The stern reception at first given to them by the Master of Ravenswood, and the difficulty he felt in explaining to that injured nobleman what guests were under the shelter of his roof, did not soothe these alarms; so that when Sir William Ashton heard the door of the court-yard shut behind him with violence, the words of Alice rung in his ears, "that he had drawn on matters too hardly with so fierce a race as those of Ravenswood, and that they would bide their time to be avenged."

The subsequent frankness of the Master's hospitality, as their acquaintance increased, abated the apprehensions these recollections were calculated to excite; and it did not escape Sir William Ashton, that it was to Lucy's grace and beauty he owed the change in their host's behaviour.

All these thoughts thronged upon him when he took possession of the secret chamber. The iron lamp, the unfurnished apartment, more resembling a prison than a place of ordinary repose, the hoarse and ceaseless sound of the waves rushing against the base of the rock on which the castle was founded, saddened and perplexed his mind. To his own successful machinations, the ruin of the family had been in a great measure owing, but his disposition was crafty and not cruel; so that actually to witness the desolation and distress he had himself occasioned, was as painful to him as it would be to the humane mistress of a family to superintend in person the execution of the lambs and poultry which are killed by her own directions. At the same time, when he thought of the alternative, of restoring to Ravenswood a large proportion of his spoils, or of adopting, as an ally and member of his own family, the heir of this impoverished house, he felt as the spider may be supposed to do, when his whole web, the intricacies of which had been planned with so much art, is destroyed by the chance sweep of a broom. And then, if he should commit himself too far in this matter, it gave rise to a perilous question, which many a good husband, when under temptation to act as a free agent, has asked himself without being able to return a satisfactory answer; "What will my wife— what will Lady Ashton say?" On the whole, he came at length to the resolution in which minds of a weaker cast so often take refuge. He resolved to watch events, to take advantage of circumstances as they occurred, and regulate his conduct accordingly. In this spirit of temporising policy, he at length composed his mind to rest.

CHAPTER XVI

"A slight note I have about me for you, for the delivery of which you must excuse me. It is an offer that friendship calls upon me to do, and no way offensive to you, since I desire nothing but right upon both sides." *King and no King.*

WHEN Ravenswood and his guest met in the morning, the gloom of the Master's spirit had in part returned. He, also, had passed a night rather of reflection than of slumber; and the feelings which he could not but entertain towards Lucy Ashton, had to support a severe conflict against those which he had so long nourished against her father. To clasp in friendship the hand of the enemy of his house, to entertain him under his roof, to exchange with him the courtesies and the kindness of domestic familiarity, was a degradation which his proud spirit could not be bent to without a struggle.

But the ice being once broken, the Lord Keeper was resolved it should not have time again to freeze. It had been part of his plan to stun and confuse Ravenswood's ideas, by a complicated and technical statement of the matters which had been in debate betwixt their families, justly thinking that it would be difficult for a youth of his age to follow the expositions of a practical lawyer, concerning actions of compt and reckoning, and of multiplepoindings, and adjudications and wadsets, proper and improper, and poindings of the ground, and declarations of the expiry of the legal. Thus, thought Sir William, I shall have all the grace of appearing perfectly communicative, while my party will derive very little advantage from any thing I may tell him. He therefore took Ravenswood aside into the deep recess of a window in the hall, and resuming the discourse of the preceding evening, expressed a hope that his young friend would assume some patience, in order to hear him enter into a minute and explanatory detail of those unfortunate circumstances, in which his late honourable father had stood at variance with the Lord Keeper. The Master of Ravenswood coloured highly, but was silent; and the Lord Keeper, though not greatly approving the sudden heightening of his auditor's complexion, commenced the history of a bond for twenty thousand marks, advanced by his father to the father of Allan Lord Ravenswood, and was proceeding to detail the executorial proceedings by which this large sum had been rendered a *debitum fundi*, when he was interrupted by the Master.

"It is not in this place," he said, "that I can hear Sir William Ashton's explanation of the matters in question between us. It is not here, where my father died of a broken heart, that I can with decency or temper investigate the cause of his distress. I might remember that I was a son, and forget the duties of a host. A time, however, there must come, when these things shall be discussed in a place and in a presence where both of us will have equal freedom to speak and to hear."

"Any time," the Lord Keeper said, "any place, was alike to those who sought nothing but justice. Yet it would seem he was, in fairness entitled to some premonition respecting the grounds upon which the Master proposed to impugn the whole train of legal proceedings, which had been so well and ripely advised in the only courts competent."

"Sir William Ashton," answered the Master, with warmth,

"the lands which you now occupy were granted to my remote ancestor for services done with his sword against the English invaders. How they have glided from us by a train of proceedings that seem to be neither sale, nor mortgage, nor adjudication for debt, but a nondescript and entangled mixture of all these rights—how annual-rent has been accumulated upon principal, and no nook or coign of legal advantage left unoccupied, until our interest in our hereditary property seems to have melted away like an icicle in thaw—all this you understand better than I do. I am willing, however, to suppose, from the frankness of your conduct towards me, that I may in a great measure have mistaken your personal character, and that things may have appeared right and fitting to you, a skilful and practised lawyer, which to my ignorant understanding seem very little short of injustice and gross oppression."

"And you, my dear Master," answered Sir William, "you, permit me to say, have been equally misrepresented to me. I was taught to believe you a fierce, imperious, hot-headed youth, ready, at the slightest provocation, to throw your sword into the scales of justice, and to appeal to those rude and forcible measures from which civil polity has long protected the people of Scotland. Then, since we were mutually mistaken in each other, why should not the young nobleman be willing to listen to the old lawyer, while, at least, he explains the points of difference betwixt them?"

"No, my lord," answered Ravenswood; "it is in the House of British Peers,[1] whose honour must be equal to their rank—it is in the court of last resort that we must parley together. The belted lords of Britain, her ancient peers, must decide, if it is their will that a house, not the least noble of their members, shall be stripped of their possessions, the reward of the patriotism of generations, as the pawn of a wretched mechanic becomes forfeit to the usurer the instant the hour of redemption has passed away. If they yield to the grasping severity of the creditor, and to the gnawing usury that eats into our lands as moths into a raiment, it will be of more evil consequence to them and their posterity than to Edgar Ravenswood—I shall still have my sword and my cloak, and can follow the profession of arms wherever a trumpet shall sound."

[1] Note III.—Appeal to Parliament.

As he pronounced these words, in a firm yet melancholy tone, he raised his eyes, and suddenly encountered those of Lucy Ashton, who had stolen unawares on their interview, and observed her looks fastened on them with an expression of enthusiastic interest and admiration, which had wrapt her for the moment beyond the fear of discovery. The noble form and fine features of Ravenswood, fired with the pride of birth and sense of internal dignity—the mellow and expressive tones of his voice, the desolate state of his fortunes, and the indifference with which he seemed to endure and to dare the worst that might befall, rendered him a dangerous object of contemplation for a maiden already too much disposed to dwell upon recollections connected with him. When their eyes encountered each other both blushed deeply, conscious of some strong internal emotion, and shunned again to meet each other's look.

Sir William Ashton had, of course, closely watched the expression of their countenances. "I need fear," said he internally, "neither Parliament nor protestation; I have an effectual mode of reconciling myself with this hot-tempered young fellow, in case he shall become formidable. The present object is, at all events, to avoid committing ourselves. The hook is fixed; we will not strain the line too soon—it is as well to reserve the privilege of slipping it loose, if we do not find the fish worth landing."

In this selfish and cruel calculation upon the supposed attachment of Ravenswood to Lucy, he was so far from considering the pain he might give to the former, by thus dallying with his affections, that he even did not think upon the risk of involving his own daughter in the perils of an unfortunate passion; as if her predilection, which could not escape his attention, were like the flame of a taper, which might be lighted or extinguished at pleasure. But Providence had prepared a dreadful requital for this keen observer of human passions, who had spent his life in securing advantages to himself by artfully working upon the passions of others.

Caleb Balderstone now came to announce that breakfast was prepared; for in those days of substantial feeding, the relics of the supper amply furnished forth the morning meal. Neither did he forget to present to the Lord Keeper, with great reverence, a morning-draught in a large pewter cup, garnished with leaves of parsley and scurvy-grass. He craved pardon, of course, for having omitted to serve it in the great silver standing cup as behoved, being that it was at present in a silversmith's in Edinburgh, for the purpose of being overlaid with gilt.

"In Edinburgh like enough," said Ravenswood; "but in what place, or for what purpose, I am afraid neither you nor I know."

"Aweel!" said Caleb, peevishly, "there's a man standing at the gate already this morning—that's ae thing that I ken —Does your honour ken whether ye will speak wi' him or no?"

"Does he wish to speak with me, Caleb?"

"Less will no serve him," said Caleb; "but ye had best take a visie of him through the wicket before opening the gate—it's no every ane we suld let into this castle."

"What! do you suppose him to be a messenger come to arrest me for debt?" said Ravenswood.

"A messenger arrest your honour for debt, and in your Castle of Wolf's-Crag!—Your honour is jesting wi' auld Caleb this morning." However, he whispered in his ear as he followed him out, "I would be loath to do ony decent man a prejudice in your honour's gude opinion; but I would tak twa looks o' that chield before I let him within these walls."

He was not an officer of the law, however; being no less a person than Captain Craigengelt, with his nose as red as a comfortable cup of brandy could make it, his laced cocked-hat set a little aside upon the top of his black riding periwig, a sword by his side, and pistols at his holsters, and his person arrayed in a riding suit, laid over with tarnished lace,—the very moral of one who would say, Stand, to a true man.

When the Master had recognised him, he ordered the gates to be opened. "I suppose," he said, "Captain Craigengelt, there are no such weighty matters betwixt you and me, but may be discussed in this place. I have company in the castle at present, and the terms upon which we last parted must excuse my asking you to make part of them."

Craigengelt, although possessing the very perfection of impudence, was somewhat abashed by this unfavourable reception. "He had no intention," he said, "to force

himself upon the Master of Ravenswood's hospitality—
he was in the honourable service of bearing a message
to him from a friend, otherwise the Master of Ravenswood should not have had reason to complain of this
intrusion."

"Let it be short, sir," said the Master, "for that will be
the best apology.   Who is the gentleman who is so fortunate
as to have your services as a messenger?"

"My friend Mr Hayston of Bucklaw," answered
Craigengelt, with conscious importance, and that confidence
which the acknowledged courage of his principal inspired,
"who conceives himself to have been treated by you with
something much short of the respect which he had reason
to demand, and therefore is resolved to exact satisfaction.
I bring with me," said he, taking a piece of paper out of
his pocket, "the precise length of his sword; and he
requests you will meet him, accompanied by a friend, and
equally armed, at any place within a mile of the castle,
when I shall give attendance as umpire, or second, on his
behoof."

"Satisfaction—and equal arms!" repeated Ravenswood,
who, the reader will recollect, had no reason to suppose he
had given the slightest offence to his late inmate—"upon
my word, Captain Craigengelt, either you have invented
the most improbable falsehood that ever came into the mind
of such a person, or your morning-draught has been somewhat of the strongest.   What could persuade Bucklaw to
send me such a message?"

"For that, sir," replied Craigengelt, "I am desired to
refer you to what, in duty to my friend, I am to term your
inhospitality in excluding him from your house, without
reasons assigned."

"It is impossible," replied the Master; "he cannot be
such a fool as to interpret actual necessity as an insult.
Nor do I believe, that, knowing my opinion of you, Captain,
he would have employed the services of so slight and inconsiderable a person as yourself upon such an errand, as
I certainly could expect no man of honour to act with you
in the office of umpire."

"I slight and inconsiderable!" said Craigengelt, raising
his voice, and laying his hand on his cutlass; "if it were not
that the quarrel of my friend craves the precedence, and it

in dependence before my own, I would give you to understand"——

"I can understand nothing upon your explanation, Captain Craigengelt. Be satisfied of that, and oblige me with your departure."

"D——n!" muttered the bully; "and is this the answer which I am to carry back to an honourable message?"

"Tell the Laird of Bucklaw," answered Ravenswood, "if you are really sent by him, that when he sends me his cause of grievance by a person fitting to carry such an errand betwixt him and me, I will either explain it or maintain it."

"Then, Master, you will at least cause to be returned to Hayston, by my hands, his property which is remaining in your possession."

"Whatever property Bucklaw may have left behind him, sir," replied the Master, "shall be returned to him by my servant, as you do not show me any credentials from him which entitle you to receive it."

"Well, Master," said Captain Craigengelt, with malice which even his fear of the consequences could not suppress, —"you have this morning done me an egregious wrong and dishonour, but far more to yourself. A castle indeed!" he continued, looking around him; "why, this is worse than a *coupe-gorge* house, where they receive travellers to plunder them of their property."

"You insolent rascal," said the Master, raising his cane, and making a grasp at the Captain's bridle, "if you do not depart without uttering another syllable, I will batoon you to death!"

At the motion of the Master towards him, the bully turned so rapidly round, that with some difficulty he escaped throwing down his horse, whose hoofs struck fire from the rocky pavement in every direction. Recovering him, however, with the bridle, he pushed for the gate, and rode sharply back again in the direction of the village.

As Ravenswood turned round to leave the courtyard after this dialogue, he found that the Lord Keeper had descended from the hall, and witnessed, though at the distance prescribed by politeness, his interview with Craigengelt.

"I have seen," said the Lord Keeper, "that gentleman's

face, and at no great distance of time—his name is Craig —Craig—something, is it not?"

"Craigengelt is the fellow's name," said the Master, "at least that by which he passes at present."

"Craig-in-guilt," said Caleb, punning upon the word *craig*, which in Scotch signifies throat; "if he is Craig-in-guilt just now, he is as likely to be Craig-in-peril as ony chield I ever saw—the loon has woodie written on his very visnomy, and I wad wager twa and a plack that hemp plaits his cravat yet."

"You understand physiognomy, good Mr Caleb," said the Keeper, smiling; "I assure you the gentleman has been near such a consummation before now—for I most distinctly recollect, that, upon occasion of a journey which I made about a fortnight ago to Edinburgh, I saw Mr Craigengelt, or whatever is his name, undergo a severe examination before the Privy Council."

"Upon what account?" said the Master of Ravenswood, with some interest.

The question led immediately to a tale which the Lord Keeper had been very anxious to introduce, when he could find a graceful and fitting opportunity. He took hold of the Master's arm, and led him back towards the hall. "The answer to your question," he said, "though it is a ridiculous business, is only fit for your own ear."

As they entered the hall, he again took the Master apart into one of the recesses of the window, where it will be easily believed that Miss Ashton did not venture again to intrude upon their conference.

CHAPTER XVII

> Here is a father now,
> Will truck his daughter for a foreign venture,
> Make her the stop-gap to some canker'd feud,
> Or fling her o'er, like Jonah, to the fishes,
> To appease the sea at highest.
>
> *Anonymous.*

THE Lord Keeper opened his discourse with an appearance of unconcern, marking, however, very carefully, the effect of his communication upon young Ravenswood.

"You are aware," he said, "my young friend, that suspicion is the natural vice of our unsettled times, and exposes the best and wisest of us to the imposition of artful rascals. If I had been disposed to listen to such the other day, or even if I had been the wily politican which you have been taught to believe me, you, Master of Ravenswood, instead of being at freedom, and with full liberty to solicit and act against me as you please, in defence of what you suppose to be your rights, would have been in the Castle of Edinburgh, or some other state prison ; or, if you had escaped that destiny, it must have been by flight to a foreign country, and at the risk of a sentence of fugitation."

"My Lord Keeper," said the Master, "I think you would not jest on such a subject—yet it seems impossible you can be in earnest."

"Innocence," said the Lord Keeper, "is also confident, and sometimes, though very excusably, presumptuously so."

"I do not understand," said Ravenswood, "how a consciousness of innocence can be, in any case, accounted presumptuous."

"Imprudent, at least, it may be called," said Sir William Ashton, "since it is apt to lead us into the mistake of supposing that sufficiently evident to others, of which, in fact, we are only conscious ourselves. I have known a rogue, for this very reason, make a better defence than an innocent man could have done in the same circumstances of suspicion. Having no consciousness of innocence to support him, such a fellow applies himself to all the advantages which the law will afford him, and sometimes (if his counsel be men of talent) succeeds in compelling his judges to receive him as innocent. I remember the celebrated case of Sir Coolie Condiddle, of Condiddle, who was tried for theft under trust, of which all the world knew him guilty, and yet was not only acquitted, but lived to sit in judgment on honester folk."

"Allow me to beg you will return to the point," said the Master ; "you seemed to say that I had suffered under some suspicion."

"Suspicion, Master ?—ay, truly—and I can show you the proofs of it ; if I happen only to have them with me.—Here, Lockhard "—His attendant came—"Fetch me the little private mail with the padlocks, that I recommended to your particular charge—d'ye hear?"

"Yes, my lord." Lockhard vanished; and the Keeper continued, as if half speaking to himself.

"I think the papers are with me—I think so, for as I was to be in this country, it was natural for me to bring them with me. I have them, however, at Ravenswood Castle, that I am sure of—so perhaps you might condescend "——

Here Lockhard entered, and put the leathern scrutoire, or mail-box, into his hands. The Keeper produced one or two papers, respecting the information laid before the Privy Council concerning the riot, as it was termed, at the funeral of Allan Lord Ravenswood, and the active share he had himself taken in quashing the proceedings against the Master. These documents had been selected with care, so as to irritate the natural curiosity of Ravenswood upon such a subject, without gratifying it, yet to show that Sir William Ashton had acted upon that trying occasion the part of an advocate and peacemaker betwixt him and the jealous authorities of the day. Having furnished his host with such subjects for examination, the Lord Keeper went to the breakfast-table, and entered into light conversation, addressed partly to old Caleb, whose resentment against the usurper of the Castle of Ravenswood began to be softened by his familiarity, and partly to his daughter.

After perusing these papers, the Master of Ravenswood remained for a minute or two with his hand pressed against his brow, in deep and profound meditation. He then again ran his eye hastily over the papers, as if desirous of discovering in them some deep purpose, or some mark of fabrication, which had escaped him at first perusal. Apparently the second reading confirmed the opinion which had pressed upon him at the first, for he started from the stone bench on which he was sitting, and, going to the Lord Keeper, took his hand, and, strongly pressing it, asked his pardon repeatedly for the injustice he had done him, when it appeared he was experiencing, at his hands, the benefit of protection to his person, and vindication to his character.

The statesman received these acknowledgments at first with well-feigned surprise, and then with an affection of frank cordiality. The tears began already to start from Lucy's blue eyes at viewing this unexpected and moving scene. To see the Master, late so haughty and reserved, and whom she had always supposed the injured person, supplicating her father for forgiveness, was a change at once surprising, flattering, and affecting.

"Dry your eyes, Lucy," said her father; "why should you weep, because your father, though a lawyer, is discovered to be a fair and honourable man?—What have you to thank me for, my dear Master," he continued, addressing Ravenswood, "that you would not have done in my case? '*Suum cuique tribuito*,' was the Roman justice, and I learned it when I studied Justinian. Besides, have you not overpaid me a thousand times, in saving the life of this dear child?"

"Yes," answered the Master, in all the remorse of self-accusation; "but the little service *I* did was an act of mere brutal instinct; *your* defence of my cause, when you knew how ill I thought of you, and how much I was disposed to be your enemy, was an act of generous, manly, and considerate wisdom."

"Pshaw!" said the Lord Keeper, "each of us acted in his own way; you as a gallant soldier, I as an upright judge and privy-councillor. We could not, perhaps, have changed parts—at least I should have made a very sorry *Tauridor*, and you, my good Master, though your cause is so excellent, might have pleaded it perhaps worse yourself, than I who acted for you before the council.

"My generous friend!" said Ravenswood;—and with that brief word, which the Keeper had often lavished upon him, but which he himself now pronounced for the first time, he gave to his feudal enemy the full confidence of an haughty but honourable heart. The Master had been remarked among his contemporaries for sense and acuteness, as well as for his reserved, pertinacious, and irascible character. His prepossessions accordingly, however obstinate, were of a nature to give way before love and gratitude; and the real charms of the daughter, joined to the supposed services of the father, cancelled in his memory the vows of vengeance which he had taken so deeply on the eve of his father's funeral. But they had been heard and registered in the book of fate.

Caleb was present at this extraordinary scene, and he could conceive no other reason for a proceeding so extraordinary than an alliance betwixt the houses, and Ravenswood Castle assigned for the young lady's dowry. As for Lucy, when Ravenswood uttered the most passionate excuses for his ungrateful negligence, she could but smile through her tears, and, as she abandoned her hand to him, assure him, in broken accents, of the delight with which she beheld the complete reconciliation between her father and her deliverer. Even the statesman was moved and affected by the fiery, unreserved, and general self-abandonment with which the Master of Ravenswood renounced his feudal enmity, and threw himself without hesitation upon his forgiveness. His eyes glistened as he looked upon a couple who were obviously becoming attached, and who seemed made for each other. He thought how high the proud and chivalrous character of Ravenswood might rise under many circumstances, in which *he* found himself " overcrowed," to use a phrase of Spenser, and kept under, by his brief pedigree, and timidity of disposition. Then his daughter—his favourite child—his constant playmate— seemed formed to live happy in a union with such a commanding spirit as Ravenswood; and even the fine, delicate, fragile form of Lucy Ashton seemed to require the support of the Master's muscular strength and masculine character. And it was not merely during a few minutes that Sir William Ashton looked upon their marriage as a probable and even desirable event, for a full hour intervened ere his imagination was crossed by recollection of the Master's poverty, and the sure displeasure of Lady Ashton. It is certain, that the very unusual flow of kindly feeling with which the Lord Keeper had been thus surprised, was one of the circumstances which gave much tacit encouragement to the attachment between the Master and his daughter, and led both the lovers distinctly to believe that it was a connexion which would be most agreeable to him. He himself was supposed to have admitted this in effect, when, long after the catastrophe of their love, he used to warn his hearers against permitting their feelings to obtain an ascendancy over their judgment, and affirm, that the greatest misfortune of his life was owing to a very temporary predominance, of sensibility over self-interest.

It must be owned, if such was the case, he was long and severely punished for an offence of very brief duration.

After some pause, the Lord Keeper resumed the conversation.—"In your surprise at finding me an honester man than you expected, you have lost your curiosity about this Craigengelt, my good Master; and yet your name was brought in, in the course of that matter too."

"The scoundrel!" said Ravenswood; "my connexion with him was of the most temporary nature possible; and yet I was very foolish to hold any communication with him at all.—What did he say of me?"

"Enough," said the Keeper, "to excite the very loyal terrors of some of our sages, who are for proceeding against men on the mere grounds of suspicion or mercenary information.—Some nonsense about your proposing to enter into the service of France, or of the Pretender, I don't recollect which, but which the Marquis of A——, one of your best friends, and another person, whom some call one of your worst and most interested enemies, could not, somehow, be brought to listen to."

"I am obliged to my honourable friend—and yet"—shaking the Lord Keeper's hand—"and yet I am still more obliged to my honourable enemy."

"*Inimicus amicissimus*," said the Lord Keeper, returning the pressure; "but this gentleman—this Mr Hayston of Bucklaw—I am afraid the poor young man—I heard the fellow mention his name—is under very bad guidance."

"He is old enough to govern himself," answered the Master.

"Old enough, perhaps, but scarce wise enough, if he has chosen this fellow for his *fidus Achates*. Why, he had lodged an information against him—that is, such a consequence might have ensued from his examination, had we not looked rather at the character of the witness than the tenor of his evidence."

"Mr Hayston of Bucklaw," said the Master, "is, I believe, a most honourable man, and capable of nothing that is mean or disgraceful."

"Capable of much that is unreasonable, though; that you must needs allow, Master. Death will soon put him in possession of a fair estate, if he hath it not already; old Lady Girnington—an excellent person, excepting that her inveterate ill-nature rendered her intolerable to the whole world—is probably dead by this time. Six heirs portioners have successively died to make her wealthy. I know the estates well; they march[1] with my own—a noble property."

"I am glad of it," said Ravenswood, "and should be more so, were I confident that Bucklaw would change his company and habits with his fortunes. This appearance of Craigengelt, acting in the capacity of his friend, is a most vile augury for his future respectability."

"He is a bird of evil omen, to be sure," said the Keeper, "and croaks of jail and gallows-trees.—But I see Mr Caleb grows impatient for our return to breakfast."

CHAPTER XVIII

Sir, stay at home and take an old man's counsel;
Seek not to bask you by a stranger's hearth;
Our own blue smoke is warmer than their fire.
Domestic food is wholesome, though 'tis homely,
And foreign dainties poisonous, though tasteful.
                    The French Courtezan.

THE Master of Ravenswood took an opportunity to leave his guests to prepare for their departure, while he himself made the brief arrangements necessary previous to his absence from Wolf's Crag for a day or two. It was necessary to communicate with Caleb on this occasion, and he found that faithful servitor in his sooty and ruinous den, greatly delighted with the departure of their visitors, and computing how long, with good management, the provisions which had been unexpended might furnish forth the Master's table. "He's nae belly god, that's ae blessing; and Bucklaw's gane, that could have eaten a horse behind the saddle. Cresses or water-purpie, and a bit ait-cake, can serve the Master for breakfast as weel as Caleb. Then for dinner—there's no muckle left on the spule-bane; it will brander, though—it will brander very weel."

His triumphant calculations were interrupted by the Master, who communicated to him, not without some hesitation, his purpose to ride with the Lord Keeper as

[1] *i.e.* They are bounded by my own.

far as Ravenswood Castle, and to remain there for a day or two.

"The mercy of Heaven forbid!" said the old serving-man, turning as pale as the table-cloth which he was folding up.

"And why, Caleb?" said his master, "why should the mercy of Heaven forbid my returning the Lord Keeper's visit?"

"Oh, sir!" replied Caleb—"O Mr Edgar! I am your servant, and it ill becomes me to speak—but I am an auld servant—have served baith your father and gudesire, and mind to have seen Lord Randal, your great-grandfather—but that was when I was a bairn."

"And what of all this, Balderstone?" said the Master; "what can it possibly have to do with me paying some ordinary civility to a neighbour?"

"O Mr Edgar,—that is, my lord!" answered the butler, "your ain conscience tells you it isna for your father's son to be neighbouring wi' the like o' him—it isna for the credit of the family. An he were ance come to terms, and to gie ye back your ain, e'en though you suld honour his house wi' your alliance, I suldna say na—for the young leddy is a winsome sweet creature—But keep your ain state wi' them—I ken the race o' them weel—they will think the mair o' ye."

"Why, now, you go farther than I do, Caleb," said the Master, drowning a certain degree of consciousness in a forced laugh; "you are for marrying me into a family that you will not allow me to visit—how's this?—and you look as pale as death besides."

"O, sir," repeated Caleb again, "you would but laugh if I tauld it; but Thomas the Rhymer, whose tongue couldna be fause, spoke the word of your house that will e'en prove ower true if you go to Ravenswood this day—O, that it should e'er have been fulfilled in my time!"

"And what is it, Caleb?" said Ravenswood, wishing to soothe the fears of his old servant.

Caleb replied, "he had never repeated the lines to living mortal—they were told to him by an auld priest that had been confessor to Lord Allan's father when the family were catholic. But mony a time," he said, "I hae soughed thae dark words ower to mysell, and, well-a-day! little did I think of their coming round this day."

"Truce with your nonsense, and let me hear the doggerel which has put it into your head," said the Master, impatiently.

With a quivering voice, and a cheek pale with apprehension, Caleb faltered out the following lines:—

"When the last Laird of Ravenswood to Ravenswood shall ride,
  And woo a dead maiden to be his bride,
  He shall stable his steed in the Kelpie's flow,
  And his name shall be lost for evermoe!"

"I know the Kelpie's flow well enough," said the Master; "I suppose, at least, you mean the quicksand betwixt this tower and Wolf's-hope; but why any man in his senses should stable a steed there"——

"O never speer ony thing about that, sir—God forbid we should ken what the prophecy means—but just bide you at hame, and let the strangers ride to Ravenswood by themselves. We have done eneugh for them; and to do mair, would be mair against the credit of the family than in its favour."

"Well, Caleb," said the Master, "I give you the best possible credit for your good advice on this occasion; but as I do not go to Ravenswood to seek a bride, dead or alive, I hope I shall choose a better stable for my horse than the Kelpie's quicksand, and especially as I have always had a particular dread of it since the patrol of dragoons were lost there ten years since. My father and I saw them from the tower struggling against the advancing tide, and they were lost long before any help could reach them."

"And they deserved it weel, the southern loons!" said Caleb; "what had they ado capering on our sands, and hindering a wheen honest folk frae bringing on shore a drap brandy? I hae seen them that busy, that I wad hae fired the auld culverin, or the demisaker that's on the south bartizan at them; only I was feared they might burst in the ganging aff."

Caleb's brain was now fully engaged with abuse of the English soldiery and excisemen, so that his master found no great difficulty in escaping from him and rejoining his guests. All was now ready for their departure; and one of the Lord Keeper's grooms having saddled the Master's steed, they mounted in the court-yard.

Caleb had, with much toil, opened the double doors of the outward gate, and thereat stationed himself, endeavouring, by the reverential, and, at the same time, consequential air which he assumed, to supply, by his own gaunt, wasted, and thin person, the absence of a whole baronial establishment of porters, warders, and liveried menials.

The Keeper returned his deep reverence with a cordial farewell, stooping at the same time from his horse, and sliding into the butler's hand the remuneration, which in those days was always given by a departing guest to the domestics of the family where he had been entertained. Lucy smiled on the old man with her usual sweetness, bade him adieu, and deposited her guerdon with a grace of action, and a gentleness of accent, which could not have failed to have won the faithful retainer's heart, but for Thomas the Rhymer, and the successful lawsuit against his master. As it was, he might have adopted the language of the Duke, in *As You Like it*—

> "Thou wouldst have better pleased me with this deed,
> If thou hadst told me of another father."

Ravenswood was at the lady's bridle-rein, encouraging her timidity, and guiding her horse carefully down the rocky path which led to the moor, when one of the servants announced from the rear that Caleb was calling loudly after them, desiring to speak with his master. Ravenswood felt it would look singular to neglect this summons, although inwardly cursing Caleb for his impertinent officiousness; therefore he was compelled to relinquish to Mr Lockhard the agreeable duty in which he was engaged, and to ride back to the gate of the court-yard. Here he was beginning, somewhat peevishly, to ask Caleb the cause of his clamour, when the good old man exclaimed, "Whisht, sir! whisht, and let me speak just ae word that I couldna say afore folk —there "—(putting into his lord's hand the money he had just received)—"there's three gowd pieces—and ye'll want siller upby yonder—But stay, whisht now!"—for the Master was beginning to exclaim against this transference —"never say a word, but just see to get them changed in the first town ye ride through, for they are bran new frae the mint, and kenspeckle a wee bit."

"You forget, Caleb," said his master, striving to force

back the money on his servant, and extricate the bridle from his hold—"You forget that I have some gold pieces left of my own. Keep these to yourself, my old friend; and, once more, good day to you. I assure you I have plenty. You know you have managed that our living should cost us little or nothing."

"Aweel," said Caleb, "these will serve for you another time; but see ye hae eneugh, for, doubtless, for the credit of the family, there maun be some civility to the servants, and ye maun hae something to mak a show with when they say, Master, will you bet a broad piece? Then ye maun tak out your purse, and say, I carena if I do; and tak care no to agree on the articles of the wager, and just put up your purse again, and"——

"This is intolerable, Caleb—I really must be gone."

"And you will go, then?" said Caleb, loosening his hold upon the Master's cloak, and changing his didactics into a pathetic and mournful tone—"And you *will* go, for a' I have told you about the prophecy, and the dead bride, and the Kelpie's quicksand?—Aweel! a wilful man maun hae his way—he that will to Cupar maun to Cupar. But pity of your life, sir, if ye be fowling or shooting in the Park—beware of drinking at the Mermaiden's well——He's gane! he's down the path, arrow-flight after her!—The head is as clean taen aff the Ravenswood family this day, as I wad chap the head aff a sybo!"

The old butler looked long after his master, often clearing away the dew as it rose to his eyes, that he might, as long as possible, distinguish his stately form from those of the other horsemen. "Close to her bridle-rein—ay, close to her bridle-rein!—Wisely saith the holy man, 'By this also you may know that woman hath dominion over all men;'—and without this lass would not our ruin have been a'thegither fulfilled."

With a heart fraught with such sad auguries did Caleb return to his necessary duties at Wolf's Crag, as soon as he could no longer distinguish the object of his anxiety among the group of riders, which diminished in the distance.

In the meantime the party pursued their roue joyfully. Having once taken his resolution, the Master of Ravenswood was not of a character to hesitate or pause upon it. He abandoned himself to the pleasure he felt in Miss

Ashton's company, and displayed an assiduous gallantry, which approached as nearly to gaiety as the temper of his mind and state of his family permitted. The Lord Keeper was much struck with his depth of observation, and the unusual improvement which he had derived from his studies. Of these accomplishments Sir William Ashton's profession and habits of society rendered him an excellent judge; and he well knew how to appreciate a quality to which he himself was a total stranger,—the brief and decided dauntlessness of the Master of Ravenswood's disposition, who seemed equally a stranger to doubt and to fear. In his heart the Lord Keeper rejoiced at having conciliated an adversary so formidable, while, with a mixture of pleasure and anxiety, he anticipated the great things his young companion might achieve, were the breath of court-favour to fill his sails.

"What could she desire," he thought, his mind always conjuring up opposition in the person of Lady Ashton to his now prevailing wish—"What could a woman desire in a match, more than the sopiting of a very dangerous claim, and the alliance of a son-in-law, noble, brave, well-gifted, and highly connected—sure to float whenever the tide sets his way—strong, exactly where we are weak, in pedigree and in the temper of a swordsman?—Sure no reasonable woman would hesitate.—But, alas!"—Here this argument was stopped by the consciousness that Lady Ashton was not always reasonable, in his sense of the word. "To prefer some clownish Merse laird to the gallant young nobleman, and to the secure possession of Ravenswood upon terms of easy compromise—it would be the act of a madwoman!"

Thus pondered the veteran politician, until they reached Bittlebrains' House, where it had been previously settled they were to dine and repose themselves, and prosecute their journey in the afternoon.

They were received with an excess of hospitality; and the most marked attention was offered to the Master of Ravenswood, in particular, by their noble entertainers. The truth, was, that Lord Bittlebrains had obtained his peerage by a good deal of plausibility, an art of building up a character for wisdom upon a very trite style of commonplace eloquence, a steady observation of the changes of the times, and the power of rendering certain political services to those who could best reward them. His lady and he, not feeling quite easy under their new honours, to which use had not adapted their feelings, were very desirous to procure the fraternal countenance of those who were born denizens of the regions into which they had been exalted from a lower sphere. The extreme attention which they paid to the Master of Ravenswood, had its usual effect in exalting his importance in the eyes of the Lord Keeper, who, although he had a reasonable degree of contempt for Lord Bittlebrains' general parts, entertained a high opinion of the acuteness of his judgment in all matters of self-interest.

"I wish Lady Ashton had seen this," was his internal reflection; "no man knows so well as Bittlebrains on which side his bread is buttered; and he fawns on the Master like a beggar's messan on a cook. And my lady, too, bringing forward her beetle-browed misses to skirl and play upon the virginals, as if she said, pick and choose. They are no more comparable to Lucy than an owl is to a cygnet, and so they may carry their black brows to a farther market."

The entertainment being ended, our travellers, who had still to measure the longest part of their journey, resumed their horses; and after the Lord Keeper, the Master, and the domestics, had drunk *doch-an-dorroch*, or the stirrup-cup, in the liquors adapted to their various ranks, the cavalcade resumed its progress.

It was dark by the time they entered the avenue of Ravenswood Castle, a long straight line leading directly to the front of the house, flanked with huge elm-trees, which sighed to the night-wind, as if they compassionated the heir of their ancient proprietors, who now returned to their shades in the society, and almost in the retinue, of their new master. Some feelings of the same kind oppressed the mind of the Master himself. He gradually became silent, and dropped a little behind the lady, at whose bridle-rein he had hitherto waited with such devotion. He well recollected the period, when, at the same hour in the evening, he had accompanied his father, as that nobleman left, never again to return to it, the mansion from which he derived his name and title. The extensive front of the old castle, on which he remembered having often looked back,

was then "as black as mourning weed." The same front
now glanced with many lights, some throwing far forward
into the night a fixed and stationary blaze, and others
hurrying from one window to another, intimating the bustle
and busy preparation preceding their arrival, which had
been intimated by an avant-courier. The contrast pressed
so strongly upon the Master's heart, as to awaken some of
the sterner feelings with which he had been accustomed to
regard the new lord of his paternal domain, and to impress
his countenance with an air of severe gravity, when, alighted
from his horse, he stood in the hall no longer his own,
surrounded by the numerous menials of its present owner.

The Lord Keeper, when about to welcome him with the
cordiality which their late intercourse seemed to render
proper, became aware of the change, refrained from his
purpose, and only intimated the ceremony of reception by
a deep reverence to his guest, seeming thus delicately to
share the feelings which predominated on his brow.

Two upper.domestics, bearing each a huge pair of silver
candlesticks, now marshalled the company into a large
saloon, or withdrawing room, where new alterations
impressed upon Ravenswood the superior wealth of the
present inhabitants of the castle. The mouldering tapestry,
which, in his father's time, had half covered the walls of
this stately apartment, and half streamed from them in
tatters, had given place to a complete finishing of wainscot,
the cornice of which, as well as the frames of the various
compartments, were ornamented with festoons of flowers
and with birds, which, though carved in oak, seemed, such
was the art of the chisel, actually to swell their throats, and
flutter their wings. Several old family portraits of armed
heroes of the house of Ravenswood, together with a suit or
two of old armour, and some military weapons, had given
place to those of King William and Queen Mary, of Sir
Thomas Hope and Lord Stair, two distinguished Scottish
lawyers. The pictures of the Lord Keeper's father and
mother were also to be seen; the latter, sour, shrewish,
and solemn, in her black hood and close pinners, with a
book of devotion in her hand; the former, exhibiting
beneath a black silk Geneva cowl, or skull-cap, which sate
as close to the head as if it had been shaven, a pinched,
peevish, puritanical set of features, terminating in a hungry,

reddish, peaked beard, forming on the whole a countenance, in the expression of which the hypocrite seemed to contend with the miser and the knave. And it is to make room for such scarecrows as these, thought Ravenswood, that my ancestors have been torn down from the walls which they erected! He looked at them again, and, as he looked, the recollection of Lucy Ashton (for she had not entered the apartment with them) seemed less lively in his imagination. There were also two or three Dutch drolleries, as the pictures of Ostade and Teniers were then termed, with one good painting of the Italian school. There was, besides, a noble full-length of the Lord Keeper in his robes of office, placed beside his lady in silk and ermine. a haughty beauty, bearing in her looks all the pride of the House of Douglas, from which she was descended. The painter, notwithstanding his skill, overcome by the reality, or, perhaps, from a suppressed sense of humour, had not been able to give the husband on the canvas that air of awful rule and right supremacy, which indicates the full possession of domestic authority. It was obvious, at the first glance, that, despite mace and gold frogs, the Lord Keeper was somewhat henpecked. The floor of this fine saloon was laid with rich carpets, huge fires blazed in the double chimneys, and ten silver sconces, reflecting with their bright plates the lights which they supported, made the whole seem as brilliant as day.

"Would you choose any refreshment, Master?" said Sir William Ashton, not unwilling to break the awkward silence

He received no answer, the Master being so busily engaged in marking the various changes which had taken place in the apartment, that he hardly heard the Lord Keeper address him. A repetition of the offer of refreshment, with the addition, that the family meal would be presently ready, compelled his attention, and reminded him, that he acted a weak, perhaps even a ridiculous part, in suffering himself to be overcome by the circumstances in which he found himself. He compelled himself, therefore, to enter into conversation with Sir William Ashton, with as much appearance of indifference as he could well command.

"You will not be surprised, Sir William, that I am interested in the changes you have made for the better in this apartment. In my father's time, after our misfortunes compelled him to live in retirement, it was little used, except by me as a playroom, when the weather would not permit me to go abroad. In that recess was my little workshop, where I treasured the few carpenter's tools which old Caleb procured for me, and taught me how to use—there, in yonder corner, under that handsome silver sconce, I kept my fishing-rods, and hunting poles, bows, and arrows."

" I have a young birkie," said the Lord Keeper, willing to change the tone of the conversation, "of much the same turn—He is never happy, save when he is in the field—I wonder he is not here.—Here, Lockhard—send William Shaw for Mr Henry—I suppose he is, as usual, tied to Lucy's apron string—that foolish girl, Master, draws the whole family after her at her pleasure."

Even this allusion to his daughter, though artfully thrown out, did not recall Ravenswood from his own topic.

" We were obliged to leave," he said, "some armour and portraits in this apartment—may I ask where they have been removed to? "

" Why," answered the Keeper, with some hesitation, "the room was fitted up in our absence—and *cedant arma togæ*, is the maxim of lawyers, you know—I am afraid it has been here somewhat too literally complied with. I hope—I believe they are safe—I am sure I gave orders—may I hope that when they are recovered, and put in proper order, you will do me the honour to accept them at my hand, as an atonement for their accidental derangement? "

The Master of Ravenswood bowed stiffly, and, with folded arms, again resumed his survey of the room.

Henry, a spoilt boy of fifteen, burst into the room, and ran up to his father. " Think of Lucy, papa; she has come home so cross and so fractious, that she will not go down to the stable to see my new pony, that Bob Wilson brought from the Mull of Galloway."

" I think you were very unreasonable to ask her," said the Keeper.

" Then you are as cross as she is," answered the boy; " but when mamma comes home, she'll claw up both your mittens."

" Hush your impertinence, you little forward imp! " said his father; "where is your tutor? "

" Gone to a wedding at Dunbar—I hope he'll get a haggis

to his dinner;" and he began to sing the old Scottish
song,—

> "There was a haggis in Dunbar
> > Fal de ral, &c.
> Mony better and few waur,
> > Fal de ral," &c.

"I am much obliged to Mr Cordery for his attentions,"
said the Lord Keeper; "and pray who has had the charge
of you while I was away, Mr Henry?"

"Norman and Bob Wilson—forby my own self."

"A groom and a gamekeeper, and your own silly self—
proper guardians for a young advocate!—Why, you will
never know any statutes but those against shooting red-
deer, killing salmon, and "——

"And speaking of red-game," said the young scape-grace,
interrupting his father without scruple or hesitation, "Norman has shot a buck, and I showed the branches to Lucy, and
she says they have but eight tynes; and she says that you
killed a deer with Lord Bittlebrains's hounds, when you
were west away, and, do you know, she says it had ten
tynes—is it true?"

"It may have had twenty, Henry, for what I know; but
if you go to that gentleman, he can tell you all about it—
Go speak to him, Henry—it is the Master of Ravenswood."

While they conversed thus, the father and son were
standing by the fire; and the Master having walked towards the upper end of the apartment, stood with his back
towards them, apparently engaged in examining one of the
paintings. The boy ran up to him, and pulled him by the
skirt of the coat with the freedom of a spoilt child, saying,
"I say, sir—if you please to tell me"——but when the
Master turned round, and Henry saw his face, he became
suddenly and totally disconcerted—walked two or three
steps backward, and still gazed on Ravenswood with an air
of fear and wonder, which had totally banished from his
features their usual expression of pert vivacity.

"Come to me, young gentleman," said the Master, "and
I will tell you all I know about the hunt."

"Go to the gentleman, Henry," said his father; "you
are not used to be so shy."

But neither invitation nor exhortation had any effect on
the boy. On the contrary, he turned round as soon as he

had completed his survey of the Master, and walking as cautiously as if he had been treading upon eggs, he glided back to his father, and pressed as close to him as possible. Ravenswood, to avoid hearing the dispute betwixt the father and the over-indulged boy, thought it most polite to turn his face once more towards the pictures, and pay no attention to what they said.

"Why do you not speak to the Master, you little fool?" said the Lord Keeper.

"I am afraid," said Henry, in a very low tone of voice.

"Afraid, you goose!" said his father, giving him a slight shake by the collar,—"What makes you afraid?"

"What makes him so like the picture of Sir Malise Ravenswood, then?" said the boy, whispering.

"What picture, you natural?" said his father. "I used to think you only a scape-grace, but I believe you will turn out a born idiot."

"I tell you it is the picture of old Malise of Ravenswood, and he is as like it as if he had loupen out of the canvas; and it is up in the old Baron's hall that the maids launder the clothes in, and it has armour, and not a coat like the gentleman—and he has not a beard and whiskers like the picture—and it has another kind of thing about the throat, and no band-strings as he has—and "——

"And why should not the gentleman be like his ancestor, you silly boy?" said the Lord Keeper.

"Ay; but if he is come to chase us all out of the castle," said the boy, "and has twenty men at his back in disguise— and is come to say, with a hollow voice, *I bide my time*— and is to kill you on the hearth as Malise did the other man, and whose blood is still to be seen!"

"Hush! nonsense!" said the Lord Keeper, not himself much pleased to hear these disagreeable coincidences forced on his notice.—"Master, here comes Lockhard to say supper is served."

And, at the same instant, Lucy entered at another door, having changed her dress since her return. The exquisite feminine beauty of her countenance, now shaded only by a profusion of sunny tresses; the sylph-like form disencumbered of her heavy riding-skirt, and mantled in azure silk; the grace of her manner and of her smile, cleared, with a celerity which surprised the Master himself, all the gloomy

and unfavourable thoughts which had for some time overclouded his fancy. In those features, so simply sweet, he
could trace no alliance with the pinched visage of the peak-
bearded, black-capped puritan, or his starched withered
spouse, with the craft expressed in the Lord Keeper's
countenance, or the haughtiness which predominated in
that of his lady; and, while he gazed on Lucy Ashton, she
seemed to be an angel descended on earth, unallied to the
coarser mortals among whom she deigned to dwell for a
season. Such is the power of beauty over a youthful and
enthusiastic fancy.

CHAPTER XIX

————————I do too ill in this,
And must not think but that a parent's plaint
Will move the heavens to pour forth misery
Upon the head of disobediency.
Yet reason tells us, parents are o'erseen,
When with too strict a rein they do hold in
Their child's affection, and control that love
Which the high powers divine inspire them with.
               The Hog hath lost his Pearl.

THE feast of Ravenswood Castle was as remarkable for its
profusion, as that of Wolf's Crag had been for its ill-veiled
penury. The Lord Keeper might feel internal pride at the
contrast, but he had too much tact to suffer it to appear.
On the contrary, he seemed to remember with pleasure
what he called Mr Balderstone's bachelor's meal, and to be
rather disgusted than pleased with the display upon his
own groaning board.

"We do these things," he said, "because others do them
—but I was bred a plain man at my father's frugal table,
and I should like well would my wife and family permit me
to return to my sowens and my poor-man-of-mutton."[1]

This was a little overstretched. The Master only
answered, "That different ranks — I mean," said he,
correcting himself, "different degrees of wealth require a
different style of housekeeping."

This dry remark put a stop to further conversation on
the subject, nor is it necessary to record that which was

[1] Note IV.—Poor-Man-of-Mutton.

substituted in its place. The evening was spent with freedom, and even cordiality; and Henry had so far overcome his first apprehensions, that he had settled a party for coursing a stag with the representative and living resemblance of grim Sir Malise of Ravenswood, called the Revenger. The next morning was the appointed time. It rose upon active sportsmen and successful sport. The banquet came in course; and a pressing invitation to tarry yet another day was given and accepted. This Ravenswood had resolved should be the last of his stay; but he recollected he had not yet visited the ancient and devoted servant of his house, old Alice, and it was but kind to dedicate one morning to the gratification of so ancient an adherent.

To visit Alice, therefore, a day was devoted, and Lucy was the Master's guide upon the way. Henry, it is true, accompanied them, and took from their walk the air of a *tête-à-tête*, while, in reality, it was little else, considering the variety of circumstances which occurred to prevent the boy from giving the least attention to what passed between his companions. Now a rook settled on a branch within shot —anon a hare crossed their path, and Henry and his greyhound went astray in pursuit of it—then he had to hold a long conversation with the forester, which detained him a while behind his companions—and again he went to examine the earth of a badger, which carried him on a good way before them.

The conversation betwixt the Master and his sister, meanwhile, took an interesting, and almost a confidential turn. She could not help mentioning her sense of the pain he must feel in visiting scenes so well known to him, bearing now an aspect so different; and so gently was her sympathy expressed, that Ravenswood felt it for a moment as a full requital of all his misfortunes. Some such sentiment escaped him, which Lucy heard with more of confusion than displeasure; and she may be forgiven the imprudence of listening to such language, considering that the situation in which she was placed by her father seemed to authorise Ravenswood to use it. Yet she made an effort to turn the conversation, and she succeeded; for the Master also had advanced farther than he intended, and his conscience had instantly checked him when he found himself on the verge of speaking of love to the daughter of Sir William Ashton.

They now approached the hut of old Alice, which had of late been rendered more comfortable, and presented an appearance less picturesque, perhaps, but far neater than before. The old woman was on her accustomed seat beneath the weeping birch, basking, with the listless enjoyment of age and infirmity, in the beams of the autumn sun. At the arrival of her visitors she turned her head towards them. "I hear your step, Miss Ashton," she said, "but the gentleman who attends you is not my lord, your father."

"And why should you think so, Alice?" said Lucy; "or how is it possible for you to judge so accurately by the sound of a step, on this firm earth, and in the open air?"

"My hearing, my child, has been sharpened by my blindness, and I can now draw conclusions from the slightest sounds, which formerly reached my ears as unheeded as they now approach yours. Necessity is a stern, but an excellent schoolmistress, and she that has lost her sight must collect her information from other sources."

"Well, you hear a man's step, I grant it," said Lucy; "but why, Alice, may it not be my father's?"

"The pace of age, my love, is timid and cautious—the foot takes leave of the earth slowly, and is planted down upon it with hesitation; it is the hasty and determined step of youth that I now hear, and—could I give credit to so strange a thought—I should say it was the step of a Ravenswood."

"This is indeed," said Ravenswood, "an acuteness of organ which I could not have credited had I not witnessed it.—I am indeed the Master of Ravenswood, Alice—the son of your old master."

"You?" said the old woman, with almost a scream of surprise—"you the Master of Ravenswood—here—in this place, and thus accompanied?—I cannot believe it—Let me pass my old hand over your face, that my touch may bear witness to my ears."

The Master sate down beside her on the earthen bank, and permitted her to touch his features with her trembling hand.

"It is indeed!" she said, "it is the features as well as the voice of Ravenswood—the high lines of pride, as well as the bold and haughty tone.—But what do you here,

Master of Ravenswood?—what do you in your enemy's domain, and in company with his child?"

As old Alice spoke, her face kindled, as probably that of an ancient feudal vassal might have done, in whose presence his youthful liege-lord had showed some symptom of degenerating from the spirit of his ancestors.

"The Master of Ravenswood," said Lucy, who liked not the tone of this expostulation, and was desirous to abridge it, "is upon a visit to my father."

"Indeed!" said the old blind woman, in an accent of surprise.

"I knew," continued Lucy, "I should do him a pleasure by conducting him to your cottage."

"Where, to say the truth, Alice," said Ravenswood, "I expected a more cordial reception."

"It is most wonderful!" said the old woman, muttering to herself; "but the ways of Heaven are not like our ways, and its judgments are brought about by means far beyond our fathoming.—Hearken, young man," she said; "your fathers were implacable, but they were honourable foes; they sought not to ruin their enemies under the mask of hospitality.   What have you to do with Lucy Ashton?—why should your steps move in the same footpath with hers?— why should your voice sound in the same chord and time with those of Sir William Ashton's daughter?—Young man, he who aims at revenge by dishonourable means "——

"Be silent, woman!" said Ravenswood, sternly; "is it the devil that prompts your voice?—Know that this young lady has not on earth a friend, who would venture farther to save her from injury or from insult."

"And is it even so?" said the old woman, in an altered but melancholy tone—"Then God help you both!"

"Amen! Alice," said Lucy, who had not comprehended the import of what the blind woman had hinted, "and send you your senses, Alice, and your good-humour. If you hold this mysterious language, instead of welcoming your friends, they will think of you as other people do."

"And how do other people think?" said Ravenswood, for he also began to believe the old woman spoke with incoherence.

"They think," said Henry Ashton, who came up at that moment, and whispered into Ravenswood's ear; "that sh is a witch, that should have been burned with them that suffered at Haddington."

"What is that you say?" said Alice, turning towards the boy, her sightless visage inflamed with passion; "that I am a witch, and ought to have suffered with the helpless old wretches who were murdered at Haddington?"

"Here to that now," again whispered Henry, "and me whispering lower than a wren cheeps!"

"If the usurer, and the oppressor, and the grinder of the poor man's face, and the remover of ancient land-marks, and the subverter of ancient houses, were at the same stake with me, I could say, light the fire, in God's name!"

"This is dreadful," said Lucy; "I have never seen the poor deserted woman in this state of mind; but age and poverty can ill bear reproach.—Come, Henry, we will leave her for the present—she wishes to speak to the Master alone. We will walk homeward, and rest us," she added, looking at Ravenswood, "by the Mermaiden's Well."

"And Alice," said the boy, "if you know of any hare that comes through among the deer, and makes them drop their calves out of season, you may tell her, with my compliments to command, that if Norman has not got a silver bullet ready for her, I'll lend him one of my doublet-buttons on purpose."

Alice made no answer till she was aware that the sister and brother were out of hearing. She then said to Ravenswood, "And you, too, are angry with me for my love?—it is just that strangers should be offended, but you, too, are angry!"

"I am not angry, Alice," said the Master, "only surprised that you, whose good sense I have heard so often praised, should give way to offensive and unfounded suspicions."

"Offensive?" said Alice—"Ay, truth is ever offensive—but, surely, not unfounded."

"I tell you, dame, most groundless," replied Ravenswood.

"Then the world has changed its wont, and the Ravenswoods their hereditary temper, and the eyes of Old Alice's understanding are yet more blind than those of her countenance. When did a Ravenswood seek the house of his enemy, but with the purpose of revenge?—and hither are you come, Edgar Ravenswood, either in fatal anger, or in still more fatal love."

"In neither," said Ravenswood, "I give you mine honour —I mean, I assure you."

Alice could not see his blushing cheek, but she noticed his hesitation, and that he retracted the pledge which he seemed first disposed to attach to his denial.

"It is so, then," she said, "and therefore she is to tarry by the Mermaiden's Well! Often has it been called a place fatal to the race of Ravenswood—often has it proved so— but never was it likely to verify old sayings as much as on this day."

"You drive me to madness, Alice," said Ravenswood; "you are more silly and more superstitious than old Balderstone. Are you such a wretched Christian as to suppose I would in the present day levy war against the Ashton family, as was the sanguinary custom in elder times? or do you suppose me so foolish, that I cannot walk by a young lady's side without plunging headlong in love with her?"

"My thoughts," replied Alice, "are my own; and if my mortal sight is closed to objects present with me, it may be I can look with more steadiness into future events. Are you prepared to sit lowest at the board which was once your father's own, unwillingly, as a connexion and ally of his proud successor?—Are you ready to live on his bounty —to follow him in the bypaths of intrigue and chicane, which none can better point out to you—to gnaw the bones of his prey when he has devoured the substance?—Can you say as Sir William Ashton says—think as he thinks—vote as he votes, and call your father's murderer your worshipful father-in-law and revered patron?—Master of Ravenswood, I am the eldest servant of your house, and I would rather see you shrouded and coffined!"

The tumult in Ravenswood's mind was uncommonly great; she struck upon and awakened a chord which he had for some time successfully silenced. He strode backwards and forwards through the little garden with a hasty pace; and at length checking himself, and stopping right opposite to Alice, he exclaimed, "Woman! on the verge of the grave, dare you urge the son of your master to blood and to revenge?"

"God forbid!" said Alice solemnly; "and therefore I would have you depart these fatal bounds, where your love, as well as your hatred, threatens sure mischief, or at least disgrace, both to yourself and others. I would shield, were it in the power of this withered hand, the Ashtons from you, and you from them, and both from their own passions. You can have nothing—ought to have nothing, in common with them—Begone from among them; and if God has destined vengeance on the oppressor's house, do not you be the instrument."

"I will think on what you have said, Alice," said Ravenswood, more composedly. "I believe you mean truly and faithfully by me, but you urge the freedom of an ancient domestic somewhat too far. But farewell; and if Heaven afford me better means, I will not fail to contribute to your comfort."

He attempted to put a piece of gold into her hand, which she refused to receive; and, in the slight struggle attending his wish to force it upon her, it dropped to the earth.

"Let it remain an instant on the ground," said Alice, as the Master stooped to raise it; "and believe me, that piece of gold is an emblem of her whom you love; she is as precious, I grant, but you must stoop even to abasement before you can win her. For me, I have as little to do with gold as with earthly passions; and the best news that the world has in store for me is, that Edgar Ravenswood is an hundred miles distant from the seat of his ancestors, with the determination never again to behold it.

"Alice," said the Master, who began to think this earnestness had some more secret cause than arose from any thing that the blind woman could have gathered from this casual visit, "I have heard you praised by my mother for your sense, acuteness, and fidelity; you are no fool to start at shadows, or to dread old superstitious saws, like Caleb Balderstone; tell me distinctly where my danger lies, if you are aware of any which is tending towards me. If I know myself I am free from all such views respecting Miss Ashton as you impute to me. I have necessary business to settle with Sir William—that arranged, I shall depart; and with as little wish, as you may easily believe, to return to a place full of melancholy subjects of reflection, as you have to see me here."

Alice bent her sightless eyes on the ground, and was for some time plunged in deep meditation. " I will speak the truth," she said at length, raising up her head—" I will tell you the source of my apprehensions, whether my candour be for good or for evil.—Lucy Ashton loves you, Lord of Ravenswood !"

" It is impossible," said the Master.

" A thousand circumstances have proved it to me," replied the blind woman. " Her thoughts have turned on no one else since you saved her from death, and that my experienced judgment has won from her own conversation. Having told you this—if you are indeed a gentleman and your father's son—you will make it a motive for flying from her presence. Her passion will die like a lamp, for want of that the flame should feed upon ; but, if you remain here, her destruction or yours, or that of both, will be the inevitable consequence of her misplaced attachment. I tell you this secret unwillingly, but it could not have been hid long from your own observation ; and it is better you learn it from mine. Depart, Master of Ravenswood—you have my secret. If you remain an hour under Sir William Ashton's roof without the resolution to marry his daughter, you are a villain—if with the purpose of allying yourself with him, you are an infatuated and predestined fool."

So saying, the old blind woman arose, assumed her staff, and, tottering to her hut, entered it and closed the door, leaving Ravenswood to his own reflections.

CHAPTER XX

Lovelier in her own retired abode
——— than Naiad by the side
Of Grecian brook—or Lady of the Mere
Lone sitting by the shores of old romance.
Wordsworth.

THE meditations of Ravenswood were of a very mixed complexion. He saw himself at once in the very dilemma which he had for some time felt apprehensive he might be placed in. The pleasure he felt in Lucy's company had indeed approached to fascination, yet it had never altogether surmounted his internal reluctance to wed with the daughter

of his father's foe ; and even in forgiving Sir William Ashton
the injuries which his family had received, and giving him
credit for the kind intentions he professed to entertain, he
could not bring himself to contemplate as possible an
alliance betwixt their houses.   Still he felt that Alice spoke
truth, and that his honour now required he should take an
instant leave of Ravenswood Castle, or become a suitor
of Lucy Ashton.   The possibility of being rejected, too,
should he make advances to her wealthy and powerful
father—to sue for the hand of an Ashton and be refused—
this were a consummation too disgraceful.   "I wish her
well," he said to himself, "and for her sake I forgive the
injuries her father has done to my house ; but I will never
—no, never see her more !"

With one bitter pang he adopted this resolution, just as
he came to where two paths parted ; the one to the
Mermaiden's Fountain, where he knew Lucy waited him,
the other leading to the castle by another and more circuitous road.   He paused an instant when about to take the
latter path, thinking what apology he should make for
conduct which must needs seem extraordinary, and had
just muttered to himself, "Sudden news from Edinburgh—
any pretext will serve—only let me dally no longer here,"
when young Henry came flying up to him, half out of
breath—"Master, Master, you must give Lucy your arm
back to the castle, for I cannot give her mine ; for Norman
is waiting for me, and I am to go with him to make his
ringwalk, and I would not stay away for a gold Jacobus,
and Lucy is afraid to walk home alone, though all the
wild nowt have been shot, and so you must come away
directly."

Betwixt two scales equally loaded, a feather's weight
will turn the scale.   "It is impossible for me to leave the
young lady in the wood alone," said Ravenswood ; "to see
her once more can be of little consequence, after the frequent meetings we have had—I ought, too, in courtesy, to
apprise her of my intention to quit the castle."

And having thus satisfied himself that he was taking not
only a wise, but an absolutely necessary step, he took the
path to the fatal fountain.   Henry no sooner saw him on
the way to join his sister, than he was off like lightning in
another direction, to enjoy the society of the forester in

their congenial pursuits. Ravenswood, not allowing himself to give a second thought to the propriety of his own conduct, walked with a quick step towards the stream, where he found Lucy seated alone by the ruin.

She sate upon one of the disjointed stones of the ancient fountain, and seemed to watch the progress of its current, as it bubbled forth to daylight, in gay and sparkling profusion, from under the shadow of the ribbed and darksome vault, with which veneration, or perhaps remorse, had canopied its source. To a superstitious eye, Lucy Ashton, folded in her plaited mantle, with her long hair, escaping partly from the snood and falling upon her silver neck, might have suggested the idea of the murdered Nymph of the Fountain. But Ravenswood only saw a female exquisitely beautiful, and rendered yet more so in his eyes—how could it be otherwise—by the consciousness that she had placed her affections on him. As he gazed on her, he felt his fixed resolution melting like wax in the sun, and hastened, therefore, from his concealment in the neighbouring thicket. She saluted him, but did not arise from the stone on which she was seated.

"My mad-cap brother," she said, "has left me, but I expect him back in a few minutes—for fortunately, as any thing pleases him for a minute, nothing has charms for him much longer."

Ravenswood did not feel the power of informing Lucy that her brother meditated a distant excursion, and would not return in haste. He sate himself down on the grass, at some little distance from Miss Ashton, and both were silent for a short space.

"I like this spot," said Lucy at length, as if she had found the silence embarrassing; "the bubbling murmur of the clear fountain, the waving of the trees, the profusion of grass and wild-flowers, that rise among the ruins, make it like a scene in romance. I think, too, I have heard it is a spot connected with the legendary lore which I love so well."

"It has been thought," answered Ravenswood, "a fatal spot to my family; and I have some reason to term it so, for it was here I first saw Miss Ashton—and it is here I must take my leave of her for ever."

The blood, which the first part of this speech called into Lucy's cheeks, was speedily expelled by its conclusion.

"To take leave of us, Master!" she exclaimed; "what can have happened to hurry you away?—I know Alice hates—I mean dislikes my father—and I hardly understood her humour to-day, it was so mysterious. But I am certain my father is sincerely grateful for the high service you rendered us. Let me hope that having won your friendship hardly, we shall not lose it lightly."

"Lose it, Miss Ashton?" said the Master of Ravenswood,—"No—wherever my fortune calls me—whatever she inflicts upon me—it is your friend—your sincere friend—who acts or suffers. But there is a fate on me, and I must go, or I shall add the ruin of others to my own."

"Yet do not go from us, Master," said Lucy; and she laid her hand, in all simplicity and kindness, upon the skirt of his cloak, as if to detain him—"You shall not part from us. My father is powerful, he has friends that are more so than himself—do not go till you see what his gratitude will do for you. Believe me, he is already labouring in your behalf with the Council."

"It may be so," said the Master, proudly; "yet it is not to your father, Miss Ashton, but to my own exertions, that I ought to owe success in the career on which I am about to enter. My preparations are already made—a sword and a cloak, and a bold heart and a determined hand."

Lucy covered her face with her hands, and the tears, in spite of her, forced their way between her fingers. "Forgive me," said Ravenswood, taking her right hand, which, after slight resistance, she yielded to him, still continuing to shade her face with the left—"I am too rude—too rough—too intractable to deal with any being so soft and gentle as you are. Forget that so stern a vision has crossed your path of life—and let me pursue mine, sure that I can meet with no worse misfortune after the moment it divides me from your side."

Lucy wept on, but her tears were less bitter. Each attempt which the Master made to explain his purpose of departure, only proved a new evidence of his desire to stay; until, at length, instead of bidding her farewell, he gave his faith to her for ever, and received her troth in return. The whole passed so suddenly, and arose so much out of the immediate impulse of the moment, that ere the Master of

Ravenswood could reflect upon the consequences of the step which he had taken, their lips, as well as their hands, had pledged the sincerity of their affection.

"And now," he said, after a moment's consideration, "it is fit I should speak to Sir William Ashton—he must know of our engagement. Ravenswood must not seem to dwell under his roof, to solicit clandestinely the affections of his daughter."

"You would not speak to my father on the subject?" said Lucy, doubtingly, and then added more warmly, "O do not—do not! Let your lot in life be determined—your station and purpose ascertained, before you address my father; I am sure he loves you—I think he will consent—but then my mother!"——

She paused, ashamed to express the doubt she felt how far her father dared to form any positive resolution on this most important subject, without the consent of his lady.

"Your mother, my Lucy?" replied Ravenswood, "she is of the house of Douglas, a house that has intermarried with mine, even when its glory and power were at the highest—what could your mother object to my alliance?"

"I did not say object," said Lucy; "but she is jealous of her rights, and may claim a mother's title to be consulted in the first instance."

"Be it so," replied Ravenswood; "London is distant, but a letter will reach it and receive an answer within a fortnight—I will not press on the Lord Keeper for an instant reply to my proposal."

"But," hesitated Lucy, "were it not better to wait—to wait a few weeks?—Were my mother to see you—to know you—I am sure she would approve; but you are unacquainted personally, and the ancient feud between the families "——

Ravenswood fixed upon her his keen dark eyes, as if he was desirous of penetrating into her very soul.

"Lucy," he said, "I have sacrificed to you projects of vengeance long nursed, and sworn to with ceremonies little better than heathen—I sacrificed them to your image, ere I knew the worth which it represented. In the evening which succeeded my poor father's funeral, I cut a lock from my hair, and, as it consumed in the fire, I swore that my rage and revenge should pursue his enemies, until they shrivelled before me like that scorched-up symbol of annihilation."

"It was a deadly sin," said Lucy, turning pale, "to make a vow so fatal."

"I acknowledge it," said Ravenswood, "and it had been a worse crime to keep it. It was for your sake that I abjured these purposes of vengeance, though I scarce knew that such was the argument by which I was conquered, until I saw you once more, and became conscious of the influence you possessed over me."

"And why do you now," said Lucy, "recall sentiments so terrible—sentiments so inconsistent with those you profess for me—with those your importunity has prevailed on me to acknowledge?"

"Because," said her lover, "I would impress on you the price at which I have bought your love—the right I have to expect your constancy. I say not that I have bartered for it the honour of my house, its last remaining possession—but though I say it not, and think it not, I cannot conceal from myself that the world may do both."

"If such are your sentiments," said Lucy, "you have played a cruel game with me. But it is not too late to give it over—take back the faith and troth which you could not plight to me without suffering abatement of honour—let what is passed be as if it had not been—forget me—I will endeavour to forget myself."

"You do me injustice," said the Master of Ravenswood; "by all I hold true and honourable, you do me the extremity of injustice—if I mentioned the price at which I have bought your love, it is only to show how much I prize it, to bind our engagement by a still firmer tie, and to show by what I have done to attain this station in your regard, how much I must suffer should you ever break your faith."

"And why, Ravenswood," answered Lucy, "should you think that possible?—Why should you urge me with even the mention of infidelity?—Is it because I ask you to delay applying to my father for a little space of time? Bind me by what vows you please; if vows are unnecessary to secure constancy, they may yet prevent suspicion."

Ravenswood pleaded, apologised, and even kneeled, to appease her displeasure; and Lucy, as placable as she was single-hearted, readily forgave the offence which his doubts had implied. The dispute thus agitated, however, ended by the lovers going through an emblematic ceremony of their troth-plight, of which the vulgar still preserve some traces. They broke betw.xt them the thin broad-piece of gold which Alice had refused to receive from Ravenswood.

"And never shall this leave my bosom," said Lucy, as she hung the piece of gold round her neck, and concealed it with her handkerchief, "until you, Edgar Ravenswood, ask me to resign it to you—and, while I wear it, never shall that heart acknowledge another love than yours."

With like protestations, Ravenswood placed his portion of the coin opposite to his heart. And now, at length, it struck them, that time had hurried fast on during this interview, and their absence at the castle would be subject of remark, if not of alarm. As they arose to leave the fountain which had been witness of their mutual engagement, an arrow whistled through the air, and struck a raven perched on the sere branch of an old oak, near to where they had been seated. The bird fluttered a few yards, and dropped at the feet of Lucy, whose dress was stained with some spots of its blood.

Miss Ashton was much alarmed, and Ravenswood, surprised and angry, looked everywhere for the marksman, who had given them a proof of his skill as little expected as desired. He was not long of discovering himself, being no other than Henry Ashton, who came running up with a crossbow in his hand.

"I knew I should startle you," he said; "and do you know you looked so busy that I hoped it would have fallen souse on your heads before you were aware of it.—What was the Master saying to you, Lucy?"

"I was telling your sister what an idle lad you were, keeping us waiting here for you so long," said Ravenswood, to save Lucy's confusion.

"Waiting for me? Why, I told you to see Lucy home, and that I was to go to make the ring-walk with old Norman in the Hayberry thicket, and you may be sure that would take a good hour, and we have all the deer's marks and furnishes got, while you were sitting here with Lucy, like a lazy loon."

"Well, well, Mr Henry," said Ravenswood; "but let us

see how you will answer to me for killing the raven. Do you know the ravens are all under the protection of the Lords of Ravenswood, and, to kill one in their presence, is such bad luck that it deserves the stab?"

"And that's what Norman said," replied the boy; "he came as far with me, as within a flight-shot of you, and he said he never saw a raven sit still so near living folk, and he wished it might be for good luck; for the raven is one of the wildest birds that flies, unless it be a tame one—and so I crept on and on, till I was within three score yards of him, and then whiz went the bolt, and there he lies, faith! Was it not well shot?—and, I daresay, I have not shot in a crossbow—not ten times, maybe."

"Admirably shot indeed," said Ravenswood; "and you will be a fine marksman if you practise hard."

"And that's what Norman says," answered the boy; "but I am sure it is not my fault if I do not practise enough; for, of free will, I would do little else, only my father and tutor are angry sometimes, and only Miss Lucy there gives herself airs about my being busy, for all she can sit idle by a well-side the whole day, when she has a handsome young gentleman to prate with—I have known her do so twenty times, if you will believe me."

The boy looked at his sister as he spoke, and, in the midst of his mischievous chatter, had the sense to see that he was really inflicting pain upon her, though without being able to comprehend the cause or the amount.

"Come now, Lucy," he said, "don't greet; and if I have said any thing beside the mark, I'll deny it again—and what does the Master of Ravenswood care if you had a hundred sweethearts?—so ne'er put finger in your eye about it."

The Master of Ravenswood was, for the moment, scarce satisfied with what he heard; yet his good sense naturally regarded it as the chatter of a spoilt boy, who strove to mortify his sister in the point which seemed most accessible for the time. But, although of a temper equally slow in receiving impressions, and obstinate in retaining them, the prattle of Henry served to nourish in his mind some vague suspicion, that his present engagement might only end in his being exposed like a conquered enemy in a Roman triumph, a captive attendant on the car of a victor, who meditated only the satiating his pride at the expense of the vanquished. There was, we repeat it, no real ground whatever for such an apprehension, nor could he be said seriously to entertain such for a moment. Indeed, it was impossible to look at the clear blue eye of Lucy Ashton, and entertain the slightest permanent doubt concerning the sincerity of her disposition. Still, however, conscious pride and conscious poverty combined to render á mind suspicious, which, in more fortunate circumstances, would have been a stranger to that as well as to every other meanness.

They reached the castle, where Sir William Ashton, who had been alarmed by the length of their stay, met them in the hall.

"Had Lucy," he said, "been in any other company than that of one who had shown he had so complete power of protecting her, he confessed he should have been very uneasy, and would have dispatched persons in quest of them. But, in the company of the Master of Ravenswood, he knew his daughter had nothing to dread."

Lucy commenced some apology for their long delay, but, conscience struck, became confused as she proceeded; and when Ravenswood, coming to her assistance, endeavoured to render the explanation complete and satisfactory, he only involved himself in the same disorder, like one who, endeavouring to extricate his companion from a slough, entangles himself in the same tenacious swamp. It cannot be supposed that the confusion of the two youthful lovers escaped the observation of the subtle lawyer, accustomed, by habit and profession, to trace human nature through all her windings. But it was not his present policy to take any notice of what he observed. He desired to hold the Master of Ravenswood bound, but wished that he himself should remain free; and it did not occur to him that his plan might be defeated by Lucy's returning the passion which he hoped she might inspire. If she should adopt some romantic feelings towards Ravenswood, in which circumstances, or the positive and absolute opposition of Lady Ashton, might render it unadvisable to indulge her, the Lord Keeper conceived they might be easily superseded and annulled by a journey to Edinburgh, or even to London, a new set of Brussels lace, and the soft whispers of half a dozen lovers, anxious to replace him whom it was convenient she should renounce. This was his provision for the worst view of the case. But, according to its more probable issue, any passing favour she might entertain for the Master of Ravenswood, might require encouragement rather than repression.

This seemed the more likely, as he had that very morning, since their departure from the castle, received a letter, the contents of which he hastened to communicate to Ravenswood. A foot-post had arrived with a packet to the Lord Keeper from that friend whom we have already mentioned, who was labouring hard under-hand to consolidate a band of patriots, at the head of whom stood Sir William's greatest terror, the active and ambitious Marquis of A——. The success of this convenient friend had been such, that he had obtained from Sir William, not indeed a directly favourable answer, but certainly a most patient hearing. This he had reported to his principal, who had replied, by the ancient French adage, " *Château qui parle, et femme qui écoute, l'un et l'autre va se rendre.*" A statesman who hears you propose a change of measures without reply, was, according to the Marquis's opinion, in the situation of the fortress which parleys, and the lady who listens, and he resolved to press the siege of the Lord Keeper.

The packet, therefore, contained a letter from his friend and ally, and another from himself to the Lord Keeper, frankly offering an unceremonious visit. They were crossing the country to go to the southward—the roads were indifferent—the accommodation of the inns as execrable as possible—the Lord Keeper had been long acquainted intimately with one of his correspondents, and though more slightly known to the Marquis, had yet enough of his lordship's acquaintance to render the visit sufficiently natural, and to shut the mouths of those who might be disposed to impute it to a political intrigue. He instantly accepted the offered visit, determined, however, that he would not pledge himself an inch farther for the furtherance of their views than *reason* (by which he meant his own self-interest) should plainly point out to him as proper.

Two circumstances particularly delighted him; the presence of Ravenswood, and the absence of his own lady. By having the former under his roof, he conceived he might be able to quash all such hazardous and hostile proceedings as he might otherwise have been engaged in, under the patronage of the Marquis; and Lucy, he foresaw, would make, for his immediate purpose of delay and procrastination, a much better mistress of his family than her mother, who would, he was sure, in some shape or other, contrive to disconcert his political schemes by her proud and implacable temper.

His anxious solicitations that the Master would stay to receive his kinsman, were of course readily complied with, since the *éclaircissement* which had taken place at the Mermaiden's Fountain had removed all wish for sudden departure. Lucy and Lockhard had, therefore, orders to provide all things necessary in their different departments, for receiving the expected guests, with a pomp and display of luxury very uncommon in Scotland at that remote period.

CHAPTER XXI

Marall. Sir, the man of honour's come,
Newly alighted——
  Overreach. In without reply,
And do as I command.——
Is the loud music I gave order for
Ready to receive him?——
New Way to Pay Old Debts.

SIR WILLIAM ASHTON although a man of sense, legal information, and great practical knowledge of the world, had yet some points of character which corresponded better with the timidity of his disposition and the supple arts by which he had risen in the world, than to the degree of eminence which he had attained; as they tended to show an original mediocrity of understanding, however highly it had been cultivated, and a native meanness of disposition, however carefully veiled. He loved the ostentatious display of his wealth, less as a man to whom habit has made it necessary, than as one to whom it is still delightful from its novelty. The most trivial details did not escape him; and Lucy soon learned to watch the flush of scorn which crossed Ravenswood's cheek, when he heard her father gravely arguing with Lockhard, nay, even with the old housekeeper, upon circumstances which, in families of rank, are left uncared for, because it is supposed impossible they can be neglected.

"I could pardon Sir William," said Ravenswood, one evening after he had left the room, "some general anxiety upon this occasion, for the Marquis's visit is an honour, and should be received as such; but I am worn out by these miserable minutiæ of the buttery, and the larder, and the very hen-coop—they drive me beyond my patience; I would rather endure the poverty of Wolf's Crag, than be pestered with the wealth of Ravenswood Castle."

"And yet," said Lucy, "it was by attention to these minutiæ that my father acquired the property"——

"Which my ancestors sold for lack of it," replied Ravenswood. "Be it so; a porter still bears but a burden, though the burden be of gold."

Lucy sighed; she perceived too plainly that her lover held in scorn the manners and habits of a father, to whom she had long looked up as her best and most partial friend, whose fondness had often consoled her for her mother's contemptuous harshness.

The lovers soon discovered that they differed upon other and no less important topics. Religion, the mother of peace, was, in those days of discord, so much misconstrued and mistaken, that her rules and forms were the subject of the most opposite opinions, and the most hostile animosities. The Lord Keeper, being a whig, was, of course, a Presbyterian, and had found it convenient, at different periods, to express greater zeal for the kirk, than perhaps he really felt. His family, equally of course, were trained under the same institution. Ravenswood, as we know, was a High-Church man, or Episcopalian, and frequently objected to Lucy the fanaticism of some of her own communion, while she intimated, rather than expressed, horror at the latitudinarian principles which she had been taught to think connected with the prelatical form of church-government.

Thus, although their mutual affection seemed to increase rather than to be diminished, as their characters opened more fully on each other, the feelings of each were mingled with some less agreeable ingredients. Lucy felt a secret awe, amid all her affection for Ravenswood. His soul was of an higher, prouder character, than those with whom she had hitherto mixed in intercourse; his ideas were more fierce and free ; and he contemned many of the opinions which had been inculcated upon her, as chiefly demanding her veneration. On the other hand, Ravenswood saw in Lucy a soft and flexible character, which, in his eyes at least, seemed too susceptible of being moulded to any form by those with whom she lived. He felt that his own temper required a partner of a more independent spirit, who could set sail with him on his course of life, resolved as himself to dare indifferently the storm and the favouring breeze. But Lucy was so beautiful, so devoutly attached to him, of a temper so exquisitely soft and kind, that, while he could have wished it were possible to inspire her with a greater degree of firmness and resolution, and while he sometimes became impatient of the extreme fear which she expressed of their attachment being prematurely discovered, he felt that the softness of a mind, amounting almost to feebleness, rendered her even dearer to him, as a being who had voluntarily clung to him for protection, and made him the arbiter of her fate for weal or woe. His feelings towards her at such moments, were those which have been since so beautifully expressed by our immortal Joanna Baillie :

> ———"Thou sweetest thing,
> That e'er did fix its lightly-fibred sprays
> To the rude rock, ah ! wouldst thou cling to me ?
> Rough and storm-worn I am—yet love me as
> Thou truly dost, I will love thee again
> With true and honest heart, though all unmeet
> To be the mate of such sweet gentleness."

Thus the very points in which they differed, seemed, in some measure, to ensure the continuance of their mutual affection. If, indeed, they had so fully appreciated each other's character before the burst of passion in which they hastily pledged their faith to each other, Lucy might have feared Ravenswood too much ever to have loved him, and he might have construed her softness and docile temper as imbecility, rendering her unworthy of his regard. But they stood pledged to each other ; and Lucy only feared that her lover's pride might one day teach him to regret his attachment ; Ravenswood, that a mind so ductile as Lucy's, might, in absence or difficulties, be induced, by the entreaties or influence of those around her, to renounce the engagement she had formed.

"Do not fear it," said Lucy, when upon one occasion a hint of such suspicion escaped her lover; "the mirrors which receive the reflection of all successive objects are framed of hard materials like glass or steel—the softer substances, when they receive an impression, retain it undefaced."

"This is poetry, Lucy," said Ravenswood; "and in poetry there is always fallacy, and sometimes fiction."

"Believe me then, once more, in honest prose," said Lucy, "that, though I will never wed man without the consent of my parents, yet neither force nor persuasion shall dispose of my hand till you renounce the right I have given you to it."

The lovers had ample time for such explanations. Henry was now more seldom their companion, being either a most unwilling attendant upon the lessons of his tutor, or a forward volunteer under the instructions of the foresters or grooms. As for the Keeper, his mornings were spent in his study, maintaining correspondences of all kinds, and balancing in his anxious mind the various intelligence which he collected from every quarter concerning the expected change of Scottish politics, and the probable strength of the parties who were about to struggle for power. At other times he busied himself about arranging, and countermanding, and then again arranging, the preparations which he judged necessary for the reception of the Marquis of A——, whose arrival had been twice delayed by some necessary cause of detention.

In the midst of all these various avocations, political and domestic, he seemed not to observe how much his daughter and his guest were thrown into each other's society, and was censured by many of his neighbours, according to the fashion of neighbours in all countries, for suffering such an intimate connexion to take place betwixt two young persons. The only natural explanation was, that he designed them for each other; while, in truth, his only motive was to temporise and procrastinate, until he should discover the real extent of the interest which the Marquis took in Ravenswood's affairs, and the power which he was likely to possess of advancing them. Until these points should be made both clear and manifest, the Lord Keeper resolved that he would do nothing to commit himself, either in one shape or other ; and, like many cunning persons, he over-reached himself deplorably.

Amongst those who had been disposed to censure, with the greatest severity, the conduct of Sir William Ashton, in permitting the prolonged residence of Ravenswood under his roof, and his constant attendance on Miss Ashton, was the new Laird of Girnington, and his faithful squire and bottle-holder, personages formerly well known to us by the names of Hayston and Bucklaw, and his companion Captain Craigengelt. The former had at length succeeded to the extensive property of his long-lived grand-aunt. and to considerable wealth besides, which he had employed in redeeming his paternal acres (by the title appertaining to which he still chose to be designated), notwithstanding Captain Craigengelt had proposed to him a most advantageous mode of vesting the money in Law's scheme, which was just then broached, and offered his services to travel express to Paris for the purpose. But Bucklaw had so far derived wisdom from adversity, that he would listen to no proposal which Craigengelt could invent, which had the slightest tendency to risk his newly-acquired independence. He that had once eat pease-bannocks, drank sour wine, and slept in the secret chamber at Wolf's Crag, would, he said, prize good cheer and a soft bed as long as he lived, and take special care never to need such hospitality again.

Craigengelt, therefore, found himself disappointed in the first hopes he had entertained of making a good hand of the Laird of Bucklaw. Still, however, he reaped many advantages from his friend's good fortune. Bucklaw, who had never been at all scrupulous in choosing his companions, was accustomed to, and entertained by a fellow, whom he could either laugh with, or laugh at, as he had a mind, who would take, according to Scottish phrase, " the bit and the buffet," understood all sports, whether within or without doors, and, when the laird had a mind for a bottle of wine (no infrequent circumstance), was always ready to save him from the scandal of getting drunk by himself. Upon these terms Craigengelt was the frequent, almost the constant, inmate of the house of Girnington.

In no time, and under no possibility of circumstances. could good have been derived from such an intimacy, however its bad consequences might be qualified by the thorough knowledge which Bucklaw possessed of his dependant's character, and the high contempt in which he held it. But as circumstances stood, this evil communication was particularly liable to corrupt what good principles nature had implanted in the patron.

Craigengelt had never forgiven the scorn with which Ravenswood had torn the mask of courage and honesty from his countenance; and to exasperate Bucklaw's resentment against him, was the safest mode of revenge which occurred to his cowardly, yet cunning and malignant disposition.

He brought up, on all occasions, the story of the challenge which Ravenswood had declined to accept, and endeavoured, by every possible insinuation, to make his patron believe that his honour was concerned in bringing that matter to an issue by a present discussion with Ravenswood. But respecting this subject, Bucklaw imposed on him, at length, a peremptory command of silence.

"I think," he said, "the Master has treated me unlike a gentleman, and I see no right he had to send me back a cavalier answer when I demanded the satisfaction of one— But he gave me my life once—and, in looking the matter over at present, I put myself but on equal terms with him. Should he cross me again, I shall consider the old accompt as balanced, and his Mastership will do well to look to himself."

"That he should," re-echoed Craigengelt; "for when you are in practice, Bucklaw, I would bet a magnum you are through him before the third pass."

"Then you know nothing of the matter," said Bucklaw, "and you never saw him fence."

"And I know nothing of the matter?" said the dependant—"a good jest, I promise you!—and though I never saw Ravenswood fence, have I not been at Monsieur Sagoon's school, who was the first *maître d'armes* at Paris; and have I not been at Signor Poco's at Florence, and Meinheer Durchstossen's at Vienna, and have I not seen all their play?"

"I don't know whether you have or not," said Bucklaw; "but what about it, though you had?"

"Only that I will be d—d if ever I saw French, Italian, or High-Dutchman ever make foot, hand, and eye, keep time half so well as you, Bucklaw."

"I believe you lie, Craigie," said Bucklaw; "however, I can hold my own, both with single rapier, backsword, sword and dagger, broadsword, or case of falchions—and that's as much as any gentleman need know of the matter."

"And the double of what ninety-nine out of a hundred know," said Craigengelt; "they learn to change a few thrusts with the small sword, and then, forsooth, they understand the noble art of defence! Now when I was at Rouen in the year 1695, there was a Chevalier de Chapon and I went to the Opera, where we found three bits of English birkies"——

"Is it a long story you are going to tell?" said Bucklaw, interrupting him without ceremony.

"Just as you like," answered the parasite, "for we made short work of it."

"Then I like it short," said Bucklaw; "is it serious or merry?"

"Devilish serious, I assure you, and so they found it; for the Chevalier and I"——

"Then I don't like it at all," said Bucklaw; "so fill a brimmer of my auld auntie's claret, rest her heart! And, as the Hielandman says, *Skioch doch na skiaill*."[1]

"That was what tough old Sir Evan Dhu used to say to me when I was out with the metall'd lads in 1689. 'Craigengelt,' he used to say, 'you are as pretty a fellow as ever held steel in his grip, but you have one fault.'"

"If he had known you as long as I have done," said Bucklaw, "he would have found out some twenty more; but hang long stories, give us your toast, man."

Craigengelt rose, went a tiptoe to the door, peeped out, shut it carefully, came back again—clapped his tarnished gold-laced hat on one side of his head, took his glass in one hand, and touching the hilt of his hanger with the other, named, "The King over the water."

"I tell you what it is, Captain Craigengelt," said Bucklaw; "I shall keep my mind to myself on these subjects, having too much respect for the memory of my venerable aunt Girnington to put her lands and tenements in the way of committing treason against established authority. Bring me King James to Edinburgh, Captain, with thirty thou-

---

[1] "Cut a drink with a tale;" equivalent to the English adage of boon companions, "don't preach over your liquor."

sand men at his back, and I'll tell you what I think about his title; but as for running my neck into a noose, and my good broad lands into the statutory penalties, 'in that case made and provided,' rely upon it, you will find me no such fool. So, when you mean to vapour with your hanger and your dram-cup in support of treasonable toasts, you must find your liquor and company elsewhere."

"Well, then," said Craigengelt, "name the toast yourself, and be it what it like, I'll pledge you, were it a mile to the bottom."

"And I'll give you a toast that deserves it, my boy," said Bucklaw; "what say you to Miss Lucy Ashton?"

"Up with it," said the Captain, as he tossed off his brimmer, "the bonniest lass in Lothian. What a pity the old sneck-drawing whigamore, her father, is about to throw her away upon that rag of pride and beggary, the Master of Ravenswood!"

"That's not quite so clear," said Bucklaw, in a tone, which, though it seemed indifferent, excited his companion's eager curiosity; and not that only, but also his hope of working himself into some sort of confidence, which might make him necessary to his patron, being by no means satisfied to rest on mere sufferance, if he could form by art or industry a more permanent title to his favour.

"I thought," said he, after a moment's pause, "that was a settled matter—they are continually together, and nothing else is spoken of betwixt Lammerlaw and Traprain."

"They may say what they please," replied his patron, "but I know better; and I'll give you Miss Lucy Ashton's health again, my boy."

"And I would drink it on my knee," said Craigengelt, "if I thought the girl had the spirit to jilt that d—d son of a Spaniard."

"I am to request you will not use the word jilt and Miss Ashton's name together," said Bucklaw gravely.

"Jilt, did I say?—discard, my lad of acres—by Jove, I meant to say discard," replied Craigengelt; "and I hope she'll discard him like a small card at piquet, and take in the King of Hearts, my boy!—But yet"——

"But what?" said his patron.

"But yet I know for certain they are hours together alone, and in the woods and the fields."

"That's her foolish father's dotage—that will be soon put out of the lass's head, if it ever gets into it," answered Bucklaw. "And now fill your glass again, Captain, I am going to make you happy—I am going to let you into a secret—a plot—a nousing plot—only the noose is but typical."

"A marrying matter?" said Craigengelt, and his jaw fell as he asked the question; for he suspected that matrimony would render his situation at Girnington much more precarious than during the jolly days of his patron's bachelorhood.

"Ay, a marriage, man," said Bucklaw; "but wherefore droops thy mighty spirit, and why grow the rubies on thy cheek so pale? The board will have a corner, and the corner will have a trencher, and the trencher will have a glass beside it; and the board-end shall be filled, and the trencher and the glass shall be replenished for thee, if all the petticoats in Lothian had sworn the contrary—What, man! I am not the boy to put myself into leading strings?"

"So says many an honest fellow," says Craigengelt, "and some of my special friends; but, curse me if I know the reason, the women could never bear me, and always contrived to trundle me out of favour before the honeymoon was over."

"If you could have kept your ground till that was over, you might have made a good year's pension," said Bucklaw.

"But I never could," answered the dejected parasite; "there was my Lord Castle-Cuddy—we were hand and glove—I rode his horses—borrowed money, both for him and from him—trained his hawks, and taught him how to lay his bets; and when he took a fancy of marrying, I married him to Katie Glegg, whom I thought myself as sure of as man could be of woman. Egad, she had me out of the house, as if I had run on wheels, within the first fortnight!"

"Well!" replied Bucklaw, "I think I have nothing of Castle-Cuddy about me, or Lucy of Katie Glegg. But you see the thing will go on whether you like it or no—the only question is, will you be useful?"

"Useful?" exclaimed the Captain;—"and to thee, my lad of lands, my darling boy, whom I would tramp barefooted through the world for?—name time, place, mode, and circumstances, and see if I will not be useful in all uses that can be devised."

"Why, then, you must ride two hundred miles for me," said the patron.

"A thousand, and call them a flea's leap," answered the dependant; "I'll cause saddle my horse directly."

"Better stay till you know where you are to go, and what you are to do," quoth Bucklaw. "You know I have a kinswoman in Northumberland, Lady Blenkensop by name, whose old acquaintance I had the misfortune to lose in the period of my poverty, but the light of whose countenance shone forth upon me when the sun of my prosperity began to arise."

"D—n all such double-faced jades!" exclaimed Craigengelt, heroically; "this I will say for John Craigengelt, that he is his friend's friend through good report and bad report, poverty and riches; and you know something of that yourself, Bucklaw."

"I have not forgot your merits," said his patron; "I do remember, that, in my extremities, you had a mind to *crimp* me for the service of the French king, or of the Pretender; and, moreover, that you afterwards lent me a score of pieces, when as I firmly believe, you had heard the news that old Lady Girnington had a touch of the dead palsy. But don't be downcast, John; I believe, after all, you like me very well in your way, and it is my misfortune to have no better counsellor at present. To return to this Lady Blenkensop, you must know she is a close confederate of Duchess Sarah."

"What! of Sall Jennings?" exclaimed Craigengelt; "then she must be a good one."

"Hold your tongue, and keep your Tory rants to yourself, if it be possible," said Bucklaw; "I tell you, that through the Duchess of Marlborough has this Northumbrian cousin of mine become a crony of Lady Ashton, the Keeper's wife, or, I may say, the Lord Keeper's Lady Keeper, and she has favoured Lady Blenkensop with a visit on her return from London, and is just now at her old mansion-house on the banks of the Wansbeck. Now, sir, as it has been the use and wont of these ladies to consider their husbands as of no importance in the management of their own families, it has been their present pleasure, without consulting Sir

William Ashton, to put on the *tapis* a matrimonial alliance, to be concluded between Lucy Ashton and my own right honourable self, Lady Ashton acting a self-constituted plenipotentiary on the part of her daughter and husband, and Mother Blenkensop, equally unaccredited, doing me the honour to be my representative. You may suppose I was a little astonished when I found that a treaty, in which I was so considerably interested, had advanced a good way before I was even consulted."

"Capot me if I think that was according to the rules of the game," said his confidant; "and pray, what answer did you return?"

"Why, my first thought was to send the treaty to the devil, and the negotiators along with it, for a couple of meddling old women; my next was to laugh very heartily; and my third and last was a settled opinion that the thing was reasonable, and would suit me well enough."

"Why, I thought you had never seen the wench but once —and then he had her riding-mask on—I am sure you told me so."

"Ay—but I liked her very well then. And Ravenswood's dirty usage of me—shutting me out of doors to dine with the lackeys, because he had the Lord Keeper, forsooth, and his daughter, to be guests in his beggarly castle of starvation—D—n me, Craigengelt, if I ever forgive him till I play him as good a trick!"

"No more you should, if you are a lad of mettle," said Craigengelt, the matter now taking a turn in which he could sympathise; "and if you carry this wench from him, it will break his heart."

"That it will not," said Bucklaw; "his heart is all steeled over with reason and philosophy—things that you, Craigie, know nothing about more than myself, God help me—But it will break his pride, though, and that's what I'm driving at."

"Distance me," said Craigengelt, "but I know the reason now of his unmannerly behaviour at his own tumble-down tower yonder—Ashamed of your company?—no, no!—Gad, he was afraid you would cut in and carry off the girl."

"Eh! Craigengelt?" said Bucklaw—"do you really think so?—but no, no!—he is a devilish deal prettier man than I am."

"Who—he?" exclaimed the parasite—"he's as black as the crook; and for his size—he's a tall fellow, to be sure—but give me a light, stout, middle-sized "——

"Plague on thee!" said Bucklaw, interrupting him, "and on me for listening to you!—you would say as much if I were hunch-backed. But as to Ravenswood—he has kept no terms with me—I'll keep none with him—if I *can* win this girl from him, I *will* win her."

"Win her?—'sblood, you *shall* win her, point, quint, and quatorze, my king of trumps—you shall pique, repique, and capot him."

"Prithee, stop thy gambling cant for one instant," said Bucklaw. "Things have come thus far, that I have entertained the proposal of my kinswoman, agreed to the terms of jointure, amount of fortune, and so forth, and that the affair is to go forward when Lady Ashton comes down, for she takes her daughter and her son in her own hand. Now they want me to send up a confidential person with some writings."

"By this good wine, I'll ride to the end of the world—the very gates of Jericho, and the judgment-seat of Prester John, for thee!" ejaculated the Captain.

"Why, I believe you would do something for me, and a great deal for yourself. Now, any one could carry the writings; but you will have a little more to do. You must contrive to drop out before my Lady Ashton, just as if it were a matter of little consequence, the residence of Ravenswood at her husband's house, and his close intercourse with Miss Ashton; and you may tell her, that all the country talks of a visit from the Marquis of A——, as it is supposed, to make up the match betwixt Ravenswood and her daughter. I should like to hear what she says to all this; for, rat me, if I have any idea of starting for the plate at all if Ravenswood is to win the race, and he has odds against me already."

"Never a bit—the wench has too much sense—and in that belief I drink her health a third time; and, were time and place fitting, I would drink it on bended knees, and he that would not pledge me, I would make his guts garter his stockings."

"Hark ye, Craigengelt; as you are going into the society of women of rank," said Bucklaw, "I'll thank you to forget your strange blackguard oaths and damme's—I'll write to them, though, that you are a blunt untaught fellow."

"Ay, ay," replied Craigengelt; "a plain, blunt, honest, downright soldier."

"Not too honest, nor too much of the soldier neither; but such as thou art, it is my luck to need thee, for I must have spurs put to Lady Ashton's motions."

"I'll dash them up to the rowel-heads," said Craigengelt; "she shall come here at the gallop, like a cow chased by a whole nest of hornets, and her tail twisted over her rump like a corkscrew."

"And hear ye, Craigie," said Bucklaw; "your boots and doublet are good enough to drink in, as the man says in the play, but they are somewhat too greasy for tea-table service—prithee, get thyself a little better rigged out, and here is to pay all charges."

"Nay, Bucklaw—on my soul, man—you use me ill—However," added Craigengelt, pocketing the money, "if you will have me so far indebted to you, I must be conforming."

"Well, horse and away!" said the patron, "so soon as you have got your riding livery in trim. You may ride the black crop-ear—and, hark ye, I'll make you a present of him to boot."

"I drink to the good luck of my mission," answered the ambassador, "in a half-pint bumper."

"I thank ye, Craigie, and pledge you—I see nothing against it but the father or the girl taking a tantrum, and I am told the mother can wind them both round her little finger. Take care not to affront her with any of your jacobite jargon."

"O ay, true—she is a whig, and a friend of old Sall of Marlborough—thank my stars, I can hoist any colours at a pinch. I have fought as hard under John Churchill as ever I did under Dundee or the Duke of Berwick."

"I verily believe you, Craigie," said the lord of the mansion; "but, Craigie, do you, pray, step down to the cellar, and fetch us up a bottle of the Burgundy, 1678—it is in the fourth bin from the right-hand turn—And I say, Craigie, you may fetch up half-a-dozen whilst you are about it.—Egad, we'll make a night on't!"

CHAPTER XXII

And soon they spied the merry-men green,
And eke the coach and four.

Duke upon Duke.

CRAIGENGELT set forth on his mission as soon as his equipage was complete, prosecuted his journey with all diligence, and accomplished his commission with all the dexterity for which Bucklaw had given him credit. As he arrived with credentials from Mr Hayston of Bucklaw, he was extremely welcome to both ladies; and those who are prejudiced in favour of a new acquaintance can, for a time at least, discover excellencies in his very faults, and perfections in his deficiencies. Although both ladies were accustomed to good society, yet, being predetermined to find out an agreeable and well-behaved gentleman in Mr Hayston's friend, they succeeded wonderfully in imposing on themselves. It is true that Graigengelt was now handsomely dressed, and that was a point of no small consequence. But, independent of outward show, his blackguard impudence of address was construed into honourable bluntness, becoming his supposed military profession, his hectoring passed for courage, and his sauciness for wit. Lest, however, any one should think this a violation of probability, we must add, in fairness to the two ladies, that their discernment was greatly blinded, and their favour propitiated, by the opportune arrival of Captain Craigengelt in the moment when they were longing for a third hand to make a party at tredrille, in which, as in all games, whether of chance or skill that worthy person was a great proficient.

When he found himself established in favour, his next point was how best to use it for the furtherance of his patron's views. He found Lady Ashton prepossessed strongly in favour of the motion, which Lady Blenkensop, partly from regard to her kinsman, partly from the spirit of match-making, had not hesitated to propose to her; so that his task was an easy one. Bucklaw, reformed from his prodigality, was just the sort of husband which she desired to have for her Shepherdess of Lammermoor; and while the marriage gave her an easy fortune, and a respectable country gentleman for her husband, Lady Ashton was of opinion that her destinies would be fully and most favourably accomplished. It so chanced, also, that Bucklaw, among his new acquisitions, had gained the management of a little political interest in a neighbouring county, where the Douglas family originally held large possessions. It was one the bosom-hopes of Lady Ashton, that her eldest son, Sholto, should represent this county in the British Parliament, and she saw this alliance with Bucklaw as a circumstance which might be highly favourable to her wishes.

Craigengelt, who in his way by no means wanted sagacity, no sooner discovered in what quarter the wind of Lady Ashton's wishes sate, than he trimmed his course accordingly. " There was little to prevent Bucklaw himself from sitting for the county—he must carry the heat—must wa k the course. Two cousins-german—six more distant kinsmen, his factor and his chamberlain, were all hollow votes— and the Girnington interest had always carried, betwixt love and fear, about as many more. But Bucklaw cared no more about riding the first horse, and that sort of thing, than he, Craigengelt, did about a game at birkie—it was a pity his interest was not in good guidance."

All this Lady Ashton drank in with willing and attentive ears, resolving internally to be herself the person who should take the management of the political influence of her destined son-in-law, for the benefit of her eldest born, Sholto, and all other parties concerned.

When he found her ladyship thus favourably disposed, the Captain proceeded, to use his employer's phrase, to set spurs to her resolution, by hinting at the situation of matters at Ravenswood Castle, the long residence which the heir of that family had made with the Lord Keeper. and the reports which (though he would be d—d ere he gave credit to any of them) had been idly circulated in the neighbourhood. It was not the Captain's cue to appear himself to be uneasy on the subject of these rumours ; but he easily saw from Lady Ashton's flushed cheek, hesitating voice, and flashing eye, that she had caught the alarm which he intended to communicate. She had not heard from her husband so often or so regularly as she thought him bound in duty to have written, and of this very interesting intelligence, concerning his visit to the Tower of

Wolf's Crag, and the guest whom, with such cordiality, he had received at Ravenswood Castle, he had suffered his lady to remain altogether ignorant, until she now learned it by the chance information of a stranger. Such concealment approached, in her apprehension, to a misprision, at least, of treason, if not to actual rebellion against her matrimonial authority; and in her inward soul did she vow to take vengeance on the Lord Keeper, as on a subject detected in meditating revolt. Her indignation burned the more fiercely, as she found herself obliged to suppress it in presence of Lady Blenkensop, the kinswoman, and of Craigengelt, the confidential friend of Bucklaw, of whose alliance she now became trebly desirous, since it occurred to her alarmed imagination, that her husband might, in his policy or timidity, prefer that of Ravenswood.

The Captain was engineer enough to discover that the train was fired; and therefore heard, in the course of the same day, without the least surprise, that Lady Ashton had resolved to abridge her visit to Lady Blenkensop, and set forth with the peep of morning on her return to Scotland, using all the dispatch which the state of the roads, and the mode of travelling, would possibly permit.

Unhappy Lord Keeper!—little was he aware what a storm was travelling towards him in all the speed with which an old-fashioned coach and six could possibly achieve its journey. He, like Don Gayferos, "forgot his lady fair and true," and was only anxious about the expected visit of the Marquis of A——. Soothfast tidings had assured him that this nobleman was at length, and without fail, to honour his castle at one in the afternoon, being a late dinner-hour; and much was the bustle in consequence of the annunciation. The Lord Keeper traversed the chambers, held consultation with the butler in the cellars, and even ventured, at the risk of a *démêlé* with a cook, of a spirit lofty enough to scorn the admonitions of Lady Ashton herself, to peep into the kitchen. Satisfied, at length, that every thing was in as active a train of preparation as was possible, he summoned Ravenswood and his daughter to walk upon the terrace, for the purpose of watching, from that commanding position, the earliest symptoms of his lordship's approach. For this purpose, with slow and idle step, he paraded the terrace, which, flanked with a heavy stone battlement, stretched in front of the castle upon a level with the first story; while visitors found access to the court by a projecting gate-way, the bartizan or flat-leaded roof of which was accessible from the terrace by an easy flight of low and broad steps. The whole bore a resemblance partly to a castle, partly to a nobleman's seat; and though calculated, in some respects, for defence, evinced that it had been constructed under a sense of the power and security of the ancient Lords of Ravenswood.

This pleasant walk commanded a beautiful and extensive view. But what was most to our present purpose, there were seen from the terrace two roads, one leading from the east, and one from the westward, which, crossing a ridge opposed to the eminence on which the castle stood, at different angles, gradually approached each other, until they joined not far from the gate of the avenue. It was to the westward approach that the Lord Keeper, from a sort of fidgeting anxiety, his daughter, from complaisance to him, and Ravenswood, though feeling some symptoms of internal impatience, out of complaisance to his daughter, directed their eyes to see the precursors of the Marquis's approach.

These were not long of presenting themselves. Two running footmen, dressed in white, with black jockey-caps, and long staffs in their hands, headed the train; and such was their agility, that they found no difficulty in keeping the necessary advance, which the etiquette of their station required, before the carriage and horsemen. Onward they came at a long swinging trot, arguing unwearied speed in their long-breathed calling. Such running footmen are often alluded to in old plays (I would particularly instance Middleton's *Mad World my Masters*), and perhaps may be still remembered by some old persons in Scotland, as part of the retinue of the ancient nobility when travelling in full ceremony.[1] Behind these glancing meteors, who

[1] Hereupon I, Jedediah Cleishbotham, crave leave to remark, *primo*, which signifies, in the first place, that, having in vain enquired at the Circulating Library in Gandercleugh, albeit it aboundeth in similar vanities, for this samyn Middleton and his *Mad World*, it was at length shown unto me amongst other ancient fooleries carefully compiled by one Dodsley, who, doubtless, hath his reward for neglect of precious time; and having misused so much of mine as was necessary for the purpose, I therein found that a play-man is brought in as a footman,

footed it.as if the Avenger of Blood had been behind them,
came a cloud of dust, raised by riders who preceded,
attended, or followed, the state-carriage of the Marquis.

The privilege of nobility, in those days, had something in
it impressive on the imagination.   The dresses and liveries
and number of their attendants, their style of travelling,
the imposing, and almost warlike air of the armed men who
surrounded them, placed them far above the laird, who
travelled with his brace of footmen ; and as to rivalry from
the mercantile part of the community, these would as
soon have thought of imitating the state equipage of the
Sovereign.   At present it is different ; and I myself, Peter
Pattieson, in a late journey to Edinburgh, had the honour,
in the mail-coach phrase, to "change a leg" with a peer of
the realm.   It was not so in the days of which I write ; and
the Marquis's approach, so long expected in vain, now took
place in the full pomp of ancient aristocracy.   Sir William
Ashton was so much interested in what he beheld, and in
considering the ceremonial of reception in case any circumstance had been omitted, that he scarce heard his son
Henry exclaim, "There is another coach and six coming
down the east road, papa—can they both belong to the
Marquis of A——?"

At length, when the youngster had fairly compelled his
attention by pulling his sleeve,

> "He turned his eyes, and, as he turn'd, survey'd
> An awful vision."

Sure enough, another coach and six, with four servants
or outriders in attendance, was descending the hill from the

whom a knight is made to greet facetiously with the epithet of "linen
stocking, and three-score miles a-day."

Secundo (which is the secondly in the vernacular), under Mr Pattieson's favour, some men not altogether so old as he would represent
them, do remember this species of menial, or forerunner.   In evidence
of which, I, Jedediah Cleishbotham, though mine eyes yet do me good
service, remember me to have seen one of this tribe clothed in white,
and bearing a staff, who ran daily before the state-coach of the umquhile John, Earl of Hopeton, father of this Earl, Charles, that now is ;
unto whom it may be justly said, that Renown playeth the part of a
running footman, or precursor ; and, as the poet singeth—

> "Mars standing by asserts his quarrel,
> And Fame flies after with a laurel."

eastward, at such a pace as made it doubtful which of the carriages thus approaching from different quarters would first reach the gate at the extremity of the avenue. The one coach was green, the other blue; and not the green and blue chariots in the Circus of Rome or Constantinople excited more turmoil among the citizens than the double apparition occasioned in the mind of the Lord Keeper. We all remember the terrible exclamation of the dying profligate, when a friend, to destroy, what he supposed the hypochondriac idea of a spectre appearing in a certain shape at a given hour, placed before him a person dressed up in the manner he described. "*Mon dieu!*" said the expiring sinner, who, it seems, saw both the real and polygraphic apparition—"*il y en a deux!*"

The surprise of the Lord Keeper was scarcely less unpleasing at the duplication of the expected arrival; his mind misgave him strangely. There was no neighbour who would have approached so unceremoniously, at a time when ceremony was held in such respect. It must be Lady Ashton, said his conscience, and followed up the hint with an anxious anticipation of the purpose of her sudden and unannounced return. He felt that he was caught "in the manner." That the company in which she had so unluckily surprised him was likely to be highly distasteful to her, there was no question; and the only hope which remained for him was her high sense of dignified propriety, which, he trusted, might prevent a public explosion. But so active were his doubts and fears, as altogether to derange his purposed ceremonial for the reception of the Marquis.

These feelings of apprehension were not confined to Sir William Ashton. "It is my mother—it is my mother!" said Lucy, turning as pale as ashes, and clasping her hands together as she looked at Ravenswood.

"And if it be Lady Ashton," said her lover to her in a low tone, "what can be the occasion of such alarm?—Surely the return of a lady to the family from which she has been so long absent, should excite other sensations than those of fear and dismay."

"You do not know my mother," said Miss Ashton, in a tone almost breathless with terror; "what will she say when she sees you in this place!"

"My stay has been too long," said Ravenswood, some-

what haughtily, "if her displeasure at my presence is likely
to be so formidable. My dear Lucy," he resumed, in a
tone of soothing encouragement, "you are too childishly
afraid of Lady Ashton; she is a woman of family—a lady
of fashion—a person who must know the world, and what
is due to her husband and her husband's guests."

Lucy shook her head; and, as if her mother, still at the
distance of half a mile, could have seen and scrutinised
her deportment, she withdrew herself from beside Ravenswood, and, taking her brother Henry's arm, led him to a
different part of the terrace. The Keeper also shuffled
down towards the portal of the great gate, without inviting
Ravenswood to accompany him, and thus he remained
standing alone on the terrace, deserted and shunned, as it
were, by the inhabitants of the mansion.

This suited not the mood of one who was proud in proportion to his poverty, and who thought that, in sacrificing
his deep-rooted resentments so far as to become Sir William
Ashton's guest, he conferred a favour and received none.
"I can forgive Lucy," he said to himself; "she is young,
timid, and conscious of an important engagement assumed
without her mother's sanction; yet she should remember
with whom it has been assumed, and leave me no reason
to suspect that she is ashamed of her choice. For the
Keeper, sense, spirit, and expression seem to have left his
face and manner since he had the first glimpse of Lady
Ashton's carriage. I must watch how this is to end; and,
if they give me reason to think myself an unwelcome guest,
my visit is soon abridged."

With these suspicions floating on his mind, he left the
terrace, and, walking towards the stables of the castle,
gave directions that his horse should be kept in readiness,
in case he should have occasion to ride abroad.

In the meanwhile the drivers of the two carriages, the
approach of which had occasioned so much dismay at the
castle, had become aware of each other's presence, as they
approached upon different lines to the head of the avenue,
as a common centre. Lady Ashton's driver and postilions
instantly received orders to get foremost, if possible, her
ladyship being desirous of dispatching her first interview
with her husband before the arrival of these guests, whoever
they might happen to be. On the other hand, the coach-

man of the Marquis, conscious of his own dignity and that of his master, and observing the rival charioteer was mending his pace, resolved, like a true brother of the whip, whether ancient or modern, to vindicate his right of precedence. So that, to increase the confusion of the Lord Keeper's understanding, he saw the short time which remained for consideration abridged by the haste of the contending coachmen, who, fixing their eyes sternly on each other, and applying the lash smartly to their horses, began to thunder down the descent with emulous rapidity, while the horsemen who attended them were forced to put on to a handgallop.

Sir William's only chance now remaining was the possibility of an overturn, and that his lady or visitor might break their necks. I am not aware that he formed any distinct wish on the subject, but I have no reason to think that his grief in either case would have been altogether inconsolable. This chance, however, also disappeared; for Lady Ashton, though insensible to fear, began to see the ridicule of running a race with a visitor of distinction, the goal being the portal of her own castle, and commanded her coachman, as they approached the avenue, to slacken his pace, and allow precedence to the stranger's equipage; a command which he gladly obeyed, as coming in time to save his honour, the horses of the Marquis's carriage being better, or, at least, fresher than his own. He restrained his pace, therefore, and suffered the green coach to enter the avenue, with all its retinue, which pass it occupied with the speed of a whirlwind. The Marquis's laced charioteer no sooner found the *pas d'avance* was granted to him, than he resumed a more deliberate pace, at which he advanced under the embowering shade of the lofty elms, surrounded by all the attendants; while the carriage of Lady Ashton followed, still more slowly, at some distance.

In the front of the castle, and beneath the portal which admitted guests into the inner court, stood Sir William Ashton, much perplexed in mind, his younger son and daughter beside him, and in their rear a train of attendants of various ranks, in and out of livery. The nobility and gentry of Scotland, at this period, were remarkable even to extravagance for the number of their servants, whose services were easily purchased in a country where men were numerous beyond proportion to the means of employing them.

The manners of a man, trained like Sir William Ashton, are too much at his command to remain long disconcerted with the most adverse concurrence of circumstances. He received the Marquis, as he alighted from his equipage, with the usual compliments of welcome; and, as he ushered him into the great hall, expressed his hope that his journey had been pleasant. The Marquis was a tall, well-made man, with a thoughtful and intelligent countenance, and an eye, in which the fire of ambition had for some years replaced the vivacity of youth; a bold, proud, expression of countenance, yet chastened by habitual caution, and the desire which, as the head of a party, he necessarily entertained of acquiring popularity. He answered with courtesy the courteous enquiries of the Lord Keeper, and was formally presented to Miss Ashton, in the course of which ceremony the Lord Keeper gave the first symptom of what was chiefly occupying his mind, by introducing his daughter as "his wife, Lady Ashton."

Lucy blushed; the Marquis looked surprised at the extremely juvenile appearance of his hostess, and the Lord Keeper with difficulty rallied himself so far as to explain. "I should have said my daughter, my lord; but the truth is, that I saw Lady Ashton's carriage enter the avenue shortly after your lordship's, and "——

"Make no apology, my lord," replied his noble guest; "let me entreat you will wait on your lady, and leave me to cultivate Miss Ashton's acquaintance. I am shocked my people should have taken precedence of our hostess at her own gate; but your lordship is aware, that I supposed Lady Ashton was still in the south. Permit me to beseech you will waive ceremony, and hasten to welcome her."

This was precisely what the Lord Keeper longed to do; and he instantly profited by his lordship's obliging permission. To see Lady Ashton, and encounter the first burst of her displeasure in private, might prepare her, in some degree, to receive her unwelcome guests with due decorum. As her carriage, therefore, stopped, the arm of the attentive husband was ready to assist Lady Ashton in dismounting. Looking as if she saw him not, she put his arm aside, and requested that of Captain Craigengelt, who stood by the coach with his laced hat under his arm, having acted as *cavalière servente*, or squire in attendance, during the journey. Taking hold of this respectable person's arm as if to support her, Lady Ashton traversed the court, uttering a word or two by way of direction to the servants, but not one to Sir William, who in vain endeavoured to attract her attention, as he rather followed than accompanied her into the hall, in which they found the Marquis in close conversation with the Master of Ravenswood : Lucy had taken the first opportunity of escaping. There was embarrassment on every countenance except that of the Marquis of A——; for even Craigengelt's impudence was hardly able to veil his fear of Ravenswood, and the rest felt the awkwardness of the position in which they were thus unexpectedly placed.

After waiting a moment to be presented by Sir William Ashton, the Marquis resolved to introduce himself. "The Lord Keeper," he said, bowing to Lady Ashton, "has just introduced to me his daughter as his wife—he might very easily present Lady Ashton as his daughter, so little does she differ from what I remember her some years since.— Will she permit an old acquaintance the privilege of a guest?"

He saluted the lady with too good a grace to apprehend a repulse, and then proceeded—"This, Lady Ashton, is a peace-making visit, and therefore I presume to introduce my cousin, the young Master of Ravenswood, to your favourable notice."

Lady Ashton could not choose but curtsy; but there was in her obeisance an air of haughtiness approaching to contemptuous repulse. Ravenswood could not choose but bow; but his manner returned the scorn with which he had been greeted.

"Allow me," she said, "to present to your lordship *my* friend." Craigengelt, with the forward impudence which men of his cast mistake for ease, made a sliding bow to the Marquis, which he graced by a flourish of his gold-laced hat. The lady turned to her husband—"You and I, Sir William," she said, and these were the first words she had addressed to him, "have acquired new acquaintances since we parted—let me introduce the acquisition I have made to mine—Captain Craigengelt."

Another bow, and another flourish of the gold-laced hat, which was returned by the Lord Keeper without intimation

of former recognition, and with that sort of anxious readiness, which intimated his wish, that peace and amnesty
should take place betwixt the contending parties, including
the auxiliaries on both sides. "Let me introduce you to
the Master of Ravenswood," said he to Captain Craigengelt, following up the same amicable system. . But the
Master drew up his tall form to the full extent of his height,
and without so much as looking towards the person thus
introduced to him, he said in a marked tone, "Captain
Craigengelt and I are already perfectly well acquainted with
each other."

"Perfectly—perfectly," replied the Captain, in a mumb-
ling tone, like that of a double echo, and with a flourish of
his hat, the circumference of which was greatly abridged,
compared with those which had so cordially graced his
introduction to the Marquis and the Lord Keeper.

Lockhard, followed by three menials, now entered with
wine and refreshments, which it was the fashion to offer as
a whet before dinner; and when they were placed before
the guests, Lady Ashton made an apology for withdrawing
her husband from them for some minutes upon business of
special import. The Marquis, of course, requested her
ladyship would lay herself under no restraint; and Craigengelt, bolting with speed a second glass of racy canary,
hastened to leave the room, feeling no great pleasure in the
prospect of being left alone with the Marquis of A——
and the Master of Ravenswood; the presence of the former
holding him in awe, and that of the latter in bodily terror.

Some arrangements about his horse and baggage formed
the pretext for his sudden retreat, in which he persevered,
although Lady Ashton gave Lockhard orders to be careful
most particularly to accommodate Captain Craigengelt with
all the attendance which he could possibly require. The
Marquis and the Master of Ravenswood were thus left to
communicate to each other their remarks upon the reception which they had met with, while Lady Ashton led the
way, and her lord followed somewhat like a condemned
criminal, to her ladyship's dressing-room.

So soon as the spouses had both entered, her ladyship
gave way to that fierce audacity of temper, which she had
with difficulty suppressed, out of respect to appearances.
She shut the door behind the alarmed Lord Keeper, took

the key out of the spring-lock, and with a countenance
which years had not bereft of its haughty charms, and eyes
which spoke at once resolution and resentment, she
addressed her astounded husband in these words :—"My
lord, I am not greatly surprised at the connexions you have
been pleased to form during my absence—they are entirely
in conformity with your birth and breeding; and it I did
expect any thing else, I heartily own my error, and that I
merit, by having done so, the disappointment you had prepared for me."

"My dear Lady Ashton—my dear Eleanor," said the
Lord Keeper, "listen to reason for a moment, and I will
convince you I have acted with all the regard due to the
dignity, as well as the interest, of my family."

"To the interest of *your* family I conceive you perfectly
capable of attending," returned the indignant lady, "and
even to the dignity of your own family also, as far as it
requires any looking after—But as mine happens to be in-
extricably involved with it, you will excuse me if I choose
to give my own attention so far as that is concerned."

"What would you have, Lady Ashton ?" said the husband
—"What is it that displeases you ? Why is it, that on your
return after so long an absence, I am arraigned in this
manner ?"

"Ask your own conscience, Sir William, what has
prompted you to become a renegade to your political party
and opinions, and led you, for all I know, to be on the
point of marrying your only daughter to a beggarly jacobite
bankrupt, the inveterate enemy of your family to the
boot."

"Why, what, in the name of common sense and common
civility, would you have me do, madam ?" answered her
husband—"Is it possible for me, with ordinary decency, to
turn a young gentleman out of my house, who saved my
daughter's life and my own, but the other morning as it
were ?"

"Saved your life ! I have heard of that story," said the
lady—"the Lord Keeper was scared by a dun cow. and he
takes the young fellow who killed her for Guy of Warwick
—any butcher from Haddington may soon have an equal
claim on your hospitality."

"Lady Ashton," stammered the Keeper, "this is intolerable—and when I am desirous, too, to make you easy by any sacrifice—if you would but tell me what you would be at."

"Go down to your guests," said the imperious dame, "and make your apology to Ravenswood, that the arrival of Captain Craigengelt and some other friends renders it impossible for you to offer him lodgings at the castle—I expect young Mr Hayston of Bucklaw."

"Good heavens, madam!" ejaculated her husband— 'Ravenswood to give place to Craigengelt, a common gambler and an informer!—it was all I could do to forbear desiring the fellow to get out of my house, and I was much surprised to see him in your ladyship's train."

"Since you saw him there, you might be well assured," answered this meek helpmate, "that he was proper society. As to this Ravenswood, he only meets with the treatment which, to my certain knowledge, he gave to a much-valued friend of mine, who had the misfortune to be his guest some time since. But take your resolution; for, if Ravenswood does not quit the house, I will."

Sir William Ashton paced up and down the apartment in the most distressing agitation; fear, and shame, and anger contending against the habitual deference he was in the use of rendering to his lady. At length it ended, as is usual with timid minds placed in such circumstances, in his adopting a *mezzo termine*, a middle measure.

"I tell you frankly, madam, I neither can nor will be guilty of the incivility you propose to the Master of Ravenswood—he has not deserved it at my hand. If you will be so unreasonable as to insult a man of quality under your own roof, I cannot prevent you; but I will not at least be the agent in such a preposterous proceeding."

"You will not?" asked the lady.

"No, by heavens, madam!" her husband replied; "ask me any thing congruent with common decency, as to drop his acquaintance by degrees, or the like—but to bid him leave my house is what I will not, and cannot consent to."

"Then the task of supporting the honour of the family will fall on me, as it has often done before," said the lady.

She sat down, and hastily wrote a few lines. The Lord Keeper made another effort to prevent her taking a step so decisive, just as she opened the door to call her female attendant from the ante-room. "Think what you are doing, Lady Ashton—you are making a mortal enemy of a young man, who is like to have the means of harming us "——

"Did you ever know a Douglas who feared an enemy?" answered the lady contemptuously.

"Ay, but he is as proud and vindictive as an hundred Douglasses, and an hundred devils to boot. Think of it for a night only."

"Not for another moment," answered the lady,—"here, Mrs Patullo, give this billet to young Ravenswood."

"To the Master, madam?" said Mrs Patullo.

"Ay, to the Master, if you call him so."

"I wash my hands of it entirely," said the Keeper; "and I shall go down into the garden, and see that Jardine gathers the winter fruit for the dessert."

"Do so," said the lady, looking after him with glances of infinite contempt; "and thank God that you leave one behind you as fit to protect the honour of the family, as you are to look after pippins and pears."

The Lord Keeper remained long enough in the garden to give her ladyship's mind time to explode, and to let, as he thought, at least the first violence of Ravenswood's displeasure blow over. When he entered the hall, he found the Marquis of A—— giving orders to some of his attendants. He seemed in high displeasure, and interrupted an apology which Sir William had commenced, for having left his lordship alone.

"I presume, Sir William, you are no stranger to this singular billet with which my kinsman of Ravenswood" (an emphasis on the word *my*) "has been favoured by your lady—and, of course, that you are prepared to receive my adieus—My kinsman is already gone, having thought it unnecessary to offer any on his part, since all former civilities had been cancelled by this singular insult."

"I protest, my lord," said Sir William, holding the billet in his hand, "I am not privy to the contents of this letter. I know Lady Ashton is a warm-tempered and prejudiced woman, and I am sincerely sorry for any offence that has been given or taken; but I hope your lordship will consider that a lady "——

"Should bear herself towards persons of a certain rank

with the breeding of one," said the Marquis, completing the half-uttered sentence.

"True, my lord," said the unfortunate Keeper; "but Lady Ashton is still a woman"——

"And as such, methinks," said the Marquis, again interrupting him, "should be taught the duties which corrrespond to her station. But here she comes, and I will learn from her own mouth the reason of this extraordinary and unexpected affront offered to my near relation, while both he and I were her ladyship's guests."

Lady Ashton accordingly entered the apartment at this moment. Her dispute with Sir William, and a subsequent interview with her daughter, had not prevented her from attending to the duties of her toilette. She appeared in full dress; and, from the character of her countenance and manner, well became the splendour with which ladies of quality then appeared on such occasions.

The Marquis of A—— bowed haughtily, and she returned the salute with equal pride and distance of demeanour. He then took from the passive hand of Sir William Ashton the billet he had given him the moment before he approached the lady, and was about to speak, when she interrupted him. "I perceive, my lord, you are about to enter upon an unpleasant subject. I am sorry any such should have occurred at this time, to interrupt, in the slightest degree, the respectful reception due to your lordship—but so it is.—Mr Edgar Ravenswood, for whom I have addressed the billet in your lordship's hand, has abused the hospitality of this family, and Sir William Ashton's sortness of temper, in order to seduce a young person into engagements without her parents' consent, and of which they never can approve."

Both gentlemen answered at once,—"My kinsman is incapable,"——said the Lord Marquis.

"I am confident that my daughter Lucy is still more incapable,"——said the Lord Keeper.

Lady Ashton at once interrupted, and replied to them both.—"My Lord Marquis, your kinsman, if Mr Ravenswood has the honour to be so, has made the attempt privately to secure the affections of this young and inexperienced girl. Sir William Ashton, your daughter has been simple enough to give more encouragement than she ought to have done to so very improper a suitor."

"And I think, madam," said the Lord Keeper, losing his accustomed temper and patience, "that if you had nothing better to tell us, you had better have kept this family secret to yourself also."

"You will pardon me, Sir William," said the lady, calmly; "the noble Marquis has a right to know the cause of the treatment I have found it necessary to use to a gentleman whom he calls his blood-relation."

"It is a cause," muttered the Lord Keeper, "which has emerged since the effect has taken place; for, if it exists at all, I am sure she knew nothing of it when her letter to Ravenswood was written."

"It is the first time that I have heard of this," said the Marquis; "but since your ladyship has tabled a subject so delicate, permit me to say, that my kinsman's birth and connexions entitled him to a patient hearing, and at least a civil refusal, even in case of his being so ambitious as to raise his eyes to the daughter of Sir William Ashton."

"You will recollect, my lord, of what blood Miss Lucy Ashton is come by the mother's side," said the lady.

"I do remember your descent—from a younger branch of the house of Angus," said the Marquis—"and your ladyship—forgive me, lady—ought not to forget that the Ravenswoods have thrice intermarried with the main-stem. Come, madam—I know how matters stand—old and long-fostered prejudices are difficult to get over—I make every allowance for them—I ought not, and I would not otherwise have suffered my kinsman to depart alone, expelled, in a manner, from this house—but I had hopes of being a mediator. I am still unwilling to leave you in anger—and shall not set forward till after noon, as I rejoin the Master of Ravenswood upon the road a few miles from hence. Let us talk over this matter more coolly."

"It is what I anxiously desire, my lord," said Sir William Ashton, eagerly. "Lady Ashton, we will not permit my Lord of A—— to leave us in displeasure. We must compel him to tarry dinner at the castle."

"The castle," said the lady, "and all that it contains, are at the command of the Marquis, so long as he chooses to honour it with his residence; but touching the further discussion of this disagreeable topic"——

"Pardon me, good madam," said the Marquis; "but I cannot allow you to express any hasty resolution on a subject so important. I see that more company is arriving; and since I have the good fortune to renew my former acquaintance with Lady Ashton, I hope she will give me leave to avoid perilling what I prize so highly upon any disagreeable subject of discussion—at least, till we have talked over more pleasant topics."

The lady smiled, curtsied, and gave her hand to the Marquis, by whom, with all the formal gallantry of the time, which did not permit the guest to tuck the lady of the house under the arm, as a rustic does his sweetheart at a wake, she was ushered to the eating-room.

Here they were joined by Bucklaw, Craigengelt, and other neighbours, whom the Lord Keeper had previously invited to meet the Marquis of A——. An apology, founded upon a slight indisposition, was alleged as an excuse for the absence of Miss Ashton, whose seat appeared unoccupied. The entertainment was splendid to profusion, and was protracted till a late hour.

CHAPTER XXIII

> Such was our fallen father's fate,
> Yet better than mine own;
> He shared his exile with his mate,
> I'm banish'd forth alone.
>
> *Waller.*

I WILL not attempt to describe the mixture of indignation and regret with which Ravenswood left the seat which had belonged to his ancestors. The terms in which Lady Ashton's billet was couched rendered it impossible for him, without being deficient in that spirit of which he perhaps had too much, to remain an instant longer within its walls. The Marquis, who had his share in the affront, was, nevertheless, still willing to make some efforts at conciliation. He therefore suffered his kinsman to depart alone, making him promise, however, that he would wait for him at the small inn called the Tod's-hole, situated, as our readers may be pleased to recollect, half way betwixt Ravenswood Castle and Wolf's Crag, and about five Scottish miles distant from each. Here the Marquis proposed to join the Master of Ravenswood, either that night or the next morning. His own feelings would have induced him to have left the castle directly, but he was loath to forfeit, without at least one effort, the advantages which he had proposed from his visit to the Lord Keeper; and the Master of Ravenswood was, even in the very heat of his resentment, unwilling to foreclose any chance of reconciliation which might arise out of the partiality which Sir William Ashton had shown towards him, as well as the intercessory arguments of his noble kinsman. He himself departed without a moment's delay, farther than was necessary to make this arrangement.

At first he spurred his horse at a quick pace through an avenue of the park, as if, by rapidity of motion, he could stupefy the confusion of feelings with which he was assailed. But as the road grew wilder and more sequestered, and when the trees had hidden the turrets of the castle, he gradually slackened his pace, as if to indulge the painful reflections which he had in vain endeavoured to repress. The path in which he found himself led him to the Mermaiden's Fountain, and to the cottage of Alice; and the fatal influence which superstitious belief attached to the former spot, as well as the admonitions which had been in vain offered to him by the inhabitant of the latter, forced themselves upon his memory. "Old saws speak truth," he said to himself; "and the Mermaiden's Well has indeed witnessed the last act of rashness of the heir of Ravenswood. —Alice spoke well," he continued, "and I am in the situation which she foretold—or rather, I am more deeply dishonoured—not the dependant and ally of the destroyer of my father's house, as the old sibyl presaged, but the degraded wretch, who has aspired to hold that subordinate character, and has been rejected with disdain."

We are bound to tell the tale as we have received it; and, considering the distance of the time, and propensity of those through whose mouths it has passed to the marvellous, this could not be called a Scottish story, unless it manifested a tinge of Scottish superstition. As Ravenswood approached the solitary fountain, he is said to have met with the following singular adventure:—His horse, which was moving slowly forward, suddenly interrupted its steady and composed pace, snorted, reared, and, though urged by the spur, refused to proceed, as if some object of terror had suddenly presented itself. On looking to the fountain, Ravenswood discerned a female figure, dressed in a white, or rather greyish mantle, placed on the very spot on which Lucy Ashton had reclined while listening to the fatal tale of love. His immediate impression was, that she had conjectured by which path he would traverse the park on his departure and placed herself at this well-known and sequestered place of rendezvous, to indulge her own sorrow and his in a parting interview. In this belief he jumped from his horse, and making its bridle fast to a tree, walked hastily towards the fountain, pronouncing eagerly, yet under his breath, the words, "Miss Ashton!—Lucy!"

The figure turned as he addressed it, and displayed to his wondering eyes the features, not of Lucy Ashton, but of old blind Alice. The singularity of her dress, which rather resembled a shroud, than the garment of a living woman—the appearance of her person, larger, as it struck him, than it usually seemed to be—above all, the strange circumstance of a blind, infirm, and decrepit person being found alone and at a distance from her habitation (considerable, if her infirmities be taken into account), combined to impress him with a feeling of wonder approaching to fear. As he approached, she arose slowly from her seat, held her shrivelled hand up as if to prevent his coming more near, and her withered lips moved fast, although no sound issued from them. Ravenswood stopped; and as, after a moment's pause, he again advanced towards her, Alice, or her apparition, moved or glided backwards towards the thicket, still keeping her face turned towards him. The trees soon hid the form from his sight; and, yielding to the strong and terrific impression that the being which he had seen was not of this world, the Master of Ravenswood remained rooted to the ground whereon he had stood when he caught his last view of her. At length, summoning up his courage, he advanced to the spot on which the figure had seemed to be seated; but neither was there pressure of the grass, nor any other circumstance, to induce him to believe that what he had seen was real and substantial.

Full of those strange thoughts and confused apprehensions which awake in the bosom of one who conceives he has witnessed some preternatural appearance, the Master of Ravenswood walked back towards his horse, frequently however looking behind him, not without apprehension, as if expecting that the vision would re-appear. But the apparition, whether it was real, or whether it was the creation of a heated and agitated imagination, returned not again; and he found his horse sweating and terrified, as if experiencing that agony of fear, with which the presence of a supernatural being is supposed to agitate the brute creation. The Master mounted, and rode slowly forward, soothing his steed from time to time, while the animal seemed internally to shrink and shudder, as if expecting some new object of fear at the opening of every glade. The rider, after a moment's consideration, resolved to investigate the matter further. "Can my eyes have deceived me," he said, "and deceived me for such a space of time?—Or are this woman's infirmities but feigned, in order to excite compassion?—And even then, her motion resembled not that of a living and existing person. Must I adopt the popular creed, and think that the unhappy being has formed a league with the powers of darkness?—I am determined to be resolved—I will not brook imposition even from my own eyes."

In this uncertainty he rode up to the little wicket of Alice's garden. Her seat beneath the birch-tree was vacant, though the day was pleasant, and the sun was high. He approached the hut, and heard from within the sobs and wailing of a female. No answer was returned when he knocked, so that, after a moment's pause, he lifted the latch and entered. It was indeed a house of solitude and sorrow. Stretched upon her miserable pallet lay the corpse of the last retainer of the house of Ravenswood, who still abode on their paternal domains! Life had but shortly departed; and the little girl, by whom she had been attended in her last moments, was wringing her hands and sobbing, betwixt childish fear and sorrow, over the body of her mistress.

The Master of Ravenswood had some difficulty to compose the terrors of the poor child, whom his unexpected appearance had at first rather appalled than comforted;

and when he succeeded, the first expression which the girl used intimated that "he had come too late." Upon enquiring the meaning of this expression, he learned that the deceased, upon the first attack of the mortal agony, had sent a peasant, to the castle to beseech an interview of the Master of Ravenswood, and had expressed the utmost impatience for his return. But the messengers of the poor are tardy and negligent: the fellow had not reached the castle, as was afterwards learned, until Ravenswood had left it, and had then found too much amusement among the retinue of the strangers to return in any haste to the cottage of Alice. Meantime her anxiety of mind seemed to increase with the agony of her body; and, to use the phrase of Babie, her only attendant, "she prayed powerfully that she might see her master's son once more, and renew her warning." She died just as the clock in the distant village tolled one; and Ravenswood remembered, with internal shuddering, that he had heard the chime sound through the wood just before he had seen what he was now much disposed to consider as the spectre of the deceased.

It was necessary, as well from his respect to the departed as in common humanity to her terrified attendant, that he should take some measures to relieve the girl from her distressing situation. The deceased, he understood, had expressed a desire to be buried in a solitary churchyard, near the little inn of the Tod's-hole, called the Hermitage, or more commonly Armitage, in which lay interred some of the Ravenswood family, and many of their followers. Ravenswood conceived it his duty to gratify this predilection, so commonly found to exist among the Scottish peasantry, and dispatched Babie to the neighbouring village to procure the assistance of some females, assuring her that, in the meanwhile, he would himself remain, with the dead body, which, as in Thessaly of old, it is accounted highly unfit to leave without a watch.

Thus, in the course of a quarter of an hour or little more, he found himself sitting a solitary guard over the inanimate corse of her, whose dismissed spirit, unless his eyes had strangely deceived him, had so recently manifested itself before him. Notwithstanding his natural courage, the Master was considerably affected by a concurrence of circumstances so extraordinary. "She died expressing her eager desire to see me. Can it be, then,"—was his natural course of reflection—"can strong and earnest wishes, formed during the last agony of nature, survive its catastrophe, surmount the awful bounds of the spiritual world, and place before us its inhabitants in the hues and colouring of life? —And why was that manifested to the eye which could not unfold its tale to the ear?—and wherefore should a breach be made in the laws of nature, yet its purpose remain unknown? Vain questions, which only death, when it shall make me like the pale and withered form before me, can ever resolve."

He laid a cloth, as he spoke, over the lifeless face, upon whose features he felt unwilling any longer to dwell. He then took his place in an old carved oaken chair, ornamented with his own armorial bearings, which Alice had contrived to appropriate to her own use in the pillage which took place among creditors, officers, domestics, and messengers of the law, when his father left Ravenswood Castle for the last time. Thus seated, he banished, as much as he could, the superstitious feelings which the late incident naturally inspired. His own were sad enough, without the exaggeration of supernatural terror, since he found himself transferred from the situation of a successful lover of Lucy Ashton, and an honoured and respected friend of her father, into the melancholy and solitary guardian of the abandoned and forsaken corse of a common pauper.

He was relieved, however, from his sad office sooner than he could reasonably have expected, considering the distance betwixt the hut of the deceased and the village, and the age and infirmities of three old women, who came from thence, in military phrase, to relieve guard upon the body of the defunct. On any other occasion the speed of these reverend sibyls would have been much more moderate, for the first was eighty years of age and upwards, the second was paralytic, and the third lame of a leg from some accident. But the burial duties rendered to the deceased, are, to the Scottish peasant of either sex, a labour of love. I know not whether it is from the temper of the people, grave and enthusiastic as it certainly is, or from the recollection of the ancient Catholic opinions, when the funeral rites were always considered as a period of festival to the living; but feasting, good cheer, and even inebriety, were, and are, the frequent accompaniments of a Scottish old-fashioned burial. What the funeral feast, or *dirgie*, as it is called, was to the men, the gloomy preparations of the dead body for the coffin were to the women. To straight the contorted limbs upon a board used for that melancholy purpose, to array the corpse in clean linen, and over that in its woollen shroud, were operations committed always to the old matrons of the village, and in which they found a singular and gloomy delight.

The old women paid the Master their salutations with a ghastly smile, which reminded him of the meeting betwixt Macbeth and the witches on the blasted heath of Forres. He gave them some money, and recommended to them the charge of the dead body of their contemporary, an office which they willingly undertook; intimating to him at the same time that he must leave the hut, in order that they might begin their mournful duties. Ravenswood readily agreed to depart, only tarrying to recommend to them due attention to the body, and to receive information where he was to find the sexton, or beadle, who had in charge the deserted churchyard of the Armitage, in order to prepare matters for the reception of old Alice in the place of repose which she had selected for herself.

"Ye'll no be pinched ι find out Johnie Mortsheugh," said the elder sibyl, and still her withered cheek bore a grisly smile—"he dwells near the Tod's-hole, an house of entertainment where there has been mony a blithe birling—for death and drink-draining are near neighbours to ane anither."

"Ay! and that's e'en true, cummer," said the lame hag, propping herself with a crutch which supported the shortness of her left leg, "for I mind when the father of this Master of Ravenswood that is now standing before us, sticked young Blackhall with his whinger, for a wrang word said ower their wine, or brandy, or what not—he gaed in as light as a lark, and he came out wi' his feet foremost. I was at the winding of the corpse; and when the bluid was washed off, he was a bonny bouk of man's body."

It may be easily believed that this ill-timed anecdote hastened the Master's purpose of quitting a company so evil-omened and so odious. Yet, while walking to the tree to which his horse was tied, and busying himself with adjusting the girths of the saddle, he could not avoid hearing, through the hedge of the little garden, a conversation respecting himself, betwixt the lame woman and the octogenarian sibyl. The pair had hobbled into the garden to gather rosemary, southernwood, rue, and other plants proper to be strewed upon the body, and burned by way of fumigation in the chimney of the cottage. The paralytic wretch, almost exhausted by the journey, was left guard upon the corpse, lest witches or fiends might play their sport with it.

The following low croaking dialogue was necessarily overheard by the Master of Ravenswood:—

"That's a fresh and full-grown hemlock, Annie Winnie —mony a cummer lang syne wad hae sought nae better horse to flee over hill and how, through mist and moonlight, and light down in the King of France's cellar."

"Ay, cummer! but the very deil has turned as hardhearted now as the Lord Keeper, and the grit folk that hae breasts like whin-stane. They prick us and they pine us, and they pit us on the pinny-winkles for witches; and, if I say my prayers backwards ten times ower, Satan will never gie me amends o' them."

"Did ye ever see the foul thief?" asked her neighbour.

"Na!" replied the other spokeswoman; "but I trow I hae dreamed of him mony a time, and I think the day will come they will burn me for't.—But ne'er mind, cummer! we hae this dollar of the Master's, and we'll send doun for bread and for yill, and tobacco, and a drap brandy to burn, and a wee pickle saft sugar—and be there deil, or nae deil, lass, we'll hae a merry night o't."

Here her leathern chops uttered a sort of cackling ghastly laugh, resembling, to a certain degree, the cry of the screech-owl.

"He's a frank man, and a free-handed man, the Master," said Annie Winnie, "and a comely personage—broad in the shouthers, and narrow around the lungies—he wad mak a bonny corpse—I wad like to hae the streaking and winding o' him."

"It is written on his brow, Annie Winnie," returned the octogenarian, her companion, "that hand of woman, or of man either, will never straught him—dead-deal will never be laid on his back—make you your market of that, for I hae it frae a sure hand."

"Will it be his lot to die on the battle-ground then, Ailsie Gourlay?—Will he die by the sword or the ball, as his forbears hae dune before him, mony ane o' them?"

"Ask nae mair questions about it—he'll no be graced sae far," replied the sage.

"I ken ye are wiser than ither folk, Ailsie Gourlay—But wha tell'd ye this?"

"Fashna your thumb about that, Annie Winnie," answered the sibyl—"I hae it frae a hand sure enough."

"But ye said ye never saw the foul thief," reiterated her inquisitive companion.

"I hae it frae as sure a hand," said Ailsie, "and frae them that spaed his fortune before the sark gaed ower his head."

"Hark! I hear his horse's feet riding aff," said the other; "they dinna sound as if good luck was wi' them."

"Mak haste, sirs," cried the paralytic hag from the cottage, "and let us do what is needfu', and say what is fitting; for, if the dead corpse binna straughted, it will girn and thraw, and that will fear the best o' us."

Ravenswood was now out of hearing. He despised most of the ordinary prejudices about witchcraft, omens, and vaticination, to which his age and country still gave such implicit credit, that to express a doubt of them, was accounted a crime equal to the unbelief of Jews or Saracens; he knew also that the prevailing belief concerning witches, operating upon the hypochondriac habits of those whom age, infirmity, and poverty rendered liable to suspicion, and enforced by the fear of death, and the pangs of the most cruel tortures. often extorted those confessions which encumber and disgrace the criminal records of Scotland during the seventeenth century. But the vision of that morning, whether real or imaginary, had impressed his mind with a superstitious feeling which he in vain endeavoured to shake off. The nature of the business which awaited him at the little inn, called Tod's-hole, where he soon after arrived, was not of a kind to restore his spirits.

It was necessary he should see Mortsheugh, the sexton of the old burial-ground at Armitage, to arrange matters for the funeral of Alice; and as the man dwelt near the place of her late residence, the Master, after a slight refreshment, walked towards the place where the body of Alice was to be deposited. It was situated in the nook formed by the eddying sweep of a stream, which issued from the adjoining hills. A rude cavern in an adjacent rock, which, in the interior, was cut into the shape of a cross, formed the hermitage, where some Saxon saint had in ancient times done penance, and given name to the place. The rich Abbey of Coldinghame had, in latter days, established a chapel in the neighbourhood, of which no vestige was now visible, though the churchyard which surrounded it was still, as upon the present occasion, used for the interment of particular persons. One or two shattered yew-trees still grew within the precincts of that which had once been holy ground. Warriors and barons had been buried there of old, but their names were forgotten, and their monuments demolished. The only sepulchral memorials which remained, were the upright headstones which mark the graves of persons of inferior rank. The abode of the sexton was a solitary cottage adjacent to the ruined wall of the cemetery, but so low, that, with its thatch, which nearly reached the ground, covered with a thick crop of grass, fog, and house-leeks, it resembled an overgrown grave. On enquiry, however, Ravenswood found that the man of the last mattock was absent at a bridal, being fiddler as well as grave-digger t. the vicinity. He therefore retired to the little inn, leaving a message that early next morning he would again call for the person, whose double occupation connected him at once with the house of mourning and the house of feasting.

An outrider of the Marquis arrived at Tod's-hole shortly after, with a message, intimating that his master would join Ravenswood at that place on the following morning; and the Master, who would otherwise have proceeded to his old retreat at Wolf's Crag, remained there accordingly, to give meeting to his noble kinsman.

CHAPTER XXIV

Hamlet.   Has this fellow no feeling of his business—he sings at grave making.
Horatio.   Custom hath made it in him a property of easiness.
Hamlet.   'Tis e'en so : the hand of little employment hath the daintier sense.

Hamlet, Act V. Scene I.

THE sleep of Ravenswood was broken by ghastly and agitating visions, and his waking intervals disturbed by melancholy reflections on the past, and painful anticipations of the future.   He was perhaps the only traveller who ever slept in that miserable kennel without complaining of his lodgings, or feeling inconvenience from their deficiencies.   It is when "the mind is free the body's delicate."·   Morning, however, found the Master an early riser, in hopes that the fresh air of the dawn might afford the refreshment which night had refused him.   He took his way toward the solitary burial-ground, which lay about half a mile from the inn.

The thin blue smoke, which already began to curl upward, and to distinguish the cottage of the living from the habitation of the dead, apprized him that its inmate had returned and was stirring.   Accordingly, on entering the little churchyard, he saw the old man labouring in a half-made grave.   My destiny, thought Ravenswood, seems to lead me to scenes of fate and of death; but these are childish thoughts, and they shall not master me.   I will not again suffer my imagination to beguile my senses.— The old man rested on his spade as the Master approached him, as if to receive his commands; and as he did not immediately speak, the sexton opened the discourse in his own way.

"Ye will be a wedding customer, sir, I'se warrant?"

"What makes you think so, friend?" replied the Master.

"I live by twa trades, sir," replied the blithe old man ; "fiddle, sir, and spade ; filling the world, and emptying of it; and I suld ken baith cast of customers by head-mark in thirty years' practice."

"You are mistaken, however, this morning," replied Ravenswood.

"Am I?" said the old man, looking keenly at him, "troth and it may be; since, for as brent as your brow is, there is something sitting upon it this day, that is as near akin to death as to wedlock. Weel, weel; the pick and shovel are as ready to your order as bow and fiddle."

"I wish you," said Ravenswood, "to look after the decent interment of an old woman, Alice Gray, who lived at the Craig-foot in Ravenswood Park."

"Alice Gray! blind Alice!" said the sexton; "and is she gane at last? that's another jow of the bell to bid me be ready. I mind when Habbie Gray brought her down to this land; a likely lass she was then, and looked ower her southland nose at us a'. I trow her pride got a down-come. And is she e'en gane?"

"She died yesterday," said Ravenswood; "and desired to be buried here, beside her husband; you know where he lies, no doubt?"

"Ken where he lies?" answered the sexton, with national indirection of response, "I ken whar a' body lies, that lies here. But ye were speaking o' her grave?—Lord help us—it's no an ordinar grave that will haud her in, if a's true that folk said of Alice in her auld days; and if I gae to six feet deep,—and a warlock's grave shouldna be an inch mair ebb, or her ain witch cummers would soon whirl her out of her shroud for a' their auld acquaintance—and be't six feet, or be't three, wha's to pay the making o't, I pray ye?"

"I will pay that, my friend, and all other reasonable charges."

"Reasonable charges?" said the sexton; "ou, there's grund-mail—and bell-siller—(though the bell's broken nae doubt)—and the kist—and my day's wark—and my bit fee—and some brandy and yill to the drigie—I am no thinking that you can inter her, to ca' decently, under saxteen pund Scots."

"There is the money, my friend," said Ravenswood, "and something over. Be sure you know the grave."

"Ye'll be ane o' her English relations, I'se warrant," said the hoary man of skulls; "I hae heard she married far below her station; it was very right to let her bite on the bridle when she was living, and it's very right to gie her a decent burial now she's dead, for that's a matter o' credit to yoursell rather than to her. Folk may let their kindred shift for themsells when they are alive, and can bear the burden of their ain misdoings; but it's an unnatural thing to let them be buried like dogs, when a' the discredit gangs to the kindred—what kens the dead corpse about it?"

"You would not have people neglect their relations on a bridal occasion neither?" said Ravenswood, who was amused with the professional limitation of the grave-digger's philanthropy.

The old man cast up his sharp grey eyes with a shrewd smile, as if he understood the jest, but instantly continued, with his former gravity,—"Bridals—wha wad neglect bridals, that had ony regard for plenishing the earth? To be sure, they suld be celebrated with all manner of good cheer, and meeting of friends, and musical instruments, harp, sackbut, and psaltery; or gude fiddle and pipes, when these auld-warld instruments of melody are hard to be compassed."

"The presence of the fiddle, I daresay," replied Ravenswood, "would atone for the absence of all the others."

The sexton again looked sharply up at him, as he answered, "Nae doubt—nae doubt—if it were weel played; —but yonder," he said, as if to change the discourse, "is Halbert Gray's lang hame, that ye were speering after, just the third bourock beyond the muckle through-stane that stands on sax legs yonder, abune some ane of the Ravenswoods; for there is mony of their kin and followers here, deil lift them! though it isna just their main burial-place."

"They are no favourites, then, of yours, these Ravenswoods?" said the Master, not much pleased with the passing benediction which was thus bestowed on his family and name.

"I kenna wha should favour them," said the grave-digger; "when they had lands and power, they were ill guides of them baith, and now their head's down, there's few care how lang they may be of lifting it again."

"Indeed," said Ravenswood; "I never heard that this unhappy family deserved ill-will at the hands of their country. I grant their poverty—if that renders them contemptible."

"It will gang a far way till't," said the sexton of Hermitage, "ye may tak my word for that—at least, I ken naething else that suld mak myself contemptible, and folk are far frae respecting me as they wad do if I lived in a twa-lofted sclated house. But as for the Ravenswoods I hae seen three generations of them, and deil ane to mend other."

"I thought they had enjoyed a fair character in the country," said their descendant.

"Character! Ou, ye see, sir," said the sexton, "as for the auld gude-sire of a lord, I lived on his land when I was a swanking young chield, and could hae blawn the trumpet wi' ony body, for I had wind eneugh then—and touching this trumpeter Marine that I have heard play afore the Lords of the Circuit, I wad hae made nae mair o' him than of a bairn and a bawbee whistle—I defy him to hae played 'Boot and saddle,' or 'Horse and away,' or 'Gallants, come trot,' with me—he hadna the tones."

"But what is all this to old Lord Ravenswood, my friend?" said the Master, who, with an anxiety not unnatural in his circumstances, was desirous of prosecuting the musician's first topic—"What had his memory to do with the degeneracy of the trumpet music?"

"Just this, sir," answered the sexton, "that I lost my wind in his service. Ye see I was trumpeter at the castle, and had allowance for blawing at break of day, and at dinner-time, and other whiles when there was company about, and it pleased my lord; and when he raised his militia to caper awa to Bothwell Brigg against the wrang-headed wastland whigs, I behoved, reason or nane, to munt a horse and caper awa wi' them."

"And very reasonable," said Ravenswood; "you were his servant and vassal."

"Servitor, say ye?" replied the sexton, "and so I was—but it was to blaw folk to their warm dinner, or at the warst to a decent kirkyard, and no to skirl them awa to a bluidy brae side, where there was deal a bedral but the hooded craw. But bide ye—ye shall hear what cam o't, and how far I am bund to be bedesman to the Ravenswoods.—Till't, ye see, we gaed on a braw simmer morning, twenty-fourth of June, saxteen hundred and se'enty-nine, of a' the days of the month and year,—drums beat—guns rattled — horses kicked and trampled. Hackstoun of Ra'hillet keepit the brigg wi' musket and carabine and pike, sword and scythe for what I ken, and we horsemen

were ordered down to cross at the ford,—I hate fords at a'
times, let abe when there's thousands of armed men on the
other side. There was auld Ravenswood brandishing his
Andrew Ferrara at the head, and crying to us to come and
buckle to, as if we had been gaun to a fair,—there was Caleb
Balderstone, that is living yet, flourishing in the rear, and
swearing Gog and Magog, he would put steel through the
guts of ony man that turned bridle,—there was young Allan
Ravenswood, that was then Master, wi' a bended pistol in
his hand,—it was a mercy it gaed na aff,—crying to me
that had scarce as much wind left to serve the necessary
purpose of my ain lungs, 'Sound, you poltroon! sound,
you damned cowardly villain, or I will blow your brains out!'
and to be sure, I blew sic points of war, that the scraugh
of a clockin-hen was music to them."

"Well, sir, cut all this short," said Ravenswood.

"Short!—I had like to hae been cut short mysell, in
the flower of my youth, as Scripture says; and that's the
very thing that I compleen o'.—Weel! in to the water we
behoved a' to splash, heels ower head, sit or fa'—ae horse
driving on anither, as in the way of brute beasts, and riders
that hae as little sense,—the very bushes on the ither side
were ableeze, wi' the flashes of the whig guns; and my
horse had just taen the grund, when a blackavised westland
carle—I wad mind the face o' him a hundred years yet—
an ee like a wild falcon's, and a beard as broad as my
shovel, clapped the end o' his lang black gun within a
quarter's length of my lug!—by the grace o' Mercy, the
horse swarved round, and I fell aff at the tae side as the
ball whistled by at the tither, and the fell auld lord took
the whig such a swauk wi' his broadsword that he made
twa pieces o' his head, and down fell the lurdane wi' a' his
bowk abune me."

"You were rather obliged to the old lord, I think," said
Ravenswood.

"Was I? my sartie! first for bringing me into jeopardy,
would I nould I—and then for whomling a chield on the
tap o' me, that dang the very wind out of my body?—I hae
been short-breathed ever since, and canna gang twenty yards
without peghing like a miller's aiver."

"You lost, then, your place as trumpeter?" said Ravenswood.

"Lost it? to be sure I lost it," replied the sexton, "for I couldna hae played pew upon a dry humlock;—but I might hae dune weel enough, for I keepit the wage and the free house, and little to do but play on the fiddle to them, but for Allan, last Lord Ravenswood, that was far waur than ever his father was."

"What," said the Master, "did my father—I mean, did his father's son—this last Lord Ravenswood, deprive you of what the bounty of his father allowed you?"

"Ay, troth did he," answered the old man; "for he loot his affairs gang to the dogs, and let in this Sir William Ashton on us, that will g'e naething for naething, and just removed me and a' the puir creatures that had bite and soup at the castle, and a hole to put our heads in, when things were in the auld way."

"If Lord Ravenswood protected his people, my friend, while he had the means of doing so, I think they might spare his memory," replied the Master.

"Ye are welcome to your ain opinion, sir," said the sexton; "but ye winna persuade me that he did his duty, either to himsell or to huz puir dependent creatures, in guiding us the gate he has done—he might hae gien us life-rent tacks of our bits o' houses and yards—and me, that's an auld man, living in yon miserable cabin, that's fitter for the dead than the quick, and killed wi' rheumatise, and John Smith in my dainty bit mailing, and his window glazen, and a' because Ravenswood guided his gear like a fule!"

"It is but too true," said Ravenswood, conscience-struck; "the penalties of extravagance extend far beyond the prodigal's own sufferings."

"However," said the sexton, "this young man Edgar is likely to avenge my wrangs on the haill of his kindred."

"Indeed?" said Ravenswood; "why should you suppose so?"

"They say he is about to marry the daughter of Leddy Ashton; an' let her leddyship get his head ance under her oxter, and see you if she winna gie his neck a thraw. Sorra a bit, if I were him—Let her alane for hauding a' thing in het water that draws near her—sae the warst wish I shall wish the lad is, that he may take his ain creditable gate o't, and ally himsell wi' his father's enemies, that have taken his broad lands and my bonny kailyard from the lawful owners thereof."

Cervantes acutely remarks, that flattery is pleasing even from the mouth of a madman; and censure, as well as praise, often affects us, while we despise the opinions and motives on which it is founded and expressed. Ravenswood, abruptly reiterating his command that Alice's funeral should be attended to, flung away from the sexton, under the painful impression that the great, as well as the small vulgar, would think of his engagement with Lucy like this ignorant and selfish peasant.

"And I have stooped to subject myself to these calumnies, and am rejected notwithstanding! Lucy, your faith must be true and perfect as the diamond, to compensate for the dishonour which men's opinions, and the conduct of your mother, attach to the heir of Ravenswood!"

As he raised his eyes, he beheld the Marquis of A——, who, having arrived at the Tod's-hole, had walked forth to look for his kinsman.

After mutual greetings, he made some apology to the Master for not coming forward on the preceding evening. "It was his wish," he said, "to have done so, but he had come to the knowledge of some matters which induced him to delay his purpose. I find," he proceeded, "there has been a love affair here, kinsman; and though I might blame you for not having communicated with me, as being in some degree the chief of your family"——

"With your lordship's permission," said Ravenswood, "I am deeply grateful for the interest you are pleased to take in me—but _I_ am the chief and head of my family."

"I know it—I know it," said the Marquis; "in a strict heraldic and genealogical sense, you certainly are so—what I mean is, that being in some measure under my guardianship"——

"I must take the liberty to say, my lord," answered Ravenswood—and the tone in which he interrupted the Marquis boded no long duration to the friendship of the noble relatives, when he himself was interrupted by the little sexton, who came puffing after them, to ask if their honours would choose music at the change-house to make up for short cheer.

"We want no music," said the Master abruptly.

"Your honour disna ken what ye're refusing, then," said the fiddler, with the impertinent freedom of his profession. "I can play, 'Wilt thou do't again,' and 'the Auld Man's Mear's Dead,' sax times better than ever Pattie Birnie. I'll get my fiddle in the turning of a coffin-screw."

"Take yourself away, sir," said the Marquis.

"And if your honour be a north-country gentleman," said the persevering minstrel, "whilk I wad judge from your tongue, I can play 'Liggeram Cosh,' and 'Mullin Dhu,' and 'the Cummers of Athole.'"

"Take yourself away, friend; you interrupt our conversation."

"Or if, under your honour's favour, ye should happen to be a thought honest, I can play" (this in a low and confidential tone), "'Killiecrankie,' and 'the King shall hae his ain,' and 'the Auld Stewarts back again,'—and the wife at the change-house is a decent discreet body, neither kens nor cares what toasts are drucken, and what tunes are played in her house—she's deaf to a' thing but the clink o' the siller."

The Marquis, who was sometimes suspected of jacobitism, could not help laughing as he threw the fellow a dollar, and bid him go play to the servants if he had a mind, and leave them at peace.

"Aweel, gentlemen," said he, "I am wishing your honours gude day—I'll be a' the better of the dollar, and ye'll be the waur of wanting the music, I'se tell ye—But I'se gang hame, and finish the grave in the tuning o' a fiddle-string, lay by my spade, and then get my t'other bread-winner, and awa to your folk, and see if they hae better lugs than their masters."

CHAPTER XXV

True love, an thou be true,
  Thou has ane kittle part to play ;
For fortune, fashion, fancy, and thou,
  Maun strive for many a day.

I've kend by mony a friend's tale,
  Far better by this heart of mine,
What time and change of fancy avail
  A true-love knot to untwine.

Hendersoun.

"I WISHED to tell you, my good kinsman," said the Marquis, "now that we are quit of that impertinent fiddler, that I had tried to discuss this love affair of yours with Sir William Ashton's daughter. I never saw the young lady but for a few minutes to-day ; so, being a stranger to her personal merits, I pay a compliment to you, and offer her no offence, in saying you might do better."

"My lord, I am much indebted for the interest you have taken in my affairs," said Ravenswood. "I did not intend to have troubled you in any matter concerning Miss Ashton. As my engagement with that young lady has reached your lordship, I can only say, that you must necessarily suppose that I was aware of the objections to my marrying into her father's family, and of course must have been completely satisfied with the reasons by which these objections are overbalanced, since I have proceeded so far in the matter."

"Nay, Master, if you had heard me out," said his noble relation, "you might have spared that observation ; for, without questioning that you had reasons which seemed to you to counterbalance every other obstacle, I set myself, by every means that it became me to use towards the Ashtons, to persuade them to meet your views."

"I am obliged to your lordship for your unsolicited intercession," said Ravenswood ; "especially as I am sure your lordship would never carry it beyond the bounds which it became me to use."

"Of that," said the Marquis, "you may be confident ; I myself felt the delicacy of the matter too much to place a gentleman nearly connected with my house in a degrading or dubious situation with these Ashtons. But I pointed out all the advantages of their marrying their daughter into a house so honourable, and so nearly related with the first in Scotland; I explained the exact degree of relationship in which the Ravenswoods stand to ourselves; and I even hinted how political matters were like to turn, and what cards would be trumps next Parliament. I said I regarded you as a son—or a nephew, or so—rather than as a more distant relation; and that I made your affair entirely my own."

"And what was the issue of your lordship's explanation?" said Ravenswood, in some doubt whether he should resent or express gratitude for his interference.

"Why, the Lord Keeper would have listened to reason," said the Marquis; "he is rather unwilling to leave his place which, in the present view of a change, must {be vacated; and, to say truth, he seemed to have a liking for you, and to be sensible of the general advantages to be attained by such a match. But his lady, who is tongue of the trump, Master,"——

"What of Lady Ashton, my lord?" said Ravenswood; "let me know the issue of this extraordinary conference— I can bear it."

"I am glad of that, kinsman," said the Marquis, "for I am ashamed to tell you half what she said. It is enough— her mind is made up—and the mistress of a first-rate boarding-school could not have rejected with more haughty indifference the suit of a half-pay Irish officer, beseeching permission to wait upon the heiress of a West India planter, than Lady Ashton spurned every proposal of mediation which it could at all become me to offer in behalf of you, my good kinsman. I cannot guess what she means. A more honourable connexion she could not form, that's certain. As for money and land, that used to be her husband's business rather than hers; I really think she hates you for having the rank which her husband has not, and perhaps for not having the lands that her goodman has. But I should only vex you to say more about it—here we are at the change-house."

The Master of Ravenswood paused as he entered the cottage, which reeked through all its crevices, and they were not few, from the exertions of the Marquis's travellingcooks to supply good cheer, and spread, as it were, a table in the wilderness.

"My Lord Marquis," said Ravenswood, "I already mentioned that accident has put your lordship in possession of a secret, which, with my consent, should have remained one even to you, my kinsman, for some time. Since the secret was to part from my own custody, and that of the only person besides who was interested in it, I am not sorry it should have reached your lordship's ears, as being fully aware that you are my noble kinsman and friend."

"You may believe it is safely lodged with me, Master of Ravenswood," said the Marquis; "but I should like well to hear you say, that you renounced the idea of an alliance, which you can hardly pursue without a degree of degradation."

"Of that, my lord, I shall judge," answered Ravenswood, "and I hope with delicacy as sensitive as any of my friends. But I have no engagement with Sir William and Lady Ashton. It is with Miss Ashton alone that I have entered upon the subject, and my conduct in the matter shall be entirely ruled by hers. If she continues to prefer me in my poverty to the wealthier suitors whom her friends recommend, I may well make some sacrifice to her sincere affection—I may well surrender to her the less tangible and less palpable advantages of birth, and the deep-rooted prejudices of family hatred. If Miss Lucy Ashton should change her mind on a subject of such delicacy, I trust my friends will be silent on my disappointment, and I shall know how to make my enemies so."

"Spoke like a gallant young nobleman," said the Marquis; "for my part I have that regard for you, that I should be sorry the thing went on. This Sir William Ashton was a pretty enough pettifogging kind of a lawyer twenty years ago, and betwixt battling at the bar, and leading in committees of Parliament, he has got well on— the Darien matter lent him a lift, for he had good intelligence and sound views, and sold out in time—but the best work is had out of him. No government will take him at his own, or rather his wife's extravagant valuation; and betwixt his indecision and her insolence, from all I can guess, he will outsit his market, and be had cheap when no one will bid for him. I say nothing of Miss Ashton;

but I assure you, a connexion with her father will be neither useful nor ornamental, beyond that part of your father's spoils which he may be prevailed upon to disgorge by way of tocher good—and take my word for it, you will get more if you have spirit to bell the cat with him in the House of Peers.—And I will be the man, cousin," continued his lordship, "will course the fox for you, and make him rue the day that ever he refused a composition too honourable for him, and proposed by me on behalf of a kinsman."

There was something in all this that, as it were, overshot the mark. Ravenswood could not disguise from himself that his noble kinsman had more reasons for taking offence at the reception of his suit, than regarded his interest and honour, yet he could neither complain nor be surprised that it should be so. He contented himself therefore with repeating, that his attachment was to Miss Ashton personally; that he desired neither wealth nor aggrandisement from her father's means and influence; and that nothing should prevent his keeping his engagement, excepting her own express desire that it should be relinquished—and he requested as a favour that the matter might be no more mentioned betwixt them at present, assuring the Marquis of A—— that he should be his confidant in its progress or its interruption.

The Marquis soon had more agreeable, as well as more interesting subjects on which to converse. A foot post, who had followed him from Edinburgh to Ravenswood Castle, and had traced his steps to the Tod's-hole, brought him a packet laden with good news. The political calculations of the Marquis had proved just, both in London and at Edinburgh, and he saw almost within his grasp, the pre-eminence for which he had panted.—The refreshments which the servants had prepared were now put on the table, and an epicure would perhaps have enjoyed them with additional zest, from the contrast which such fare afforded to the miserable cabin in which it was served up.

The turn of conversation corresponded with and added to the social feelings of the company. The Marquis expanded with pleasure on the power which probable incidents were likely to assign to him, and on the use which he hoped to make of it in serving his kinsman Ravenswood. Ravenswood could but repeat the gratitude which he really felt, even when he considered the topic as too long dwelt upon. The wine was excellent, notwithstanding its having been brought in a runlet from Edinburgh; and the habits of the Marquis, when engaged with such good cheer, were somewhat sedentary. And so it fell out that they delayed their journey two hours later than was their original purpose.

"But what of that, my good young friend?" said the Marquis, "your Castle of Wolf's Crag, is but at five or six miles distance, and will afford the same hospitality to your kinsman of A——, that it gave to this same Sir William Ashton."

"Sir William took the castle by storm," said Ravenswood, "and, like many a victor, had little reason to congratulate himself on his conquest."

"Well, well!" said Lord A——, whose dignity was something relaxed by the wine he had drunk,—"I see I must bribe you to harbour me—Come, pledge me in a bumper health to the last young lady that slept at Wolf's Crag, and liked her quarters.—My bones are not so tender as hers, and I am resolved to occupy her apartment tonight, that I may judge how hard the couch is that love can soften."

"Your lordship may choose what penance you please," said Ravenswood; "but I assure you, I should expect my old servant to hang himself, or throw himself from the battlements, should your lordship visit him so unexpectedly —I do assure you, we are totally and literally unprovided."

But this declaration only brought from his noble patron an assurance of his own total indifference as to every species of accommodation, and his determination to see the Tower of Wolf's Crag. His ancestor, he said, had been feasted there, when he went forward with the then Lord Ravenswood to the fatal battle of Flodden, in which they both fell. Thus hard pressed, the Master offered to ride forward to get matters put in such preparation as time and circumstances admitted; but the Marquis protested his kinsman must afford him his company, and would only consent that an avant courier should carry to the destined Seneschal, Caleb Balderstone, the unexpected news of this invasion.

The Master of Ravenswood soon after accompanied the

Marquis in his carriage, as the latter had proposed; and when they became better acquainted in the progress of the journey, his noble relation explained the very liberal views which he entertained for his relation's preferment, in case of the success of his own political schemes. They related to a secret, and highly important commission beyond sea, which could only be intrusted to a person of rank, talent, and perfect confidence, and which, as it required great trust and reliance on the envoy employed, could not but prove both honourable and advantageous to him. We need not enter into the nature and purpose of this commission, farther than to acquaint our readers that the charge was in prospect highly acceptable to the Master of Ravenswood, who hailed with pleasure the hope of emerging from his present state of indigence and inaction, into independence and honourable exertion.

While he listened thus eagerly to the details with which the Marquis now thought it necessary to intrust him, the messenger who had been dispatched to the Tower of Wolf's Crag, returned with Caleb Balderstone's humble duty, and an assurance that "a' should be in seemly order, sic as the hurry of time permitted, to receive their lordships as it behoved."

Ravenswood was too well accustomed to his Seneschal's mode of acting and speaking, to hope much from this confident assurance. He knew that Caleb acted upon the principle of the Spanish generals, in the campaign of ——, who, much to the perplexity of the Prince of Orange, their commander-in-chief, used to report their troops as full in number, and possessed of all necessary points of equipment, not considering it consistent with their dignity, or the honour of Spain, to confess any deficiency either in men or munition, until the want of both was unavoidably discovered in the day of battle. Accordingly, Ravenswood thought it necessary to give the Marquis some hint, that the fair assurance which they had just received from Caleb, did not by any means insure them against a very indifferent reception.

"You do yourself injustice, Master," said the Marquis, "or you wish to surprise me agreeably. From this window I see a great light in the direction where, if I remember aright, Wolf's Crag lies; and, to judge from the splendour which the old Tower sheds around it, the preparations for our reception must be of no ordinary description. I remember your father putting the same deception on me, when he went to the Tower for a few days' hawking, about twenty years since, and yet we spent our time as jollily at Wolf's Crag as we could have done at my own hunting seat at B——."

"Your lordship, I fear, will experience that the faculty of the present proprietor to entertain his friends is greatly abridged," said Ravenswood; "the will, I need hardly say remains the same. But I am as much at a loss as your lordship to account for so strong and brilliant a light as is now above Wolf's Crag,—the windows of the Tower are few and narrow, and those of the lower story are hidden from us by the walls of the court. I cannot conceive that any illumination of an ordinary nature could afford such a blaze of light."

The mystery was soon explained; for the cavalcade almost instantly halted, and the voice of Caleb Balderstone was heard at the coach window, exclaiming, in accents broken by grief and fear, "Och, gentlemen—Och, my gude lords—Och, haud to the right!—Wolf's Crag is burning, bower and ha'—a' the rich plenishing outside and inside—a' the fine graith, pictures, tapestries, needle-wark, hangings, and other decorements—a' in a bleeze, as if they were nae mair than sae mony peats, or as muckle peas-strae! Haud to the right, gentlemen, I implore ye—there is some sma' provision making at Lucky Sma'trash's—but O, wae for this night, and wae for me that lives to see it!"

Ravenswood was at first stunned by this new and unexpected calamity; but after a moment's recollection, he sprang from the carriage, and hastily bidding his noble kinsman good-night, was about to ascend the hill towards the castle, the broad and full conflagration of which now flung forth a high column of red light, that flickered far to seaward upon the dashing waves of the ocean.

"Take a horse, Master," exclaimed the Marquis, greatly affected by this additional misfortune, so unexpectedly heaped upon his young protegé; "and give me my ambling palfrey;—and haste forward, you knaves, to see what can be done to save the furniture, or to extinguish the fire—ride, you knaves, for your lives!"

The attendants bustled together, and began to strike their horses with the spur, and call upon Caleb to show them the road. But the voice of that careful Seneschal was heard above the tumult, "O stop—sirs, stop—turn bridle, for the luve of mercy—add not loss of lives to the loss of warld's gear!—Thirty barrels of powther, landed out of a Dunkirk dogger in the auld lord's time—a' in the vau'ts of the auld tower,—the fire canna be far aff it, I trow—Lord's sake, to the right, lads—to the right—let's pit the hill atween us and peril,—a wap wi' a corner-stane o' Wolf's Crag wad defy the doctor!"

It will readily be supposed that this annunciation hurried the Marquis and his attendants into the route which Caleb prescribed, dragging Ravenswood along with them, although there was much in the matter which he could not possibly comprehend. "Gunpowder!" he exclaimed, laying hold of Caleb, who in vain endeavoured to escape from him, "what gunpowder? How any quantity of powder could be in Wolf's Crag without my knowledge, I cannot possibly comprehend."

"But I can," interrupted the Marquis, whispering him, "I can comprehend it thoroughly—for God's sake, ask him no more questions at present."

"There it is, now," said Caleb, extricating himself from his master, and adjusting his dress, "your honour will believe his lordship's honourable testimony—His lordship minds weel, how, in the year that him they ca'd King Willie died"——

"Hush! hush, my good friend!" said the Marquis; "I shall satisfy your master upon that subject."

"And the people in Wolf's-hope," said Ravenswood, "did none of them come to your assistance before the flame got so high?"

"Ay did they, mony ane of them, the rapscallions!" said Caleb; "but truly I was in nae hurry to let them into the Tower, where there were so much plate and valuables."

"Confound you for an impudent liar!" said Ravenswood, in uncontrollable ire, "there was not a single ounce of"——

"Forby," said the butler, most irreverently raising his voice to a pitch which drowned his master's, "the fire made fast on us, owing to the store of tapestry and carved timmer in the banqueting ha', and the loons ran like scauded rats sae sune as they heard of the gunpouther."

"I do entreat," said the Marquis to Ravenswood, "you will ask him no more questions."

"Only one, my lord—What has become of poor Mysie?"

"Mysie?" said Caleb, "I had nae time to look about ony Mysie—she's in the tower, I'se warrant, biding her awful doom."

"By heaven," said Ravenswood, "I do not understand all this! The life of a faithful old creature is at stake—my lord, I will be withheld no longer—I will at least ride up, and see whether the danger is as imminent as this old fool pretends."

"Weel, then, as I live by bread," said Caleb, "Mysie is weel and safe. I saw her out of the castle before I left it mysell. Was I ganging to forget an auld fellow-servant?"

"What made you tell me the contrary this moment?" said his master.

"Did I tell you the contrary?" said Caleb; "then I maun hae been dreaming surely, or this awsome night has turned my judgment—but safe she is, and ne'er a living soul in the castle, a' the better for them—they wad have gotten an unco heezy."

The Master of Ravenswood, upon this assurance being solemnly reiterated, and notwithstanding his extreme wish to witness the last explosion, which was to ruin to the ground the mansion of his fathers, suffered himself to be dragged onward towards the village of Wolf's-hope, where not only the change-house, but that of our well-known friend the cooper, were all prepared for reception of himself and his noble guest, with a liberality of provision which requires some explanation.

We omitted to mention in its place, that Lockhard, having fished out the truth concerning the mode by which Caleb had obtained the supplies for his banquet, the Lord Keeper, amused with the incident, and desirous at the time to gratify Ravenswood, had recommended the cooper of Wolf's-hope to the official situation under government, the prospect of which had reconciled him to the loss of his wild-fowl. Mr Girder's preferment had occasioned a pleasing surprise to old Caleb; for when, some days after his master's departure, he found himself absolutely compelled, by some necessary business, to visit the fishing hamlet, and was gliding like a ghost past the door of the cooper, for fear of being summoned to give some account of the progress of the solicitation in his favour, or, more probably, that the inmates might upbraid him with the false hope he had held out upon the subject, he heard himself not without some apprehension, summoned at once in treble, tenor, and bass,—a trio performed by the voices of Mrs Girder, old Dame Loup-the-dike, and the good-man of the dwelling —"Mr Caleb—Mr Caleb—Mr Caleb Balderstone! I hope ye arena ganging dry-lipped by our door, and we sae muckle indebted to you?"

This might be said ironically as well as in earnest. Caleb augured the worst, turned a deaf ear to the trio aforesaid, and was moving doggedly on, his ancient castor pulled over his brows, and his eyes bent on the ground, as if to count the flinty pebbles with which the rude pathway was causewayed. But on a sudden he found himself surrounded in his progress, like a stately merchantman in the Gut of Gibraltar (I hope the ladies will excuse the tarpaulin phrase) by three Algerine galleys.

"Gude guide us, Mr Balderstone!" said Mrs Girder.

"Wha wad hae thought it of an auld and kend friend!" said the mother:

"And no sae muckle as stay to receive our thanks," said the cooper himself, "and frae the like o' me that seldom offers them! I am sure I hope there's nae ill seed sawn between us, Mr Balderstone—Ony man that has said to ye, I am no gratefu' for the situation of Queen's cooper, let me hae a whample at him wi' mine eatche—that's a'."

"My good friends—my dear friends," said Caleb, still doubting how the certainty of the matter might stand, "what needs a' this ceremony?—ane tries to serve their friends, and sometimes they may happen to prosper, and sometimes to misgie—naething I care to be fashed wi' less than thanks—I never could bide them."

"Faith, Mr Balderstone, ye suld hae been fashed wi' few o' mine," said the downright man of staves and hoops, "if I had only your gude-will to thank ye for—I suld e'en hae set the guse, and the wild-deukes, and the runlet of sack, to balance that account. Gude-will, man, is a geizen'd tub, that hauds in nae liquor—but gude deed's like the cask, tight, round, and sound, that will haud liquor for the king."

"Have ye no heard of our letter," said the mother-in-law, "making our John the Queen's cooper for certain?—and scarce a chield that had ever hammered gird upon tub but was applying for it?"

"Have I heard!!!" said Caleb (who now found how the wind set), with an accent of exceeding contempt at the doubt expressed—"Have I heard, quo' she!!!"—and as he spoke, he changed his shambling, skulking, dodging pace, into a manly and authoritative step, re-adjusted his cocked hat, and suffered his brow to emerge from under it in all the pride of aristocracy, like the sun from behind a cloud."

"To be sure, he canna but hae heard," said the good woman.

"Ay, to be sure, it's impossible but I should," said Caleb; "and sae I'll be the first to kiss ye, joe, and wish you, cooper, much joy of your preferment, naething doubting but ye ken wha are your friends, and *have* helped ye, and *can* help ye. I thought it right to look a wee strange upon it at first," added Caleb, "just to see if ye were made of the right mettle—but ye ring true, lad, ye ring true!"

So saying, with a most lordly air he kissed the women, and abandoned his hand, with an air of serene patronage, to the hearty shake of Mr Girder's horn-hard palm. Upon this complete, and to Caleb most satisfactory, information, he did not, it may readily be believed, hesitate to accept an invitation to a solemn feast, to which were invited, not only all the *notables* of the village, but even his ancient antagonist, Mr Dingwall himself. At this festivity he was, of course, the most welcome and most honoured guest; and so well did he ply the company with stories of what he could do with his master, his master with the Lord Keeper, the Lord Keeper with the Council, and the Council with the King, that before the company dismissed (which was, indeed, rather at an early hour than a late one), every man of note in the village was ascending to the top-gallant of some ideal preferment by the ladder of ropes which Caleb had presented to their imagination. Nay, the cunning butler regained in that moment, not only all the influence he possessed formerly over the villagers, when the baronial family which he served were at the proudest, but acquired even an accession of importance. The writer—the very attorney himself—such is the thirst of preferment—felt the force of the attraction, and taking an opportunity to draw Caleb into a corner, spoke, with affectionate regret, of the declining health of the sheriff-clerk of the county.

"An excellent man—a most valuable man, Mr Caleb—but fat sall I say!—we are peer feckless bodies—here the day, and awa by cock-screech the morn—and if he failzies, there maun be somebody in his place—and gif that ye could airt it my way, I sall be thankful, man—a gluve stuffed wi' gowd nobles—an' hark ye, man, something canny till yoursell—and the Wolf's-hope carles to settle kindly wi' the Master of Ravenswood—that is, Lord Ravenswood—God bless his lordship!"

A smile, and a hearty squeeze by the hand, was the suitable answer to this overture—and Caleb made his escape from the jovial party, in order to avoid committing himself by any special promises.

"The Lord be gude to me," said Caleb, when he found himself in the open air, and at liberty to give vent to the self-exultation with which he was, as it were, distended; "did ever ony man see sic a set of green-gaislings!—the very pick-maws and solan-geese outby yonder at the Bass hae ten times their sense!—God, an I had been the Lord High Commissioner to the Estates o' Parliament, they couldna hae beflumm'd me mair—and, to speak Heaven's truth, I could hardly hae beflumm'd them better neither! But the writer—ha! ha! ha!—ah, ha! ha! ha! mercy on me, that I suld live in my auld days to gie the gang-by to the very writer!—Sheriff-clerk!!!—But I hae an auld account to settle wi' the carle; and to make amends for by-ganes, the office shall just cost him as much time-serving and tide-serving, as if he were to get it in gude earnest—of whilk there is sma' appearance, unless the Master learns mair the ways of this warld, whilk it is muckle to be doubted that he never will do."—

CHAPTER XXVI

Why flames yon far summit—why shoot to the blast
Those embers, like stars from the firmament cast?—
'Tis the fire-shower of ruin, all dreadfully driven
From thine eyry, that beacons the darkness of Heaven.

Campbell.

THE circumstances announced in the conclusion of the
last chapter, will account for the ready and cheerful reception of the Marquis of A—— and the Master of Ravenswood
in the village of Wolf's-hope.   In fact, Caleb had no sooner
announced the conflagration of the tower, than the whole
hamlet were upon foot to hasten to extinguish the flames.
And although that zealous adherent diverted their zeal by
intimating the formidable contents of the subterranean
apartments, yet the check only turned their assiduity into
another diection.   Never had there been such slaughtering
of capons, and fat geese, and barn-door fowls,—never such
boiling of *reested* hams,—never such making of car-cakes
and sweet scones, Selkirk bannocks, cookies, and petticoat-
tails,—delicacies little known to the present generation.
Never had there been such a tapping of barrels, and such
uncorking of greybeards, in the village of Wolf's-hope.
All the inferior houses were thrown open for the reception
of the Marquis's dependants, who came, it was thought, as
precursors of the shower of preferment, which hereafter
was to leave the rest of Scotland dry, in order to distil its
rich dews on the village of Wolf's-hope under Lammermoor.
The minister put in his claim to have the guests of distinction lodged at the Manse, having his eye, it was thought,
upon a neighbouring preferment, where the incumbent was
sickly; but Mr Balderstone destined that honour to the
cooper, his wife, and wife's mother, who danced for joy at
the preference thus assigned them.

Many a beck and many a bow welcomed these noble
guests to as good entertainment as persons of such rank
could set before such visitors; and the old dame, who had
formerly lived in Ravenswood Castle, and knew, as she
said, the ways of the nobility, was in no whit wanting in
arranging matters, as well as circumstances permitted,
according to the etiquette of the times.   The cooper's

house was so roomy, that each guest had his separate retiring room, to which they were ushered with all due ceremony, while the plentiful supper was in the act of being placed upon the table.

Ravenswood no sooner found himself alone, than, impelled by a thousand feelings, he left the apartment, the house, and the village, and hastily retraced his steps to the brow of the hill, which rose betwixt the village, and screened it from the tower, in order to view the final fall of the house of his fathers. Some idle boys from the hamlet had taken the same direction out of curiosity, having first witnessed the arrival of the coach-and-six and its attendants. As they ran one by one past the Master, calling to each other to "come and see the auld tower blaw up in the lift like the peelings of an ingan," he could not but feel himself moved with indignation. "And these are the sons of my father's vassals," he said—"of men bound, both by law and gratitude, to follow our steps through battle, and fire, and flood ; and now the destruction of their liege-lord's house is but a holiday's sight to them !"

These exasperating reflections were partly expressed in the acrimony with which he exclaimed, on feeling himself pulled by the cloak,—"What do you want, you dog ?"

"I am a dog and an auld dog too," answered Caleb, for it was he who had taken the freedom, "and I am like to get a dog's wages—but it does not signification a pinch of sneeshing, for I am ower auld a dog to learn new tricks, or to follow a new master."

As he spoke, Ravenswood attained the ridge of the hill from which Wolf's Crag was visible ; the flames had entirely sunk down, and, to his great surprise, there was only a dusky reddening upon the clouds immediately over the castle, which seemed the reflection of the embers of the sunken fire.

"The place cannot have blown up," said the Master ; "we must have heard the report—if a quarter of the gunpowder was there you tell me of, it would have been heard twenty miles off."

"It's very like it wad," said Balderstone, composedly.

"Then the fire cannot have reached the vaults ?"

"It's like no," answered Caleb, with the same impenetrable gravity.

"Hark ye, Caleb," said his master, "this grows a little too much for my patience. I must go and examine how matters stand at Wolf's Crag myself."

"Your honour is ganging to gang nae sic gate," said Caleb, firmly.

"And why not?" said Ravenswood, sharply; "who or what shall prevent me?"

"Even I mysell," said Caleb, with the same determination.

"You, Balderstone!" replied the Master; "you are forgetting yourself, I think."

"But I think no," said Balderstone; "for I can just tell ye a' about the castle on this knowe-head as weel as if ye were at it. Only dinna pit yoursell into a kippage, and expose yoursell before the weans, or before the Marquis, when ye gang down-by."

"Speak out, you old fool," replied his master, "and let me know the best and the worst at once."

"Ou, the best and the warst is, just that the tower is standing hail and feir, as safe and as empty as when ye left it."

"Indeed!—and the fire?" said Ravenswood.

"Not a gleed of fire, then, except the bit kindling peat, and maybe a spunk in Mysie's cutty-pipe," replied Caleb.

"But the flame?" demanded Ravenswood; "the broad blaze which might have been seen ten miles off—what occasioned that?"

"Hout awa! it's an auld saying and a true,—

> "Little's the light
> Will be seen far in a mirk night.

A wheen fern and horse litter that I fired in the court-yard, after sending back the loun of a footman; and, to speak heaven's truth, the next time that ye send or bring ony body here, let them be gentles allenarly, without ony fremd servants, like that chield Lockhard, to be gledging and gleeing about, and looking upon the wrang side of ane's housekeeping, to the discredit of the family, and forcing ane to damn their souls wi' telling ae lee after another faster than I can count them—I wad rather set fire to the tower in gude earnest, and burn it ower my ain head into the bargain, or I see the family dishonoured in the sort."

"Upon my word, I am infinitely obliged by the proposal, Caleb," said his master, scarce able to restrain his laughter, though rather angry at the same time. "But the gun-powder?—is there such a thing in the tower?—The Marquis seemed to know of it."

"The pouther—ha! ha! ha!—the Marquis—ha! ha! ha!" replied Caleb; "if your honour were to brain me, I behooved to laugh—the Marquis—the pouther!—was it there? ay, it was there. Did he ken o't? my certie! the Marquis kend o't, and it was the best o' the game; for, when I couldna pacify your honour wi' a' that I could say, I aye threw out a word mair about the gunpouther, and garr'd the Marquis tak the job in his ain hand."

"But you have not answered my question," said the Master, impatiently; "how came the powder there, and where is it now?"

"Ou, it came there, an ye maun needs ken," said Caleb, looking mysteriously, and whispering, "when there was like to be a wee bit rising here; and the Marquis, and a' the great lords of the north, were a' in it, and mony a gudely gun and broadsword were ferried ower frae Dunkirk forby the pouther—awfu' wark we had getting them into the tower under cloud o' night, for ye maun think it wasna every body could be trusted wi' sic kittle jobs—But if ye will gae hame to your supper, I will tell you a' about it as ye gang down."

"And these wretched boys," said Ravenswood, "is it your pleasure they are to sit there all night, to wait for the blowing up of a tower that is not even on fire?"

"Surely not, if it is your honour's pleasure that they suld gang hame; although," added Caleb, "it wadna do them a grain's damage—they wad screigh less the next day, and sleep the sounder at e'en—But just as your honour likes."

Stepping accordingly towards the urchins who manned the knolls near which they stood, Caleb informed them, in an authoritative tone, that their Honours Lord Ravenswood and the Marquis of A—— had given orders that the tower was not to blow up till next day at noon. The boys dispersed upon this comfortable assurance. One or two, however, followed Caleb for more information, particularly the urchin whom he had cheated while officiating as turnspit, who screamed, "Mr Balderstone! Mr Balderstone! then the castle's gane out like an auld wife's spunk?"

"To be sure it is, callant," said the butler; "do ye think the castle of as great a lord as Lord Ravenswood wad continue in a bleeze, and him standing looking on wi' his ain very een?—It's aye right," continued Caleb, shaking off his ragged page, and closing in to his master, "to train up weans, as the wise man says, in the way they should go, and, aboon a', to teach them respect to their superiors."

"But all this while, Caleb, you have never told me what became of the arms and powder," said Ravenswood.

"Why, as for the arms," said Caleb, "it was just like the bairn's rhyme—

> "'Some gaed east, and some gaed west,
> And some gaed to the craw's nest:'

And for the pouther, I e'en changed it, as occasion served, with the skippers o' Dutch luggers and French vessels, for gin and brandy, and it served the house mony a year—a gude swap too, between what cheereth the soul of man and that which dingeth it clean out of his body; forby, I keepit a wheen pounds of it for yoursell when ye wanted to take the pleasure o' shooting—whiles, in these latter days, I wad hardly hae kend else whar to get pouther for your pleasure.—And now that your anger is ower, sir, wasna that weel managed o' me, and arena ye far better sorted doun yonder, than ye could hae been in your ain auld ruins upby youder, as the case stands wi' us now?— the mair's the pity."

"I believe you may be right, Caleb; but, before burning down my castle, either in jest or in earnest," said Ravenswood, "I think I had a right to be in the secret."

"Fie for shame, your honour!" replied Caleb; "it fits an auld carle like me weel eneugh to tell lees for the credit of the family, but it wadna beseem the like o' your honour's sell; besides, young folk are no judicious—they cannot make the maist of a bit figment. Now this fire—for a fire it sall be, if I suld burn the auld stable to make it mair feasible—this fire, besides that it will be an excuse for asking ony thing we want through the country, or doun at the haven—this fire will settle mony things on an honourable footing for the family's credit, that cost me telling twenty daily lees to a wheen idle chaps and queans, and, what's waur, without gaining credence."

"That was hard indeed, Caleb; but I do not see how this fire should help your veracity or your credit."

"There it is now!" said Caleb; "wasna I saying that young folk had a green judgment?—How suld it help me, quotha?—it will be a creditable apology for the honour of the family for this score of years to come, if it is weel guided. Where's the family pictures? says ae meddling body—the great fire at Wolf's Crag, answers I. Where's the family plate? says another—the great fire, says I; wha was to think of plate, when life and limb were in danger? —Where's the wardrobe and the linens?—where's the tapestries and the decorements?—beds of state, twilts, pands and testors, napery and broidered wark?—The fire —the fire—the fire. Guide the fire weel, and it will serve ye for a' that ye suld have and have not—and, in some sort, a gude excuse is better than the things themselves; for they maun crack and wear out, and be consumed by time, whereas a gude offcome, prudently and creditably handled, may serve a nobleman and his family, Lord kens how lang!"

Ravenswood was too well acquainted with his butler's pertinacity and self-opinion, to dispute the point with him any farther. Leaving Caleb, therefore, to the enjoyment of his own successful ingenuity, he returned to the hamlet, where he found the Marquis and the good women of the mansion under some anxiety—the former on account of his absence, the others for the discredit their cookery might sustain by the delay of the supper. All were now at ease, and heard with pleasure that the fire at the castle had burned out of itself without reaching the vaults, which was the only imformation that Ravenswood thought it proper to give in public concerning the event of his butler's stratagem.

They sat down to an excellent supper. No invitation could prevail on Mr and Mrs Girder, even in their own house, to sit down at table with guests of such high quality. They remained standing in the apartment, and acted the part of respectful and careful attendants on the company. Such were the manners of the time. The elder dame, confident through her age and connexion with the Ravenswood family, was less scrupulously ceremonious. She played a mixed part betwixt that of the hostess of an inn, and the mistress of a private house, who receives guests above her own degree. She recommended, and even pressed, what she thought best, and was herself easily entreated to take a moderate share of the good cheer, in order to encourage her guests by her own example. Often she interrupted herself, to express her regret that "my Lord did not eat—that the Master was pyking a bare bane—that, to be sure, there was naething there fit to set before their honours—that Lord Allan, rest his saul, used to like a pouthered guse, and said it was Latin for a tass o' brandy—that the brandy came frae France direct; for, for a' the English laws and gaugers, the Wolf's-hope brigs hadna forgotten the gate to Dunkirk."

Here the cooper admonished his mother-in-law with his elbow, which procured him the following special notice in the progress of her speech.

"Ye needna be dunshin that gate, John," continued the old lady; "naebody says that *ye* ken whar the brandy comes frae; and it wadna be fitting ye should, and you the queen's cooper; and what signifies't," continued she, addressing Lord Ravenswood, "to king, queen, or keiser, whar an auld wife like me buys her pickle sneeshin, or her drap brandy-wine, to haud her heart up?"

Having thus extricated herself from her supposed false step, Dame Loup-the-dyke proceeded, during the rest of the evening, to supply, with great animation, and very little assistance from her guests, the funds necessary for the support of the conversation, until, declining any further circulation of their glass, her guests requested her permission to retire to their apartments.

The Marquis occupied the chamber of dais, which, in every house above the rank of a mere cottage, was kept sacred for such high occasions as the present. The modern finishing with plaster was then unknown, and tapestry was confined to the houses of the nobility and superior gentry. The cooper, therefore, who was a man of some vanity, as well as some wealth, had imitated the fashion observed by the inferior landholders and clergy, who usually ornamented their state apartments with hangings of a sort of stamped leather, manufactured in the Netherlands, garnished with trees and animals executed in copper foil, and with many a pithy sentence of morality, which, although couched in Low Dutch, were perhaps as much attended to in practice as if written in broad Scotch. The whole had somewhat of a gloomy aspect; but the fire, composed of old pitch-barrel staves, blazed merrily up the chimney; the bed was decorated with linen of most fresh and dazzling whiteness, which had never before been used, and might, perhaps, have never been used at all, but for this high occasion. On the toilette beside, stood an old-fashioned mirror, in a fillagree frame, part of the dispersed finery of the neighbouring castle. It was flanked by a long-necked bottle of Florence wine, by which stood a glass nearly as tall, resembling in shape that which Teniers usually places in the hands of his own portrait, when he paints himself as mingling in the revels of a country village. To counterbalance those foreign centinels, there mounted guard on the other side of the mirror two stout warders of Scottish lineage; a jug, namely, of double ale, which held a Scotch pint, and a quegh, or bicker, of ivory and ebony, hooped with silver, the work of John Girder's own hands, and the pride of his heart. Besides these preparations against thirst, there was a goodly diet-loaf, or sweet cake; so that, with such auxiliaries, the apartment seemed victualled against a siege of two or three days.

It only remains to say, that the Marquis's valet was in attendance, displaying his master's brocaced night-gown, and richly embroidered velvet cap, lined and faced with Brussels lace, upon a huge leathern easy chair, wheeled round so as to have the full advantage of the comfortable fire which we have already mentioned. We therefore commit that eminent person to his night's repose, trusting he profited by the ample preparations made for his accommodation,—preparations which we have mentioned in detail, as illustrative of ancient Scottish manners.

It is not necessary we should be equally minute in describing the sleeping apartment of the Master of Ravenswood, which was that usually occupied by the goodman and goodwife themselves. It was comfortably hung with a sort of warm-coloured worsted, manufactured in Scotland, approaching in texture to what is now called shaloon. A staring picture of John Girder himself ornamented this dormitory, painted by a starving Frenchman, who had, God

knows how or why, strolled over from Flushing or Dunkirk
to Wolf's-hope in a smuggling dogger. The features were,
indeed, those of the stubborn, opinionative, yet sensible
artisan, but Monsieur had contrived to throw a French
grace into the look and manner, so utterly inconsistent with
the dogged gravity of the original, that it was impossible to
look at it without laughing. John and his family, however,
piqued themselves not a little upon this picture, and were
proportionably censured by the neighbourhood, who pronounced that the cooper, in sitting for the same, and yet
more in presuming to hang it up in his bedchamber, had
exceeded his privilege as the richest man of the village; at
once stept beyond the bounds of his own rank, and en-
croached upon those of the superior orders; and, in fine,
had been guilty of a very overweening act of vanity and
presumption. Respect for the memory of my deceased
friend, Mr Richard Tinto, has obliged me to treat this
matter at some length; but I spare the reader his prolix,
though curious observations, as well upon the character of
the French school, as upon the state of painting in Scotland,
at the beginning of the eighteenth century.

The other preparations of the Master's sleeping apartment were similar to those in the chamber of dais.

At the usual early hour of that period, the Marquis of
A—— and his kinsman prepared to resume their journey.
This could not be done without an ample breakfast, in
which cold meat and hot meat, and oatmeal flummery, wine
and spirits, and milk varied by every possible mode of preparation, evinced the same desire to do honour to their
guests, which had been shown by the hospitable owners of
the mansion upon the evening before. All the bustle of
preparation for departure now resounded through Wolf's-
hope. There was paying of bills and shaking of hands,
and saddling of horses, and harnessing of carriages, and
distributing of drink-money. The Marquis left a broad
piece for the gratification of John Girder's household, which
he, the said John, was for some time disposed to convert
to his own use; Dingwall the writer assuring him he was
justified in so doing, seeing he was the disburser of those
expenses which were the occasion of the gratification. But,
notwithstanding this legal authority, John could not find in
his heart to dim the splendour of his late hospitality, by

pocketing any thing in the nature of a gratuity. He only
assured his menials he would consider them as a damned
ungrateful pack, if they bought a gill of brandy elsewhere
than out of his own stores; and as the drink-money was
likely to go to its legitimate use, he comforted himself that,
in this manner, the Marquis's donative would, without any
impeachment of credit and character, come ultimately into
his own exclusive possession.

While arrangements were making for departure, Ravenswood made blithe the heart of his ancient butler, by informing him, cautiously however (for he knew Caleb's
warmth of imagination), of the probable change which was
about to take place in his fortunes. He deposited with
Balderstone, at the same time, the greater part of his
slender funds, with an assurance, which he was obliged to
reiterate more than once, that he himself had sufficient
supplies in certain prospect. He, therefore, enjoined Caleb,
as he valued his favour, to desist from all farther manœuvres
against the inhabitants of Wolf's-hope, their cellars, poultry-
yards, and substance whatsoever. In this prohibition, the
old domestic acquiesced more readily than his master expected. "It was doubtless," he said, "a shame, a discredit, and a sin, to harry the puir creatures, when the
family were in circumstances to live honourably on their ain
means; and there might be wisdom," he added, "in giving
them a whiles breathing time at any rate, that they might be
the more readily brought forward upon his honour's future
occasions."

This matter being settled, and having taken an affectionate farewell of his old domestic, the Master rejoined
his noble relative, who was now ready to enter his carriage.
The two landladies, old and young, having received in all
kindly greeting, a kiss from each of their noble guests,
stood simpering at the door of their house, as the coach-
and-six, followed by its train of clattering horsemen,
thundered out of the village. John Girder also stood upon
his threshold, now looking at his honoured right hand,
which had been so lately shaken by a marquis and a lord,
and now giving a glance into the interior of his mansion,
which manifested all the disarray of the late revel, as if
balancing the distinction which he had attained with the
expenses of the entertainment.

At length he opened his oracular jaws. "Let every man and woman here set about their ain business, as if there was nae sic thing as marquis or master, duke or drake, laird or lord, in this world. Let the house be redd up, the broken meat set by, and if there is ony thing totally uneatable, let it be gien to the puir folk; and, gudemother and wife, I hae just ae thing to entreat ye, that ye will never speak to me a single word, good or bad, anent a' this nonsense wark, but keep a' your cracks about it to yoursells and your kimmers, for my head is weelnigh dung donnart wi' it already."

As John's authority was tolerably absolute, all departed to their usual occupations, leaving him to build castles in the air, if he had a mind, upon the court favour which he had acquired by the expenditure of his worldly substance.

CHAPTER XXVII

Why, now I have Dame Fortune by the forelock,
And if she escapes my grasp, the fault is mine;
He that hath buffeted with stern adversity,
Best knows to shape his course to favouring breezes.
Old Play.

OUR travellers reached Edinburgh without any farther adventure, and the Master of Ravenswood, as had been previously settled, took up his abode with his noble friend.

In the meantime, the political crisis which had been expected, took place, and the Tory party obtained, in the Scottish, as in the English councils of Queen Anne, a short-lived ascendency, of which it is not our business to trace either the cause or consequences. Suffice it to say, that it affected the different political parties according to the nature of their principles. In England, many of the High Church party, with Harley, afterwards Earl of Oxford, at their head, affected to separate their principles from those of the Jacobites, and, on that account, obtained the denomination of Whimsicals. The Scottish High Church party, on the contrary, or, as they termed themselves, the Cavaliers, were more consistent, if not so prudent, in their politics, and viewed all the changes now made, as preparatory to calling to the throne, upon the queen's demise, her brother, the Chevalier de St George. Those who had suffered in his service, now entertained the most unreasonable hopes, not only of indemnification, but of vengeance upon their political adversaries ; while families attached to the Whig interest, saw nothing before them but a renewal of the hardships they had undergone during the reigns of Charles the Second and his brother, and a retaliation of the confiscation which had been inflicted upon the Jacobites during that of King William.

But the most alarmed at the change of system, was that prudential set of persons, some of whom are found in all governments, but who abound in a provincial administration like that of Scotland during the period, and who are what Cromwell called waiters upon Providence or, in other words, uniform adherents to the party who are uppermost. Many of these hastened to read their recantation to the Marquis of A——; and, as it was easily seen that he took a deep interest in the affairs of his kinsman, the Master of Ravenswood, they were the first to suggest measures for retrieving at least a part of his property, and for restoring him in blood against his father's attainder.

Old Lord Turntippet professed to be one of the most anxious for the success of these measures; for "it grieved him to the very saul," he said, " to see so brave a young gentleman, of sic auld and undoubted nobility, and, what was mair than a' that, a bluid relation of the Marquis of A——, the man whom," he swore, " he honoured most upon the face of the yearth, brought to so severe a pass. For his ain puir peculiar," as he said, " and to contribute something to the rehabilitation of sae auld ane house," the said Turntippet sent in three family pictures lacking the frames, and six high-backed chairs, with worked Turkey cushions, having the crest of Ravenswood broidered thereon, without charging a penny either of the principal or interest they had cost him, when he bought them, sixteen years before, at a roup of the furniture of Lord Ravenswood's lodgings in the Canongate.

Much more to Lord Turntippet's dismay than to his surprise, although he affected to feel more of the latter than the former, the Marquis received his gift very drily, and observed, that his lordship's restitution, if he expected it to be received by the Master of Ravenswood and his friends, must comprehend a pretty large farm, which, having been mortgaged to Turntippet for a very inadequate sum, he had contrived, during the confusion of the family affairs, and by means well understood by the lawyers of that period, to acquire to himself in absolute property.

The old time-serving lord winced excessively under this requisition, protesting to God, that he saw no occasion the lad could have for the instant possession of the land, seeing he would doubtless now recover the bulk of his estate from Sir William Ashton, to which he was ready to contribute by every means in his power, as was just and reasonable; and finally declaring, that he was willing to settle the land on the young gentleman, after his own natural demise.

But all these excuses availed nothing, and he was compelled to disgorge the property, on receiving back the sum for which it had been mortgaged. Having no other means of making peace with the higher powers, he returned home sorrowful and malcontent, complaining to his confidants, "that every mutation or change in the state had hitherto been productive of some sma' advantage to him in his ain quiet affairs; but that the present had (pize upon it!) cost him one of the best pen-feathers o' his wing."

Similar measures were threatened against others who had profited by the wreck of the fortune of Ravenswood; and Sir William Ashton, in particular, was menaced with an appeal to the House of Peers against the judicial sentences under which he held the Castle and Barony of Ravenswood. With him, however, the Master, as well for Lucy's sake as on account of the hospitality he had received from him, felt himself under the necessity of proceeding with great candour. He wrote to the late Lord Keeper, for he no longer held that office, stating frankly the engagement which existed between him and Miss Ashton, requesting his permission for their union, and assuring him of his willingness to put the settlement of all matters between them upon such a footing, as Sir William himself should think favourable.

The same messenger was charged with a letter to Lady Ashton, deprecating any cause of displeasure which the Master might unintentionally have given her, enlarging upon his attachment to Miss Ashton, and the length to which it had proceeded, and conjuring the lady, as a

Douglas in nature as well as in name, generously to forget ancient prejudices and misunderstandings; and to believe that the family had acquired a friend, and she herself a respectful and attached humble servant, in him who subscribed himself Edgar, Master of Ravenswood.

A third letter Ravenswood addressed to Lucy, and the messenger was instructed to find some secret and secure means of delivering it into her own hands. It contained the strongest protestations of continued affection, and dwelt upon the approaching change of the writer's fortunes, as chiefly valuable by tending to remove the impediments to their union. He related the steps he had taken to overcome the prejudices of her parents, and especially of her mother, and expressed his hope they might prove effectual. If not, he still trusted that his absence from Scotland upon an important and honourable mission might give time for prejudices to die away; while he hoped and trusted Miss Ashton's constancy, on which he had the most implicit reliance, would baffle any effort that might be used to divert her attachment. Much more there was, which, however interesting to the lovers themselves, would afford the reader neither interest nor information. To each of these three letters the Master of Ravenswood received an answer, but by different means of conveyance, and certainly couched in very different styles.

Lady Ashton answered his letter by his own messenger, who was not allowed to remain at Ravenswood a moment longer than she was engaged in penning these lines. "For the hand of Mr Ravenswood of Wolf's Crag—These:

"SIR, UNKNOWN,

"I have received a letter, signed Edgar, Master of Ravenswood, concerning the writer whereof I am uncertain, seeing that the honours of such a family were forfeited for high treason in the person of Allan, late Lord Ravenswood. Sir, if you shall happen to be the person so subscribing yourself, you will please to know, that I claim the full interest of a parent in Miss Lucy Ashton, which I have disposed of irrevocably in behalf of a worthy person. And, sir, were this otherwise, I would not listen to a proposal from you, or any of your house, seeing their hand has been uniformly held up against the freedom of the subject, and the immunities of God's kirk. Sir, it is not a flightering blink of prosperity which can change my constant opinion in this regard, seeing it has been my lot before now, like holy David, to see the wicked great in power, and flourishing like a green bay tree; nevertheless I passed, and they were not, and the place thereof knew them no more. Wishing you to lay these things to your heart for your own sake, so far as they may concern you, I pray you to take no farther notice of her, who desires to remain your unknown servant,

> "MARGARET DOUGLAS,
> "otherwise ASHTON."

About two days after he had received this very unsatisfactory epistle, the Master of Ravenswood, while walking up the High Street of Edinburgh, was jostled by a person, in whom, as the man pulled off his hat to make an apology, he recognised Lockhard, the confidential domestic of Sir William Ashton. The man bowed, slipt a letter into his hand, and disappeared. The packet contained four close-written folios, from which, however, as is sometimes incident to the compositions of great lawyers, little could be extricted, excepting that the writer felt himself in a very puzzling predicament.

Sir William spoke at length of his high value and regard for his dear young friend, the Master of Ravenswood, and of his very extreme high value and regard for the Marquis of A——, his very dear old friend;—he trusted that any measures that they might adopt, in which he was concerned, would be carried on with due regard to the sanctity of decreets, and judgments obtained *in foro contentioso*; protesting, before men and angels, that if the Law of Scotland, as declared in her supreme courts, were to undergo a reversal in the English House of Lords, the evils which would thence arise to the public would inflict a greater wound upon his heart, than any loss he might himself sustain by such irregular proceedings. He flourished much on generosity and forgiveness of mutual injuries, and hinted at the mutability of human affairs, always favourite topics with the weaker party in politics. He pathetically lamented, and gently censured, the haste which had been used in depriving him of his situation of Lord Keeper, which his experience had enabled him to fill with some advantage to the public, without so much as giving him an opportunity of explaining how far his own views of general politics might essentially differ from those now in power. He was convinced the Marquis of A—— had as sincere intentions towards the public, as himself or any man ; and if, upon a conference, they could have agreed upon the measures by which it was to be pursued, his experience and his interest should have gone to support the present administration. Upon the engagement betwixt Ravenswood and his daughter, he spoke in a dry and confused manner. He regretted so premature a step as the engagement of the young people should have been taken, and conjured the Master to remember he had never given any encouragement thereunto ; and observed, that, as a transaction *inter minores*, and without concurrence of his daughter's natural curators, the engagement was inept, and void in law. This precipitate measure, he added, had produced a very bad effect upon Lady Ashton's mind, which it was impossible at present to remove. Her son, Colonel Douglas Ashton, had embraced her prejudices in the fullest extent, and it was impossible for Sir William to adopt a course disagreeable to them, without a fatal and irreconcilable breach in his family ; which was not at present to be thought of. Time, the great physician, he hoped, would mend all.

In a postscript, Sir William said something more explicitly, which seemed to intimate, that rather than the law of Scotland should sustain a severe wound through his sides, by a reversal of the judgment of her supreme courts, in the case of the Barony of Ravenswood, through the intervention of what, with all submission, he must term a foreign court of appeal, he himself would extrajudicially consent to considerable sacrifices.

From Lucy Ashton, by some unknown conveyance, the Master received the following lines :—"I received yours, but it was at the utmost risk ; do not attempt to write again till better times. I am sore beset, but I will be true to my word, while the exercise of my reason is vouchsafed to me. That you are happy and prosperous is some consolation, and my situation requires it all." The note was signed L. A.

This letter filled Ravenswood with the most lively alarm.

He made many attempts, notwithstanding her prohibition, to convey letters to Miss Ashton, and even to obtain an interview; but his plans were frustrated, and he had only the mortification to learn, that anxious and effectual precautions had been taken to prevent the possibility of their correspondence. The Master was the more distressed by these circumstances, as it became impossible to delay his departure from Scotland, upon the important mission which had been confided to him. Before his departure, he put Sir William Ashton's letter into the hands of the Marquis of A——, who observed with a smile, that Sir William's day of grace was past, and that he had now to learn which side of the hedge the sun had got to. It was with the greatest difficulty that Ravenswood extorted from the Marquis a promise, that he would compromise the proceedings in Parliament, providing Sir William should be disposed to acquiesce in a union between him and Lucy Ashton.

"I would hardly," said the Marquis, "consent to your throwing away your birth-right in this manner, were I not perfectly confident that Lady Ashton, or Lady Douglas, or whatever she calls herself, will, as Scotchmen say, keep her threep; and that her husband dares not contradict her."

"But yet," said the Master, "I trust your lordship will consider my engagement as sacred?"

"Believe my word of honour," said the Marquis, "I would be a friend even to your follies; and having thus told you *my* opinion, I will endeavour, as occasion offers, to serve you according to your own."

The Master of Ravenswood could but thank his generous kinsman and patron, and leave him full power to act in all his affairs. He departed from Scotland upon his mission, which, it was supposed, might detain him upon the continent for some months.

CHAPTER XXVIII

Was ever woman in this humour wooed?
Was ever woman in this humour won?
I'll have her.

Richard the Third.

TWELVE months had passed away since the Master of Ravenswood's departure for the continent, and, although his return to Scotland had been expected in a much shorter space, yet the affairs of his mission, or, according to a prevailing report, others of a nature personal to himself, still detained him abroad. In the meantime, the altered state of affairs in Sir William Ashton's family may be gathered from the following conversation which took place betwixt Bucklaw and his confidential bottle companion and dependant, the noted Captain Craigengelt.

They were seated on either side of the huge sepulchral-looking freestone chimney in the low hall at Girnington. A wood fire blazed merrily in the grate; a round oaken table, placed between them, supported a stoup of excellent claret, two rummer glasses, and other good cheer; and yet, with all these appliances and means to boot, the countenance of the patron was dubious, doubtful, and unsatisfied, while the invention of his dependant was taxed to the utmost, to parry what he most dreaded, a fit, as he called it, of the sullens, on the part of his protector. After a long pause, only interrupted by the devil's tattoo, which Bucklaw kept beating against the hearth with the toe of his boot, Craigengelt at last ventured to break silence. "May I be double distanced," said he, "if ever I saw a man in my life have less the air of a bridegroom! Cut me out of feather, if you have not more the look of a man condemned to be hanged!"

"My kind thanks for the compliment," replied Bucklaw; "but I suppose you think upon the predicament in which you yourself are most likely to be placed;—and pray, Captain Craigengelt, if it please your worship, why should I look merry, when i'm sad, and devilish sad too?"

"And that's what vexes me," said Craigengelt. "Here is this match, the best in the whole country, and which you were so anxious about, is on the point of being concluded, and you are as sulky as a bear that has lost its whelps."

"I do not know," answered the laird, doggedly, "whether I should conclude it or not, if it was not that I am too far forwards to leap back."

"Leap back!" exclaimed Craigengelt, with a well-assumed air of astonishment, "that would be playing the back-game with a witness! Leap back! Why, is not the girl's fortune"——

"The young lady's, if you please," said Hayston, interrupting him.

"Well, well, no disrespect meant—Will Miss Ashton's tocher not weigh against any in Lothian?"

"Granted," answered Bucklaw; "but I care not a penny for her tocher—I have enough of my own."

"And the mother, that loves you like her own child?"

"Better than some of her children, I believe," said Bucklaw, "or there would be little love wared on the matter."

"And Colonel Sholto Douglas Ashton, who desires the marriage above all earthly things?"

"Because," said Bucklaw, "he expects to carry the county of ——— through my interest."

"And the father, who is as keen to see the match concluded, as ever I have been to win a main?"

"Ay," said Bucklaw, in the same disparaging manner, "it lies with Sir William's policy to secure the next best match, since he cannot barter his child to save the great Ravenswood estate, which the English House of Lords are about to wrench out of his clutches."

"What say you to the young lady herself?" said Craigengelt; "the finest young woman in all Scotland, one that you used to be so fond of when she was cross, and now she consents to have you, and gives up her engagement with Ravenswood, you are for jibbing—I must say, the devil's in ye, when ye neither know what you would have, nor what you would want."

"I'll tell you my meaning in a word," answered Bucklaw, getting up and walking through the room; "I want to know what the devil is the cause of Miss Ashton's changing her mind so suddenly?"

"And what need you care," said Craigengelt, "since the change is in your favour?"

"I'll tell you what it is," returned his patron, "I never knew much of that sort of fine ladies, and I believe they may be as capricious as the devil; but there is something in Miss Ashton's change, a devilish deal too sudden, and too serious for a mere flisk of her own. I'll be bound Lady Ashton understands every machine for breaking in the human mind, and there are as many as there are cannon-bits, martingales, and cavessons for young colts."

"And if that were not the case," said Craigengelt, "how the devil should we ever get them into training at all?"

"And that's true too," said Bucklaw, suspending his march through the dining-room, and leaning upon the back of a chair.—"And besides, here's Ravenswood in the way still; do you think he'll give up Lucy's engagement?"

"To be sure he will," answered Craigengelt; "what good can it do him to refuse, since he wishes to marry another woman, and she another man?"

"And you believe seriously," said Bucklaw, "that he is going to marry the foreign lady we heard of?"

"You heard yourself," answered Craigengelt, "what Captain Westenho said about it, and the great preparation made for their blithesome bridal."

"Captain Westenho," replied Bucklaw, "has rather too much of your own cast about him, Craigie, to make what Sir William would call a 'famous witness.' He drinks deep, plays deep, swears deep, and I suspect can lie and cheat a little into the bargain. Useful qualities, Craigie, if kept in their proper sphere, but which have a little too much of the freebooter to make a figure in a court of evidence."

"Well, then," said Craigengelt, "will you believe Colonel Douglas Ashton, who heard the Marquis of A—— say in a public circle, but not aware that he was within ear-shot, that his kinsman had made a better arrangement for himself than to give his father's land for the pale-cheeked daughter of a broken-down fanatic, and that Bucklaw was welcome to the wearing of Ravenswood's shaughled shoes."

"Did he say so, by heavens!" cried Bucklaw, breaking out into one of those uncontrollable fits of passion to which he was constitutionally subject,—"if I had heard him, I would have torn the tongue out of his throat before all his peats and minions, and Highland bullies into the bargain. Why did not Ashton run him through the body?"

"Capote me if I know," said the Captain. "He deserved it sure enough; but he is an old man, and a minister of state, and there would be more risk than credit in meddling with him. You had more need to think of making up to Miss Lucy Ashton the disgrace that's like to fall upon her, than of interfering with a man too old to fight, and on too high a stool for your hand to reach him."

"It *shall* reach him, though, one day," said Bucklaw, "and his kinsman Ravenswood to boot. In the meantime, I'll take care Miss Ashton receives no discredit for the slight they have put upon her. It's an awkward job, however, and I wish it were ended; I scarce know how to talk to her,—but fill a bumper, Craigie, and we'll drink her health. It grows late, and a night-cowl of good claret is worth all the considering-caps in Europe."

CHAPTER XXIX

> " It was the copy of our conference.
> In bed she slept not, for my urging it;
> At board she fed not, for my urging it;
> Alone, it was the subject of my theme;
> In company I often glanced at it."
> *Comedy of Errors.*

THE next morning saw Bucklaw, and his faithful Achates, Craigengelt, at Ravenswood Castle. They were most courteously received by the knight and his lady, as well as by their son and heir, Colonel Ashton. After a good deal of stammering and blushing,—for Bucklaw, notwithstanding his audacity in other matters, had all the sheepish bashfulness common to those who have lived little in respectable society,—he contrived at length to explain his wish to be admitted to a conference with Miss Ashton upon the subject of their approaching union. Sir William and his son looked at Lady Ashton, who replied with the greatest composure, "that Lucy would wait upon Mr Hayston directly. I hope," she added with a smile, "that as Lucy is very young, and has been lately trepanned into an engagement, of which she is now heartily ashamed, our dear Bucklaw will excuse her wish, that I should be present at their interview?"

"In truth, my dear lady," said Bucklaw, "it is the very thing that I would have desired on my own account; for I have been so little accustomed to what is called gallantry, that I shall certainly fall into some cursed mistake, unless I have the advantage of your ladyship as an interpreter."

It was thus that Bucklaw, in the perturbation of his embarrassment upon this critical occasion, forgot the just apprehensions he had entertained of Lady Ashton's over-bearing ascendency over her daughter's mind, and lost an opportunity of ascertaining, by his own investigation, the real state of Lucy's feelings.

The other gentlemen left the room, and in a short time, Lady Ashton, followed by her daughter, entered the apartment. She appeared, as he had seen her on former occasions, rather composed than agitated; but a nicer judge than he could scarce have determined, whether her calmness was that of despair, or of indifference. Bucklaw was too much agitated by his own feelings minutely to scrutinise those of the lady. He stammered out an unconnected address, confounding together the two or three topics to which it related, and stopt short before he brought it to any regular conclusion. Miss Ashton listened, or looked as if she listened, but returned not a single word in answer, continuing to fix her eyes on a small piece of embroidery, on which, as if by instinct or habit, her fingers were busily employed. Lady Ashton sat at some distance, almost screened from notice by the deep embrasure of the window in which she had placed her chair. From this she whispered, in a tone of voice, which, though soft and sweet, had something in it of admonition, if not command,—"Lucy, my dear, remember—have you heard what Bucklaw has been saying?"

The idea of her mother's presence seemed to have slipped from the unhappy girl's recollection. She started, dropped her needle, and repeated hastily, and almost in the same breath, the contradictory answers, "Yes, madam—no, my lady—I beg pardon, I did not hear."

"You need not blush, my love, and still less need you look so pale and frightened," said Lady Ashton, coming forward; "we know that maiden's ears must be slow in receiving a gentleman's language; but you must remember Mr Hayston speaks on a subject on which you have long since agreed to give him a favourable hearing. You know how much your father and I have our hearts set upon an event so extremely desirable."

In Lady Ashton's voice, a tone of impressive, and even stern innuendo was sedulously and skilfully concealed, under an appearance of the most affectionate maternal tenderness. The manner was for Bucklaw, who was easily enough imposed upon; the matter of the exhortation was for the terrified Lucy, who well knew how to interpret her mother's hints, however skilfully their real purport might be veiled from general observation.

Miss Ashton sat upright in her chair, cast round her a glance, in which fear was mingled with a still wilder expression, but remained perfectly silent. Bucklaw, who had in the meantime paced the room to and fro, until he had recovered his composure, now stopped within two or three yards of her chair, and broke out as follows :—" I believe I have been a d—d fool, Miss Ashton ; I have tried to speak to you as people tell me young ladies like to be talked to, and I don't think you comprehend what I have been saying ; and no wonder, for d—n me if I understand it myself! But, however, once for all, and in broad Scotch, your father and mother like what is proposed, and if you can take a plain young fellow for your husband, who will never cross you in any thing you have a mind to, I will place you at the head of the best establishment in the three Lothians ; you shall have Lady Girnington's lodging in the Canongate of Edinburgh, go where you please, do what you please, and see what you please, and that's fair. Only I must have a corner at the board-end for a worthless old play-fellow of mine, whose company I would rather want than have, if it were not that the d—d fellow has persuaded me that I can't do without him ; and so I hope you won't except against Craigie, although it might be easy to find much better company."

" Now, out upon you, Bucklaw," said Lady Ashton, again interposing,—" how can you think Lucy can have any objection to that blunt, honest, good-natured creature, Captain Craigengelt ?"

" Why, madam," replied Bucklaw, "as to Craigie's sincerity, honesty, and good-nature, they are, I believe, pretty much upon a par—but that's neither here nor there —the fellow knows my ways, and has got useful to me, and I cannot well do without him, as I said before. But all this is nothing to the purpose ; for, since I have mustered up courage to make a plain proposal, I would fain hear Miss Ashton, from her own lips give me a plain answer."

"My dear Bucklaw," said Lady Ashton, "let me spare Lucy's bashfulness. I tell you, in her presence, that she has already consented to be guided by her father and me in this matter.—Lucy, my love," she added, with that singular combination of suavity of tone and pointed energy which we have already noticed—"Lucy, my dearest love! speak for yourself, is it not as I say?"

Her victim answered in a tremulous and hollow voice— "I *have* promised to obey you,—but upon one condition."

"She means," said Lady Ashton, turning to Bucklaw, "she expects an answer to the demand which she has made upon the man at Vienna, or Ratisbon, or Paris—or where is he—for restitution of the engagement in which he had the art to involve her. You will not, I am sure, my dear friend, think it is wrong that she should feel much delicacy upon this head; indeed, it concerns us all."

"Perfectly right—quite fair," said Bucklaw, half humming, half speaking the end of the old song—

> "It is best to be off wi' the old love
> Before you be on wi' the new.

"But I thought," said he, pausing, "you might have had an answer six times told from Ravenswood. D—n me, if I have not a mind to go and fetch one myself, if Miss Ashton will honour me with the commission."

"By no means," said Lady Ashton, "we have had the utmost difficulty of preventing Douglas (for whom it would be more proper) from taking so rash a step; and do you think we could permit you, my good friend, almost equally dear to us, to go to a desperate man upon an errand so desperate? In fact, all the friends of the family are of opinion, and my dear Lucy herself ought so to think, that, as this unworthy person has returned no answer to her letter, silence must on this, as in other cases, be held to give consent, and a contract must be supposed to be given up, when the party waives insisting upon it. Sir William, who should know best, is clear upon this subject; and therefore, my dear Lucy"——

"Madam," said Lucy, with unwonted energy, "urge me no farther—if this unhappy engagement be restored, I have already said you shall dispose of me as you will—till then

I should commit a heavy sin in the sight of God and man, in doing what you require."

"But, my love, if this man remains obstinately silent "——

"He will *not* be silent," answered Lucy; "it is six weeks since I sent him a double of my former letter by a sure hand."

"You have not—you could not—you durst not," said Lady Ashton, with violence inconsistent with the tone she had intended to assume; but instantly correcting herself, "My dearest Lucy," said she, in her sweetest tone of expostulation, "how could you think of such a thing?"

"No matter," said Bucklaw; "I respect Miss Ashton for her sentiments, and I only wish I had been her messenger myself."

"And pray how long, Miss Ashton," said her mother, ironically, "are we to wait the return of your Pacolet—your fairy messenger—since our humble couriers of flesh and blood could not be trusted in this matter?"

"I have numbered weeks, days, hours, and minutes," said Miss Ashton; "within another week I shall have an answer, unless he is dead.—Till that time, sir," she said, addressing Bucklaw, "let me be thus far beholden to you, that you will beg my mother to forbear me upon this subject."

"I will make it my particular entreaty to Lady Ashton," said Bucklaw. "By my honour, madam, I respect your feelings; and, although the prosecution of this affair be rendered dearer to me than ever, yet as I am a gentleman, I would renounce it, were it so urged as to give you a moment's pain."

"Mr Hayston, I think, cannot apprehend that," said Lady Ashton, looking pale with anger, "when the daughter's happiness lies in the bosom of the mother.—Let me ask you, Miss Ashton, in what terms your last letter was couched?"

"Exactly in the same, madam," answered Lucy, "which you dictated on a former occasion."

"When eight days have elapsed, then," said her mother, resuming her tone of tenderness, "we shall hope, my dearest love, that you will end this suspense."

"Miss Ashton must not be hurried, madam," said Bucklaw, whose bluntness of feeling did not by any means arise from want of good-nature—"messengers may be stopped or delayed. I have known a day's journey broke by the casting off a fore-shoe.—Stay, let me see my calendar—the 20th day from this is St Jude's, and, the day before, I must be at Caverton Edge to see the match between the Laird of Kittlegirth's black mare, and Johnston the meal-monger's four-year-old colt; but I can ride all-night, or Craigie can bring me word how the match goes; and I hope, in the meantime, as I shall not myself distress Miss Ashton with any further importunity, that your ladyship yourself, and Sir William, and Colonel Douglas, will have the goodness to allow her uninterrupted time for making up her mind."

"Sir," said Miss Ashton, "you are generous."

"As for that, madam," answered Bucklaw, "I only pretend to be a plain good-humoured young fellow, as I said before, who will willingly make you happy if you will permit him, and show him how to do so."

Having said this, he saluted her with more emotion than was consistent with his usual train of feeling, and took his leave; Lady Ashton, as she accompanied him out of the apartment, assuring him that her daughter did full justice to the sincerity of his attachment, and requesting him to see Sir William before his departure, "since," as she said, with a keen glance reverting towards Lucy, "against St Jude's day, we must all be ready to *sign and seal*."

"To sign and seal!" echoed Lucy in a muttering tone, as the door of the apartment closed—"To sign and seal—to do and die!" and, clasping her extenuated hands together, she sunk back on the easy-chair she occupied, in a state resembling stupor.

From this she was shortly after awakened by the boisterous entry of her brother Henry, who clamorously reminded her of a promise to give him two yards of carnation ribbon to make knots to his new garters. With the most patient composure Lucy arose, and opening a little ivory-cabinet, sought out the ribbon the lad wanted, measured it accurately, cut it off into proper lengths, and knotted into the fashion his boyish whim required.

"Dinna shut the cabinet yet," said Henry, "for I must have some of your silver wire to fasten the bells to my hawk's jesses,—and yet the new falcon's not worth them neither ; for do you know, after all the plague we had to get her from an eyry, all the way at Posso, in Mannor Water, she's going to prove, after all, nothing better than a rifler— she just wets her singles in the blood of the partridge, and then breaks away, and lets her fly ; and what good can the poor bird do after that, you know, except pine and die in the first heather-cow or whin-bush she can crawl into ?"

"Right, Henry—right, very right," said Lucy, mournfully, holding the boy fast by the hand, after she had given him the wire he wanted ; "but there are more riflers in the world than your falcon, and more wounded birds that seek but to die in quiet, that can find neither brake nor whin-bush to hide their heads in."

"Ah ! that's some speech out of your romances," said the boy ; "and Sholto says they have turned your head. But I hear Norman whistling to the hawk—I must go fasten on the jesses."

And he scampered away with the thoughtless gaiety of boyhood, leaving his sister to the bitterness of her own reflections.

"It is decreed," she said, "that every living creature, even those who owe me most kindness, are to shun me, and leave me to those by whom I am beset. It is just it should be thus. Alone and uncounselled, I involved myself in these perils—alone and uncounselled, I must extricate myself or die."

CHAPTER XXX

———————— What doth ensue
But moody and dull melancholy,
Kinsman to grim and comfortless despair,
And, at her heels, a huge infectious troop
Of pale distemperatures, and foes to life ?
Comedy of Errors.

As some vindication of the ease with which Bucklaw (who otherwise, as he termed himself, was really a very good-humoured fellow) resigned his judgment to the management of Lady Ashton, while paying his addresses to her daughter, the reader must call to mind the strict domestic discipline, which, at this period, was exercised over the females of a Scottish family.

The manners of the country in this, as in many other respects, coincided with those of France before the revolution. Young women of the higher ranks seldom mingled in society until after marriage, and, both in law and fact, were held to be under the strict tutelage of their parents, who were too apt to enforce the views for their settlement in life, without paying any regard to the inclination of the parties chiefly interested. On such occasions, the suitor expected little more from his bride than a silent acquiescence in the will of her parents; and as few opportunities of acquaintance, far less of intimacy, occurred, he made his choice by the outside as the lovers in the *Merchant of Venice* select the casket, contented to trust to chance the issue of the lottery, in which he had hazarded a venture.

It was not therefore surprising, such being the general manners of the age, that Mr Hayston of Bucklaw, whom dissipated habits had detached in some degree from the best society, should not attend particularly to those feelings in his elected bride, to which many men of more sentiment, experience, and reflection, would, in all probability, have been equally indifferent. He knew what all accounted the principal point, that her parents and friends, namely, were decidedly in his favour, and that there existed most powerful reasons for their predilection.

In truth, the conduct of the Marquis of A——, since Ravenswood's departure, had been such as almost to bar the possibility of his kinsman's union with Lucy Ashton. The Marquis was Ravenswood's sincere, but misjudging friend; or rather, like many friends and patrons, he consulted what he considered to be his relation's true interest, although he knew that in doing so he ran counter to his inclinations.

The Marquis drove on, therefore, with the plentitude of ministerial authority, an appeal to the British House of Peers against those judgments of the courts of law, by which Sir William became possessed of Ravenswood's hereditary property. As this measure, enforced with all the authority of power, was new in Scottish judicial proceedings, though now so frequently resorted to, it was exclaimed against by the lawyers on the opposite side of politics, as an interference with the civil judicature of the country, equally new, arbitrary, and tyrannical. And if it thus affected even strangers connected with them only by political party, it may be guessed what the Ashton family themselves said and thought under so gross a dispensation. Sir William, still more worldly minded than he was timid, was reduced to despair by the loss by which he was threatened. His son's haughtier spirit was exalted into rage at the idea of being deprived of his expected patrimony. But to Lady Ashton's yet more vindictive temper, the conduct of Ravenswood, or rather of his patron, appeared to be an offence challenging the deepest and most immortal revenge. Even the quiet and confiding temper of Lucy herself, swayed by the opinions expressed by all around her, could not but consider the conduct of Ravenswood as precipitate, and even unkind. "It was my father," she repeated with a sigh, "who welcomed him to this place, and encouraged, or at least allowed, the intimacy between us. Should he not have remembered this, and requited it with at least some moderate degree of procrastination in the assertion of his own alleged rights? I would have forfeited for him double the value of these lands, which he pursues with an ardour that shows he has forgotten how much I am implicated in the matter."

Lucy, however, could only murmur these things to herself, unwilling to increase the prejudices against her lover entertained by all around her, who exclaimed against the steps pursued on his account, as illegal, vexatious, and tyrannical, resembling the worst measures in the worst times of the worst Stewarts, and a degradation of Scotland, the decisions of whose learned judges were thus subjected to the review of a court, composed indeed of men of the highest rank, but who were not trained to the study of any municipal law, and might be supposed specially to hold in contempt that of Scotland. As a natural consequence of the alleged injustice meditated towards her father, every means was resorted to, and every argument urged, to induce Miss Ashton to break off her engagement with Ravenswood, as being scandalous, shameful, and sinful, formed with the mortal enemy of her family, and calculated to add bitterness to the distress of her parents.

Lucy's spirit, however, was high; and although unaided

and alone, she could have borne much—she could have endured the repinings of her father—his murmurs against what he called the tyrannical usage of the ruling party—his ceaseless charges of ingratitude against Ravenswood—his endless lectures on the various means by which contracts may be voided and annulled—his quotations from the civil, the municipal, and the canon law—and his prelections upon the *patria potestas*.

She might have borne also in patience, or repelled with scorn, the bitter taunts and occasional violence of her brother Colonel Douglas Ashton, and the impertinent and intrusive interference of other friends and relations. But it was beyond her power effectually to withstand or elude the constant and unceasing persecution of Lady Ashton, who, laying every other wish aside, had bent the whole efforts of her powerful mind to break her daughter's contract with Ravenswood, and to place a perpetual bar between the lovers, by effecting Lucy's union with Bucklaw. Far more deeply skilled than her husband in the recesses of the human heart, she was aware, that in this way she might strike a blow of deep and decisive vengeance upon one, whom she esteemed as her mortal enemy; nor did she hesitate at raising her arm, although she knew that the wound must be dealt through the bosom of her daughter. With this stern and fixed purpose, she sounded every deep and shallow of her daughter's soul, assumed alternately every disguise of manner which could serve her object, and prepared at leisure every species of dire machinery, by which the human mind can be wrenched from its settled determination. Some of these were of an obvious description, and require only to be cursorily mentioned; others were characteristic of the time, the country, and the persons engaged in this singular drama.

It was of the last consequence, that all intercourse betwixt the lovers should be stopped, and, by dint of gold and authority, Lady Ashton contrived to possess herself of such a complete command of all who were placed around her daughter, that, in fact, no leaguered fortress was ever more completely blockaded; while, at the same time, to all outward appearance, Miss Ashton lay under no restriction. The verge of her parents' domains became, in respect to her, like the viewless and enchanted line drawn around a fairy castle, where nothing unpermitted can either enter from without, or escape from within. Thus every letter, in which Ravenswood conveyed to Lucy Ashton the indispensable reasons which detained him abroad, and more than one note which poor Lucy had addressed to him through what she thought a secure channel, fell into the hands of her mother. It could not be, but that the tenor of these intercepted letters, especially those of Ravenswood, should contain something to irritate the passions, and fortify the obstinacy, of her into whose hands they fell; but Lady Ashton's passions were too deep-rooted to require this fresh food. She burnt the papers as regularly as she perused them; and as they consumed into vapour and tinder, regarded them with a smile upon her compressed lips, and an exultation in her steady eye, which showed her confidence that the hopes of the writers should soon be rendered equally unsubstantial.

It usually happens, that fortune aids the machinations of those who are prompt to avail themselves of every chance that offers. A report was wafted from the Continent, founded, like others of the same sort, upon many plausible circumstances, but without any real basis, stating the Master of Ravenswood to be on the eve of marriage with a foreign lady of fortune and distinction. This was greedily caught up by both the political parties, who were at once struggling for power and for popular favour, and who seized, as usual, upon the most private circumstances in the lives of each other's partisans, to convert them into subjects of political discussion.

The Marquis of A—— gave his opinion aloud and publicly, not indeed in the coarse terms ascribed to him by Captain Craigengelt, but in a manner sufficiently offensive to the Ashtons:—"He thought the report," he said, "highly probable, and heartily wished it might be true. Such a match was fitter and far more creditable for a spirited young fellow, than a marriage with the daughter of an old whig lawyer, whose chicanery had so nearly ruined his father."

The other party, of course, laying out of view the opposition which the Master of Ravenswood received from Miss Ashton's family, cried shame upon his fickleness and perfidy, as if he had seduced the young lady into an engagement, and wilfully and causelessly abandoned her for another.

Sufficient care was taken that this report should find its way to Ravenswood Castle through every various channel, Lady Ashton being well aware, that the very reiteration of the same rumour from so many quarters could not but give it a semblance of truth. By some it was told as a piece of ordinary news, by some communicated as serious intelligence; now it was whispered to Lucy Ashton's ear in the tone of malignant pleasantry, and now transmitted to her as a matter of grave and serious warning.

Even the boy Henry was made the instrument of adding to his sister's torments. One morning he rushed into the room with a willow branch in his hand, which he told her had arrived that instant from Germany for her special wearing. Lucy, as we have seen, was remarkably fond of her younger brother, and at that moment his wanton and thoughtless unkindness seemed more keenly injurious than even the studied insults of her elder brother. Her grief, however, had no shade of resentment; she folded her arms about the boy's neck, and saying, faintly, "Poor Henry! you speak but what they tell you," she burst into a flood of unrestrained tears. The boy was moved, notwithstanding the thoughtlessness of his age and character. "The devil take me," said he, "Lucy, if I fetch you any more of these tormenting messages again; for I like you better," said he, kissing away the tears, "than the whole pack of them; and you shall have my grey pony to ride on, and you shall canter him if you like,—ay, and ride beyond the village, too, if you have a mind."

"Who told you," said Lucy, "that I am not permitted to ride where I please?"

"That's a secret," said the boy; "but you will find you can never ride beyond the village but your horse will cast a shoe, or fall lame, or the castle bell will ring, or something will happen to bring you back.—But if I tell you more of these things, Douglas will not get me the pair of colours they have promised me, and so good-morrow to you."

This dialogue plunged Lucy in still deeper dejection, as it tended to show her plainly what she had for some time suspected, that she was little better than a prisoner at large in her father's house. We have described her in the outset of our story as of a romantic disposition, delighting in tales of love and wonder, and readily identifying herself with the situation of those legendary heroines, with whose adventures, for want of better reading, her memory had become stocked. The fairy wand, with which in her solitude she had delighted to raise visions of enchantment, became now the rod of a magician, the bond slave of evil genii, serving only to invoke spectres at which the exorcist trembled. She felt herself the object of suspicion, of scorn, of dislike at least, if not of hatred, to her own family; and it seemed to her that she was abandoned by the very person on whose account she was exposed to the enmity of all around her. Indeed, the evidence of Ravenswood's infidelity began to assume every day a more determined character.

A soldier of fortune, of the name of Westenho, an old familiar of Craigengelt's, chanced to arrive from abroad about this time. The worthy Captain, though without any precise communication with Lady Ashton, always acted most regularly and sedulously in support of her plans, and easily prevailed upon his friend, by dint of exaggeration of real circumstances, and coining of others, to give explicit testimony to the truth of Ravenswood's approaching marriage.

Thus beset on all hands, and in a manner reduced to despair, Lucy's temper gave way under the pressure of constant affliction and persecution. She became gloomy and abstracted, and, contrary to her natural and ordinary habit of mind, sometimes turned with spirit, and even fierceness, on those by whom she was long and closely annoyed. Her health also began to be shaken, and her hectic cheek and wandering eye gave symptoms of what is called a fever upon the spirits. In most mothers this would have moved compassion; but Lady Ashton, compact and firm of purpose, saw these waverings of health and intellect with no greater sympathy than that with which the hostile engineer regards the towers of a beleaguered city as they reel under the discharge of his artillery; or rather, she considered these starts and inequalities of temper as symptoms of Lucy's expiring resolution; as the angler, by the throes and convulsive exertions of the fish which he has hooked, becomes aware that he soon will be able to land him. To accelerate the catastrophe in the present case, Lady Ashton had recourse to an expedient very consistent with the temper and credulity of those times, but which the reader will probably pronounce truly detestable and diabolical.

CHAPTER XXXI

> In which a witch did dwell, in loathly weeds,
> And wilful want, all careless of her needs;
> So choosing solitary to abide,
> Far from all neighbours, that her devilish deeds
> And hellish arts from people she might hide,
> And hurt far off, unknown, whome'er she envied.
>
> *Fairy Queen.*

THE health of Lucy Ashton soon required the assistance of a person more skilful in the office of a sick nurse than the female domestics of the family. Ailsie Gourlay, sometimes called the Wise Woman of Bowden, was the person whom, for her own strong reasons, Lady Ashton selected as an attendant upon her daughter.

This woman had acquired a considerable reputation among the ignorant by the pretended cures which she performed, especially in *oncomes*, as the Scotch call them, or mysterious diseases, which baffle the regular physician. Her pharmacopeia consisted partly of herbs selected in planetary hours, partly of words, signs, and charms, which sometimes, perhaps, produced a favourable influence upon the imagination of her patients. Such was the avowed profession of Lucky Gourlay, which, as may well be supposed, was looked upon with a suspicious eye, not only by her neighbours, but even by the clergy of the district. In private, however, she traded more deeply in the occult sciences; for, notwithstanding the dreadful punishments inflicted upon the supposed crime of witchcraft, there wanted not those who, steeled by want and bitterness of spirit, were willing to adopt the hateful and dangerous character, for the sake of the influence which its terrors enabled them to exercise in the vicinity, and the wretched emolument which they could extract by the practice of their supposed art.

Ailsie Gourlay was not indeed fool enough to acknowledge a compact with the Evil One, which would have been a swift and ready road to the stake and tar-barrel. Her fairy, she said, like Caliban's, was a harmless fairy. Nevertheless, she "spaed fortunes," read dreams, composed philtres, discovered stolen goods, and made and dissolved matches as successfully as if, according to the belief of the whole neighbourhood, she had been aided in those arts by Beelzebub himself. The worst of the pretenders to these sciences was, that they were generally persons who, feeling themselves odious to humanity, were careless of what they did to deserve the public hatred. Real crimes were often committed under pretence of magical imposture; and it somewhat relieves the disgust with which we read, in the criminal records, the conviction of these wretches, to be aware that many of them merited, as poisoners, suborners, and diabolical agents in secret domestic crimes, the severe fate to which they were condemned for the imaginary guilt of witchcraft.

Such was Ailsie Gourlay, whom, in order to attain the absolute subjugation of Lucy Ashton's mind, her mother thought it fitting to place near her person. A woman of less consequence than Lady Ashton had not dared to take such a step; but her high rank and strength of character set her above the censure of the world, and she was allowed to have selected for her daughter's attendant the best and most experienced sick-nurse "and mediciner" in the neighbourhood, where an inferior person would have fallen under the reproach of calling in the assistance of a partner and ally of the great Enemy of mankind.

The beldam caught her cue readily and by innuendo, without giving Lady Ashton the pain of distinct explanation. She was in many respects qualified for the part she played, which indeed could not be efficiently assumed without some knowledge of the human heart and passions. Dame Gourlay perceived that Lucy shuddered at her external appearance, which we have already described when we found her in the death-chamber of blind Alice; and while internally she hated the poor girl for the involuntary horror with which she saw she was regarded, she commenced her operations by endeavouring to efface or overcome those prejudices which, in her heart, she resented as mortal offences. This was easily done, for the hag's external ugliness was soon balanced by a show of kindness and interest, to which Lucy had of late been little accustomed; her attentive services and real skill gained her the ear, if not the confidence, of her patient; and under pretence of diverting the solitude of a sick room, she soon led her attention captive by the legends in which she was well skilled, and to which Lucy's habits of reading and reflection induced her to "lend an attentive ear." Dame Gourlay's tales were at first of a mild and interesting character—

> Of fays that nightly dance upon the wold,
> And lovers doomed to wander and to weep,
> And castles high, where wicked wizards keep
> Their captive thralls.

Gradually, however, they assumed a darker and more mysterious character, and became such as, told by the midnight lamp, and enforced by the tremulous tone, the quivering and livid lip, the uplifted skinny fore-finger, and the shaking head of the blue-eyed hag, might have appalled a less credulous imagination, in an age more hard of belief. The old Sycorax saw her advantage, and gradually narrowed her magic circle around the devoted victim on whose spirit she practised. Her legends began to relate to the fortunes of the Ravenswood family, whose ancient grandeur and portentous authority, credulity had graced with so many superstitious attributes. The story of the fatal fountain was narrated at full length, and with formidable additions, by the ancient sibyl. The prophecy, quoted by Caleb, concerning the dead bride, who was to be won by the last of the Ravenswoods, had its own mysterious commentary; and the singular circumstance of the apparition, seen by the Master of Ravenswood in the forest, having partly transpired through his hasty enquiries in the cottage of old Alice, formed a theme for many exaggerations.

Lucy might have despised these tales, if they had been related concerning another family, or if her own situation had been less despondent. But circumstanced as she was the idea that an evil fate hung over her attachment, became predominant over her other feelings; and the gloom of superstition darkened a mind, already sufficiently weakened by sorrow, distress, uncertainty, and an oppressive sense of desertion and desolation.   Stories were told by her attendant so closely resembling her own in their circumstances, that she was gradually led to converse upon such tragic and mystical subjects with the beldam, and to repose a sort of confidence in the sibyl, whom she still regarded with involuntary shuddering.   Dame Gourlay knew how to avail herself of this imperfect confidence.   She directed Lucy's thoughts to the means of enquiring into futurity,—the surest mode, perhaps, of shaking the understanding and destroying the spirits.   Omens were expounded, dreams were interpreted, and other tricks of jugglery perhaps resorted to, by which the pretended adepts of the period deceived and fascinated their deluded followers.   I find it mentioned in the articles of dittay against Ailsie Gourlay —(for it is some comfort to know that the old hag was tried, condemned, and burned on the top of North Berwick Law, by sentence of a commission from the Privy Council), —I find, I say, it was charged against her, among other offences, that she had, by the aid and delusions of Satan, shown to a young person of quality, in a mirror glass, a gentleman then abroad, to whom the said young person was betrothed, and who appeared in the vision to be in the act of bestowing his hand upon another lady.   But this and some other parts of the record appear to have been studiously left imperfect in names and dates, probably out of regard to the honour of the families concerned.   If Dame Gourlay was able actually to play off such a piece of jugglery, it is clear she must have had better assistance to practise the deception, than her own skill or funds could supply.   Meanwhile, this mysterious visionary traffic had its usual effect, in unsettling Miss Ashton's mind.   Her temper became unequal, her health decayed daily, her manners grew moping, melancholy, and uncertain.   Her father, guessing partly at the cause of these appearances, and exerting a degree of authority unusual with him, made a point of banishing Dame Gourlay from the castle ; but the arrow was shot, and was rankling barb-deep in the side of the wounded deer.

It was shortly after the departure of this woman, that Lucy Ashton, urged by her parents, announced to them, with a vivacity by which they were startled, "that she was conscious heaven and earth and hell had set themselves against her union with Ravenswood; still her contract," she said, "was a binding contract, and she neither would nor could resign it without the consent of Ravenswood. Let me be assured," she concluded, "that he will free me from my engagement, and dispose of me as you please, I care not how. When the diamonds are gone, what signifies the casket?"

The tone of obstinacy with which this was said, her eyes flashing with unnatural light, and her hands firmly clenched precluded the possibility of dispute; and the utmost length which Lady Ashton's art could attain, only got her the privilege of dictating the letter by which her daughter required to know of Ravenswood, whether he intended to abide by, or to surrender, what she termed, "their unfortunate engagement." Of this advantage Lady Ashton so far and so ingeniously availed herself, that, according to the wording of the letter, the reader would have supposed Lucy was calling upon her lover to renounce a contract which was contrary to the interests and inclinations of both. Not trusting even to this point of deception, Lady Ashton finally determined to suppress the letter altogether, in hopes that Lucy's impatience would induce her to condemn Ravenswood unheard and in absence. In this she was disappointed. The time, indeed, had long elapsed, when answer should have been received from the Continent. The faint ray of hope which still glimmered in Lucy's mind was wellnigh extinguished. But the idea never forsook her, that her letter might not have been duly forwarded. One of her mother's new machinations unexpectedly furnished her with the means of ascertaining what she most desired to know.

The female agent of hell having been dismissed from the castle, Lady Ashton, who wrought by all variety of means, resolved to employ, for working the same end on Lucy's mind, an agent of a very different character. This was no other than the Reverend Mr Bide-the-bent, a Presbyterian clergyman, formerly mentioned, of the very strictest order, and the most rigid orthodoxy, whose aid she called in, upon the principle of the tyrant in the tragedy :—

> "I'll have a priest shall preach her from her faith,
> And make it sin not to renounce that vow
> Which I'd have broken."

But Lady Ashton was mistaken in the agent she had selected. His prejudices, indeed, were easily enlisted on her side, and it was no difficult matter to make him regard with horror, the prospect of a union betwixt the daughter of a God-fearing, professing, and presbyterian family of distinction, with the heir of a bloodthirsty prelatist and persecutor, the hands of whose fathers had been dyed to the wrists in the blood of God's saints. This resembled, in the divine's opinion, the union of a Moabitish stranger with a daughter of Zion. But with all the more severe prejudices and principles of his sect, Bide-the-bent possessed a sound judgment and had learnt sympathy even in that very school of persecution, where the heart is so frequently hardened. In a private interview with Miss Ashton, he was deeply moved by her distress, and could not but admit the justice of her request to be permitted a direct communication with Ravenswood, upon the subject of their solemn contract. When she urged to him the great uncertainty under which she laboured, whether her letter had been ever forwarded, the old man paced the room with long steps, shook his grey head, rested repeatedly for a space on his ivory-headed staff, and, after much hesitation, confessed that he thought her doubts so reasonable, that he would himself aid in the removal of them.

"I cannot but opine, Miss Lucy," he said, "that your worshipful lady mother hath in this matter an eagerness, whilk, although it ariseth doubtless from love to your best interests here and hereafter,—for the man is of persecuting blood, and himself a persecutor, a cavalier or malignant, and a scoffer, who hath no inheritance in Jesse,—nevertheless, we are commanded to do justice unto all, and to fulfil our bond and covenant, as well to the stranger, as to him who is in brotherhood with us. Wherefore myself, even I myself, will be aiding unto the delivery of your letter to the man Edgar Ravenswood, trusting that the issue thereof may be your deliverance from the nets in which he hath sinfully engaged you. And that I may do in this neither more nor less than hath been warranted by your honourable parents, I pray you to transcribe, without increment or subtraction, the letter formerly exped under the dictation of your right honourable mother; and I shall put it into such sure course of being delivered, that if, honoured young madam, you shall receive no answer, it will be necessary that you conclude that the man meaneth in silence to abandon that naughty contract, which, peradventure, he may be unwilling directly to restore."

Lucy eagerly embraced the expedient of the worthy divine. A new letter was written in the precise terms of the former, and consigned by Mr Bide-the-bent to the charge of Saunders Moonshine, a zealous elder of the church when on shore, and, when on board his brig, as bold a smuggler as ever ran out a sliding bowsprit to the winds that blow betwixt Campvere and the east coast of Scotland. At the recommendation of his pastor, Saunders readily undertook that the letter should be securely conveyed to the Master of Ravenswood at the court where he now resided.

This retrospect became necessary to explain the conference betwixt Miss Ashton, her mother, and Bucklaw, which we have detailed in a preceding chapter.

Lucy was now like the sailor, who, while drifting through a tempestuous ocean, clings for safety to a single plank, his powers of grasping it becoming every moment more feeble, and the deep darkness of the night only checkered by the flashes of lightning, hissing as they show the white tops of the billows, in which he is soon to be engulfed.

Week crept away after week, and day after day. St Jude's day arrived, the last and protracted term to which Lucy had limited herself, and there was neither letter nor news of Ravenswood.

CHAPTER XXXII

> How fair these names, how much unlike they look
> To all the blurr'd subscriptions in my book!
> The bridegroom's letters stand in row above,
> Tapering, yet straight, like pine-trees in his grove;
> While tree and fine the bride's appear below,
> As light and slender as her jessamines grow.
>
> *Crabbe.*

St Jude's day came, the term assigned by Lucy herself as the furthest date of expectation, and, as we have already said, there were neither letters from, nor news of, Ravenswood.   But there were news of Bucklaw, and of his trusty associate Craigengelt, who arrived early in the morning for the completion of the proposed espousals, and for signing the necessary deeds.

These had been carefully prepared under the revisal of Sir William Ashton himself, it having been resolved, on account of the state of Miss Ashton's health, as it was said, that none save the parties immediately interested should be present when the parchments were subscribed.   It was further determined, that the marriage should be solemnised upon the fourth day after signing the articles, a measure adopted by Lady Ashton, in order that Lucy might have as little time as possible to recede, or relapse into intractability. There was no appearance, however, of her doing either. She heard the proposed arrangement with the calm indifference of despair, or rather with an apathy arising from the oppressed and stupefied state of her feelings.   To an eye so unobserving as that of Bucklaw, her demeanour had little more of reluctance than might suit the character of a bashful young lady, who, however, he could not disguise from himself, was complying with the choice of her friends, rather than exercising any personal predilection in his favour.

When the morning compliments of the bridegroom had been paid, Miss Ashton was left for some time to herself; her mother remarking, that the deeds must be signed before the hour of noon, in order that the marriage might be happy.

Lucy suffered herself to be attired for the occasion as the taste of her attendants suggested, and was of course splendidly arrayed.   Her dress was composed of white satin and Brussels lace, and her hair arranged with a profusion of jewels, whose lustre made a strange contrast to the deadly paleness of her complexion, and to the trouble which dwelt in her unsettled eye.

Her toilette was hardly finished, ere Henry appeared, to conduct the passive bride to the state apartment, where all was prepared for signing the contract.   "Do you know, sister," he said, "I am glad you are to have Bucklaw after all, instead of Ravenswood, who looked like a Spanish grandee come to cut our throats, and trample our bodies under foot.   And I am glad the broad seas are between us this day, for I shall never forget how frightened I was when I took him for the picture of old Sir Malise walked out of the canvas. Tell me true, are you not glad to be fairly shot of him?"

"Ask me no questions, dear Henry," said his unfortunate sister; "there is little more can happen to make me either glad or sorry in this world."

"And that's what all young brides say," said Henry; "and so do not be cast down, Lucy, for you'll tell another tale a twelvemonth hence—and I am to be bride's-man, and ride before you to the kirk, and all our kith, kin, and allies, and all Bucklaw's, are to be mounted and in order—and I am to have a scarlet laced coat, and a feathered hat, and a sword-belt, double bordered with gold, and *point d'espagne*, and a dagger instead of a sword; and I should like a sword much better, but my father won't hear of it. All my things, and a hundred besides, are to come out from Edinburgh to-night with old Gilbert, and the sumpter mules—and I will bring them, and show them to you the instant they come."

The boy's chatter was here interrupted by the arrival of Lady Ashton, somewhat alarmed at her daughter's stay. With one of her sweetest smiles, she took Lucy's arm under her own, and led her to the apartment where her presence was expected.

There were only present, Sir William Ashton, and Colonel Douglas Ashton, the last in full regimentals—Bucklaw, in bridegroom trim—Craigengelt, freshly equipt from top to toe by the bounty of his patron, and bedizened with as much lace as might have become the dress of the Copper Captain, together with the Rev. Mr Bide-the-bent; the presence of a minister being, in strict Presbyterian families, an indispensable requisite upon all occasions of unusual solemnity.

Wines and refreshments were placed on a table, on which the writings were displayed, ready for signature.

But before proceeding either to business or refreshment, Mr Bide-the-bent, at a signal from Sir William Ashton, invited the company to join him in a short extemporary prayer, in which he implored a blessing upon the contract now to be solemnised between the honourable parties then present. With the simplicity of his times and profession, which permitted strong personal allusions, he petitioned, that the wounded mind of one of these noble parties might be healed, in reward of her compliance with the advice of her right honourable parents; and that, as she had proved herself a child after God's commandment, by honouring her father and mother, she and hers might enjoy the promised blessing—length of days in the land here, and a happy portion hereafter in a better country. He prayed farther, that the bridegroom might be weaned from those follies which seduce youth from the path of knowledge; that he might cease to take delight in vain and unprofitable company, scoffers, rioters, and those who sit late at the wine (here Bucklaw winked to Craigengelt), and cease from the society that causeth to err. A suitable supplication in behalf of Sir William and Lady Ashton, and their family, concluded this religious address, which thus embraced every individual present, excepting Craigengelt, whom the worthy divine probably considered as past all hopes of grace.

The business of the day now went forward; Sir William Ashton signed the contract with legal solemnity and precision; his son, with military *nonchalance*; and Bucklaw, having subscribed as rapidly as Craigengelt could manage to turn the leaves, concluded by wiping his pen on that worthy's new laced cravat.

It was now Miss Ashton's turn to sign the writings, and she was guided by her watchful mother to the table for that purpose. At her first attempt, she began to write with a dry pen, and when the circumstance was pointed out, seemed unable, after several attempts, to dip it in the massive silver ink-standish, which stood full before her. Lady Ashton's vigilance hastened to supply the deficiency. I have myself seen the fatal deed, and in the distinct characters in which the name of Lucy Ashton is traced on each page, there is only a very slight tremulous irregularity, indicative of her state of mind at the time of the subscription. But the last signature is incomplete, defaced and blotted; for, while her hand was employed in tracing it, the hasty tramp of a horse was heard at the gate, succeeded by a step in the outer gallery, and a voice, which, in a commanding tone, bore down the opposition of the menials. The pen dropped from Lucy's fingers, as she exclaimed with a faint shriek—" He is come—he is come!"

CHAPTER XXXIII

This by his tongue should be a Montague !
Fetch me my rapier, boy ;
Now, by the faith and honour of my kin,
To strike him dead I hold it not a sin.

Romeo and Juliet.

HARDLY had Miss Ashton dropped the pen, when the door of the apartment flew open, and the Master of Ravenswood entered the apartment.

Lockhard and another domestic, who had in vain attempted to oppose his passage through the gallery or antechamber, were seen standing on the threshold transfixed with surprise, which was instantly communicated to the whole party in the state-room. That of Colonel Douglas Ashton was mingled with resentment ; that of Bucklaw, with haughty and affected indifference ; the rest, even Lady Ashton herself, showed signs of fear, and Lucy seemed stiffened to stone by this unexpected apparition. Apparition it might well be termed, for Ravenswood had more the appearance of one returned from the dead, than of a living visitor.

He planted himself full in the middle of the apartment, opposite to the table at which Lucy was seated, on whom, as if she had been alone in the chamber, he bent his eyes with a mingled expression of deep grief and deliberate indignation. His dark-coloured riding cloak, displaced from one shoulder, hung around one side of his person in the ample folds of the Spanish mantle. The rest of his rich dress was travel-soil'd, and deranged by hard riding. He had a sword by his side, and pistols in his belt. His slouched hat, which he had not removed at entrance, gave an additional gloom to his dark features, which, wasted by sorrow, and marked by the ghastly look communicated by long illness, added to a countenance naturally somewhat stern and wild, a fierce and even savage expression. The matted and dishevelled locks of hair which escaped from under his hat, together with his fixed and unmoved posture, made his head more resemble that of a marble bust than that of a living man. He said not a single word, and there was a deep silence in the company for more than two minutes.

It was broken by Lady Ashton, who in that space partly recovered her natural audacity. She demanded to know the cause of this unauthorised intrusion.

"That is a question, madam," said her son, "which I have the best right to ask—and I must request of the Master of Ravenswood to follow me, where he can answer it at leisure."

Bucklaw interposed, saying, "No man on earth should usurp his previous right in demanding an explanation from the Master.—Craigengelt," he added, in an under tone, "d—n ye, why do you stand staring as if you saw a ghost? fetch me my sword from the gallery."

"I will relinquish to none," said Colonel Ashton, "my right of calling to account the man who has offered this unparalleled affront to my family."

"Be patient, gentlemen," said Ravenswood, turning sternly towards them, and waving his hand as if to impose silence on their altercation. "If you are as weary of your lives as I am, I will find time and place to pledge mine against one or both; at present, I have no leisure for the disputes of triflers."

"Triflers!" echoed Colonel Ashton, half unsheathing his sword, while Bucklaw laid his hand on the hilt of that which Craigengelt had just reached him.

Sir William Ashton, alarmed for his son's safety, rushed between the young men and Ravenswood, exclaiming "My son, I command you—Bucklaw, I entreat you—keep the peace, in the name of the Queen and of the law!"

"In the name of the law of God," said Bide-the-bent, advancing also with uplifted hands between Bucklaw, the Colonel, and the object of their resentment—"In the name of Him who brought peace on earth, and good-will to mankind, I implore—I beseech—I command you to forbear violence towards each other! God hateth the bloodthirsty man—he who striketh with the sword, shall perish with the sword."

"Do you take me for a dog, sir," said Colonel Ashton, turning fiercely upon him, "or something more brutally stupid, to endure this insult in my father's house?—Let me go, Bucklaw! He shall account to me, or, by Heaven, I will stab him where he stands!"

"You shall not touch him here," said Bucklaw; "he once gave me my life, and were he the devil come to fly away with the whole house and generation, he shall have nothing but fair play."

The passions of the two young men thus counteracting each other, gave Ravenswood leisure to exclaim, in a stern and steady voice, "Silence!—let him who really seeks danger, take the fitting time when it is to be found; my mission here will be shortly accomplished.—Is *that* your handwriting, madam?" he added in a softer tone, extending towards Miss Ashton her last letter.

A faltering "Yes," seemed rather to escape from her lips, than to be uttered as a voluntary answer.

"And is *this* also your handwriting?" extending towards her the mutual engagement.

Lucy remained silent. Terror, and a yet stronger and more confused feeling, so utterly disturbed her understanding, that she probably scarcely comprehended the question that was put to her.

"If you design," said Sir William Ashton, "to found any legal claim on that paper, sir, do not expect to receive any answer to an extrajudicial question."

"Sir William Ashton," said Ravenswood, "I pray you, and all who hear me, that you will not mistake my purpose. If this young lady, of her own free will, desires the restoration of this contract, as her letter would seem to imply— there is not a withered leaf which this autumn wind strews on the heath, that is more valueless in my eyes. But I must and will hear the truth from her own mouth—without this satisfaction I will not leave this spot. Murder me by numbers you possibly may; but I am an armed man—I am a desperate man—and I will not die without ample vengeance. This is my resolution, take it as you may. I WILL hear her determination from her own mouth; from her own mouth, alone, and without witnesses, will I hear it. Now, choose," he said, drawing his sword with the right hand, and, with the left, by the same motion taking a pistol from his belt and cocking it, but turning the point of one weapon and the muzzle of the other to the ground, —"Choose if you will have this hall floated with blood, or if you will grant me the decisive interview with my affianced bride, which the laws of God and the country alike entitle me to demand."

All recoiled at the sound of his voice, and the determined action by which it was accompanied; for the ecstasy of real desperation seldom fails to overpower the less energetic passions by which it may be opposed. The clergyman was the first to speak. "In the name of God," he said, "receive an overture of peace from the meanest of his servants. What this honourable person demands, albeit it is urged with over violence, hath yet in it something of reason. Let him hear from Miss Lucy's own lips that she hath dutifully acceded to the will of her parents, and repenteth her of her covenant with him; and when he is assured of this, he will depart in peace unto his own dwelling, and cumber us no more. Alas! the workings of the ancient Adam are strong even in the regenerate—surely we should have long suffering with those who, being yet in the gall of bitterness and bond of iniquity, are swept forward by the uncontrollable current of worldly passion. Let, then, the Master of Ravenswood have the interview on which he insisteth; it can but be as a passing pang to this honourable maiden, since her faith is now irrevocably pledged to the choice of her parents. Let it, I say, be thus: it belongeth to my functions to entreat your honour's compliance with this healing overture."

"Never!" answered Lady Ashton, whose rage had now overcome her first surprise and terror—"never shall this man speak in private with my daughter, the affianced bride of another! Pass from this room who will, I remain here. I fear neither his violence nor his weapons, though some," she said, glancing a look towards Colonel Ashton, "who bear my name, appear more moved by them."

"For God's sake, madam," answered the worthy divine, "add not fuel to firebrands. The Master of Ravenswood cannot, I am sure, object to your presence, the young lady's state of health being considered, and your maternal duty. I myself will also tarry; peradventure my grey hairs may turn away wrath."

"You are welcome to do so, sir," said Ravenswood; "and Lady Ashton is also welcome to remain, if she shall think proper; but let all others depart."

"Ravenswood," said Colonel Ashton, crossing him as he went out, "you shall account for this ere long."

"When you please," replied Ravenswood.

"But I," said Bucklaw, with a half smile, "have a prior demand on your leisure, a claim of some standing."

"Arrange it as you will," said Ravenswood; "leave me but this day in peace, and I will have no dearer employment on earth, to-morrow, than to give you all the satisfaction you can desire."

The other gentlemen left the apartment; but Sir William Ashton lingered.

"Master of Ravenswood," he said, in a conciliating tone, "I think I have not deserved that you should make this scandal and outrage in my family. If you will sheath your sword, and retire with me into my study, I will prove to you, by the most satisfactory arguments, the inutility of your present irregular procedure"——

"To-morrow, sir—to-morrow—to-morrow, I will hear you at length," reiterated Ravenswood, interrupting him; "this day has its own sacred and indispensable business."

He pointed to the door, and Sir William left the apartment.

Ravenswood sheathed his sword, uncocked and returned his pistol to his belt, walked deliberately to the door of the apartment, which he bolted—returned, raised his hat from his forehead, and gazing upon Lucy with eyes in which an expression of sorrow overcame their late fierceness, spread his dishevelled locks back from his face, and said, "Do you know me, Miss Ashton?—I am still Edgar Ravenswood." She was silent, and he went on with increasing vehemence—"I am still that Edgar Ravenswood, who, for your affection, renounced the dear ties by which injured honour bound him to seek vengeance. I am that Ravenswood, who, for your sake, forgave, nay, clasped hands in friendship with the oppressor and pillager of his house—the traducer and murderer of his father."

"My daughter," answered Lady Ashton, interrupting him, "has no occasion to dispute the identity of your person; the venom of your present language is sufficient to remind her, that she speaks with the mortal enemy of her father."

"I pray you to be patient, madam," answered Ravenswood; "my answer must come from her own lips.—Once more, Miss Lucy Ashton, I am that Ravenswood to whom you granted the solemn engagement, which you now desire to retract and cancel."

Lucy's bloodless lips could only falter out the words, "It was my mother."

"She speaks truly," said Lady Ashton, "it *was* I, who, authorised alike by the laws of God and man, advised her, and concurred with her, to set aside an unhappy and precipitate engagement, and to annul it by the authority of Scripture itself."

"Scripture!" said Ravenswood, scornfully.

"Let him hear the text," said Lady Ashton, appealing to the divine, "on which you yourself, with cautious reluctance, declared the nullity of the pretended engagement insisted upon by this violent man."

The clergyman took his clasped Bible from his pocket, and read the following words: "*If a woman vow a vow unto the Lord, and bind herself by a bond, being in her father's house in her youth; and her father hear her vow, and her bond wherewith she hath bound her soul, and her father shall hold his peace at her: then all her vows shall stand, and every vow wherewith she hath bound her soul shall stand.*"

"And was it not even so with us?" interrupted Ravenswood.

"Control thy impatience, young man," answered the divine, "and hear what follows in the sacred text:—'*But if her father disallow her in the day that he heareth; not any of her vows, or of her bonds wherewith she hath bound her soul, shall stand: and the Lord shall forgive her, because her father disallowed her.*'"

"And was not," said Lady Ashton, fiercely and triumphantly breaking in,—"was not ours the case stated in the holy writ?—Will this person deny, that the instant her parents heard of the vow, or bond, by which our daughter had bound her soul, we disallowed the same in the most express terms, and informed him by writing of our determination?"

"And is this all?" said Ravenswood, looking at Lucy—"Are you willing to barter sworn faith, the exercise of free will, and the feelings of mutual affection, to this wretched hypocritical sophistry?"

"Hear him!" said Lady Ashton, looking to the clergy-man—"hear the blasphemer!"

"May God forgive him," said Bide-the-bent, "and enlighten his ignorance!"

"Hear what I have sacrificed for you," said Ravenswood, still addressing Lucy, "ere you sanction what has been done in your name. The honour of an ancient family, the urgent advice of my best friends, have been in vain used to sway my resolution; neither the arguments of reason, nor the portents of superstition, have shaken my fidelity. The very dead have arisen to warn me, and their warning has been despised. Are you prepared to pierce my heart for its fidelity, with the very weapon which my rash confidence intrusted to your grasp?"

"Master of Ravenswood," said Lady Ashton, "you have asked what questions you thought fit. You see the total incapacity of my daughter to answer you. But I will reply for her, and in a manner which you cannot dispute. You desire to know whether Lucy Ashton, of her own free will, desires to annul the engagement into which she has been trepanned. You have her letter under her own hand, demanding the surrender of it; and, in yet more full evi-dence of her purpose, here is the contract which she has this morning subscribed, in presence of this reverend gentleman, with Mr Hayston of Bucklaw."

Ravenswood gazed upon the deed, as if petrified. "And it was without fraud or compulsion," said he, looking towards the clergyman, "that Miss Ashton subscribed this parchment?"

"I vouch it upon my sacred character."

"This is indeed, madam, an undeniable piece of evi-dence," said Ravenswood, sternly; "and it will be equally unnecessary and dishonourable to waste another word in useless remonstrance or reproach. There, madam," he said, laying down before Lucy the signed paper and the broken piece of gold—"there are the evidences of your first engagement; may you be more faithful to that which you have just formed. I will trouble you to return the corresponding tokens of my ill-placed confidence—I ought rather to say, of my egregious folly."

Lucy returned the scornful glance of her lover with a gaze, from which perception seemed to have been banished.

yet she seemed partly to have understood his meaning, for she raised her hands as if to undo a blue ribbon which she wore around her neck. She was unable to accomplish her purpose but Lady Ashton cut the ribbon asunder, and detached the broken piece of gold which Miss Ashton had till then worn concealed in her bosom; the written counterpart of the lovers' engagement she for some time had had in her own possession. With a haughty curtsy, she delivered both to Ravenswood, who was much softened when he took the piece of gold.

"And she could wear it thus," he said—speaking to himself—"could wear it in her very bosom—could wear it next to her heart—even when—But complaint avails not," he said, dashing from his eye the tear which had gathered in it, and resuming the stern composure of his manner. He strode to the chimney, and threw into the fire the paper and piece of gold, stamping upon the coals with the heel of his boot, as if to ensure their destruction. "I will be no longer," he then said, "an intruder here—Your evil wishes, and your worse offices, Lady Ashton. I will only return, by hoping these will be your last machinations against your daughter's honour and happiness.—And to you madam," he said, addressing Lucy, "I have nothing farther to say, except to pray to God that you may not become a world's wonder for this act of wilful and deliberate perjury."— Having uttered these words, he turned on his heel, and left the apartment.

Sir William Ashton, by entreaty and authority, had detained his son and Bucklaw in a distant part of the castle, in order to prevent their again meeting with Ravenswood; but as the Master descended the great staircase, Lockhard delivered him a billet, signed Sholto Douglas Ashton, requesting to know where the Master of Ravenswood would be heard of four or five days from hence, as the writer had business of weight to settle with him, so soon as an important family event had taken place.

"Tell Colonel Ashton," said Ravenswood, composedly, "I shall be found at Wolf's Crag when his leisure serves him."

As he descended the outward stair which led from the terrace, he was a second time interrupted by Craigengelt, who, on the part of his principal, the Laird of Bucklaw, expressed a hope, that Ravenswood would not leave Scotland within ten days at least, as he had both former and recent civilities for which to express his gratitude.

"Tell your master," said Ravenswood, fiercely, "to choose his own time. He will find me at Wolf's Crag, if his purpose is not forestalled."

"*My* master?" replied Craigengelt, encouraged by seeing Colonel Ashton and Bucklaw at the bottom of the terrace; "give me leave to say, I know of no such person upon earth, nor will I permit such language to be used to me!"

"Seek your master, then, in hell!" exclaimed Ravenswood, giving way to the passion he had hitherto restrained, and throwing Craigengelt from him with such violence, that he rolled down the steps, and lay senseless at the foot of them.—"I am a fool," he instantly added, "to vent my passion upon a caitiff so worthless."

He then mounted his horse, which at his arrival he had secured to a balustrade in front of the castle, rode very slowly past Bucklaw and Colonel Ashton, raising his hat as he passed each, and looking in their faces steadily while he offered this mute salutation, which was returned by both with the same stern gravity. Ravenswood walked on with equal deliberation until he reached the head of the avenue, as if to snow that he rather courted than avoided interruption. When he had passed the upper gate, he turned his horse, and looked at the castle with a fixed eye; then set spurs to his good steed, and departed with the speed of a demon dismissed by the exorcist.

CHAPTER XXXIV

Who comes from the bridal chamber?
It is Azrael, the angel of death.

Thalaba.

AFTER the dreadful scene that had taken place at the castle, Lucy was transported to her own chamber, where she remained for some time in a state of absolute stupor. Yet afterwards, in the course of the ensuing day, she seemed to have recovered, not merely her spirits and resolution, but a sort of flighty levity, that was foreign to her character and situation, and which was at times chequered by fits of deep silence and melancholy and of capricious pettishness. Lady Ashton became much alarmed, and consulted the family physicians. But as her pulse indicated no change, they could only say that the disease was on the spirits, and recommended gentle exercise and amusement. Miss Ashton never alluded to what had passed in the state-room. It seemed doubtful even if she was conscious of it, for she was often observed to raise her hands to her neck, as if in search of the ribbon that had been taken from it, and mutter, in surprise and discontent, when she could not find it, " It was the link that bound me to life."

Notwithstanding all these remarkable symptoms, Lady Ashton was too deeply pledged, to delay her daughter's marriage even in her present state of health. It cost her much trouble to keep up the fair side of appearances towards Bucklaw. She was well aware, that if he once saw any reluctance on her daughter's part, he would break off the treaty, to her great personal shame and dishonour. She therefore resolved, that, if Lucy continued passive, the marriage should take place upon the day that had been previously fixed, trusting that a change of place, of situation, and of character, would operate a more speedy and effectual cure upon the unsettled spirits of her daughter, than could be attained by the slow measures which the medical men recommended. Sir William Ashton's views of family aggrandisement, and his desire to strengthen himself against the measures of the Marquis of A——, readily induced him to acquiesce in what he could not have perhaps resisted if willing to do so. As for the young men, Bucklaw and Colonel Ashton, they protested, that after what had happened it would be most dishonourable to postpone for a single hour the time appointed for the marriage, as it would be generally ascribed to their being intimidated by the instrusive visit and threats of Ravenswood.

Bucklaw would indeed have been incapable of such precipitation, had he been aware of the state of Miss Ashton's health, or rather of her mind. But custom, upon these occasions, permitted only brief and sparing intercourse between the bridegroom and the betrothed ; a circumstance so well improved by Lady Ashton, that Bucklaw neither saw nor suspected the real state of the health and feelings of his unhappy bride.

On the eve of the bridal day, Lucy appeared to have one of her fits of levity, and surveyed with a degree of girlish interest the various preparations of dress, &c. &c., which the different members of the family had prepared for the occasion.

The morning dawned bright and cheerily. The bridal guests assembled in gallant troops from distant quarters. Not only the relations of Sir William Ashton, and the still more dignified connexions of his lady, together with the numerous kinsmen and allies of the bridegroom, were present upon this joyful ceremony, gallantly mounted, arrayed, and caparisoned, but almost every presbyterian family of distinction, within fifty miles, made a point of attendance upon an occasion which was considered as giving a sort of triumph over the Marquis of A——, in the person of his kinsman. Splendid refreshments awaited the guests on their arrival, and after these were finished, the cry was to horse. The bride was led forth betwixt her brother Henry and her mother. Her gaiety of the preceding day had given rise to a deep shade of melancholy, which, however, did not misbecome an occasion so momentous. There was a light in her eyes, and a colour in her cheek, which had not been kindled for many a day, and which, joined to her great beauty, and the splendour of her dress, occasioned her entrance to be greeted with an universal murmur of applause, in which even the ladies could not refrain from joining. While the cavalcade were getting to horse, Sir William Ashton, a man of peace and of form, censured his son Henry for having begirt himself with a military sword of preposterous length, belonging to his brother, Colonel Ashton.

"If you must have a weapon," he said, "upon such a peaceful occasion, why did you not use the short poniard sent from Edinburgh on purpose?"

The boy vindicated himself, by saying it was lost.

"You put it out of the way yourself, I suppose," said his father, "out of ambition to wear that preposterous thing, which might have served Sir William Wallace—But never mind, get to horse now, and take care of your sister."

The boy did so, and was placed in the centre of the

gallant train. At the time, he was too full of his own appearance, his sword, his laced cloak, his feathered hat, and his managed horse, to pay much regard to any thing else; but he afterwards remembered to the hour of his death, that when the hand of his sister, by which she supported herself on the pillion behind him, touched his own, it felt as wet and cold as sepulchral marble.

Glancing wide over hill and dale, the fair bridal procession at last reached the parish church, which they nearly filled; for, besides domestics, above a hundred gentlemen and ladies were present upon the occasion. The marriage ceremony was prformed according to the rites of the Presbyterian persuasion, to which Bucklaw of late had judged it proper to conform.

On the outside of the church, a liberal dole was distributed to the poor of the neighbouring parishes, under the direction of Johnny Mortsheugh, who had lately been promoted from his desolate quarters at the Hermitage, to fill the more eligible situation of sexton at the parish church of Ravenswood. Dame Gourlay, with two of her contemporaries, the same who assisted at Alice's late-wake, seated apart upon a flat monument, or *through-stane*, sate enviously comparing the shares which had been allotted to them in dividing the dole.

" Johnny Mortsheugh," said Annie Winnie, " might hae minded auld lang syne, and thought of his auld kimmers, for as braw as he is with his new black coat. I hae gotten but five herring instead o' sax, and this disna look like a gude saxpennys, and I daresay this bit morsel o' beef is an unce lighter than ony that's been dealt round; and it's a bit o' the tenony hough, mair by token, that yours, Maggie, is out o' the back sey."

" Mine, quo' she?" mumbled the paralytic hag, " mine is half banes, I trow. If grit folk gie poor bodies ony thing for coming to their weddings and burials, it suld be something that wad do them gude, I think."

" Their gifts," said Ailsie Gourlay, " are dealt for nae love of us—nor out of respect for whether we feed or starve. They wad gie us whinstanes for loaves, if it would serve their ain vanity, and yet they expect us to be as grateful, as they ca' it, as if they served us for true love and liking."

" And that's truly said," answered her companion.

"But, Ailsie Gourlay, ye're the auldest o' us three, did ye ever see a mair grand bridal?"

"I winna say that I have," answered the hag; "but I think soon to see as braw a burial."

"And that wad please me as weel," said Annie Winnie; "for there's as large a dole, and folk are no obliged to girn and laugh, and mak murgeons, and wish joy to these hellicat quality, that lord it ower us like brute beasts. I like to pack the dead-dole in my lap, and rin ower my auld rhyme,—

"'My loaf in my lap, my penny in my purse,
Thou art ne'er the better, and I'm ne'er the worse.'"[1]

"That's right, Annie," said the paralytic woman; "God send us a green Yule and a fat kirkyard!"

"But I wad like to ken, Lucky Gourlay, for ye're the auldest and wisest amang us, whilk o' these revellers' turns it will be to be streekit first?"

"D'ye see yon dandilly maiden," said Dame Gourlay, "a' glistenin' wi' goud and jewels, that they are lifting up on the white horse behind that harebrained callant in scarlet, wi' the lang sword at his side?"

"But that's the bride!" said her companion, her cold heart touched with some sort of compassion; "that's the very bride hersell! Eh, whow! sae young, sae braw, and sae bonny—and is her time sae short?"

"I tell ye," said the sibyl, "her winding sheet is up as high as her throat already, believe it wha list. Her sand has but a few grains to rin out, and nae wonder—they've been weel shaken. The leaves are withering fast on the trees, but she'll never see the Martinmas wind gar them dance in swirls like the fairy rings."

"Ye waited on her for a quarter," said the paralytic woman, "and got twa red pieces, or I am far beguiled."

"Ay, ay," answered Ailsie, with a bitter grin; "and Sir William Ashton promised me a bonny red gown to the boot o' that—a stake, and a chain, and a tar barrel, lass! —what think ye o' that for a propine?—for being up early

---

[1] Reginald Scott tells of an old woman who performed so many cures by means of a charm, that she was suspected of witchcraft. Her mode of practice being enquired into, it was found, that the only fee which she would accept of, was a loaf of bread and a silver penny; and that the potent charm with which she wrought so many cures, was the doggerel couplet in the text.

and doun late for fourscore nights and mair wi' his dwining
daughter. But he may keep it for his ain leddy,
cummers."

"I hae heard a sough," said Annie Winnie, "as if Leddy
Ashton was nae canny body."

"D'ye see her yonder," said Dame Gourlay, "as she
prances on her grey gelding out at the kirkyard?—there's
mair o' utter deevilry in that woman, as brave and fair-
fashioned as she rides yonder, than in a' the Scotch
witches that ever flew by moonlight ower North-Berwick
Law."

"What's that ye say about witches, ye damned hags?"
said Johnny Mortsheugh; "are ye casting yer cantrips in
the very kirkyard, to mischieve the bride and bridegroom?
Get awa hame, for if I tak my souple t'ye, I'll gar ye find
the road faster than ye wad like."

"Hech, sirs!" answered Ailsie Gourlay; "how bra' are
we wi' our black coat and our weel-pouthered head, as if
we had never kend hunger nor thirst oursells! and we'll be
screwing up our bit fiddle, doubtless, in the ha' the night,
amang a' the other elbo'-jiggers for miles round. Let's see
if the pins haud, Johnny—that's a', lad."

"I take ye a' to witness, gude people," said Mortsheugh,
"that she threatens me wi' mischief, and forespeaks me.
If ony thing but gude happens to me or my fiddle this
night, I'll make it the blackest night's job she ever stirred
in. I'll hae her before Presbytery and Synod—I'm half a
minister mysell, now that I'm a bedral in an inhabited
parish."

Although the mutual hatred betwixt these hags and the
rest of mankind had steeled their hearts against all impressions of festivity, this was by no means the case with
the multitude at large. The splendour of the bridal
retinue—the gay dresses—the spirited horses—the blithesome appearance of the handsome women and gallant
gentlemen assembled upon the occasion, had the usual
effect upon the minds of the populace. The repeated
shouts, of "Ashton and Bucklaw for ever!"—the discharge
of pistols, guns, and musketoons, to give what was called
the bridal-shot, evinced the interest the people took in the
occasion of the cavalcade, as they accompanied it upon
their return to the castle. If there was here and there an

elder peasant or his wife who sneered at the pomp of the upstart family, and remembered the days of the long-descended Ravenswoods, even they, attracted by the plentiful cheer which the castle that day afforded to rich and poor, held their way thither, and acknowledged, notwithstanding their prejudices, the influence of *l'Amphitrion où l'on dîne*.

Thus accompanied with the attendance both of rich and poor, Lucy returned to her father's house. Bucklaw used his privilege of riding next to the bride, but, new to such a situation, rather endeavoured to attract attention by the display of his person and horsemanship, than by any attempt to address her in private. They reached the castle in safety, amid a thousand joyous acclamations.

It is well known, that the weddings of ancient days were celebrated with a festive publicity rejected by the delicacy of modern times. The marriage-guests, on the present occasion, were regaled with a banquet of unbounded profusion, the relics of which, after the domestics had feasted in their turn, were distributed among the shouting crowd, with as many barrels of ale as made the hilarity without correspond to that within the castle. The gentlemen, according to the fashion of the times, indulged, for the most part, in deep draughts of the richest wines, while the ladies, prepared for the ball which always closed a bridal entertainment, impatiently expected their arrival in the state gallery. At length the social party broke up at a late hour, and the gentlemen crowded into the saloon, where, enlivened by wine and the joyful occasion, they laid aside their swords, and handed their impatient partners to the floor. The music already rung from the gallery, along the fretted roof f the ancient state apartment. According to strict etiquette, the bride ought to have opened the ball, but Lady Ashton, making an apology on account of her daughter's health, offered her own hand to Bucklaw as substitute for her daughter's.

But as Lady Ashton raised her head gracefully, expecting the strain at which she was to begin the dance, she was so much struck by an unexpected alteration in the ornaments of the apartment, that she was surprised into an exclamation,—"Who has dared to change the pictures?"

All looked up, and those who knew the usual state of the

apartment, observed, with surprise, that the picture of Sir William Ashton's father was removed from its place, and in its stead that of old Sir Malise Ravenswood seemed to frown wrath and vengeance upon the party assembled below. The exchange must have been made while the apartments were empty, but had not been observed until the torches and lights in the sconces were kindled for the ball. The haughty and heated spirits of the gentlemen led them to demand an immediate enquiry into the cause of what they deemed an affront to their host and to themselves; but Lady Ashton, recovering herself, passed it over as the freak of a crazy wench who was maintained about the castle, and whose susceptible imagination had been observed to be much affected by the stories which Dame Gourlay delighted to tell concerning "the former family," so Lady Ashton named the Ravenswoods. The obnoxious picture was immediately removed, and the ball was opened by Lady Ashton, with a grace and dignity which supplied the charms of youth, and almost verified the extravagant encomiums of the elder part of the company, who extolled her performance as far exceeding the dancing of the rising generation.

When Lady Ashton sat down, she was not surprised to find that her daughter had left the apartment, and she herself followed, eager to obviate any impression which might have been made upon her nerves by an incident so likely to affect them as the mysterious transposition of the portraits. Apparently she found her apprehensions groundless, for she returned in about an hour, and whispered the bridegroom, who extricated himself from the dancers, and vanished from the apartment. The instruments now played their louder strains—the dancers pursued their exercise with all the enthusiasm inspired by youth, mirth, and high spirits, when a cry was heard so shrill and piercing, as at once to arrest the dance and the music. All stood motionless; but when the yell was again repeated, Colonel Ashton snatched a torch from the sconce, and demanding the key of the bridal-chamber from Henry, to whom, as bride's-man, it had been intrusted, rushed thither, followed by Sir William and Lady Ashton, and one or two others, near relations of the family. The bridal guests waited their return in stupefied amazement.

Arrived at the door of the apartment, Colonel Ashton

knocked and called, but received no answer except stifled groans. He hesitated no longer to open the door of the apartment, in which he found opposition from something which lay against it. When he had succeeded in opening it, the body of the bridegroom was found lying on the threshold of the bridal chamber, and all around was flooded with blood. A cry of surprise and horror was raised by all present; and the company, excited by this new alarm, began to rush tumultuously towards the sleeping apartment. Colonel Ashton, first whispering to his mother, —"Search for her—she has murdered him!" drew his sword, planted himself in the passage, and declared he would suffer no man to pass excepting the clergyman, and a medical person present. By their assistance, Bucklaw, who still breathed, was raised from the ground, and transported to another apartment, where his friends, full of suspicion and murmuring, assembled round him to learn the opinion of the surgeon.

In the meanwhile Lady Ashton, her husband, and their assistants, in vain sought Lucy in the bridal bed and in the chamber. There was no private passage from the room, and they began to think that she must have thrown herself from the window, when one of the company, holding his torch lower than the rest, discovered something white in the corner of the great old-fashioned chimney of the apartment. Here they found the unfortunate girl, seated, or rather couched like a hare upon its form—her head-gear dishevelled; her night-clothes torn and dabbled with blood,—her eyes glazed, and her features convulsed into a wild paroxysm of insanity. When she saw herself discovered, she gibbered, made mouths, and pointed at them with her bloody fingers, with the frantic gestures of an exulting demoniac.

Female assistance was now hastily summoned; the unhappy bride was overpowered, not without the use of some force. As they carried her over the threshold, she looked down, and uttered the only articulate words that she had yet spoken, saying, with a sort of grinning exultation,— "So, you have ta'en up your bonny bridegroom?" She was by the shuddering assistants conveyed to another and more retired apartment, where she was secured as her situation required, and closely watched. The unutterable agony of the parents—the horror and confusion of all who were in the castle—the fury of contending passions between the friends of the different parties, passions augmented by previous intemperance, surpass description.

The surgeon was the first who obtained something like a patient hearing ; he pronounced that the wound of Bucklaw, though severe and dangerous, was by no means fatal, but might readily be rendered so by disturbance and hasty removal. This silenced the numerous party of Bucklaw's friends, who had previously insisted that he should, at all rates, be transported from the castle to the nearest of their houses. They still demanded, however, that, in consideration of what had happened, four of their number should remain to watch over the sick-bed of their friend, and that a suitable number of their domestics, well armed, should also remain in the castle. This condition being acceded to on the part of Colonel Ashton and his father, the rest of the bridegroom's friends left the castle, notwithstanding the hour and the darkness of the night. The cares of the medical man were next employed in behalf of Miss Ashton, whom he pronounced to be in a very dangerous state. Farther medical assistance was immediately summoned. All night she remained delirious. On the morning, she fell into a state of absolute insensibility. The next evening, the physicians said, would be the crisis of her malady. It proved so ; for although she awoke from her trance with some appearance of calmness, and suffered her night-clothes to be changed, or put in order, yet so soon as she put her hand to her neck, as if to search for the fatal blue ribbon, a tide of recollections seemed to rush upon her, which her mind and body were alike incapable of bearing. Convulsion followed convulsion, till they closed in death, without her being able to utter a word explanatory of the fatal scene.

The provincial judge of the district arrived the day after the young lady had expired, and executed, though with all possible delicacy to the afflicted family, the painful duty of enquiring into this fatal transaction. But there occurred nothing to explain the general hypothesis, that the bride, in a sudden fit of insanity, had stabbed the bridegroom at the threshold of the apartment. The fatal weapon was found in the chamber, smeared with blood. It was the same poniard which Henry should have worn on the wedding-day, and which his unhappy sister had probably contrived to secrete on the succeeding evening, when it had been shown to her among other articles of preparation for the wedding.

The friends of Bucklaw expected that on his recovery he would throw some light upon this dark story, and eagerly pressed him with enquiries, which for some time he evaded under pretext of weakness. When, however, he had been transported to his own house, and was considered as in a state of convalescence, he assembled those persons, both male and female, who had considered themselves as entitled to press him on this subject, and returned them thanks, for the interest they had exhibited in his behalf, and their offers of adherence and support. "I wish you all," he said, "my friends, to understand, however, that I have neither story to tell, nor injuries to avenge. If a lady shall question me henceforward upon the incidents of that unhappy night, I shall remain silent, and in future consider her as one who has shown herself desirous to break off her friendship with me; in a word, I will never speak to her again. But if a gentleman shall ask me the same question, I shall regard the incivility as equivalent to an invitation to meet him in the Duke's Walk,[1] and I expect that he will rule himself accordingly."

A declaration so decisive admitted no commentary; and it was soon after seen that Bucklaw had arisen from the bed of sickness a sadder and a wiser man than he had hitherto shown himself. He dismissed Craigengelt from his society, but not without such a provision as, if well employed, might secure him against indigence, and against temptation.

Bucklaw afterwards went abroad, and never returned to Scotland; nor was he known ever to hint at the circumstance attending his fatal marriage. By many readers this may be deemed overstrained, romantic, and composed by the wild imagination of an author, desirous of gratifying the popular appetite for the horrible; but those who are read in the private family history of Scotland during the period in

---

[1] A walk in the vicinity of Holyrood-house, so called, because often frequented by the Duke of York, afterwards James II., during his residence in Scotland. It was for a long time the usual place of rendezvous for settling affairs of honour.

which the scene is laid, will readily discover, through the disguise of borrowed names, and added incidents, the leading particulars of AN OWER TRUE TALE.

CHAPTER XXXV

Whose mind's so marbled, and his heart so hard,
That would not, when this huge mishap was heard,
To th' utmost note of sorrow set their song,
To see a gallant, with so great a grace,
So suddenly unthought on, so o'erthrown,
And so to perish, in so poor a place,
By too rash riding in a ground unknown!
Poem, in Nisbet's Heraldry, Vol. II.

WE have anticipated the course of time to mention Bucklaw's recovery and fate, that we might not interrupt the detail of events which succeeded the funeral of the unfortunate Lucy Ashton. This melancholy ceremony was performed in the misty dawn of an autumnal morning, with such moderate attendance and ceremony as could not possibly be dispensed with. A very few of the nearest relations attended her body to the same churchyard to which she had so lately been led as a bride, with as little free will, perhaps, as could be now testified by her lifeless and passive remains. An aisle adjacent to the church had been fitted up by Sir William Ashton as a family cemetery; and here, in a coffin bearing neither name nor date, were consigned to dust the remains of what was once lovely, beautiful, and innocent, though exasperated to frenzy by a long tract of unremitting persecution. While the mourners were busy in the vault, the three village hags, who, notwithstanding the unwonted earliness of the hour, had snuffed the carrion like vultures, were seated on the "through-stane," and engaged in their wonted unhallowed conference.

"Did not I say," said Dame Gourlay, "that the braw bridal would be followed by as braw a funeral?"

"I think," answered Dame Winnie, "there's little bravery at it; neither meat nor drink, and just a wheen silver tippences to the poor folk; it was little worth while to come sae far road for sae sma' profit, and us sae frail."

"Out, wretch!" replied Dame Gourlay, "can a' the

dainties they could gie us be half sae sweet as this hour's vengeance? There they are that were capering on their prancing nags four days since, and they are now ganging as dreigh and sober as oursells the day. They were a' glistening wi' gowd and silver—they're now as black as the crook. And Miss Lucy Ashton, that grudged when an honest woman came near her, a taid may sit on her coffin the day, and she can never scunner when he croaks. And Lady Ashton has hell-fire burning in her breast by this time; and Sir William, wi' his gibbets, and his faggots, and his chains, how likes he the witcheries of his ain dwelling-house?"

"And is it true, then," mumbled the paralytic wretch, "that the bride was trailed out of her bed and up the chimley by evil spirits, and that the bridegroom's face was wrung round ahint him?"

"Ye needna care wha did it, or how it was done," said Ailsie Gourlay; "but I'll uphaud it for nae stickit job, and that the lairds and leddies ken weel this day."

"And was it true," said Annie Winnie, "sin ye ken sae mickle about it, that the picture of Auld Sir Malise Ravenswood came down on the ha' floor, and led out the brawl before them a'?"

"Na," said Ailsie; "but into the ha' came the picture—and I ken weel how it came there—to gie them a warning that pride would get a fa'. But there's as queer a ploy, cummers, as ony o' thae, that's gaun on even now in the burial vault yonder—ye saw twall mourners, wi' crape and cloke, gang down the steps pair and pair?"

"What should ail us to see them?" said the one old woman.

"I counted them," said the other, with the eagerness of a person to whom the spectacle had afforded too much interest to be viewed with indifference.

"But ye did not see," said Ailsie, exulting in her superior observation, "that there's a thirteenth amang them that they ken naething about; and, if auld freets say true, there's ane o' that compiny that'll no be lang for this warld. But come awa, cummers; if we bide here, I'se warrant we get the wyte o' whatever ill comes of it, and that gude will come of it nane o' them need ever think to see."

And thus, croaking like the ravens when they anticipate

pestilence, the ill-boding sibyls withdrew from the church-yard.

In fact, the mourners, when the service of interment was ended, discovered that there was among them one more than the invited number, and the remark was communicated in whispers to each other. The suspicion fell upon a figure, which, muffled in the same deep mourning with the others, was reclined, almost in a state of insensibility, against one of the pillars of the sepulchral vault. The relatives of the Ashton family were expressing in whispers their surprise and displeasure at the intrusion, when they were interrupted by Colonel Ashton, who, in his father's absence, acted as principal mourner. "I know," he said in a whisper, "who this person is ; he has, or shall soon have, as deep cause of mourning as ourselves—leave me to deal with him, and do not disturb the ceremony by unnecessary exposure." So saying, he separated himself from the group of his relations, and taking the unknown mourner by the cloak, he said to him, in a tone of suppressed emotion, "Follow me."

The stranger, as if starting from a trance at the sound of his voice, mechanically obeyed, and they ascended the broken ruinous stair which led from the sepulchre into the churchyard. The other mourners followed, but remained grouped together at the door of the vault, watching with anxiety the motions of Colonel Ashton and the stranger, who now appeared to be in close conference beneath the shade of a yew-tree, in the most remote part of the burial-ground.

To this sequestered spot Colonel Ashton had guided the stranger, and then turning round, addressed him in a stern and composed tone.—"I cannot doubt that I speak to the Master of Ravenswood?" No answer was returned. "I cannot doubt," resumed the Colonel, trembling with rising passion, "that I speak to the murderer of my sister?"

"You have named me but too truly," said Ravenswood, in a hollow and tremulous voice.

"If you repent what you have done," said the Colonel, "may your penitence avail you before God ; with me it shall serve you nothing. Here," he said, giving a paper, "is the measure of my sword, and a memorandum of the time and place of meeting. Sunrise to-morrow morning, on the links to the east of Wolf's-hope."

The Master of Ravenswood held the paper in his hand, and seemed irresolute. At length he spoke—"Do not," he said, "urge to farther desperation a wretch who is already desperate. Enjoy your life while you can, and let me seek my death from another."

"That you never, never shall!" said Douglas Ashton. "You shall die by my hand, or you shall complete the ruin of my family by taking my life. If you refuse my open challenge, there is no advantage I will not take of you, no indignity with which I will not load you, until the very name of Ravenswood shall be the sign of every thing that is dishonourable, as it is already of all that is villainous."

"That it shall never be," said Ravenswood, fiercely; "if I am the last who must bear it, I owe it to those who once owned it, that the name shall be extinguished without infamy. I accept your challenge, time, and place of meeting. We meet, I presume, alone?"

"Alone we meet," said Colonel Ashton, "and alone will the survivor of us return from that place of rendezvous."

"Then God have mercy on the soul of him who falls!" said Ravenswood.

"So be it!" said Colonel Ashton; "so far can my charity reach even for the man I hate most deadly, and with the deepest reason. Now, break off, for we shall be interrupted. The links, by the sea-shore to the east of Wolf's-hope—the hour, sunrise—our swords our only weapons."

"Enough," said the Master, "I will not fail you."

They separated; Colonel Ashton joining the rest of the mourners, and the Master of Ravenswood taking his horse, which was tied to a tree behind the church. Colonel Ashton returned to the castle with the funeral guests, but found a pretext for detaching himself from them in the evening, when, changing his dress to a riding habit, he rode to Wolf's-hope that night, and took up his abode in the little inn, in order that he might be ready for his rendezvous in the morning.

It is not known how the Master of Ravenswood disposed of the rest of that unhappy day. Late at night, however, he arrived at Wolf's Crag, and aroused his old domestic,

Caleb Balderstone, who had ceased to expect his return. Confused and flying rumours of the late tragical death of Miss Ashton, and of its mysterious cause, had already reached the old man, who was filled with the utmost anxiety, on account of the probable effect these events might produce upon the mind of his master.

The conduct of Ravenswood did not alleviate his apprehensions. To the butler's trembling entreaties, that he would take some refreshment, he at first returned no answer, and then suddenly and fiercely demanding wine, he drank, contrary to his habits, a very large draught. Seeing that his master would eat nothing, the old man affectionately entreated that he would permit him to light him to his chamber. It was not until the request was three or four times repeated, that Ravenswood made a mute sign of compliance. But when Balderstone conducted him to an apartment which had been comfortably fitted up, and which, since his return, he had usually occupied, Ravenswood stopped short on the threshold.

"Not here," said he, sternly; "show me the room in which my father died; the room in which SHE slept the night they were at the castle."

"Who, sir?" said Caleb, too terrified to preserve his presence of mind.

"*She*, Lucy Ashton!—would you kill me, old man, by forcing me to repeat her name?"

Caleb would have said something of the disrepair of the chamber, but was silenced by the irritable impatience which was expressed in his master's countenance; he lighted the way trembling and in silence, placed the lamp on the table of the deserted room, and was about to attempt some arrangement of the bed, when his master bid him begone in a tone that admitted of no delay. The old man retired, not to rest, but to prayer; and from time to time crept to the door of the apartment, in order to find out whether Ravenswood had gone to repose. His measured heavy step upon the floor was only interrupted by deep groans; and the repeated stamps of the heel of his heavy boot, intimated too clearly, that the wretched inmate was abandoning himself at such moments to paroxysms of uncontrolled agony. The old man thought that the morning, for which he longed, would never have dawned;

but time, whose course rolls on with equal current, however it may seem more rapid or more slow to mortal apprehension, brought the dawn at last, and spread a ruddy light on the broad verge of the glistening ocean. It was early in November, and the weather was serene for the season of the year. But an easterly wind had prevailed during the night, and the advancing tide rolled nearer than usual to the foot of the crags on which the castle was founded.

With the first peep of light, Caleb Balderstone again resorted to the door of Ravenswood's sleeping apartment, through a chink of which he observed him engaged in measuring the length of two or three swords which lay in a closet adjoining to the apartment. He muttered to himself, as he selected one of these weapons, "It is shorter— let him have this advantage, as he has every other."

Caleb Balderstone knew too well, from what he witnessed, upon what enterprise his master was bound, and how vain all interference on his part must necessarily prove. He had but time to retreat from the door, so nearly was he surprised by his master suddenly coming out, and descending to the stables. The faithful domestic followed; and, from the dishevelled appearance of his master's dress, and his ghastly looks, was confirmed in his conjecture that he had passed the night without sleep or repose. He found him busily engaged in saddling his horse, a service from which Caleb, though with faltering voice and trembling hands, offered to relieve him. Ravenswood rejected his assistance by a mute sign, and having led the animal into the court, was just about to mount him, when the old domestic's fear giving way to the strong attachment which was the principal passion of his mind, he flung himself suddenly at Ravenswood's feet, and clasped his knees, while he exclaimed, "Oh, sir! oh, master! kill me if you will, but do not go out on this dreadful errand! Oh! my dear master, wait but this day—the Marquis of A—— comes to-morrow, and a' will be remedied."

"You have no longer a master, Caleb," said Ravenswood, endeavouring to extricate himself; "why, old man, would you cling to a falling tower?"

"But I *have* a master," cried Caleb, still holding him fast, "while the heir of Ravenswood breathes. I am but a servant; but I was born your father's—your grand-

father's servant—I was born for the family—I have lived
for them—I would die for them!—Stay but at home, and
all will be well!"

"Well, fool! well?" said Ravenswood; "vain old man,
nothing hereafter in life will be well with me, and happiest
is the hour that shall soonest close it!"

So saying, he extricated himself from the old man's hold,
threw himself on his horse, and rode out at the gate; but
instantly turning back, he threw towards Caleb, who
hastened to meet him, a heavy purse of gold.

"Caleb!" he said, with a ghastly smile, "I make you
my executor;" and again turning his bridle, he resumed
his course down the hill.

The gold fell unheeded on the pavement, for the old
man ran to observe the course which was taken by his
master, who turned to the left down a small and broken
path, which gained the seashore through a cleft in the rock,
and led to a sort of cove, where, in former times, the boats
of the castle were wont to be moored. Observing him take
this course, Caleb hastened to the eastern battlement,
which commanded the prospect of the whole sands, very
near as far as the village of Wolf's-hope. He could easily
see his master riding in that direction, as fast as the horse
could carry him. The prophecy at once rushed on
Balderstone's mind, that the Lord of Ravenswood should
perish on the Kelpie's Flow, which lay half way betwixt
the tower and the links, or sand knolls, to the northward of
Wolf's-hope. He saw him accordingly reach the fatal spot,
but he never saw him pass further.

Colonel Ashton, frantic for revenge, was already in the
field, pacing the turf with eagerness, and looking with impatience towards the tower for the arrival of his antagonist.
The sun had now risen, and showed its broad disk above
the eastern sea, so that he could easily discern the horseman who rode towards him with speed which argued
impatience equal to his own. At once the figure became
invisible, as if it had melted into the air. He rubbed his
eyes, as if he had witnessed an apparition, and then
hastened to the spot, near which he was met by Balderstone, who came from the opposite direction. No trace
whatever of horse or rider could be discerned; it only
appeared, that the late winds and high tides had greatly

extended the usual bounds of the quicksand, and that the
unfortunate horseman, as appeared from the hoof-tracks, in
his precipitated haste, had not attended to keep on the firm
sands on the foot of the rock, but had taken the shortest
and most dangerous course. One only vestige of his fate
appeared. A large sable feather had been detached from
his hat, and the rippling waves of the rising tide wafted it
to Caleb's feet. The old man took it up, dried it, and
placed it in his bosom.

The inhabitants of Wolf's-hope were now alarmed, and
crowded to the place, some on shore, and some in boats,
but their search availed nothing. The tenacious depths of
the quicksand, as is usual in such cases, retained its prey.

Our tale draws to a conclusion. The Marquis of
A——, alarmed at the frightful reports that were current, and
anxious for his kinsman's safety, arrived on the subsequent
day to mourn his loss; and, after renewing in vain a search
for the body, returned to forget what had happened amid
the bustle of politics and state affairs.

Not so Caleb Balderstone. If worldly profit could have
consoled the old man, his age was better provided for than
his earlier life had ever been; but life had lost to him its
salt and its savour. His whole course of ideas, his feelings,
whether of pride or of apprehension, of pleasure or of pain,
had all arisen from his close connexion with the family
which was now extinguished. He held up his head no
longer—forsook all his usual haunts and occupations, and
seemed only to find pleasure in moping about those apartments in the old castle, which the Master of Ravenswood
had last inhabited. He ate without refreshment, and
slumbered without repose; and, with a fidelity sometimes
displayed by the canine race, but seldom by human beings,
he pined and died within a year after the catastrophe which
we have narrated.

The family of Ashton did not long survive that of
Ravenswood. Sir William Ashton outlived his eldest son,
the Colonel, who was slain in a duel in Flanders; and,
Henry, by whom he was succeeded, died unmarried.
Lady Ashton lived to the verge of extreme old age, the
only survivor of the group of unhappy persons, whose misfortunes were owing to her implacability. That she might
internally feel compunction, and reconcile herself with

Heaven whom she had offended, we will not, and we dare not, deny; but to those around her, she did not evince the slightest symptom either of repentance or remorse. In all external appearance, she bore the same bold, haughty, unbending character, which she had displayed before these unhappy events. A splendid marble monument records her name, titles, and virtues, while her victims remain undistinguished by tomb or epitaph.

NOTES

Note I. p. 148.—RAID OF CALEB BALDERSTONE

The raid of Caleb Balderstone on the cooper's kitchen, has been universally considered on the southern side of the Tweed as grotesquely and absurdly extravagant. The author can only say, that a similar anecdote was communicated to him, with date and names of the parties, by a noble Earl lately deceased, whose remembrances of former days, both in Scotland and England, while they were given with a felicity and power of humour never to be forgotten by those who had the happiness of meeting his lordship in familiar society, were especially invaluable from their extreme accuracy.

Speaking after my kind and lamented informer, with the omission of names only, the anecdote ran thus :—There was a certain bachelor gentleman in one of the midland counties of Scotland, second son of an ancient family, who lived on the fortune of a second son, *videlicet*, upon some miserably small annuity, which yet was so managed and stretched out by the expedients of his man John, that his master kept the front rank with all the young men of quality in the county, and hunted, dined, diced and drank with them, upon apparently equal terms.

It is true, that as the master's society was extremely amusing, his friends contrived to reconcile his man John to accept assistance of various kinds under the rose, which they dared not to have directly offered to his master. Yet, very consistently with all this good inclination to John, and John's master, it was thought among the young fox-hunters, that it would be an excellent jest, if possible, to take John at fault.

With this intention, and, I think, in consequence of a bet, a party of four or five of these youngsters arrived at the bachelor's little mansion, which was adjacent to a considerable village. Here they alighted a short while before the dinner hour—for it was judged regular to give John's ingenuity a fair start—and, rushing past the astonished domestic, entered the little parlour ; and, telling some concerted story of the cause of their invasion, the self-invited guests asked their landlord if he could let them have some dinner. Their friend gave them a hearty and unembarrassed reception, and, for the matter of dinner, referred them to John. He was summoned accordingly—received his master's orders to get dinner ready for the party who had thus unexpectedly arrived ; and, without changing a muscle of his countenance, promised prompt obedience. Great was the speculation of the visitors, and probably of the landlord also, what was to be the issue of John's fair promises. Some of the more curious had taken a peep into the kitchen and could see nothing there to realise the prospect held out by the *Major Domo*. But punctual as the dinner hour struck on the village clock, John placed before them a stately rump of boiled beef, with a proper accompaniment of greens, amply sufficient to dine the whole party, and to decide the bet against those among the visitors who expected to take John napping. The explanation was the same as in the case of Caleb Balderstone. John had used the freedom to carry off the *kail-pot* of a rich old chuff in the village, and brought it to his master's house, leaving the proprietor and his friends to dine on bread and cheese; and, as John said, "good enough for them." The fear of giving offence to so many persons of distinction, kept the poor man sufficiently quiet, and he was afterwards remunerated by some indirect patronage, so that the jest was admitted a good one on all sides. In England, at any period, or in some parts of Scotland at the present day it might not have passed off so well.

Note II. p. 151.—Ancient Hospitality

It was once the universal custom to place ale, wine, or some strong liquor, in the chamber of an honoured guest, to assuage his thirst should he feel any on awaking in the night, which, considering that the hospitality of that period often reached excess, was by no means unlikely. The author has met some instances of it in former days, and in old-fashioned families. It was, perhaps, no poetic fiction that records how

> "My cummer and I lay down to sleep
> With two pint stoups at our bed-feet:
> And aye when we waken'd we drank them dry:
> What think you o' my cummer and I?"

It is a current story in Teviotdale, that in the house of an ancient family of distinction, much addicted to the Presbyterian cause, a Bible was always put into the sleeping apartment of the guests, along with a bottle of strong ale. On some occasion there was a meeting of clergymen in the vicinity of the castle, all of whom were invited to dinner by the worthy Baronet, and several abode all night. According to the fashion of the times, seven of the reverend guests were allotted to one large barrack-room, which was used on such occasions of extended hospitality. The butler took care that the divines were presented, according to custom, each with a Bible and a bottle of ale. But after a little consultation among themselves, they are said to have recalled the domestic as he was leaving the apartment. "My friend," said one of the venerable guests, "you must know, when we meet together as brethren, the youngest minister reads aloud a portion of Scripture to the rest;—only one Bible, therefore, is necessary; take away the other six, and in their place bring six more bottles of ale."

This synod would have suited the "hermit sage" of Johnson, who answered a pupil who enquired for the real road to happiness, with the celebrated line,

> "Come, my lad, and drink some beer!"

Note III. p. 165.—Appeal to Parliament

The power of appeal from the Court of Session, the supreme Judges of Scotland, to the Scottish Parliament, in cases of civil right, was fiercely debated before the Union. It was a privilege highly desirable for the subject, as the examination and occasional reversal of their sentences in Parliament, might serve as a check upon the judges, which they greatly required at a time when they were much more distinguished for legal knowledge than for uprightness and integrity.

The members of the Faculty of Advocates (so the Scottish barristers are termed), in the year 1674, incurred the violent displeasure of the Court of Session, on account of their refusal to renounce the right of appeal to Parliament ; and, by a very arbitrary procedure, the majority of the number were banished from Edinburgh, and consequently deprived of their professional practice for several sessions, or terms. But, by the articles of the Union, an appeal to the British House of Peers has been secured to the Scottish subject, and that right has, no doubt, had its influence in forming the impartial and independent character which, much contrary to the practice of their predecessors, the Judges of the Court of Session have since displayed.

It is easy to conceive, that an old lawyer like the Lord Keeper in the text, should feel alarm at the judgments given in his favour, upon grounds of strict penal law, being brought to appeal under a new and dreaded procedure in a Court eminently impartial, and peculiarly moved by considerations of equity.

In earlier editions of this Work, this legal distinction was not sufficiently explained.

Note IV. p. 188.—POOR-MAN-OF-MUTTON

The blade-bone of a shoulder of mutton is called in Scotland "a poor man," as in some parts of England it is termed a "poor knight of Windsor" ; in contrast, it must be presumed, to the baronial Sir Loin. It is said, that in the last age an old Scottish peer, whose conditions (none of the most gentle) were marked by a strange and fierce-looking exaggeration of the Highland countenance, chanced to be indisposed while he was in London attending Parliament. The master of the hotel where he lodged, anxious to show attention to his noble guest, waited on him to enumerate the contents of his well-stocked larder, so as to endeavour to hit on something which might suit his appetite. "I think, landlord," said his lordship, rising up from his couch, and throwing back the tartan plaid with which he had screened his grim and ferocious visage—"I think I could eat a morsel of a *poor man*." The landlord fled in terror, having no doubt that his guest was a cannibal, who might be in the habit of eating a slice of a tenant, as light food, when he was under regimen.

GLOSSARY

ABOON, ABUNE, *above.*
AE; *one.*
AHINT, *behind.*
AIRT, *direct.*
AITS, *oats.*
AIVER, *cart-horse.*
ALLENARLY, *solely.*

BACK SEY, *sirloin.*
BANNOCKS, *flat round cakes.*
BAWBEE, *halfpenny.*
BEDESMAN, *poor pensioner.*
BEDRAL, *grave-digger.*
BEFLUMM'D, *made a fool of.*
BELL SILLER, *fee for bell-ringing.*
BELL - THE - CAT, *use strong measures.*
BEND-LEATHER, *thick sole leather.*
BICKER, *wooden bowl for liquor.*
BIDE A WEE, *wait a little.*
BIGGONETS, *linen caps of the style worn by the Beguine sisterhood.*
BIRKIE, *lively young fellow.*
BIRLING, *drinking bout.*
BIT AND BUFFET, *support given side by side with ill-usage.*
BITS O' PIGS, *pieces of crockery.*
BLACKAVISED, *swarthy.*
BLINK, *glance, a twinkling.*
BLITHE, *glad, pleasant, happy.*
BOGLE, *hobgoblin, spectre.*
BOUK, BOWK, *body, bulk.*
BOUROCK, *mound.*
BRACH, *hound.*
BRAES, *hill-sides.*
BRANDER, *gridiron.*
BRAW, *fine, brave.*
BRENT, *straight.*
BREWIS, *soup.*
BRISKET, *the breast.*
BROCHE, *spit.*

BUSK, *dress.*

CADGY, *lively, frisky, cheerful.*
CAITIFF, *mean, despicable person.*
CALLANT, *lad.*
CANTRIPS, *spells.*
CANTY, *cheery.*
CARCAKES, *cakes made with eggs, etc.*
CARLE, *fellow, gruff old man.*
CARLINE, *old woman.*
CAUK, *lime, chalk.*
CERTIE! *gracious!*
CHAMBER OF DAIS, *best chamber.*
CHANGE-HOUSE, *roadside inn where horses are changed on a journey.*
CHAPPINS, *quarts.*
CHAPPIT, *struck.*
CHAUMER, *chamber.*
CHEEK, *side.*
CHEEPS, *chirps.*
CHIEL, CHIELD, *young fellow.*
CLAVERS, *talk, idle gossip.*
CLAW UP BOTH YOUR MITTENS, *upset your arrangements.*
COCKERNONY, *young woman's head-dress.*
CRACKS, *conversation.*
CRAIG, *neck.*
CRIMP, *seize.*
CROOK, *pot-hook.*
CROWDY, *a kind of porridge.*
CUITTLE, *diddle.*
CUMMERS, *gossips.*
CUTTY, *short.*

DAFFING, *foolery.*
DAFT, *mad, crazed.*
DANG, *drove.*
DECORED, *adorned.*
DECOREMENTS, *decorations adornments.*

DIKE, *stone-wall fence.*

DINK, *dainty.*

DITTAY, *indictment.*

DOCH-AN-DORROCH, *a parting cup.*

DOGGER, *Dutch fishing vessel.*

DOITED, *stupid.*

DOOCOT, *pigeon-house.*

DOOS, *pigeons.*

DOUR, *obstinate.*

DRAP-DE-BERRY, *fine woollen cloth from France.*

DREIGH, *slow.*

DRIBBLE, *tipple.*

DRIGIE, *burial service.*

DROUGHT, *thirst.*

DUNG DONNART, *driven stupid.*

DUNSHIN, *pushing.*

DWINING, *declining in health.*

EATCHE, *adze.*

EBB, *shallow.*

ELBO-JIGGERS, *fiddlers.*

EXIES, *hysterics.*

FASH, *trouble.*

FASHED, *bothered.*

FECKLESS, *weak, feeble.*

FEE, *wages.*

FEIR, *unharmed.*

FELL, *stout.*

FEUARS, *holders of land subject to payment of a feu or fief.*

FLIGHTERING BLINK, *wavering glance.*

FLISK, *whisk, caper.*

FLYTING, *scolding.*

FORBY, *besides.*

FOREGATHER, *meet.*

FOUS O' AITS, *bushels of oats.*

FOY, *parting feast.*

FRAE, *from.*

FREETS, FREITS, *superstitious observances.*

FREMD, *strange.*

GABERLUNZIE, *mendicant.*

GABS, *palates.*

GAED, *went.*

GAR, *make.*

GAR'D, *made.*

GATE, *way.*

GAWSIE, *jolly, pert.*

GEAR, *property.*

GEIZEN'D, *leaky.*

GENTLES, *gentlefolk.*

GETT, *urchin.*

GIED, *gave.*

GIRN, *grin.*

GLEDGING AND GLEEING, *spying and peeping.*

GLENT, *pass quickly.*

GLOWERS, *stares.*

GOB-BOX, *mouth.*

GOWKS, *fools.*

GRAITH, *harness.*

GRAVANIMOUS, *serious, grave.*

GREET, *cry.*

GREETING, *weeping.*

GRUND-MAIL, *ground rent.*

GUSTING, *pleasing.*

GUTS, *stomach.*

HAGGIS, *the pluck, etc., of a sheep, minced with suet, onions, etc., boiled in its stomach.*

HALLAN, *partition between the door and fire-place.*

HANGER, *short broad-sword.*

HATTED KITT, *a mixture of milk warm from the cow, and butter-milk.*

HEEZY, *tossing.*

HELLICAT, *half-witted.*

HOUT AWA! *nonsense!*

HOW, *valley.*

HUMLOCK, *hemlock.*

HUZ, *us.*

ILK, ILKA, *each, every.*

ILL-CLECKIT, *ill-hatched.*

INGAN, *onion.*

INLAKE, *want.*

I'SE, *I will, I shall.*

JOW, *toll of the bell.*

KAIL, *broth.*

KAILYARD, *cabbage or kitchen garden.*

KAIN, *duty paid by a tenant to his landlord in eggs, fowls, etc.*

KEBBUCK, *a cheese.*
KEEKIT, *peeped.*
KEEL, *ruddle.*
KENSPECKLE, *noticeable.*
KIMMERS, *v.* CUMMERS.
KIPPAGE, *rage, passion.*
KIPPER, *dried fish, or salted salmon.*
KIRK, *church.*
KIST, *coffin.*
KITCHEN-LUMM, *kitchen vent or chimney.*
KITTLE, *ticklish.*
KITTLES, *tickles.*
KNOWE-HEAD, *top of the hillock.*

LAIRD, *squire.* lauch p139 *
LAMMER, *amber.*
LANDWARD, *country.*
LAWING, *reckoning.*
LIFT, *air, sky.*
LIPPENING, *trusting.*
LOON, LOUN, *rascal.*
LOUPEN, *sprung.*
LOWE, *flame.*
LURDANE, *blockhead.*

MAILING, *farm.*
MEAL-POKE, *meal-bag.*
MERK, *a Scottish coin, value 13s. 4d.*
MESSAN, *cur.*
MIRK, *dark.*
MUCKLE, *much, great.*
MURGEONS, *wry faces.*
MY CERTIE! *my gracious!*

NAPERY, *table-linen.*
NATHELESS, *nevertheless.*
NEEST TILL'T, *next to it.*
NEVOY, *nephew.*
NOURICESHIP, *nurse.*

OF THAT ILK, *the same, e.g. Tinto of Tinto.*
OXTER, *arm.*

PAROCHINE, *parish.*
PATTER, *chatter.*
PEARLINGS, *lace decorations.*
PEGHING, *breathing hard.*

PETTICOAT-TAILS, *cakes made with butter.*
PICKLE, *small quantity.*
PICK-MAWS, *small sea-gulls.*
PIGS, *crockery ware.*
PINCHED, *at a difficulty.*
PINNYWINKLES, *a board with holes into which the fingers are thrust and pressed upon with pegs, as a species of torture.*
PIRN, *reel.*
PIT-MIRK, *pitch dark.*
PLACK, *a copper coin, value the third part of an English penny.*
PLENISHING, *furniture.*
PLISKIE, *mischievous trick.*
PLOY, *employment.*
POCK-PUDDINGS, *bag-puddings.*
POOR-MAN-OF-MUTTON, *the blade bone of a shoulder of mutton.*
POUTHERED, *slightly salted.*
PRENT, *print.*
PROPINE, *a present.*

QUAIGH, *small drinking cup.*
QUEAN, *wench, girl.*
QUICK, *living.*

RAILLY, *woman's upper garment.*
REAVING, *thieving.*
REDD UP, *cleared up, tidied.*
RED WUD, *stark mad.*
REESTED, *smoke-dried.*
RIGS, *ridges.*
ROUND, *whisper.*
ROUP, *sale by auction.*
RUDAS, *scold.*

SAUT-SAUMON, *salt salmon.*
SCLATED, *slated.*
SCLATER-LOOMS, *slater rascals.*
SCRAUGH, SCREIGH, *scream.*
SCUNNER, *loathe.*
SENESCHAL, *steward.*
SHAUGHLED, *well-worn.*
SKARTS, *scratches.*
SKIRL, *shrill cry.*
SLIDDERY, *slippery.*
SLOCKEN, *slake.*
SNAP, *nut.*
SNECK-DRAWER, *sly, artful fellow.*

SNEESHING, SNISHING, *snuff.*
SOOTHFAST, *honest.*
SOPITE, *quash.*
SORTED, *accommodated.*
SOUGH, *whisper.*
SOUGHED, *thought over.*
SOUP, *sup, allowance.*
SOUP BRANDY, *cup of brandy.*
SOUPLE, *hand-staff.*
SOWENS, *flummery of oatmeal dust.*
SPEER, *ask.*
SPULE-BANE, *blade-bone.*
SPUNK, *spark.*
STEER, *molest.*
STICKIT, *imperfect.*
STOUTHRIEF, *robbery.*
STREEKIT, *stretched.*
SUMPH, *sulky fellow.*
SUTE AND THE ASS, *soot and ashes.*
SWANK, *stroke.*
SWAP, *exchange.*
SWIRE, *declination of a mountain or hill near its summit.*
SYBO, *onion.*
SYND, *rinse.*

TACKS, *leases.*
TASS O'BRANDY, *cup of brandy.*
TENT, *attend to.*
THOWLESS, *useless.*
THRAW, *twist.*
THREEP, *threat.*
THROUGH - STANE, *flat monument.*
THUNNER, *thunder.*
TILL'T, *to it, towards it.*
TOCHER-GOOD, *dowry.*
TOD, *fox.*
TOLBOOTH, *gaol.*
TOUT, *sulks.*
TROW, *believe, consider.*

TWAL, *twelve.*
TWA-LOFTED, *two-storied.*

UMQUHILE, *late, deceased.*
UNCO, *strange, uncommon.*
UPBY, *a little way up.*

VISIE, *sight.*
VIVERS, *victuals.*

WADSETTERS, *lenders on heritable bonds.*
WAE, *sorry.*
WAMES, *stomachs.*
WAP, *blow.*
WARED, *spent.*
WARLOCK, *witch.*
WAUR, *worse.*
WEAN, *child.*
WEID, *a feverish cold.*
WHAMPLE, *stroke, slash.*
WHEEN, *few.*
WHIGMALEERIES, *trinkets, nicknacks.*
WHILK, *which.*
WHIN-BUSH, *gorse bush.*
WHINGER, *a large knife used at meals and in broils.*
WHITE - HASS, *sausages stuffed with oatmeal and suet.*
WHOLMING, *upsetting.*
WITHIE, *halter.*
WOODIE, *the gallows, gallows-rope.*
WRAITH, *spectre, apparition.*
WUD, *mad.*
WULL-A-WINS! *well-a-day!*
WYTE, *blame.*

YESTREEN, *last night.*
YILL, *ale.*
YOWLING, *yelling.*